Emily

A [illegible]

Against the Pain

NEWFOUNDLAND WRITERS' GUILD PUBLICATIONS

Newfoundland Writers 1974

A Way with Words:
An Anthology for the 20th Anniversary of the
Newfoundland Writers' Guild

Life Sentences:
25 Years with the Newfoundland Writers' Guild

A Charm Against the Pain

29 VOICES FROM NEWFOUNDLAND

An Anthology of New Writing from the Newfoundland Writers' Guild

Edited by
Georgina Olivere Queller, Roberta Buchanan, and Geraldine Chafe Rubia

With an Introduction by Joan Clark

PENNYWELL BOOKS
ST. JOHN'S, NL

Library and Archives Canada Cataloguing in Publication

A charm against the pain : 29 voices from Newfoundland / edited by Georgina Olivere Queller, Roberta Buchanan and Geraldine Chafe Rubia ; with an introduction by Joan Clark.

"Newfoundland Writers' Guild".
ISBN 1-894463-96-X

1. Canadian literature (English)--Newfoundland and Labrador. 2. Canadian literature (English)--21st century. 3. Newfoundland and Labrador--Literary collections. I. Queller, Georgina Olivere, 1943- II. Buchanan, Roberta III. Rubia, Geraldine IV. Newfoundland Writers' Guild

PS8255.N4C43 2006 C810.8'09718 2006-906252-8

"Percy Janes Boarding the Bus" by Agnes Walsh is reprinted from *In the Old Country of My Heart* by Agnes Walsh (St. John's: Killick Press, 1996) by permission of the author.

PRINTED IN CANADA

PENNYWELL BOOKS
AN IMPRINT OF FLANKER PRESS LTD.
P.O. BOX 2522, STATION C
ST. JOHN'S, NL, CANADA A1C 6K1
TOLL FREE: 1-866-739-4420
WWW.FLANKERPRESS.COM

Cover Design: Adam Freake
freakdesignstudios@nl.rogers.com 709-745-6803

First Canadian edition printed November 2006

10 9 8 7 6 5 4 3 2 1

Canada | Canada Council for the Arts | Conseil des Arts du Canada | Government of Newfoundland and Labrador

We acknowledge the financial support of: the Government of Canada through the Book Publishing Industry Development Program (BPIDP); the Canada Council for the Arts which last year invested $20.0 million in writing and publishing throughout Canada; the Government of Newfoundland and Labrador, Department of Tourism, Culture and Recreation.

Dedication

In Memoriam

Cassie Brown
Isobel Brown
Grace Butt
Carol Devine
Andrew Horwood
Harold Horwood
Joan Horwood
Vina Horwood
Consie Howley
Percy Janes
Peggy Smith Krachun
Eleanor Orchard McKim
Rev. J. A. (Art) McKim
Neil Murray
Millicent Penney
Rae Perlin
Dorothy W. Riach

CONTENTS

INTRODUCTION / xv
Joan Clark

PREFACE / xix

A Charm Against the Pain ~ Title Poem / xxiii
Geraldine Chafe Rubia

SPRING – SHEILAGH'S BRUSH

I'm Here to Teach ~ Short Story / 3
Fran Baird Innes

Through a Glass, Darkly ~ Short Story / 15
Trudy J. Morgan-Cole

Sheilagh's Brush ~ Poem / 29
Marilyn Porter

Baked Beans and Gingerbread ~ Memoir / 30
Esther Slaney-Brown

Like Air-Bubbles ~ Poem / 34
Lillian Bouzane

My Old Gaiters ~ Short Story / 35
Geraldine Flannigan

Boxing Arena ~ Poem / 38
Anne Ferncase

Follow the Crows ~ Short Story / 39
Hilda Chaulk Murray

The Gingerbread Man ~ Short Story / 47
Danette Dooley

Three Haiku / 61
Geraldine Flannigan

reading between the lines ~ Poem / 62
Anne Ferncase

Circle Game ~ Poem / 65
Helen Fogwill Porter

What is a Lawyer? ~ Poem / 66
Danette Dooley

The Shroud ~ Short Story / 67
Lillian Bouzane

Perennial Anxiety ~ Poem / 77
Laura Morry Williams

My Ferryland Childhood:
A Memoir / 78
Laura Morry Williams

Silver Poetry / 87
Roberta Buchanan

Rosie ~ Short Story / 89
Alison Melvin

The Killing-Jar ~ Memoir / 99
Roberta Buchanan

New Gower Street 1962 ~ Poem / 105
Geraldine Chafe Rubia

Surfaces ~ Short Story / 107
Maggie Heneghan

SUMMER – GARDEN PARTY

The Summer of Lannie Ramunski ~ Short Story / 115
M. T. Dohaney

Summer Love ~ Poem / 127
Lillian Bursey

Clematis ~ Poem / 128
Janet McNaughton

First Night ~ Poem / 129
Georgina Olivere Queller

Ten Thousand Years ~ Short Story / 132
Trudy J. Morgan-Cole

Lost Love, A Proposal ~ 2 Poems / 144
Laura Morry Williams

Night Train ~ Poem / 145
Eileen Dicks

Garden Party ~ Poem / 146
Eileen Dicks

The Pilgrim of Eternity ~ Excerpt from a novel-in-progress / 147
Paul O'Neill

By Sliding Rock ~ Poem / 158
Paul O'Neill

Beatrice ~ Poem / 160
Eileen Dicks

A High Romance ~ Short Story / 161
Bernice Morgan

Stamp Collecting Newfoundland ~ Memoir / 175
Georgina Olivere Queller

The Hundred Black Ducks ~ Poem / 181
Lillian Bouzane

The Heron ~ Excerpt
from a novel-in-progress / 182
Libby Creelman

Three Bird Haiku / 192
Kathleen Knowles

Historical Sites, 1992 ~ Non-Fiction / 193
Bernice Morgan

Seasonal Rites ~ Poem / 199
Geraldine Chafe Rubia

All in a Day's Work ~ Short Story / 201
Kathleen Knowles

Writer Wanted ~ Poem / 212
Anne Ferncase

Practical Catholics, Budding Atheists ~ Essay / 213
Peggy Smith Krachun

Who I Am ~ Poem / 218
Laura Morry Williams

Only One Regret ~ Short Story / 219
Fran Baird Innes

A Life Well Lived ~ Memoir / 225
Esther Slaney-Brown

Swimmer's Prayer ~ Poem / 228
Laura Morry Williams

Hard Light ~ Poem / 229
Georgina Olivere Queller

I Have Forgotten the Way to Beachy Cove ~ Poem / 230
Roberta Buchanan

Intemperate Zone: A Suite of Poems About Belonging / 232
Janet McNaughton

Stone ~ Poem / 235
Grace Butt

AUTUMN – STARLINGS EVERYWHERE THEN GONE

The Series ~ Poem / 239
Helen Fogwill Porter

Driving to Maberly, Harvest Sounds ~ 2 Poems / 241
Hilda Chaulk Murray

Guilty as Hell ~ Excerpt from a novel-in-progress / 242
Helen Fogwill Porter

Untitled ~ Poem / 250
Joan Scott

My Mother's Poem / 251
Bernice Morgan

I Curse this Body ~ Poem / 253
Georgina Olivere Queller

Three Poems about My Relationship with My Body / 254
Marilyn Porter

when I finally saw an elephant ~ Poem / 256
Georgina Olivere Queller

Work Poem / 259
Michael Bruce-Lockhart

Women's Work ~ Poem / 262
Helen Fogwill Porter

on retiring ~ Poem / 263
Anne Ferncase

Blood-Red Poppies ~ Poem / 265
Fran Baird Innes

Music to Lie in Bed By ~ Poem / 266
Geraldine Chafe Rubia

Starlings Everywhere
Then Gone ~ Poem / 268
Joan Scott

WINTER – SHIVERING THOUGHTS

Two Haiku / 273
Geraldine Flannigan

Speaking as Settlers ~ Poem / 274
Paul O'Neill

The Ghost of Cim ~ Poem / 276
Marilyn Porter

Trapped ~ Short Story / 278
Kathleen Knowles

A Privilege of Birth ~ Memoir / 286
Jennifer Morgan

Haiku / 293
Marilyn Porter

Viewing Not Advised ~ Short Story / 294
M. T. Dohaney

A Mostly One-Sided Dialogue ~ Poem / 305
Geraldine Chafe Rubia

Fir Trees Dark Against the Sky ~ Poem / 308
Eileen Dicks

Goodbye Percy Janes ~ Memoir / 309
Danette Dooley

And a Wife Shall Cleave to her Husband ~ Poem / 323
Anne Ferncase

Slaughter on Franklyn Avenue ~ Poem / 324
Helen Fogwill Porter

Beast-ridden ~ Double Haiku / 325
Helen Fogwill Porter

Erotic Lines in the Junior Common Room ~ Poem / 326
Bernice Morgan

The Two Dresses ~ Memoir / 329
Alison Melvin

The Visitor ~ Journal Entry / 331
Grace Butt

CONTRIBUTOR BIOGRAPHIES / 333

CONTRIBUTOR INDEX / 341

Introduction

IN RECENT YEARS much has been said about the flowering of literature in Newfoundland. Like musicians, actors, and visual artists, writers are often asked to explain why this burst of energy comes from an island in the North Atlantic populated by something over half a million people. Is it the sea and the salt air? The Irish and English genes? The isolation? It is certainly true that living on the edge of a country and a continent motivates creative energy, if for no other reason than to wave a flag reminding mainlanders that we're here. At the same time, it's misleading to regard the creative output as a recent phenomenon that owes nothing to the tradition of Newfoundlanders and Labradorians, who for centuries have been entertaining themselves with music-making and storytelling in outport kitchens. Though largely invisible, the fact is writers have been beavering away for years without attracting attention outside the province.

Because our writers are isolated by geography as well as profession, many of us have coalesced into writers' groups whose primary purpose is encouragement and the sharing of work in progress. In St. John's alone there have been four such groups: the now defunct Thursday Collective, The Burning Rock, which began as the nucleus of Memorial University's creative writing class, the Feminist Writers' Group which became East Coast Women and Words, and The Newfoundland Writers' Guild. Although The Burning Rock has attracted more attention through the success of its starred writers, Lisa Moore and Michael Winter, the Newfoundland Writers' Guild has been more inclusive and enduring. Working on the premise that everyone has a story worth telling, for thirty-eight years the Guild has developed dozens of writers of all ages. Nowhere is its wide-ranging eclecticism more evident than in the all-new work in its fourth anthology, *A Charm Against the Pain*, which is organized by season, underscoring the generational intent of celebrating the work of young writers as well as writers who have been Guild members from the beginning.

In *Spring*, the energetic story, "Through a Glass Darkly," by Trudy J. Morgan-Cole, raises the interesting question of where truth is to be found in fiction. After Morgan-Cole's story, the emphasis is often on the past as fiction and poetry are viewed through young-old eyes. Although the stories are often cushioned with nostalgia, the subject matter is tough-minded as writers delve into family breakups, sexual abuse and madness. Priests and teachers play a big part in these stories which are inspired by events that predate the Mount Cashel scandal. *Spring* is not confined to Newfoundland childhoods, however, and includes a wonderfully realized story, "The Killing-Jar," by Roberta Buchanan that takes place far from Newfoundland, in what was once Rhodesia.

Appropriately, *Summer* kicks off with "The Summer of Lannie Rumunski," by a consummate storyteller, M. T. Dohaney. Still in the season of youth, this story is soon followed by "Ten Thousand Years" in which Trudy J. Morgan-Cole confronts the unfashionable idea of religious truth, asking questions that are seldom found in today's literary magazines. This summer section of the anthology also includes a brave story by Paul O'Neill about youthful self-recrimination. There is also a previously unpublished, understated story by Bernice Morgan about a gay friendship in hidebound, pre-Confederation St. John's.

Summer being a season of burgeoning growth, it is hardly surprising that this part of the anthology is populated by an eclectic mix of poetry and fiction. It is as if a handful of wildflower seeds was widely distributed by the wind, seeding stories about icebergs, the lost fishery, the Regatta, and a grandfather who loved his garden as much as his granddaughter loved him. *Summer* also includes a very fine excerpt, "The Heron," from a novel-in-progress by Libby Creelman. As well, Janet McNaughton offers a suite of poems, "The Intemperate Zone," which explores her attachment to this place. Moving on, Georgina Olivere Queller's poem, inspired by Michael Crummy's *Hard Light*, expresses the undeniable and obdurate love of Newfoundland:

> Some of my rocks, like gems,
> fit into a child's pocket,
> hard as light can be.

Autumn is launched by an excerpt from Helen Fogwill Porter's novel-in-progress in which middle-aged Eileen wrestles with the hard knocks and responsibilities of grown children and needy friends. As in the poetry that follows, there is a sense of resignation in the excerpt that comes from the tacit acknowledgement that time is running out. Autumn is the season in which colours fade and the body breaks down, as Olivere Queller writes about skin pattern in her elephant poem:

> the same one
> I see on my own hands
> criss-crossed leatherlike
> harbinger of the wizened woman
> I will become.

More upbeat, Marilyn Porter puts it this way:

> After so many years of ricocheting
> from bulge to dip and back again
> here I am in middle age, without
> much shape at all. So free at last
> from tyranny, let's warmly welcome
> stretchy waistbands and comfy shoes.

Anne Ferncase confronts the compromises imposed by time another way:

> One day I woke up
> realized
> I had nothing
> if not time.

Winter, the final section of the book, a culmination of life's journey, begins with the deft and gentle touch of Marilyn Porter's, "The Ghost of Cim," in which a woman, once perhaps the mistress of the house, makes her departure, "quietly in her silent slippers." Reading this fine poem, and the fiction that follows, the significance of the anthology's title, *A Charm*

Against the Pain, resonates, as it acknowledges the power of literature to navigate travellers through the valleys and peaks of life.

But all is not gloom and doom. In the hands of M. T. Dohaney and Gerry Rubia, humour and hilarity enliven the anthology. Humour is very much present in "Goodbye Percy Janes," a mix of reportage and homage, in which Danette Dooley presents both an interview with the late author of the Newfoundland classic, *House of Hate*, as well as a eulogy. *Winter* ends as gently as it begins, with "The Visitor," written by longtime Guild member, Grace Butt, who, before she died in January 2005 in her 95th year, wrote this about death:

> Maybe I'll fill up the kettle and lay out some baked things so I'll be relaxed in his company, drinking tea and eating tiny pieces of white cake. Some people have told me this guy is arrogant, taking charge of the whole conversation. Others say he is gentle and soft-spoken. I'll see when the time comes.

There's no smokescreen, no artifice or trickery in "The Visitor." The writing is direct, honest, courageous and in its simplicity, provides a powerful and moving conclusion to an anthology written by a remarkable group of writers, some of whom have been together for nearly forty years and have done more than any other group to nurture, share and support writing in Newfoundland and Labrador. When casting around for answers to explain what on the surface may appear to be a recent flourishing of our literature, we need look no further than the Newfoundland Writers' Guild, whose contribution to the prose and poetry of our province has been as stalwart and generous as it has been significant.

Joan Clark
St. John's

Preface

A *Charm Against the Pain* presents all new work from some of Newfoundland's best-loved, as well as emerging writers. The book is structured around the four seasons–spring, summer, autumn, winter–which serve as a framework for the four phases of human life, from childhood to old age, and for the seasonal round ranging from caplin sculls to berry picking. Each section contains a mixture of fiction, poetry, memoir, and other prose, reflecting the Newfoundland environment with nuanced poignancy and a wry, at times rollicking, wit. Happy families and abusive families, at least one wake and a birth, hatred of "beasties" and the love of nature, religious pessimism, and eternal optimism–the writing runs the gamut of emotions from tragedy to ecstasy.

The book started as a Millennium Project. Submissions were juried by Janet McNaughton, Libby Creelman, and Geraldine Chafe Rubia. Members' work was accepted, rejected, or accepted subject to mentoring. Guild mentors were provided. This manuscript next went to an external editor, Carmelita McGrath, for evaluation and restructuring. Some of her recommendations were then used to compile a second draft of the manuscript. At that stage, the present editorial committee, consisting of Geraldine Chafe Rubia, Georgina Olivere Queller, and Roberta Buchanan, took over. A variety of new material was added, some by new members of the Guild. The manuscript was restructured into its present format and sequence and further edited.

Readers will find contributions by well-known, award-winning writers, such as Bernice Morgan, Helen Fogwill Porter, Paul O'Neill, M. T. Dohaney, Janet McNaughton, Grace Butt, and Lillian Bouzane, alongside names which will be new to them.

This is the fourth anthology by members of the Newfoundland Writers' Guild, following *Newfoundland Writers 1974* (Newfoundland Writers' Guild, 1974); *A Way with Words: An Anthology for the 20th*

Anniversary of the Newfoundland Writers' Guild (Jesperson Press, 1987); and *Life Sentences: 25 Years with the Newfoundland Writers' Guild* (Creative Publishers, 1993). In addition, to celebrate International Women's Year, members Bernice Morgan, Helen Fogwill Porter, and Geraldine Chafe Rubia compiled an anthology celebrating our province's women writers: *From This Place* (Jesperson Press, 1977).

The Guild is a unique phenomenon in the lively Newfoundland writing scene. It is open to all levels of expertise. It contains nervous beginners anxious to hone their skills, as well as established writers who have published widely. Peggy Krachun wrote in her introduction to *Life Sentences*: "It's not an elitist organization where 'accomplished authors' massage each others' (and their own) egos. It is, and has been from the very start, a place to help and encourage writers at all levels, a place where veterans work side by side with fledglings and where no one is ever too 'accomplished' to benefit from a bit of constructive criticism." For a modest yearly fee of twenty dollars, members can participate in monthly workshops, as well as two annual writers' retreats held at Eastport in spring and fall. The Eastport retreats are occasions of hilarity as well as serious writing:

> Sing a song of Eastport
> A pocket full of pens
> Nearly twenty writers
> Clucking like hens.
> When the wine is opened
> The writers start to sing
> Gather for a verbal feast
> In autumn or in spring!
>
> —*Trudy Morgan-Cole*

and,

> A feisty old writer named Mart
> Said I don't give a fig or a fart
> I comes to the Inn
> Cause the food is a sin
> And the company's good for me 'art
>
> —*Geraldine Chafe Rubia*

The workshop process is strictly democratic: each member reads their work, and receives constructive feedback from all. Experienced writers mentor and encourage new ones. The atmosphere is positive and friendly. Once a year an Awards Brunch celebrates the achievements of members, and all rejoice in the success of others. At the Annual General Meeting a small prize is given to the member with the most rejection slips: in this way, members are encouraged to submit their work to magazines and publishers for wider scrutiny.

The Guild takes a proactive stance to its members, and to writing in general in the province. It has sponsored a high school short story contest; a writing competition, the Margaret Duley Short Story Contest, named for one of our first Newfoundland novelists; a play reading (and writing) group; and coffee house poetry readings. During the Cabot 500 year celebrations we sponsored local "Waterfront Writing Festivals" and offered writing workshops in Ferryland, Happy Valley-Goose Bay, Sheshatshit, and St. John's. The Festivals celebrated local writers with public readings of their work. On a more political note, the Guild lobbied for the formation of the Newfoundland and Labrador Arts Council; protested against literary censorship; assisted in removing the provincial government sales tax on books; and was involved in the formation of the Writers' Alliance of Newfoundland and Labrador (WANL), an organization devoted to the professional concerns of writers in the province. Many members of the Guild became founding members of WANL, and several have served on its board (Lillian Bouzane was its first president). The Guild's latest project has been to donate books by Guild members to the Agnes Cowan Hostel for families of patients at the Janeway Children's Hospital (which it is hoped will become an annual event). Also, two members of the Guild have undertaken to begin work on a biography and study of one founding member, pioneer dramatist, Grace Butt. For more information on the multifarious activities of the Guild and its members, readers should consult Bouzane's informative "History of the Newfoundland Writers' Guild, 1968–1993," in *Life Sentences*. Short bios of the authors included in this anthology can be found at the back of this book.

The Guild does no advertising, yet it has had a flourishing existence since 1968, largely through word of mouth recommendation. People join because they see it as a practical way to get feedback on their writing, and to meet in a relaxed atmosphere with those of similar interests. The Guild has no office, no paid secretary, or executive assistant. Those serving on its board are volunteers. It meets in members' houses; or, when the number of those attending gets too large to manage comfortably in a private home, space is rented for meetings. Refreshment is provided by the host or hosts of the meeting, ensuring no overheads. Membership fees pay for small incidental expenses and a newsletter, *The Page*, which is either mailed or emailed to members.

The editors would like to thank the board of the Guild for their unfailing and practical support for this project; our contributors for their enduring patience and good faith; Joan Scott and Kathleen Knowles for help with the manuscript; and special thank-yous to Joan Clark for graciously agreeing to write the introduction, to Ed Kavanagh for his editorial assistance, and to Jennifer Morgan for her designs of the section title pages. To the management and staff of Flanker Press, we express our gratitude for their faith in this manuscript, and for their generosity and patience with our editorial committee of three.

Roberta Buchanan
with Geraldine Chafe Rubia
and Georgina Olivere Queller

A Charm Against the Pain

(For Bernice Morgan)

GERALDINE CHAFE RUBIA

She has a raging sorrow
An unaccepted cross
Before she was an orphan
She knew the shape of loss

Why has God forsaken
Why is blood the price
Why do thieves and tyrants
Ransack Paradise

She weaves a frieze of custom
A charm against the pain
Nubbed with thorn and tansy
And names we take in vain

She is a witting witness
Of a stoic race
She has a raging sorrow
She has unwitting grace

Spring

Sheilagh's Brush

I'm Here to Teach

FRAN BAIRD INNES

AS SOON AS I jumped off the rig I saw her. She was perched on top of a big steamer trunk in front of the railway station and not another creature in sight. Course I didn't know who she was right away. What with her stocking cap pulled down around her ears and a long, red wool scarf wound up to her chin, I could hardly see her face.

"Hello, boy," she said without moving an inch. "I hope you've come to get me? I told the stationmaster I was expected, so he went on home. I'm nearly perished, waiting here this past hour."

"No, Miss, I came for the mail. That's the mailbag you're resting your feet on. Do you want to go to Arnot Cove then?"

"Well, I'm certainly not sitting here for my health," she snapped. "Of course I want to go to Arnot Cove. I'm Miss Matthews, your new teacher."

"Well blessie lard! Oh pardon me, Miss, but we didn't know you was coming today."

"What do you mean, you didn't know? I'll be staying with Mrs. Saunders and I sent her a telegram."

"Well, she's my mother, Miss, and she didn't get no message. Mom's the postmistress and she only sent me in for the mail. Course, I'll take you back with me, Miss, except for that trunk. The catamaran isn't big enough for you, me and that trunk." She pushed her cap back and gave me such an angry look.

"I'll sit on it, that way it won't take up extra space," she snapped.

"I think, Miss, you'll have to sit on the mailbag if you don't mind."

"But what if it's stolen? All my things are in it."

"Don't worry, it will be safe here. The stationmaster will send it in tomorrow."

"Isn't this the limit," she grumbled. "No one here to meet me, I'm not even expected and now I have to leave my trunk behind."

She slid to the ground and did I ever get a surprise. So help me, I never saw a teacher so short! She stood no taller than me, and for sure I'm no fourteen-year-old giant. She picked up a black cane and lurching from side to side, made her way to the catamaran. Cripes, I thought, she's a cripple. See, I only came to the station for the mail, and here I was with the new teacher and she a cripple and mad as a hornet over her old trunk. I figured she should have been darn glad I showed up at all.

As Miss Matthews lumbered towards me, a picture of a waddling duck popped into my head. I had to smother a laugh.

"What's your name boy?" Her eyes were blazing.

"Tommy Saunders, Miss."

"Well, Tommy, I promise you, someone is going to hear about this."

I threw the mailbag on the catamaran and offered Teacher a hand up.

"I can manage better on my own, thank you." She caught hold of the post and hauled herself up.

It was jeezly cold and I was anxious to get home to supper and a warm fire. Patch, my pony, was restless too. He snorted and pawed the frozen ground when I jumped aboard the rig. The strong smell rising from the pony's steaming flanks made me haul my scarf over my nose. I looked back to make sure Teacher was settled on the mailbag.

"How far to the Cove?" she asked.

"About a mile, Miss, and you better hold on to them posts."

With a flick of the reins, old Patch started off with a jerk. The trail was rough and real slippery in places from the sea spray. The worst thing was swerving to miss the snow-covered tuckamore that stuck up like ghosts along the way. When I glanced back, Teacher was holding on to them posts for dear life. Once Patch hit his stride, the clop, clop of hooves, the crunch of runners on frozen snow and the tinkling of harness bells were the only sounds, the air was that still.

When we reached home, I jumped off and ran to tell Mom I had the new teacher aboard.

"The new teacher. What do you mean, the new teacher? I'm not expecting no new teacher today."

"Miss Matthews says she sent you a telegram. But that's not the worst of it, Mom, she's a funny-looking cripple."

"A cripple. You mean her leg is broke?"

"No, it's not that. She's real short and walks funny."

"Good Lord, Tommy, why didn't you help her in for heaven's sake?"

Mom bolted out the door and me right behind her. Teacher was leaning kinda stiff-like against the sleigh. Mom took hold of her.

"You poor thing. I expects you're nearly gone with the cold. Tommy, quick, give me a hand. We got to get her into the house before she perishes altogether."

I felt some embarrassed helping Mom carry her into the kitchen, but she was so cold she couldn't speak or move her legs. Dad was at the kitchen table waiting for his supper, and the smell of rabbit soup and bread, fresh from the oven, made my stomach growl.

"Gus, Miss Matthews is the new teacher and she's fair froze because we wasn't expecting her today. Lucky, Tommy went for the mail. Fetch me that big enamel basin in the pantry and fill it with warm water. We got to get her thawed out."

Mom sat Teacher on a chair in front of the wood stove, pulled off her boots and black stockings and eased her feet into the water. Dad wrapped a heavy wool blanket around her shoulders. "Don't you worry, Miss," he said. "Daisy will have you thawed out in no time. There's no heat upstairs, so you sleep on the settle in here by the kitchen fire tonight. When you feel like it, a good bowl of rabbit soup will warm your insides."

All this time, Teacher didn't say a word. She just sat huddled in the quilt with her feet to the stove. She looked more like an elf than a teacher.

Next morning, I got my first good look at Miss Matthews. She wasn't so white anymore but her cheeks weren't exactly rosy either. Her hair was pulled back except for a few frizzy bits that escaped the elastic and curled around her face. She didn't look much older than some of the girls at school.

"Good morning, Tommy." Her voice was low and hoarse. "I want to thank you for all your help yesterday even though I nearly perished. Anyway, there's no point dwelling on that, because now I have to see to my school. I need to get started as soon as possible."

"Why don't you take it easy today and get your bones warmed through? You still looks a little pale," Mom remarked.

"I'm all right now, thanks to your expert care. It's best if I keep on the move, else I'll stiffen right up. Once things are in order at school we can let everyone know I'm here. It's already two weeks into 1934, and with their teacher leaving before Christmas, the children have missed enough school already."

"You'll never get to that school on your own, me maid. All the lower land hereabouts was built up or taken for fish stages and such, so the school had to go on top of the hill back of here."

"Well, it can't be far away, then."

"It's not the distance," Mom explained, "there's no road up the hill, just a lot of steps."

"If that's the only way to get to school, I may as well go now and see what I'm up against."

"I don't know what that St. John's crowd is thinking about sending a young girl like yourself out here. It's hard enough for the men and they don't stay long."

"I came because I finished my teacher training before Christmas, and since you have no teacher, this school was available. Now, Mrs. Saunders, if you don't mind showing me the way, I want to see my school."

"Then I'll get my coat and come with you and Tommy will give us a hand, won't you, son?"

I hate it when Mom corners me like that but what could I say? Anyway, I figured once she saw them steep steps, it would be the last straw and she would hightail it back to St. John's.

"I guess so," I mumbled, "and I'll take a few splits and birch junks to light the fire. School's been closed so long it will be colder than death in there."

So off the three of us went, teacher lurching along with her walking stick, which wasn't much help in the snow, and Mom hitched tight to her other arm. When we reached the steps, I figured she would take one look and give up then and there. We could kiss school goodbye for the rest of the year. Well, sir, she was stopped right in her tracks when she saw them forty steps.

"Glory be," she said, "they are steep, aren't they?"

"There's no way you can climb them steps. No one in their right mind would expect you to. Come on, we'll go home and . . . " That's as far as Mom got.

"Go home? Indeed we won't go home. You go on ahead, Tommy. These aren't the first steps I've managed and they won't be the last."

Lucky thing the wind had blown away the snow, so the steps were bare at least. I went on up aways, and when I glanced back, she was down on her hands and knees, working herself up, step by step. Mom stayed close behind in case she fell. Teacher's face was all red from the effort, but I have to admit, she was some determined. No way would she quit.

The school was freezing. I found some dry strips of birch bark in the woodbox, lit them under the splits and in jigtime the old pot-belly stove was throwing off a good heat. As soon as she came in the door, Teacher flopped down on a bench in front of the stove. Mom, all out of puff, was right behind her. The two of them just sat there until, finally, the heat began to revive them. Teacher stood up and looked around. This was the only school I had ever been in, and I guess until that minute I hadn't paid much heed to how it looked. My eyes followed hers up the dingy walls to the windows where peeling paint, covered in cobwebs, fluttered in the draft. Some windowpanes were bust out and the holes covered with cardboard. "This can't possibly be my school. Where's the new school Dr. Blackall promised me? He said you built a new school here. That's where I'm supposed to teach. Where is it?" She was livid.

"So we did build a new one, Miss," Mom explained, "but when the men got her finished, they decided it was too good for a school, so they made her into a church. Now the poor children are back in this old barn."

I figured that would be the end of it. Sure as anything she would be on the next train to St. John's.

"Well, I certainly didn't expect anything like this."

Here it comes, I thought.

"But I guess we'll have to make the best of it. Now let's see what needs to be done. First thing is to replace those broken windowpanes, and a lick of paint will do wonders."

Mom was as surprised as I was. "You mean you're willing to stay?"

"I told you, I'm here to teach. Now, can you persuade your husband to round up enough men to get this place in shape?"

By Saturday the inside looked pretty good. Teacher sent me off to tell everyone school would open on Monday.

I was in a dead sleep on Monday morning when Mom's whisper finally got through to me.

"Tommy, come on you young 'angashore, get up out of that bed."

Drifting out of the fog, it took a few minutes to get my wits about me. "What's the matter? Is the house on fire?"

"No, but keep your voice down. We have to take Miss Matthews to school early, to get herself sorted out before the youngsters get there."

That woke me up in a hurry.

"Ah, Mom, you don't expect me to take her to school every day do you? I won't have a dog's life once it gets around. Bram and his crowd will say I'm sucking up to the new teacher."

"Now listen here, Tommy," Mom said. "That spit of a girl is a cripple and look how determined she is to get you young ones back to school. If I was her I'd head right back home on the next train."

I almost said I hoped she'd go, but instead I told Mom she'd likely leave once she came up against Bram's bunch.

"All the more reason to help her all we can," Mom replied. "Some things, son, are worth fighting for."

Fighting is right, I thought, but I held my tongue. Once Mom's mind was made up, there was no use arguing.

We must have been a comical sight, the three of us trudging through the snow. I prayed no one would see me, but just my luck, Will Barnes was in his yard chopping splits. When we came to the steps, I couldn't get free of Teacher's arm fast enough.

"Now me maid, hitch up your coat and I'll see ya safe to the top. I'll be here to give ya a hand getting back this afternoon."

When I saw my mother off she whispered to me, "Tommy, mind you stay around to walk Miss Matthews home."

I felt a knot form in my stomach. " Ah Mom," I pleaded, "do I have to?"

"As long as the snow is around you will."

"I feel sorry for her being a cripple and all, Mom," I said, "but I don't want to be stuck to her like paper to a glue pot. The boys will never let up, *'teacher's pet . . . sooky baby.'* There'll be no end to it."

The very first day it started. Teacher was hanging a map of Newfoundland on the blackboard, and while her back was turned, Bram, who sat behind me, grabbed my arm and twisted it behind my back.

"*Teacher's pet*," he hissed. He tightened his grip and it hurt so bad I let out a yell. As teacher turned around and headed towards us, he let go of my arm.

"What is going on here?"

"Nothing, Miss." Bram looked as if he was about to sprout a halo.

"Really?" she said.

I started to sweat. I knew if she asked was it me who yelled, I'd have to tell the truth, and if I told, Bram, who is older and bigger than me, would skin me.

She looked right at me but she didn't ask.

"Now you boys might as well know I will not tolerate any nonsense in my school. You are here to learn and you, Bramwell, had better apply yourself to your work. Didn't you fail last year?" Bram nodded. "Well then, you surely want to pass your grade and move on, don't you?"

"Oh yes, I wants to move on all right—right out of here," he muttered.

His seatmate, Lal, and his buddies Will and Harv who sat next to him smothered their laughs. Everyone knew that, more than anything, Bram wanted to be at the fishing with his father.

"What did you say, Bramwell?" Her eyes were blazing.

"Oh yes, Miss, that's what I wants, Miss, to move on."

"All right then. Now get busy with your work." With that, she headed back to her desk.

"There goes ducky," Lal whispered. That brought a fit of coughing to cover the laughs. She really did waddle like a duck.

To avoid trouble, I tried to stay out of Bram's way. By Thursday I guess I got careless, and during recess the boys were laying for me in the playground behind the school.

"Well, if it ain't teacher's pet," Lal said. I tried to run, but Harv blocked me.

"How's Duckie's *little ducky* today? Not in cleaning the blackboard?" Bram said. He grabbed me and slapped me against the wall. I lashed out with my boot and tried to break away.

"Where do you think yer going, *sooky baby*. Inside to complain to Miss Ducky? Ain't nothing a cripple teacher can do to me and the boys."

I pounded him as hard as I could but Bram, the big lug, had me on the ground real quick. Then we heard the clang-clang of the bell. You never saw anyone move so fast. Bram was off me and at the door just as teacher stepped outside. I lagged behind him.

"I'll take a turn around the playground with the bell for you, Miss. Save you standing here in the cold." Bram could look so darn innocent.

"Thank you, Bramwell. That's very thoughtful of you."

When everyone was back in school, Bram strolled in, put the bell on teacher's desk, and grinning from ear to ear, took his seat behind me.

Then I got the jab in the back.

"Hey *sooky baby*, ain't Teach the soft touch though?"

I wasn't sure what he meant until lunchtime. Miss Matthews picked up the brass bell and gave it a shake. Dead silence, nothing, not a tinkle. She shook it again. Not a sound. She turned it up and looked inside.

"Bramwell, come here at once." Bram rushed to her desk.

"What is it, Miss?"

"I expect you know very well what it is. You were the last one to touch this bell. What happened to the clapper?"

"The clapper, Miss?"

"Yes, the clapper. You know, the little metal ball that hits the sides to make it ring?"

"Oh I know what the clapper is, Miss. Is something wrong with it?"

"It isn't there, Bramwell, that's what's wrong with it. Where is it?"

"I don't know, Miss. I suppose it must have fallen out. I'll go look for it." He bolted out the door.

Teacher clapped her hands for attention. "Now children, eat your lunch and stay inside until Bramwell returns with the clapper."

Of course Bram didn't find the clapper, and it was a week before Teacher got another school bell. In the meantime, everything was thrown off schedule. No matter who Teacher sent to round us up, we took our own sweet time getting back to work.

Each day, Teacher's temper got worse. I thought she would have a fit the day one of the girls spotted the mouse. Harv brought it to school in a box. I saw him showing it to Bram, but I never thought he would let it loose. It was during morning prayers, and in no time the place was in an uproar. Us boys were running around trying to corner the mouse. Most of the girls were sitting on their desks, skirts hugged tight around their legs, screaming their heads off. No one paid any attention to Teacher. Suddenly she banged the desk several times with her cane. That got our attention.

"Well I never. Such a commotion over a little mouse. All of you sit down at once." No one moved. "Sit down, I said. At once, do you hear me?" We scurried back to our seats. Teacher looked ready to explode.

Someone shouted. "There it goes. Look, over there."

"Don't anyone move," she yelled. "What nonsense, as if a mouse could hurt you. Girls, get down off your desks this instant. Sit properly in your seats. I don't want to see any more of this foolishness."

Teacher was still agitated when we left for home that afternoon. Mom was waiting at the steps as usual.

"How are ya doing, me maid? You looks as if ya had a rough day."

"A rough day. It's been rough ever since I got here. No new school as I was promised, the clapper mysteriously gone out of the school bell and today . . . " she started to sob, "today, the place was bedlam."

Mom put her arms around her. "There, there now. It's too much for ya, ya poor young thing. No one could blame ya if ya got on the next train and went home out of it."

This is it, I thought, she'll quit now for sure.

Teacher stopped sniffling and faced Mom. "No, they will not drive me out. Not as long as I can still crawl up those steps, they won't." She blew her nose and dried her eyes. "I'm sure Bramwell and his friends are behind all this, but, Tommy, I know you are having your own problems with them, so it's not fair to ask you to tell. Somehow I have to gain their respect on my own."

Right then, I had to admit she was one spunky lady.

She took hold of Mom's arm, I offered her my arm and the three of us walked home. But, for the life of me, I couldn't see how she would get the better of Bram and his buddies.

The rest of the week was pretty quiet in school. The mouse was caught, Teacher had her new bell, and except for the usual spitballs and paper planes flying about, things had returned to normal.

Monday was a different story. It was a cold, windy day and Teacher told us older boys to keep the wood to the fire. After recess, Bram left his seat and went to add more birch junks to the stove. Suddenly there were three loud bangs.

"Bramwell, what on earth are you doing?"

"This junk is stuck, Miss. I'm trying to knock it in." Using another junk as a hammer, he hit it again and again.

"Stop that at once, you'll shake the stovepipe apart."

"Just one more crack, Miss, that should do the trick." We all started to giggle as Bram gave it one more whack. The pipe broke open. Giggles turned into coughs, sneezes and runny eyes, as smoke and soot poured into the classroom. Bram coughed so hard you would swear he was choking. When he saw Teacher coming he went into his angel act.

"Gee, Miss, I got the junk in, see. Too bad the pipe broke. Guess there's nothing for it but for all hands to go home."

"Go home. Indeed you won't go home. You young devil, you did that on purpose." Holding a handkerchief over her nose, she slammed the stove door shut. "Some of you boys open the windows to help clear the air."

"Hurrah, a holiday," the children shouted.

"Oh no, there will be no holiday. Get into your coats, then return to your seats. Now Bramwell, since you caused this problem, you can jolly well put it right."

"You want me to go for Mr. Ray, Miss? He usually fixes the stove."

"No you won't go for Mr. Ray or anyone else. You, Bramwell, are going to fix it."

"Me, Miss? I don't know nothing about fixing stovepipes."

"Well since you are so good at knocking them apart, let's see how good you are at knocking them together again. Get the stepladder, roll up your sleeves and get started. It's getting cold in here. Wear your mitts so you don't burn yourself. Lal, you can give him a hand."

"Why me, Miss? I didn't do nothin."

"Surely, Lal, you would like to help your best friend. Get to it and no more fooling around. Now children we'll continue with our lessons."

There were loud groans of "Oh heck" and "Ah Miss, have a heart."

"Put on your coats and try to keep warm because there will be no holiday today. We will carry on as usual. Primary, get out your copybooks and practice your letters. Preliminary, continue with your sums and brush up on your multiplication tables. Intermediates, go over the poem I assigned yesterday. Who can tell me which poem it is?"

Emily, who was always smart in English literature, jumped to her feet. "'The Charge of the Light Brigade,' Miss. By Tennyson."

"Absolutely right, Emily. Now, everyone get to work, and in a while we will do some marching and singing to warm us up."

It took a long, cold hour for Bram and Lal to fit the pieces of stovepipe back together. Bram, soot from head to toe, stood before Teacher.

"It's all fixed, Miss, so I'll run on home now. I needs to get a wash."

"You'll get a wash, but I'm afraid you will have to make do with the soap and water here. And when you finish washing, take your seat with the others."

Now everyone knows cold water is next to useless against soot. A laugh went up when Bram, still looking like someone just come up out of a coal mine, flopped down in his seat. Teacher clapped her hands for attention.

"Now then, Bramwell, open your Royal Reader to the poem you have to memorize before next lesson. Bram shuffled the pages and found the poem. He started reading to himself.

"No, no, stand up Bramwell and read it out loud to the class." Snickers came from all around the room as Bram, his face streaked with soot and looking very sheepish, got slowly to his feet and started to read. "'Half a league, half a league/Half a league onward/All in the valley of Death/Rode the six hundred . . .'"

Through a Glass, Darkly

Trudy J. Morgan-Cole

My life began in October of grade eight. I'd been expecting this. In January I had a feeling, an idea, that Something Would Happen in October. I opened the gold clasp on my new Holly Hobbie diary and flipped ahead to October, wondering what it would bring. Jeff Harris would finally notice me and go out with me. Neil Diamond would come to St. John's for a concert. Something. Anything. I drew a red star next to every day in October.

The day, when it arrives, is an ordinary one—a gray-white sky and the wind cool enough to need the mitts I have shoved deep in my jacket pockets. I'm not wearing them because the new girl isn't wearing hers. The metal railing burns cold under my fingers as I watch her. I usually get the bus home with my best friend, but today she's sick. And the new girl is sitting beside me on the concrete steps of the Salvation Army Citadel where Route 7 stops, saying, "Mom and Dad usually drive me home, but they've got a staff meeting or something today and Mom wants me home early to vacuum the living room."

On the bus, she leads the way to a seat much farther in the back than where I usually sit. She gets the window seat and stares out the window intently, her arms clasped around her dark green bookbag. She's shorter than me and I find myself staring down at her hair. It's long, straight, sheer black. I want hair like hers, skin like hers, a soft raspy voice like hers.

"I love riding buses," she says at last. "I like looking down at the cars."

"Yeah—I do too."

"Did you ever look at people in other cars and wonder about them? I mean like there they are, in their little cars, behind their windshields, and we only see the outside. But in there, they've got lives of their own—every one of them has their own thoughts, their own friends and family—a whole *world* of their own." Her brown eyes, dark-browed and forceful, brighten as she turns to me.

"I know," I say. "That just hit me one day when I was in the mall, looking at people. It made me feel weird." My best friend was with me then, but I didn't tell her about it.

"Everything makes me feel weird," the new girl says.

"Me too," I say. "Sometimes, anyway."

"Do you ever write poems, Shannon?"

I say, "Sometimes."

Right away I know this is it. Something Has Happened. The window of the bus closes in like the coverslip on one of Mr. Redmond's microscope slides, suspending me and the new girl in this moment, while I answer the question I've been waiting all my life for someone to ask.

"Yeah, do you?"

"Yeah . . . I wrote one today in science. While Mr. Redmond was droning on. Want to see it?"

Out of her binder comes a smudged and crumpled sheet of loose leaf. I'm almost scared to read it. The moment seems as fragile and perfect as the wind chimes Aunt Gladys brought from Florida, all made of creamy pink shells, and if her poem is one of those sappy things like Sandra McKinnon writes for her boyfriend (*I love you more and more each day, Please don't ever go away*), everything will be spoiled. I hold my breath, and the paper in my hands.

Her poem shimmers through the blurry pencil. It's free verse, better than any of my poems. I read the last four lines over again and again.

I have secrets
That you cannot see
I have dreams
You will never believe.

When I give it back I can't think what to say. "This is *so* good," I manage finally.

She folds it up and sticks it back in her binder.

"Can I have a copy?" I ask.

"Sure." She looks pleased, flattered. She isn't perfect and distant after all. She needs me. Then she says, "Can I see your poems someday?"

"Oh, sure."

~~~

The bus pulls into the Village Mall lot. "We've got to change here to Number 6," I say, "or else walk home."

"It's not that far. Let's walk."

We get off, but instead of going towards the road she heads for the doors of the mall. "Let's go shopping!"

"I thought you had to vacuum for your mother."

"Aw, I'll get home in time to do that." Inside the Village she goes straight for the phones. "Have you got two dimes?" she asks.

I find two dimes in my purse and hand them to her. She puts them in the phone, dials, waits, and asks for a guy whose name I don't recognize. Rolls her eyes while she waits for him to answer. Then says, "Hi, it's me. Whatcha doin'?"

Pause. "I'm at the Village. Wanna come over?" She grabs my wrist to see my watch. "OK, meet me by the fountain at quarter to four."

"Who's that?" I ask when she hangs up.

"My boyfriend. He lives up by us. He doesn't go to our school."

Well, that's pretty obvious. Our school is small—I know everyone in it. We go over to sit by the fountain.

When the boyfriend shows up, he has dark hair parted in the middle, wears a black KISS shirt under a denim jacket, and is about as tall as I am. I've never had a boyfriend and neither has my best friend, so I'm not sure how the new girl and her boyfriend will act. But they don't hug or kiss or anything. She just introduces us and we get up and start drifting through the mall.
~~~

We go into Smart Set because she sees some jeans she wants to try. While she's in the fitting room, I try to look interested in stuff on the racks. I flip through a rack of blouses, each one looking pretty much like the others. Her boyfriend stands with his hands in his pockets, looking as bored as I feel. Neither of us says anything.

She comes back out. "They didn't fit," she says. "I need to lose weight."

"That's stupid," her boyfriend says, and he's right. She's even skinnier than I am.

"Oh *look*," she says, lunging at a rack. "And it's in my size. Oh, I've *got* to try it on." The dress is red lace over a red slip, with spaghetti straps and a drop waist. She pulls out another dress—black—and thrusts it at me. "Here, I'll try it on if you try this one."

Fitting rooms have always been for me to stand in while my mother sends the salesgirl for another size of that navy blue skirt or another colour sweater. I had no idea they were places where you could have fun, trying on clothes you never intended to buy, costuming for roles you might never play. I let the new girl steer me towards the fitting room, but just as we get there she breaks away. "I have to grab something else," she says.

The black dress, after I twist myself like a pretzel to zip it up, doesn't look right. It's strapless and I have nothing yet to hold it up with. The scratchy material stands stiffly away from where my bust should be. My chest and shoulders look startlingly white against the black material. The dress is glamorous but the parts sticking out still look like me. I come out and stand in the little hallway.

"Just a second, I'll be right out," she calls from the next stall. I wait because I don't want to go out alone in the black dress, to let her boyfriend see me.

She comes out walking slowly, almost like a model. She wears a huge, broad-brimmed black hat and a double strand of beads, and with the red dress they make her look about seventeen. She isn't exactly pretty but she is glamorous.

Her boyfriend grins when he sees us. He has a hat in his hand, a black fedora that looks OK for a guy even though this is a women's store. He takes a pair of sunglasses out of his pocket, puts them on, and tilts the hat forward on his head. The three of us stand in front of the three-way mirror and he puts his arms around both of us, one on either side. "Now I look like a gangster, and ye're my two ladies," he says.

"Molls," I say. "I think gangsters' women are called molls." I read that somewhere.

"Moll One and Moll Two," the new girl says, and we all stand staring at our reflections and giggling till a salesgirl looks over at us and starts to walk in our direction.

I'm giddy as we reel out into the mall again. My shoulder still seems warm where the boyfriend's arm was. We go into a bookstore and he starts flipping through MAD magazine, showing me different parts he likes. The new girl goes off to look for something in another section. When she comes back to where we're laughing at the comics, she walks up behind us. She tugs at my sleeve and says loudly in a fake accent, "Pliss, can you tell me vere da books on SEX are?"

She says the word sex loudly, and a man in the next aisle glances over. We double over laughing but she keeps on. "No, pliss, I must find dese SEX books. I vant a book dat vill tell me how to haff goot SEX—" Her eyes are very wide and she keeps a perfectly straight face until we're all outside the store.

Weak with laughter, we stumble over to the railing where we can look down at the fountain on the first floor. Huge jets of rainbow water shoot up into the second storey. The boyfriend takes three pennies out of his pocket and hands one to each of us. "Make a wish," he says.

The new girl and I drop our pennies into the water below, but he flips his so it spins up, curves, and falls spinning down. Then we both want to try that, so he pulls out more pennies. But ours don't spin like his did. Finally I get it right and my penny—a brilliant new one—spins up into the air. Just as it passes the top of its copper arc and starts to fall, the boy reaches out over the rail and snatches that shining thing out of the air. He opens his fist to show it gleaming in his palm.

We don't leave the Village till five o'clock. I know my mother will be wondering where I am. My street is beyond theirs, so I walk the last few blocks alone, staring at the houses and streets I see every day. They look as different as they did when I came home wearing my first pair of glasses and saw for the first time blades of grass, leaves on trees, where before I had seen only a flat green blur. When I get in the house my mother tells me my best friend called three times. I promised to phone her as soon as I got home from school.

~~~

That's not the way it happened, of course. That's what I've just written, glowing words on the screen in front of me. Where do the memories leave off and the lies begin?

So much gets left out this way. I'm trying to make our school, my adolescence, sound as generic as possible, maybe thinking of the market for my story. But really, how do I capture the feel of a small, church-run school, a tightly-knit evangelical community where everything centred on those two brick buildings, church, and school, at opposite ends of the parking lot? A world so tiny and self-contained you could drop a plastic dome over it and sell it for a souvenir. Turn it upside down to make it snow.

Also, this business of not using names isn't working. I don't know if I'm striving for a certain effect, but I'm writing "the new girl," "her boyfriend," "my best friend," when what I'm meaning is "Liz," "Derek," "Kathy." I was afraid of making up names, afraid it wouldn't seem real. And I thought of writing in their real names and changing them after. The wordsearch could do it. "Change all Liz to"—to—to "Jessica." That would be a good name for Liz, though not so popular as it became ten years later. But if I wrote their real names, I'd feel tied to the facts.

And facts are not what I'm writing, are they? I don't even remember the facts. It's true I did meet Liz and Derek one day in October, 1978. Liz and I took the bus home together and met Derek at the Village. And it's true I knew right away that they were different from anyone I'd ever known before. I don't remember what Liz said to me on the bus. That thing about the people in cars, I think she said that later. Another time. She did show me her poem, though. And we did try on clothes, though that red dress is one I remember from another time and place. And talking about the sex books in her fake-German accent—that's factual. But most of the details of that day are fuzzy, lost to view.

Another thing—Kathy must not have ridden the bus with me that
~~~

day, but I don't remember why. She could have been sick. I don't know if she called or not. She was in grade nine, a year ahead of me, and we didn't always hang around together although we were still best friends. She had friends in her own class, too. My story makes it sound like I made a clear-cut choice of one friendship over another, but that's not how it was.

The poem, at least, is authentic. I kept Liz's poems, though she did not keep mine. From the pile of old diaries, notes, and letters on the floor at my feet, round grade-eight handwriting stares up at me, a real document from an unreal past, as eerie as manuscripts in glass cases at the museum. Next to that pencilled, adolescent scrawl, the neat lines I've written here look as orderly as interpretive plaques next to those glass cases, telling who wrote this and in what year. As orderly, and as irrelevant. Why not let the documents tell their own story, if there is a story to be told?

My fingers slip from the keys. As usual, I'm easily distracted from a story that isn't working. Liz's poem blinks up at me, the real past challenging my story. Next to it, one of my poems—mine always in pen, hers always in pencil.

> Wild as the wind and free you are,
> My friend, as you go your way,
> And the path you travel will lead you on
> 'Neath skies of blue or grey.

I probably gave Liz a copy of this one, since I wrote it for her. Maybe I gave it to her at lunchtime, when we sat on the fire escape stairs eating our lunches, my tuna sandwich making the air pungent. Or perhaps it was after school as we hung around an empty classroom, waiting for her mother to finish grading so we could go home. I wrote many of my poems to her, to the wild dancing creature I saw in her and so badly wanted to see in myself.

Beneath the poem, old science class notes. I wrote "ROCKS" neatly at the top of the page, but my handwriting grew looser and swirled as my hand drifted down the page and my mind drifted away from Mr. Redmond's dry commentary on igneous and sedimentary rocks. Behind me Jeff Harris says, "My sediments exactly," and I crack up quietly because Jeff said it and it's funny. Little shaded hearts tumble down the margin of the paper. I can see where I've written "JH" in one of them, then scratched it out, wanting and not wanting Jeff to see. In one corner I've doodled the face of a girl with long eyelashes, huge lips, long flowing hair. Was I looking at Liz then, back when she was still The New Girl, wondering if I'd ever get to know her? So far she didn't seem to have any special close friends, though lots of girls wanted to be friends with her. I wondered what she was really like—if, underneath her black hair, she might be the friend I'd dreamed of meeting.

I turn back to the poem on the top of my pile, run my finger along its ragged spiral-bound edges. No date on it, but I know this is the first one she gave me—that much I remember, no embellishments. That day on the bus, riding home. Even now the smudged, blurry lines dance on the page, charged with possibility.

You speak of rocks and mountains
You don't know that
I am a rock.
You can see me but
You can't get inside.
You can touch me
But you shall never break me
For I am strong
I have power
I have secrets
That you cannot see
I have dreams
You will never believe.

On the corner of the page she has written "LM+DD" inside a red heart. Derek Drake. She writes that while we're waiting at the Village for Derek to show up. Later I will see her inscribe "DD" on her arm in red pen, a makeshift tattoo, and say she plans to get a real tattoo when she's fourteen. (She does.) I may not remember the exact details of that day at the Village, but this paper still pulses with the energy that surged through me as I ran home that day, the three of us shouting with laughter as Derek chased us around the monkey bars in the playground behind Liz's house. I was afraid to slip and fall: the day might shatter.

Once again I click the lock on the Holly Hobbie diary and leaf through its pages. The entries were terse, shaped to fit on the tiny lined sheets. I purposely wrote only summaries of the day's events, leaving out anything private in case Kathy ever wanted to read my diary. I riffle my finger along the gilt edges of the pages, looking for October. By then, near the end of the year, I was less conscientious about writing. Days, sometimes weeks, are blank, always followed by an entry that begins: "Sorry I haven't written in so long." Sure enough, the days of October are spangled with red stars. On the third: *In January I had a premonition that something nice—no, maybe something bad—but, anyway, something that will change my life, would happen in October. Something MAY happen, but I suspect I shall have to bring it about myself. Keep you posted.* I think I was still expecting to entice Jeff Harris into falling in love with me. When I read my diary now, I wonder, what could I have been reading then? *Emily of New Moon*, probably.

When I find the eighteenth, it's marked as a "Super Day" (I coded the days—Super, Good, OK, Bad, Awful), but the entry says only, *Went to the Village after school with Liz Leary and her boyfriend DD. They're crazy. We had fun.*

Is that *all*? How did I not know, why didn't I write, *My life began today?* I pick up my journal, the shabby spiral-bound notebook that lived between the mattress and box spring while my diary sat proudly next to my Bible and alarm clock. The entries here are fewer but longer, the handwriting messier. That summer before grade eight I wrote, *Even though Kathy is my best friend I feel there are so many things I can never share with her. Sometimes I feel she doesn't really know me at all. I wish I had a true kindred spirit.* There's no entry at all for October, though. Liz and Derek don't even get mentioned till November. I've copied out one of Liz's poems on the pages of my journal. *How can the wind/Sing so freely/When I am in a cage?* Something she must have written in class.

From the pile of loose pages on the floor I pull out one creased from being folded over and over before it was surreptitiously passed across the aisle in class. My writing, tall and spiky; Liz's rounded and full of swirls and curlicues.

Shannon, what was it you were
going to ask me this morning?

What was wrong with DD last
night? He seemed in a real bad
mood when he left your place.
Did you guys have a fight?

I guess you could call it a
fight. He's driving me
crazy. He acts like he owns
me. We fight about it all
the time. You know I can't
stand feeling trapped.

I smooth out the page and place it next to my poem: *Wild as the wind and free you are.* Already my mind is juxtaposing them, making a story. Did I write this poem for Liz after she wrote me that note?

I know, anyway, that shortly after this note came the long, scrawled journal entry that begins: *Liz and DD broke up today. She talked to me for a long time after school and then, much to my surprise, he called me tonight.* I can still hear his voice, feel the hot phone pressed to my ear and chin as I sit curled against the wall in our hall. He talks to me for an hour, talks about Liz and the necklace he bought her for Christmas that he can't give her now. In his story there haven't been any fights; he loves her and can't understand why she would want to break up. In my journal I have written things like: *I hope I can still be friends with both of them* and *I didn't know what to say to Derek, I hope the little I did say helped.* But nowhere have I written what I'm sure I remember feeling: balancing between my after-school talk with Liz in the playground, muffled in scarves to our ears, and my nighttime conversation with

Derek, I felt strangely elated. They both needed me; I was important to both of them; I was on the inside of something at last.

~~~

These shabby and smudged papers—*Memoirs of a Poetess at Thirteen*—and the sharp fragments of memory I have preserved through the years. No more the real story than the one I tried to write. What *really* happened has disappeared like the coins in the fountain at the Village.

There's another version of this story—no, there are many others. Liz's version? Derek's? Does that afternoon at the Village exist at all in their memories? Where are their turning points marked? Now that I think about it, I see all our different stories, like huge panes of glass, intersecting here and there, stretching off into infinity. Each tilted at a slightly different angle. Despite what Liz and I knew at thirteen about the people in other cars, I didn't really see the separateness of those planes until ten years later. Until the night I heard another version of this story.

~~~

Kathy and I sit on the fold-out bed in my first apartment. It is 2:15 a.m. and we're eating potato chips. We don't see each other often these days, and when we do we frantically talk through the night, storing up moments of friendship.

The summer I was eleven-turning-twelve, the summer before grade seven, I went to camp and Kathy was in my cabin, although she was a year older. We knew each other because we were both from town and went to the same church and school. The other four girls in our cabin were all from around the bay and Kathy and I used to laugh when one of them would say, "Go in the cabin and get that machine off my bunk for me," and it could be a camera or a swimsuit or anything. We were partners for canoeing and had to tip the canoe over together. Kathy told me that she had her period and couldn't go swimming the whole week of camp. Neither of us had a boyfriend.

So we became best friends, and stayed best friends in September when I started grade seven, though we weren't in the same grade. You couldn't really have a best friend outside of your own grade but Kathy and I were an exception to that rule. The next summer we went to camp again and both had a crush on Barry West from Bay Roberts. We stole his baseball cap and took turns sleeping with it until Rhonda Bragg found it and told on us.

Somehow, sitting on the fold-out bed, we get to remembering this. What our lives were like before everything. We both remember Barry West's cap and laugh over it. Why did we stop being best friends after that? I say maybe because she was in grade nine; grade nines always seemed so much older than grade eights.

She wrinkles her brow. "Sure that's when you started hanging out with Liz and Derek. You never had time for anyone else. Don't you remember that time Derek cursed at me down to church?"

"Derek *cursed* at you? At *church*?"

"You don't mean to say you don't remember that. It was at that party they had for the young people, where Heather and them put on that skit?"

Heather and her crowd were older than us and were always putting on skits. At any party with them, we would have been the little kids. I remember parties in the church basement and in people's rec rooms, for ages thirteen to seventeen. The sixteens and seventeens were the centre of attention and we younger ones lived our vivid lives in the margins. Kids like Derek who didn't go to our church, but knew people who did, came along and were closely watched by the adults.

But I don't remember any party where Derek cursed at Kathy.

"Go on, Shannon, you must remember." There is something like shock or disappointment on Kathy's face—maybe how I would look if Liz told me she didn't remember asking for sex books at Coles. "You and Liz and Derek were out in the hall laughing and carrying on, making a whole lot of noise, and they were starting up some kind of game inside. Mrs. Spencer sent me out to tell whoever was in the hall to get inside. So I came out and asked you to come in, and Liz just laughed at me. I said, 'No, come on in, they're starting a game and they want everyone in here.' And she said they could go on without you, and Derek said he didn't want to play no kids' games."

This scene doesn't exist in my memory at all, but as Kathy talks it begins to take shape. I can see Derek leaning against the wall, collar of his denim jacket turned up (this would be before he took to wearing black leather), hands deep in his pockets, eyes rolled back in his head.

"So then I started to get mad," Kathy goes on. "I guess I felt stupid. I didn't care about Liz and Derek, but I wasn't used to you getting on like that, making trouble. So I looked over at you, thinking you'd back me up, and you just shrugged. And Derek said, 'Why don't you mind your own damn business, bitch?' And I just stood there, like I was too shocked to move."

I shake my head. I cannot believe this. This is not a scene I played in. Nothing sounds familiar.

"So I looked back at you, because I couldn't believe you'd put up with that. I thought you'd stand up for me, I thought for sure you'd leave them and come back in to the party with me. But you didn't say anything, and I turned and walked away. Even when I got back in I couldn't believe you were still out there with them."

"I don't remember any of that at all."

Kathy shakes her head, reaches for a chip from the half-empty bag. "Well, that's what happened. I can still hear it clear as day—mind your own damn business, bitch."

"Did we get in any trouble—did anyone say anything to Derek?"

"No, I never told—I think I was too shocked. Or maybe I just didn't want to look like a sook."

"Well—I'm sorry."

Kathy laughs. "Not much odds now, girl."

But I am, belatedly, terribly sorry. It's a stranger's story to me: I still can't remember being me, Shannon, in that hallway. Instead I feel like I'm inside Kathy's skin, walking away alone from the cold eyes of my best friend. It's so much like the sort of thing that would happen—did happen—to me. I can't believe it happened to Kathy. I can't believe I had the power—or the need—to do that to her.

We shake our heads and try to laugh over it. But can't, quite. "Mind your own damn business, bitch." "Vere are da sex books, pliss?" The words that hang on in our memories, on which we hang everything that ever happens to us.

~~~

And here I am with my fingers on the keys, the letters dancing behind their glass screen, trying to write a story. But whose story? Where do they end, these intersecting panes of glass? If I could see them all, what would I know?

I scroll back up through the pages, trying to read my story through Kathy's eyes, through Derek's or Liz's. But of course I can't; I can't even see it through my own eyes anymore. All I see are details I've invented, blanks I've filled in. Conversations I don't remember having, a dress I'm not sure I wore.

Oh, and that part about throwing pennies in the fountain? I made that up—but it's the truest part of the whole story.
~~~

Sheilagh's Brush

Marilyn Porter

The March of the year, it is winter still,
with Sheilagh to come, and her last-minute Brush,
to crash down the cliff, in a mad, wild rush
and a dump of snow right up to the sill.

Brings a bitter wind to bewilder and chill,
the tender buds to wither and crush.
The March of the year, it is winter still,
with Sheilagh to come, and her last-minute Brush.

Then as fast as she came, she goes over the hill,
leaving behind the grey mounds of slush.
Sheilagh has gone, having taken her fill
Galumping around, birch broom in the fits.

The March of the year, it is winter still,
with Sheilagh to come, and her last-minute Brush.

Baked Beans and Gingerbread

Esther Slaney-Brown

It was a marvelous winter. We didn't eat many pork chops or roasts that year. It also proved to be a harder season than usual on the henhouse population. The big cellar on the side of the hill emptied earlier than usual. Mondays, Wednesdays, and Saturdays the kitchen was filled with the pungent odour of baked beans and gingerbread. There was no need to complain. An hour or two of flying down the hill on the slides, Dad, a carpenter by trade, had built for us, and we were ready for any fare.

We seldom saw our father. He worked "with the Americans" at an air force base on the Labrador. A few weeks a year, usually in July, he made an appearance. It didn't do us children a whole lot of good. He spent that time making repairs to the old country house my parents bought when they were first married. Fathers, back then, showed their love by putting food on the table and a roof over the heads of their ever-expanding family. Sunday afternoon drives in the resurrected Ford, which spent forty-nine weeks a year propped up on blocks in the garage was our only "quality time."

Ours was an old-fashioned kitchen known to us as "the house," probably because we did all our living in that one room. It was large enough to contain an enormous wood range—a monstrosity of steel and cream-coloured enamel. On each edge of the warming oven were stuck three red carnations I had cut from the Carnation Milk can. Beside the stove stood a small crib, a snug spot for the newest addition. Over the stove was a clothesline. Its purpose was to finish drying the clothes brought in from outside, or on rainy days to dry the few baby napkins my mother rinsed out to tide her over.

One corner was designated for a table big enough, when the leaves were up, to feed a dozen or more. After supper, it was converted to a desk for homework with enough room at one end for Mom's sewing machine.

Sitting against the wall, under the window, was the daybed. My father spent one winter on that daybed. It never occurred to our parents to tell us children that he was recuperating from a serious illness. We went to school as usual. Our mother busied herself with her family. When Christmas came, we killed one of the hens. Santa brought less—we didn't even notice. A small bow and arrow with a little suction cup on its tip had been my brother's gift that year.

What we did notice was the times my father, while lying on the bed, got our mother in the bum with one of the arrows. He would wink at us children. We pressed our fists to curling lips trying not to let our giggles give him away. Dad would quickly take aim and—swoosh—the little arrow would find its target. After a few hundred times, Mom decided to ignore him.

"Men are like children," she would say, grinning. "The more attention you give them the worse they get."

The weather turned harsh that year. We managed more than a few reprieves from the dreaded schoolhouse. On long winter days we would climb on the daybed while Dad sang songs or recited silly poems he could make up at the drop of a hat. When the bedlam got to Mom she would light the parlour stove and drive out the lot of us.

Spring broke and Dad's health improved. He was up and around helping Mom in the kitchen, slicing the turnips or peeling potatoes. He never changed the baby's napkin; neither of my parents would consider this appropriate work for a man. Slicing the turnips, which proved particularly hard that year, or peeling a few spuds were his domestic limits.

One evening when a strong March wind threatened to put out our electricity, Dad took over. He got bundled up and went to the store in search of kerosene. He pulled on his oilskins, gathered up a couple of old bottles to hold the oil, and was out the door before Mom could stop him. Ten minutes later the bulb flickered and died. Mom lit the only lamp still containing oil. We sat around the table, watching the flame throwing strange shadows around the room. I can honestly say it was the first time that winter I saw my mother worried.

We children sat around the table trying to concentrate on our homework. The baby cried, Mom picked him up. She pulled a napkin from the line, changed him, and put him down again without saying a word. We looked at each other and went back to our struggle by lamplight.

Storms had always been fun in our home. Mom would stoke the old stove and put the kettle on to boil. With the wind howling, it was our custom to sit around the table drinking cocoa and munching on Purity Milk Lunch biscuits. Not so this night. Rain pelted against the windows. It sent a strange, uncomfortable chill through our souls. The safe, cosy kitchen didn't exist that evening.

After an hour or so we heard a noise in the back porch. Mom stared expectantly at the kitchen door. Dad stepped into the house and shook the water from his sou'wester. He passed the two bottles to Mom. Then he reached inside his rubber jacket and pulled out the biggest sack of candy we ever saw. It wasn't the usual, small, brown-paper bag; this one could hold a whole pound of onions.

"My God, Mike! What were you thinking about?" Mom sat at the table watching us clamouring for the long-forgotten treat. My sister and I, being the oldest, dug in first, looking for our favourite colours. I loved the white ones, she the red. Our oldest brother managed to get a few purple ones. Then we contrived to convince the younger children that the yellow and green ones were their favourites. Dad sat at the table wiping the rain from his face, a big grin reaching from ear to ear. Mom finally got in the mood and reached for a black candy. We children always left the black ones for her. They were her favourite.

We sat around the table while the wind huffed and puffed at our sturdy old house. The baby gurgled in his crib. The rain danced on the windowpane. Wood crackled in the big Avalon stove. Dad just sat there grinning. Now I understand. That night my father realized he had weathered the storm.

Summer arrived early that year. We pulled out the skipping ropes from the garage, careful not to rub up against the dusty black Ford. We played hopscotch in the gravel driveway while tantalizing odours of fresh meat and onions frying drifted out the open kitchen window. Our lives were as before.

This past fall, long before the first snow fell, as we sat around his bed, reminiscing about the good times, our father peacefully weathered his final storm.

It's Saturday afternoon. I sit in my modern kitchen. A computer has replaced the sewing machine. The aroma of baked beans and gingerbread permeates the entire house. I am comforted.

Like Air-Bubbles

LILLIAN BOUZANE

Like air-bubbles
        our days in the mud
                come back to me

In a thin vein
        near the riverbank
                we found white clay for our pies

My Old Gaiters

GERALDINE FLANNIGAN

BECAUSE IT BEGINS to snow, Mrs. Wall lets us out ten minutes early. I noticed it had rained just before we got back in school, leaving a sunny, icy sheen on everything. But now, a thin sheet of fresh white snow covers the ground.

Mom told me to go to the store on the way home to get a loaf of bread for supper. I bundle up—snow pants, jacket, scarf, cap, two pairs of mittens. Finally, I pull on my gaiters. I head for the door, thinking about the candy I will buy out of the four cents that's left over. Before I leave, I make sure the quarter is safe in my pocket.

My gaiters are old, but I don't realize they have no grips on them. Just as I step out the door, down I go. I get up, steady myself, but down I slide again. The road is a complete sheet of ice. I can't find a good place to walk. My feet won't hold me up. They are so wobbly that every step I take, I slip. I will never reach the store at this speed, let alone home. My God, please, what can I do? This road is so slippery, lovely glitter Mom would call it, but it's not pretty to me. Even these baby steps can't hold me upright. There's not a soul in sight. No one to see, let alone help. Perhaps when I get to the store Mrs. Perry will see my misery and do something. Maybe she will ask Mr. Perry to give me a drive home.

Thank you, God. I can see the shop. It seems to take forever to reach the door. When I step in, I'm surprised to feel the safety of the floor not moving. I'm sure the quarter is not in my pocket. I'm certain that it has bounced out.

Thank heavens, it's there. I'm surprised at its warmth. "Gee, Mrs. Perry, it's some slippery out there. I must have fell down a thousand times. Mom needs a loaf of bread and I'll have four cents worth of jaw breakers."

I take the bread off the counter and put the candies snug in my pocket. I head for the door but the memory of that road makes me hesitate. I doubt that even the candy will bring sweet joy. I know I can't manage eating with the road a sheet of ice. I'll probably bite my tongue off. Maybe I'll sit by the side of the road . . . gee I can't do that, Mom will be waiting for the bread. I comfort myself with the thought that I'll eat the candy when I get home. Before I leave, I turn around. In desperation, I look straight into Mrs. Perry's eyes. She just stands there and murmurs, "Goodbye Jeanie."

I step outside. I move carefully to the roadway. I'm no sooner on the road when I slide down again. My God, don't let me squash the bread. We need the bread for supper and Mom will bawl me out if it is all squished up.

Now I can't stand on my feet at all. Will I ever get home? What am I going to do? I look up at the sky. I notice it's getting dark. Have I been on the road that long? Oh God, please send someone to get me, please. How come Mom hasn't sent someone to find me? This road is so icy; I'll never get there. The road holds no pity. It's still a sheet of grease. Nanny would call this something wicked and I fully agree with her. I look around to see if there is any gravel. There is none . . . not one rock, not even a spot of clay. I slither to one side of the road . . . then to the other. But nothing makes any difference. The friggin' ice. I have no way out. I have to walk. I have no other choice. I wonder if my legs were normal would I be going through this? I look up and down the road again. There's still no one to help. I pray again, but my prayers aren't answered. I'll never get home. I'll never get this bread home in time.

Each time I fall, I throw the bread aside. I can't land on the bread. Ouch, now there is a sharp pain in my hip. I can feel hot tears running down my cheeks. Maybe if I crawl, I'll get home quicker. No. I can't do that. That looks worse than falling down. I'm not going to get home. Damn these gaiters. I'm throwing them away when I get home. This up and down, up and down. I have no use for this darn game. Oh thank

God. I can see my house. As I think warm thoughts of home, I lose my footing again. Oh no, God, I fell on the bread. Mom is going to smack me.

The smell of supper greets my nose. I'm only a few feet away. Now if I cry out, someone will hear me. Carefully and slowly I stand on my feet, yell, but fall flat on my face. That's it; I'm going to crawl home. The bread is already squashed, so who cares?

At last, I make it to the door and bang on it. Mom comes and takes the bread. "What happened to you, Jeanie? We're waiting for the bread. What happened to it?" When I hear these words, tears stream from my eyes. I get to my feet, go inside, pull off the gaiters, head straight for the kitchen, open the damper on the stove and throw them in. The kitchen fills with the smell of burning rubber. I wipe the tears away, take my jaw breakers and sit in the little corner by the stove savouring their sweetness.

Boxing Arena

ANNE FERNCASE

My baby sister and me,
fat-packed & pugnacious,
shared the last bed,
parked in the hall.
We were the bump
in the night
between the bathroom
and the laundry.

Each night we'd fight over
Gramma's blue square of wool
which never quite covered
our two bulbous bums
until sleep, like a good right hook,
knocked us out.

Follow the Crows

Hilda Chaulk Murray

"Come on, Sare. We'll be all day 'fore we gets on the berry hills." Practical, serious Hetty, anxious to start picking berries, was feeling annoyed with her red-haired younger companion who was dilly-dallying more than usual. When they went berry picking Hetty usually led the way if the path would not let them walk side by side. They didn't talk much so she had gone a hundred feet or more before she realized Sarah was not right behind her. Instead, when she looked around there was Sarah standing stock-still watching a flock of crows wheeling over a small patch of trees in an overgrown, disused garden about a half mile away to their left.

At Hetty's call, Sarah came running up to her. "I was jus' wonderin', Hetty, why do you think the crows are makin' such a racket over there in Jabe's old garden?"

Concerned only with picking as many berries as she could, Hetty replied rather sharply, "P'raps there's a dead cat or somethin' fer 'em to pick at. Anyway, we don't have time to be gaping at crows. We've got to figure out the best spot for us to go to today. Everyone else went off early but Mam wanted *me* to help with the Saturday cleanin' and half the day is gone."

"Evelyn and that crowd've gone in to Tumbledown Rocks, I think," volunteered Sarah.

"There's lots in there, but that's too far fer us to go. Mam wants me back in time to help get supper fer Pap and the boys. Let's try that little dry hill over there in the middle of the mesh. Old Addie used to pick berries there all the time. Mam calls it 'Addie's Purley'."

Walking carefully around bushes and small bog holes, the girls followed the meandering, single-file path across the marsh to the dry hillock. This little "island" was separated from the low rocky ridge that went all the way to Flowers Pond by about twenty feet of bog that had no clearly defined path between it and the ridge. They found the "island" was indeed a choice spot for berries and both set to work gathering the small ruby-red berries that formed a lustrous carpet beneath their feet.

Now, picking partridgeberries keeps the fingers busy but frees the mind, and Sarah's thoughts flitted from one subject to another as the berries mounted in her emper. She saw herself grown-up, leaving Muddy Brook, fashionably dressed in a suit with a frilly, high-collared blouse like the teacher sometimes wore, she thought of the people she knew in that small community and in the nearby cove—her aunt, her cousins, Hetty's family, the missing Sal Brown—and the crows. Aloud she said: "Hetty, did your mother say anything 'bout Sal Brown lately?"

"No," replied Hetty, "'cept to warn me to be awful careful round the cliffs and the bogholes and to keep an eye out fer the fog. That's partly why she don't want us goin' farther in the country. 'Fraid we'd lose our way and never be seen again, like Sal."

"P'raps she's run away with some man. That's what I heard Evelyn and them sayin'."

"No one round 'ere left 'ome at that time. And there was no ol' man goin' aroun' to the doors at that time o' year. They only comes in the summer."

"Yes, don't I know that! Aunt Ann near frightened the life out o' me las' summer. 'Member? She got a bigger fright then me though, 'cause I keeled over in a faint and she had a hard job to get me to come to. She's full of devilment, Aunt Ann is. Can you picture your Mam dressin' up like that and goin' from 'ouse to 'ouse tryin' to frighten the other women? You know she put her shirt-tail out through the front of her trousers and shook it at Aunt Polly. She knowed Aunt Polly wouldn' let 'er in the 'ouse but'd be peekin' at 'er from behin' the curtains. Aunt Polly tol' everyone down on the flakes that evenin' how scandalized she was. Aunt Ann heard all about what the man done and more he hadn', and kep' a straight face."

"Yer Aunt Ann kin get away wid it 'cause a day or so 'forehand she brings up that der's a ol' man goin' round out in the Cove. And yer 'ouse is 'id from everyone else's by the droke up in the garden. She kin dress up and come roun' the shore road jist as if she was comin' from the Cove."

"Aunt Ann is a great one to poke fun and I'm glad she took me in when . . ." Sarah's voice trailed off.

Hetty knew full well how Sarah pined for a mother's love, the kind she herself and the rest of the seven Pace children received from her roly-poly, easier-to-jump-over-than-walk-around, mother. The contrast with Sarah's angular aunt was extreme. Both girls sighed and resumed berry picking.

Topmost in Sarah's mind was her position in her aunt's home. Her Aunt Ann had taken her in after her parents died within a month of each other three long years ago when Sarah was ten. She was sure she hadn't been happy since. Aunt Ann and Uncle Bill saw she had proper clothes and had enough to eat but she longed for the love she saw lavished in Hetty's home. Her three cousins—Joe, Matt, and Jack—they were loved. But Matt was the only kind one of her cousins, the only one that seemed to care about her. He was the same age as herself, and stood up for her when she was being tormented and teased by the other two. Like her, Matt chafed under Joe's bossy ways. And because Jack, the youngest, was his mother's darling, many times she and Matt got blamed for something Jack had done. Perhaps her aunt only looked after her because she was entitled to the orphan's allowance; how she hated having to go to stern old Zeke Baker to collect that every quarter. Other things bothered her too—she was terribly afraid of the dark; she hated being alone in the house; and she disliked being the first one up in the morning and having to get the fire going in the kitchen wood stove. Getting up early . . . that brought up another picture—one she had seen from her bedroom window one chilly, grey, misty morning in April of this year. A man, half-running, half-walking up the path over White Head. Soon he topped the hill and was out of sight. She had thought, "Someone's up earlier than me," as she hurried down to the kitchen.

Sarah recalled how a week later the news went round that Sal Brown was missing from the cove. Both Sal's widowed father and her older brother told people that Sal had left home in the early morning of April 17. She was going up to the Bight to see her married sister but she never reached Bess's place.

For the rest of that month there had been an all-out search for the fifteen-year-old girl. The constable from Bona had organized all the men and teenaged boys into teams. They had looked down all the gulches between Muddy Brook and the Bight; they had walked along every beach, and had studied the margins of every pond and flashet for footprints. Any clue. Anything. Because it was often foggy on that stretch of coast, they feared she had lost her way, strayed off the path and had either fallen over a cliff or into some quicksand-like bog hole. But finding no trace of her, people began saying that perhaps she had run off with someone. After all, she had a hard life of it with her surly father and mean brother.

"Well, anyway, I guess I got it good compared to poor Sal. They say her father and brother didn't treat her right. Only raggedy clothes to wear and not allowed to go out for a walk in the evenings like the other girls," she mused. Back to Sal Brown again. Why couldn't she get the girl out of her mind? To Hetty she said: "Did you ever speak to Jake Brown?"

"Are you still thinkin' 'bout Sal Brown?" Hetty queried. Knowing that Sarah was keen on getting any information she could about the Browns, she suggested, "We've been pickin' steady fer a few hours now. I'm starved. Time we had a bite t'eat. Let's sit down and have our lunch. I'll tell you what I heard."

Seated comfortably on a large, rounded, chair-height boulder with its patches of grey-green lichen, they opened their small cloth lunch sacks and munched on their "dry lunch," slices of buttered homemade bread topped with molasses. Had they gone in the country in the early morning with the older girls, they would have stopped at noon and boiled the kettle over an open fire. Between bites, Hetty continued: "People says that Jethro Brown is a hard man to deal with. His wife has been dead a long time—seven or eight years. Bess, Sal's sister, was eleven. Her father made her stay out of school and look after the house. Jake and Sal stopped goin' to school when Bess got married. That was three year ago. Mam says they're the worst-off fam'ly in the Cove. P'raps they got to stay home in the winter 'cause they don't have any clothes, that's what Mam thinks."

"But I heared even when she was goin' to school, she wasn't ever allowed to go out playin' aroun' like we do in the evenin'," said Sarah. "Sure, when 'tis duckish that's the best time to play Ol' Daddy, cause whoever is Ol' Daddy can't see you to catch you if you can't run fast and get home."

"P'raps if her mother . . ." Hetty stopped. "Let's see if we can pick another gallon or two each 'fore we leave," she finished lamely.

The evening sun was a hand's breadth high when they stopped picking berries, pleased with their day's work. Their shadows stretched long before them as they trudged along the winding path, their berry sacks heavy on their shoulders.

The path they chose to follow homeward was nearer the cliffs and went fairly close to Jabe's garden. None of the wooden fence was left upright. All that remained to show the southern boundary of the garden was a rock wall some four-by-ten feet. As they broke over the hill leading past the garden, they were startled by the sudden flight of some dozen crows that rose from the top of the wall.

"Are you afraid of crows, Hetty?"

"Noo . . . but they gives me a quare feelin'. Mam sez somethin' 'bout 'one fer sorrow, two fer joy' but she didn't say nuttin' 'bout a dozen."

"Me, too, Hetty. But I got t' find out what they're all on that wall fer. Comin'?"

Sarah laid her berries on the turf and headed for the wall. Hetty followed more slowly. To get to the inner side of the wall they had to climb over hummocks and push through low-growing bushes and low, wind-damaged trees. Hetty was directly behind Sarah when the latter drew back, gasped, and turned an ashen face to Hetty. Hetty pushed forward, and she too stood transfixed. They clung to each other trembling, yet their eyes were drawn inexorably to the base of the old wall. There, some twelve inches from the wall, lay exposed a girl's leg still wearing the everyday shoemaker's boot that reached just above the ankle. From the top of the boot to the kneecap, the leg had been stripped bare. The rest of the body was covered with several layers of loose rock that had foundered from the top of the wall. Some rocks were strewn around the ground close by the protruding leg.

"No, Sare! Don't you faint, don't!" hissed Hetty.

Her friend's voice roused Sarah. Grabbing hands, they fairly flew back to the path. Fear propelled them over all obstacles. Berries forgotten, they tore pell-mell to the crest of White Head and down the equally steep northern slope into Muddy Brook.

They burst into the Pace's kitchen, just as Hetty's mother was pouring boiling water into an old brown teapot on the back of the stove. "What's wrong, Het?" she said, at the same time opening her arms. She locked her arms around them both and waited for them to speak. Worried about Hetty's lateness—she had promised to help get supper—she was ready to go looking for them herself when they passed the kitchen window in their headlong flight home.

They were still standing by the stove when Hetty's father and her brothers got out of berry picking. They all heard the girls gasp out their gruesome tale ending with "'n we left our berries up on the path!"

"I'd better get home. Aunt Ann'll be mad at me. Late gettin' home and no berries. I'm scared . . ."

"Sam, walk Sare over to Bill's, will you? 'Tis gettin' duckish out and she's had a big fright. We'll go up and get yer berries, me maid," he added kindly. "Sam, you tell 'em what happened. And ask Bill to go fer the constable in Bona. We'll take a lantern and go fer the berries and have a look at what the young maids found."

"C'mon, Sare!" snarled the disgruntled fifteen-year-old Sam, who wanted to be one of the party going to the scene of the crime. "Kin ya' run? I wants to get back quick so's I kin go with the crowd."

Taking Sarah's small berry-stained hand in his own calloused, equally berry-stained one, he set a fast pace around the shore road to the Chards. The family was just beginning supper, and on Sarah's entrance a black-browed Aunt Ann opened her mouth to speak . . . and closed it. What she saw written in Sarah's eyes touched her deeply. She crossed to the girl quickly and folded her in her arms.

"What's wrong, Sam?" queried Sarah's Uncle Bill. "Why is Sare in that state?"

Briefly and bluntly the boy told of the girls' gruesome find, adding, "Pap wants you to go fer the constable. We's goin' to git the berries and have a look." With that he was off. Right behind him were the three Chard boys.

Sarah took her place at the table and her aunt put a bowl of pea soup in front of her. It had lots of small bits of salt beef swimming in it, just the way Sarah liked it. But she couldn't eat. Her stomach urged. She was afraid she'd be sick. She got away from the table and her aunt made her lie down for a while on the kitchen settle and tucked a quilt around her.

Within ten minutes of hearing the news, Bill Chard was moving at a fast clip towards Bona. Less than two hours later, burly, ruddy-cheeked Constable Dalton was in Muddy Brook. He listened carefully as Sarah told her story once again.

"You've had a bad fright, little maid, and your friend Hetty, too," he said gravely. "I'd 've left me berries behin' too if I'd come across somethin' like that."

Carrying lanterns and any implements they felt might be needed, some dozen men and older boys accompanied the constable to Jabe's garden. They also carried the stretcher and a sheet the constable had brought with him. While several men held the lanterns, the others, under Dalton's supervision, carefully removed the layers of rock covering the body. In the combined light of the lanterns and the full moon, the grisly spectacle was revealed, a length of heavy trawl line encircling the neck lay loosely on the ground.

They laid the remains on the stretcher and covered it with the sheet. Walking with sure, firm strides along the narrow, well-worn path in bright moonlight, they bore Sal's body into Muddy Brook. Everyone but the very babes in their cradles watched mutely as the stretcher was placed in the constable's cart. The doctor would have to examine the body in his surgery in Bona. Then . . .

The constable knew the Browns were not Methodists, but only that minister resided in the Cove so he went to the parsonage. Old Mr. House accompanied him to Jethro Brown's house and knocked gently. As tactfully as they could, they broke the news to the father and brother.

Next morning everyone was asking, "Who done it?"

Sally Brown was buried in St. Anne's graveyard in Bona. The small chapel could not hold the hundreds that turned out for the funeral. People commented that her father and brother looked decent for once in their lives.

A week later while Constable Dalton methodically carried out his investigations, it came out that Sal Brown had been "in the family way."

Again they asked: "Who done it? Whose baby?" No one knew of her keeping company with any young fella. Tongues wagged.

~~~

On a Sunday evening in late October, young Jake Brown tied a small grapnel round his waist and threw it and himself over Peter Hobbs's stagehead into two fathoms of water. A demented Jethro was carried off to the asylum in St. John's.
~~~

The Gingerbread Man

DANETTE DOOLEY

MISSY'S THREE YEARS old, asleep on her Daddy's shoulder. Daddy's rocking her gently in Nanny's wooden chair. Her nightgown is Daddy's undershirt, clean but tattered. She's not quite sound asleep yet. Her Daddy's calloused hands are caressing her damp neck, under her curls. He's singing softly in her ear.

> I peeped in to say goodnight
> then I heard my child in prayer
> and for me some scarlet ribbons
> scarlet ribbons for my hair . . .

When Melissa Dawn Evans goes from elementary to junior high school, she abandons her ribbons. Yes, even her lovely scarlet ribbons. Scarlet red for the month of June, the Feast of Christ the King. Pigtails are much too childish for a big girl going to junior high. Missy puts her shoebox filled with coloured ribbons on her bookshelf in the corner of her room.

"If you're not going to use those ribbons, Missy, get rid of them," her Mom says one day while tidying Missy's room. Missy can't bear to throw them out. She hides the box in her closet next to the doll Santa brought her last year . . .

"Nearly ten years old and still playing with dollies, sooky baby

Missy," her sister Jennifer teases. Jenny is eleven and a half. She never plays with dollies any more. Not even Barbies. So when Missy's mother asks if she wants a doll for Christmas, Missy has to tell her no. Cause Jenny is listening, all ears.

But there she is under the tree Christmas morning. Straight out of Bowring's window. Beautiful Sarah Jane. Three feet high. Golden ringlets, Newfoundland tartan dress, little black plastic shoes, white ankle socks and a tartan tam with a red wool pompom on top.

"I s'pose I'll keep her," Missy tells her sister with a frown. "For Mom's sake, not mine," she whispers.

Missy is tickled pink . . .

Now, one year later, her ribbon box and Sarah Jane lie side by side behind closed closet doors. Some nights Missy longs for both though she never touches her doll again. She wouldn't dare. Sara Jane's too clean. What if Missy's dirt rubs off?

Sarah Jane's what Missy once was, but can never be again.

Missy tried so hard to wash him from her body. She pokes a worn face cloth into her privates when she's in the bath. She scrubs and scrubs and scrubs her neck. But still the smell of Brylcreem lingers.

Missy sits in her Nan's big kitchen staring at her grandmother washing clothes in their ancient wringer washer. Her Pop's old work pants yanked through the wringer. All the greyish water pouring back into the washer, to be flushed away forever, out in the ocean. Missy wishes she could put her body through the wringer too. Squeeze out all the badness. All the dirt. All the shame. All the pain. Out. Out. Out. Into the sea. Never to return again. Then she'd be clean too. Just like Sarah Jane.

Alone in her room, Missy reaches for her shoe box. She loves those ribbons dearly. No, that's a lie. She hates them. Missy's so confused. She tears into a ribbon with her teeth. She desperately needs someone or something to blame.

Oh how she longs to tell her Dad. But Uncle Bill's not just her coach. He's Daddy's brother. They both love to watch her outrace all the others. Even Jenny couldn't catch her on the track. But Missy thinks that's cause Jenny bundles up too much. She wears at least two pairs of sweatpants all the time.

"Missy's only eleven, Bill, but my girl is going places," Dad often tells his brother.

"And that she is," is Bill's reply.

Missy yearns to put her ribbons in her hair and keep them there forever. She sits in front of her mirror and runs her fingers down the back of her head. She brings her long brown hair to the front of her shoulders and makes two expert plaits. She picks two coloured ribbons and ties them on the ends. Missy loves the image that stares back at her. Missy's face. With two beautiful braids resting on her shoulders. But when she stands back from the mirror, Missy's long lanky legs and budding breasts tell her she's outgrown her plaits. She unties the pale blue ribbons and puts them in her box. Blue for the month of May, the Blessed Virgin's month . . .

"Are you a virgin, Melissa?" Uncle Bill asks Missy often when he drives her home from practice.

"Yes," she replies, thinking of her pale blue ribbons. She knew she was. She'd never forget her most embarrassing moment . . .

Easter morning. Last year. Missy's running around the living room in her short nightie. Nan and Pop are staying at her house. She and Jenny are hunting for eggs. She's on her hands and knees groping under the chesterfield, when her Nan says sternly, "Melissa Dawn Evans, go change your underwear. A big girl like you should know how to wipe her bum."

But when she goes upstairs to the bathroom Missy's terrified. She's bleeding to death. She knows Jenny sometimes doesn't go to gym cause it's the wrong time of the month. But Missy's sure this much blood means something terrible has happened. She screeches for her mother. Her Mom comes in, looks at Missy standing there, blood running down her scrawny legs, her panties at her ankles, her face white with fright. Her mother disappears and comes back with a long thick pad. And a white elastic belt with two little hooks. She mutters something about Missy being a virgin and staying that way. Then she shows Missy where the box of pads are hidden, under the spare towels in the closet. A big blue cardboard box marked Kotex.

"You'll have to use these every month now, girl," her mother mutters. "And don't flush them down the toilet or leave them in the garbage for your brothers to see," she warns before leaving the bathroom, slamming the door behind her.

What is she supposed to do with them, Missy wonders. She stands staring at her stained white panties. Her favourite pair. Mr. Hamburger on the front is still smiling up at her. "What's happening to me?" she asks him. She doesn't want this bloody mess. She wants to go back downstairs. She knows by now Jenny has probably found all the hidden eggs.

If only she'd said no. Maybe Uncle Bill would have left her alone. But she never thought in a million years that her uncle would ever hurt her. Uncle Bill was good. Uncle Bill was just like Daddy . . .

But her uncle wants to teach Missy more than how to run. Other things. Their little secret things. And that's when Missy knows her uncle is not like Daddy at all . . .

Uncle Bill starts lying on top of Missy all the time. In his van. After practice. And one night he gets really mad at her. "I was inside you a bit that time, Melissa. You said you were a virgin but there isn't any blood," he said. His eyes squint in anger. Missy doesn't understand. Why does he want to see blood? Blood reminds her of all the little football eggs poking up from the yellow straw in Jenny's little basket. And why is he so mad at her?

He sits up behind the steering wheel and looks over at Missy, fixing her sweatpants.

"Did it hurt?" he asks.

"No," Missy blurts out. She knows he'd never hurt her. He's been lying on top of her a lot lately, hauling down her sweatpants over her bum. But she didn't know he was inside her. She didn't know it was supposed to hurt.

He slaps her face, fast. Her lip spurts blood. No one ever hit Melissa Dawn Evans in her life.

"You're not allowed to hit me," Missy yells. "I'm telling Dad. And when I see a policeman, I . . . I'm going to tell him too."

Missy is all mixed up about what Uncle Bill is teaching her but she knows for sure he isn't allowed to hit her. No siree. No one is allowed to hit anybody in her family. When her brothers get into a fight, her Dad always says, "Don't ever raise your hand to one another. That's the one thing I won't put up with in this house."

Missy knows her Dad is going to be ripping at Uncle Bill. Even though she's a big girl now, she is still her Daddy's favourite. They still joke about when Missy was a little girl . . .

The youngest of nine, Missy's speech comes slower than her brothers and sisters. At four, she still struggles with the simplest of words. But she loves to please her Daddy. And she practises hard to say the words her Daddy loves to hear.

Missy crawls upon her Daddy's lap and waits until he notices her slapping his neck. Daddy's neck. Sunlight soap. Her favourite smell. Her Daddy.

She has his full attention now. Her Daddy's looking down at her perched upon his lap. Their eyes are locked together. Her Daddy starts to sing.

"Whose girlie?"

"Da D girlie"

"Girlie what?"

"G . . . Girlie good."

Missy claps her hands.

"G . . . Girlie good. G . . . Girlie good," she stammers.

Missy's soon rewarded for her efforts as her Daddy wraps her tightly in a bear hug.

Missy loves being Da D girlie. G . . . Girlie good.

But as she sits in her uncle's van wiping her swollen lip on the sleeve of her sweat jacket, Missy knows that Uncle Bill has somehow turned girlie good into girlie bad.

She is so busy daydreaming, she doesn't even notice that he's turned the van around. Missy daydreams a lot when she's with her uncle. Especially when he's doing it. She always counts gingerbread men hopping from the oven and running away. Her counting takes her mind off Uncle Bill's grunting noises. Sometimes when he's doing it, Missy counts up to fifty piping hot gingerbread men running across their canvas kitchen floor, out into the clean fresh air. Away, away, away.

Uncle Bill is speeding up Military Road, his hands gripping the steering wheel. The van comes to a quick stop not far from the fire station, across from the Basilica. There are police cars everywhere. That's how Missy knows that big building is the police station. Because of all the cop cars and motorcycles.

"Go in and tell," Uncle Bill says calmly. "And when they ask if you kicked and screamed when I stuck it in you, make sure you tell the truth. They'll hook you up to a machine. They'll know you're lying. They'll send you off to jail," he screams.

Missy knows she didn't kick and scream. She knows now she should have. The police will never believe me, Missy thinks. Uncle Bill has friends in that building. He talks about his buddy Constable White all the time. They play ball together in the summer. And hockey in the winter time.

Missy's so confused. Everyone keeps saying Uncle Bill is good. Except that once, when Missy heard her sister yelling at their uncle, after practice. Something about him being a pervert. That's because he used to be an Anglican, Missy thinks. Now he's a Catholic. And ever since he perverted, he gets to give out Holy Communion with Father Hickey every Sunday. So he can't be bad. And he gave Missy her dog, Sammy, last year when she broke the 800-metre record. And he lets her take Sam to practice every day.

"Bill's never had time to marry, he's too busy with the church," Mom always tells her friends.

Uncle Bill is right. Whatever is happening, is Missy's own fault.

Missy begs her uncle not to make her go inside and talk to a policeman. "Pl . . . please just take me home. I'll stop crying. I'll be good."

Her uncle smiles and says, "That's better." But there's something in his eyes that scares Missy. Something bad. Is she bad too? If only she had kicked and screamed. Like a good girl would have done.

From that day on, Missy does everything her uncle tells her. She doesn't ever want to make him angry again. But he always finds some reason to be mad at her. Some reason why she deserves to be hit . . .

She's running on the grass. Warming up for a big cross-country race.

"Get your eyes off Bob Andrews, whore," her uncle warns. "He's the new coach in town. Coming here from away, trying to take over the whole fucking track club. You like him don't you, whore? You . . ."

"No," Missy blurts out quickly. "I . . . I wasn't looking at him, honest."

"I saw you looking, whore. Staring at his crotch."

As quick as a wink, when no one's looking, Uncle Bill spits in Missy's face, hissing the word whore. Quickly, Missy wipes him from her cheek. She knows she is a whore. He calls her that all the time now. She doesn't know how she got to be a whore. But when he spits at her, the slime on her cheek always smells like him and reminds her she's that bad word—whore.

Taking Missy by the arm her uncle walks her away from the other runners. No one notices the grimace on her face as his fingers dig into the flesh of her bony arm. Finally he releases her.

"Karla Adams is your stiffest competition today," he tells Missy as she continues with her warm-up exercises. "She's over there. The tall redhead. Her coach has been training her hard. This is a tough course—three miles, mostly wet marsh around Burton's Pond, then back to finish in front of the Arts Building."

Missy's jumping up and down, running on the spot. She has to keep her muscles warm.

"Listen to me, Melissa. Stay tucked behind the Adams kid. Let her set the pace. When the finish line's in sight make your move. Save your kick for the last one hundred yards. You know you can out-sprint them all. Remember, girl, don't let me down," he warns.

"I won't," she says as the starter announces the race will begin in five minutes.

Missy tries to concentrate on the race she's about to run. She sits on the grass and begins to take her sweatpants off. Though the sun is shining brightly, the air is cool and crisp. Missy sees a shadow on the ground next to her left foot. A giant. She looks up. Uncle Bill is staring down at her new white terry cloth shorts. His hands are on his hips. He's squinting. He's licking his lips. Uncle Bill's just like the fox in Daddy's Gingerbread Man story, Missy thinks. He's tricked her into believing he's good. But, like the mean old fox, he's just waiting for his chance to gobble her up . . .

Sixty schoolgirls line up at the starting line.

On your mark, get set, the gun is fired.

Elbows bump together. Feet collide. But Missy knows just what she has to do. She's just like the gingerbread man. Faster than the others. Missy sticks her arms out from her sides to protect her upper body from the elbows of the other runners. Her stride is short and quick as she battles towards the front of the pack. Soon she's among the leaders. Missy's stride has lengthened now. Cold mud splashes on her legs as she glides through the long grass around the pond. Missy loves this feeling of freedom only racing brings.

The pack has thinned now. Eight runners out in front. Missy's following on Karla Adams's heels. Though she knows the pace is much too slow, she stays in second where she's been told to stay.

Remember, girl, don't let me down.

Run, run as fast as you can, he can't catch you, you're the gingerbread man.

About two miles into the race, Karla Adams's stride has shortened. She's gasping for air. Missy knows her strongest competitor is fading. She glances over her shoulder. There's no one else in sight. Missy's gained her second wind. She can easily lengthen her stride even farther and take the lead. But he said to wait until the end. She must remember to do as he says.

Soon Missy sees some spectators up ahead. A volunteer offers the two leading runners water. Missy accepts but knows better than to drink it. She pours the water over her head, being careful not to break her stride. The icy coldness runs down her top, cooling her hot body.

Missy and the Adams girl are running neck and neck. The finish line's in sight now. About a hundred yards in front of them. Missy makes her move. Her legs lift high, her arms move in perfect motion with her legs. Pumping, pumping, pumping. She's in the lead now. She's running, nearly flying.

Remember, girl, don't let me down.

Run, run as fast as you can, he can't catch you, you're the gingerbread man.

Missy sees her Dad among the crowd clapping and cheering her on. Uncle Bill's there, too, staring at his stopwatch. It can't get any better than this, Missy thinks as she raises her arms in victory, breaking through the finish line.

"The Evans kid has done it again," someone shouts. "She's the smallest in the pack but no one else can touch her."

Missy's legs are all rubbery. She's bending at the waist. Her elbows resting on her knees. Though she's exhausted, she knows she can't sit down yet. "Keep walking, Missy," her Dad shouts from the sideline as Uncle Bill approaches. His eyes are angry. But why? What did she do wrong? She stayed behind the Adams girl.

Her uncle takes her by the arm, his grip tightening. Everyone just thinks he's helping her recover from the race. But Missy knows she's in trouble. She sees it in his eyes.

"Get the fuck in the van," he hisses through his teeth.

"I want to talk to Dad first," Missy says, trying to catch her breath.

"Get the fuck in the van, whore," he whispers, steering Missy by the arm in the direction of the parking lot.

He yells to her Dad that they're going to drive down the road, to see how the other runners are doing.

Missy knows she's going to be beat.

As soon as they drive away he reaches over quickly and punches her arm. Hard.

"Wh . . . what did I do?" she asks him.

"Fucking whore," he screams, leaning forward on the steering wheel. Missy wishes he would sit back in his seat. His punches are always harder when he's leaning ahead. Cause he's more angry. Missy wishes she wasn't so tired.

Uncle Bill's next punch hits Missy just above her ear. Her hand moves quickly to her head. She feels a lump popping out. Thank God it's hidden under her hair.

"Pl . . . please just tell me what did I do? I stayed behind her like . . ."

"Stupid slut," he yells as he punches her ribs under her raised arm. Missy scolds herself for keeping her hand up to her aching head. But she's too tired to try to guess where his fists are going to hit next.

"Your nipples are showing right through your top. Fucking whore . . ."

Missy glances down. Uncle Bill is right. Her top's all wet from the cold water she poured over her head. And her titties are sticking out like two tiny unripe berries. Missy can't hold back her tears any longer. She's too exhausted to even try.

"I . . . I'm sorry," Missy cries as she scurries to the corner of the van out of his reach. Missy gets down on the floor and curls into a little ball. She needs to become smaller. If only she could be invisible when Uncle Bill is mad like this. Cause Missy knows it's all her fault he's hitting her.

"Fucking cockteaser," he screams. Missy's never heard that word before. But she knows what a cock is. And she knows what a teaser is.

Melissa Dawn Evans is a whore.

Melissa Dawn Evans is a stupid slut.

Melissa Dawn Evans is a cockteaser.

Melissa Dawn Evans is definitely GIRLIE BAD!

When they return, the last of the runners are crossing the finish line. Missy's Dad comes over and gives her a big hug. He doesn't notice her face is all red and blotchy from crying. Her face is always flushed after a hard race. But Missy's safe at last. Her arms are wrapped around her Daddy, tightly. She wishes she could glue them there forever.

"Good job, Flash. Another provincial record. I knew you could do it," her Dad says, releasing her from his hold. He turns to his brother, patting him on the back.

"You're a great coach, Bill. Missy's going places," he tells him proudly.

"And that she is," is his reply.

Missy's teammates gather round to congratulate her on her new record. But she doesn't care about the race. She has too much on her mind. Her arm is aching. She must remember to wear long-sleeved tops now, for a couple of weeks. Her head is throbbing. The lump on the side of her head feels like a hard-boiled egg. But at least she doesn't have to worry about it showing. But she'll have to be careful when she washes her hair tonight. Cause touching her scalp, even lightly to rub in shampoo, always makes her head ache when the bumps are there.

Missy now hates running. She's petrified her titties are going to stick out again. But Missy is a smart girl. She'll think of something . . .

Every day before practice, Missy covers each tittie with a Band-Aid. Sometimes she leaves the same ones on for a couple of days. Cause her Mom keeps asking what's happening to all the Band-Aids. And besides, it hurts a lot when she has to pull them off. Missy can't decide if it's easier to rip them off quickly or ease them off slowly. Either way her titties are always sore and ooze tiny drops of yellow stuff. But that doesn't bother Missy one bit. Missy's proud that she has found a clever way to take away a reason for Uncle Bill to hit her. And she's positive her uncle won't ever catch on to her little secret. He's not interested in her tops or sweat jackets. He only pulls her sweatpants down when he's doing it. Sometimes he makes her take one leg out but most of the time he just lies on top of her and does it. Cause they don't have much time. Practice is over and her Mom and Dad are home waiting. Waiting for Uncle Bill and their pride and joy, their youngest, Melissa Dawn.

Missy heard her Mom explain to a lady in Mass once why they named her Dawn. She didn't really understand what her Mom was saying. Something about Dawn bringing change and Missy being unexpected. A change of life baby.

Missy wonders if her life is ever going to change. For no matter how hard she tries not to upset her uncle, he always finds an excuse to hit her. She looked at another man, she cried when he was doing it. Sometimes when Missy loses count of her gingerbread men, Uncle Bill's grunting scares her and she starts to cry. Missy knows she deserves to be hit then because Uncle Bill always warns, "No fucking tears, whore."

Missy can't convince her uncle she isn't interested in men. Men are giants. Bad giants. Men know how to trick little girls. Turn them into whores without them even knowing.

Whenever Uncle Bill's fists leave a mark that Missy can't hide, he tells her what to say. You hurt yourself in gym. You bumped into the van door. You jammed your hand in the kitchen drawer . . . Just last week her Daddy called her "clumsy Missy," when she told him the great big bruise on her arm was because she fell down the stairs at school.

Maybe Daddy's right. Maybe she is just too stunned. But not too stunned for Sam. She talks to him all the time . . .

"Turn out, Sam," she tells him when they're settled in bed. Sam's breath reminds Missy of Jim Shields' meat market. Raw meat and sawdust. But Sam likes to face her. He knows her tears will start soon. He loves to lick her salty tears.

Missy strokes her doggy's silky ears. She wipes the yucky guck from the corner of his eyes.

"You have sad eyes too," Missy tells him. She sees her forlorn face in Sam's chocolate glassy eyes. Her tears begin.

"We're some lot alike, you and me, Sam," Missy whispers.

"Sometimes when he kicks me now, I sound just like you. I think it's because I'm not allowed to cry. But a sob always sneaks out. Sometimes I don't know who's moaning. Me or you. Oh, Sammy, Sammy, Sammy . . ."

Missy wipes her tears in Sammy's neck. She remembers earlier tonight. Sam's whimpers in the van.

"You have to learn to be braver, Sam. Try not to cry when he kicks you. That only makes him madder," she explains. Missy's face is buried deep in Sammy's neck. She cannot let her Mom and Dad hear her sobs. Missy likes her uncle a lot for giving her Sam. Sam's with her all the time. Sam knows it's not her fault. But sometimes she's real angry with her uncle. Cause if she didn't have Sammy to protect she'd be able to run away. Away, away, away. Just like her gingerbread men. But Uncle Bill says Sammy will be history if she ever tries to run away. Missy knows she'll never let that happen.

And she knows there's no way she can tell anyone what Uncle Bill is doing. What she's letting him do. She likes it, he keeps telling her. Could he be right, Missy wonders? Then why does she always get butterflies in her stomach as soon as she sees him? Or even when Dad says his name. Bill. She could throw up right now, just thinking of him.

Missy's body begins to tremble. She hugs Sam even tighter round his neck. His sharp stubbly hairs poke up Missy's nose. She starts to sneeze. She's all snotty now. Sam licks her snots. Slurp, slurp, slurp. Gross, she tells him but doesn't move her face away. No one loves her quite like Sammy. He's in it with her. He's sticking by her. It's Missy and Sam against the world . . .

Then one day a lady from the police station visits Missy's school. Her name is Constable Lynn. She talks all about good touching and bad touching. And tells girls it's very important to tell if someone makes them feel uncomfortable. Missy shivers but doesn't say a word.

"Do you like Uncle Bill?" Jenny asks that afternoon as they are skipping home from school. Constable Lynn spoke to Jenny's class too.

"Yeah, I spose," Missy replies.

"Uncle Bill's a pervert. He makes me feel sick," Jenny yells, throwing down her skipping rope. Missy stops dead in her tracks. Her know-it-all big sister doesn't seem so brazen any more. She looks frightened to death, Missy thinks.

The next day the two girls visit their guidance counsellor, Mrs. Ryan. "We want to talk about our Uncle Bill," Missy tells the teacher. Mrs. Ryan says it's better if she talks to them one at a time. She tells Jenny to go wait in the library. Then she closes her office door and asks Missy what's on her mind.

Telling is just like going through her Nan's old wringer washer. Out it spills. All the dirt. All the shame. All the pain. Out. Out. Out.

When Missy's finally quiet, Mrs. Ryan stands up from behind her desk and sits in the empty chair next to Missy. The teacher reaches out her hand and gently raises the little girl's chin. She tells Missy to listen very carefully to what she's going to say. Mrs. Ryan looks Missy right in the face.

"I'm very proud of you, Melissa," the teacher says. "You're a brave little girl. And always remember, this is not your fault. You've done nothing wrong."

When Missy leaves the guidance counsellor's office she sees her sister coming down the corridor. Jenny's wiping her nose in the sleeve of her blouse. Her eyes are all watery, like she was swimming all afternoon in Bannerman Park. Missy can't believe Uncle Bill was after Jenny too. Missy knows that mean old fox will never, ever, ever, get a chance to gobble them up again.

That night before she crawls under her blankets, Missy opens her closet door and peeps inside. Sarah Jane's plastic arms are extended in the air, beckoning Missy to pick her up. Slowly Missy reaches down and strokes a dusty golden curl.

Three Haiku

Geraldine Flannigan

blue spots in fresh snow
prancing around my meadow
. . . crocus blossoms

~~~

silver gleams on shore
twisting, turning, arching—splash
. . . caplin scull

~~~

look up my Daddy
is that red and yellow kite
stuck there in the sky?

reading between the lines

ANNE FERNCASE

Spot was never
my dog
but Dick grew up
to be my dad
he married Jean
sired his own little Dick
and Mary this and Mary that

as his third Mary
I loved him
until I was five
and he got mad
whipped
my neck around
I faced
my mother's cries
    stop
save yourself
run Dick run

Spot
wet the new
living room rug
Dick destroyed Spot

that fall
my sisters and I
knelt rosary-like
silent
pigtailed
four dents in the rug
spotted
again
no dog to blame

when you're five
almost six
time is not counted
on clocks

we four Marys
waited forever
under his gaze
no one would tell

I headed
for the hall
I thought
how long can dark eyes rage
I never
really thought at all

my thirty pounds
became a ball
fell soundless
from my father's
hands
nestled crumpled
against the floor

stay Mary stay

Circle Game

(A partly found poem)

HELEN FOGWILL PORTER

After I wet my bed
she made them form a circle
with me in the middle
and she began to beat me

when I could no longer stand
she ordered two of the girls
to hold me up

she kept on hitting me
until she'd had enough

I was seven years old
she was a Sister of Mercy

What is a lawyer?

Danette Dooley

A child with orange-red Brillo-pad curls raises her arm, fingers dancing.
    "It's someone you call when you are in big trouble.
    Like when your Daddy beats up your Mommy, right?"
Eyes as dark as overripe blueberries await my answer.

The Shroud

LILLIAN BOUZANE

MY GRANDMOTHER WAS the only member of our family left on Handy Harbour Island. She wouldn't leave; she wanted to be buried there with my grandfather.

The summer between high school and university, my parents sent me back home to be with her. Every evening of that long, drought-filled season we sat on her back porch in the fading light and I listened to her stories. As she often said: "All stories will out sooner or later."

"Grandma, wasn't there one about Mainze Stewart?"

"Yes, it was the year we got our new young priest. His first parish."

"Something happened?"

"It's a knotted story. Mainze Stewart was an orphan who had come over from Ming's Bight to work with the Ryles. They used to own the business that the Trahanes now run. She was only thirteen. A bright young thing."

"What happened to her?"

"Well, as she told it to me, Jock Ryle forced her and made her pregnant. She went to see the young priest. He accused her of starting it all and for her sins ordered her to go to Mass every Sunday with a shroud over her head—until the child was born."

"How shocking!"

"Yes, priests had a lot of power then and some of them used it, not always wisely. As I was the nurse, Mainze naturally came to me with her problem. She was more upset by having to wear the shroud, poor child, than what was ahead of her, for God knows she was too young to imagine it. The business of the shroud troubled me too. No one on Handy Harbour Island had ever been given a public penance. And Mainze was so young.

"I calmed her and took her over to the nursing station to confirm she was pregnant. I imagine Jock Ryle saw us go. We had to pass his store. After I examined Mainze I sent her back here and went in to see Jock.

"There were a number of men sitting around the stove in his store. I went up to Jock. He blushed and took me by the arm and directed me into the backroom.

'Mainze is pregnant. She said you forced her.'

"His face turned savage. He hissed a curse at me. He cursed Mainze. He said we were all liars.

'Why did you take me in here then if you're so innocent?'

'Get out of my sight.'

'Jock this won't go well for you. She's underage. You've got children of your own.'

"He was beet red. He wouldn't listen. He wanted me out of there. I left. I kept Mainze with me that night and the next morning I went to see the priest. I told him of my visit to Jock and described the panic Mainze was in and suggested it might not be good for her health to do public penance. He asked me if I were questioning his authority. I said I was only interested in the state of health of a poor orphan who had been molested, was pregnant, and had come to me for help.

'There'll be no scandal in my parish.'

'But there already is.'

"He looked at me for a long moment, then he got up from behind his desk and opened the door of his study. For the second time in twenty-four hours I was being thrown out of a room. As I passed through the door, and I remember it as if it were yesterday, I said to myself—*then there'll be court work over this*."

"You were brave, Grandma."

"I didn't feel brave. In those days you didn't go against the wishes of a priest. But I was needed on the Island as much as he was and I think our young priest understood that. I didn't know much about court, as we rarely had cause for a magistrate to come to Handy Harbour Island, and I had paid very little attention to the few cases that did occur. Of course, I had read of court cases and heard about them on the radio but I knew nothing about how you went about getting one started.

"The next day I didn't go to the nursing station. The only other times I stayed away from work were when my children were being born. I wanted to be with Mainze. I wasn't sure of her state of mind and I wanted time to think how I should proceed. Finally, I decided I would do two things: send Mainze out of Handy Harbour Island to my mother in St. John's, and consult my uncle Stephen, who was a lawyer, although he had been retired for years."

"Did you think you were taking a chance by sending Mainze out of the place, Grandma? After all, she wasn't related to you."

"It was the public penance that was causing Mainze misery. I knew I had to get her out. When I told her she was going to my mother's and wouldn't have to attend even one Mass with the shroud over her head, she calmed down and her considerable common sense took over. I felt I wasn't taking too much of a chance with her. And as for anybody interfering? I figured only Jock Ryle or the priest would do that; and some instinct told me that neither of them would make a move to stop her, or me.

"The coastal boat used to call every Saturday then. That Saturday, I put Mainze on the boat with a letter to my mother, and one for Uncle Stephen. I thought Suse Ryle would come to see me about Mainze. But she didn't, and not once in all that happened afterwards did she speak to me. In fact, the whole family avoided me, and as you know, that is hard to do on Handy Harbour Island with only a few hundred people. And of course on Sunday, Jock was sitting in his usual place in the front pew with all his family around him. No public penance for him."

"How lucky Mainze was to have you on her side."

"I didn't think about that then; I was too caught up in getting something done about the situation. The next Saturday when the boat returned, Uncle Stephen was aboard, so was Mainze, and a magistrate. It was Magistrate Wells from St. John's. I was glad to see him. The district magistrate was related to many of us and had a little too much respect for Jock and Suse's money. With a neutral magistrate, and Uncle

Stephen to support Mainze, I thought the child had a fair chance. Again Mainze stayed with me and so did Uncle Stephen. I could see he enjoyed being back in harness. Enjoyed being needed."

"How was Mainze taking it?"

"The trip out to visit my mother helped. She was calmer. She was hopeful, I think. She understood that she wasn't alone. I kept her close to the house. I wasn't sure how she would be treated. By this time it was obvious that everyone on the Island knew what was going on. Every time I looked out the front window there was somebody passing by the house and staring in."

"Grandma, you came from outside; were you resented?"

"No, I never felt resented. I had born half the youngsters on the Island by that time and there's a closeness you feel that one court case couldn't wipe out. No, only Jock resented what I was doing. At least I thought so at the time.

"The case was set for the middle of the week and as it was August almost every able-bodied man, woman, and child was at the fish; that saved us from a crush of Ryle relatives. Court was held in the schoolhouse on a Wednesday morning. Other than Mainze, Jock and Suse, Uncle Stephen and myself, there were only a few old sea captains and one or two very old women in the school. I was glad both for the child and myself, although I knew every word would be repeated a hundred times by the few who were there.

"The case started. Magistrate Wells sat at the teacher's desk and the rest of us sat around in the school desks. The magistrate didn't recognise Uncle Stephen or any of us. He picked up his book and read: 'Case of child molesting and pregnancy brought against Jock Ryle by Bridget Mercier. First witness.' My name was called. I had expected to be sworn in but there was nothing like that. From where I sat, I said what I had been told by Mainze and what I had discovered through the medical examination.

"Next, Mainze's name was called and like me she told her story from where she sat. She did well. Uncle Stephen had coached her, I discovered, and she used some technical terms she hadn't known before she left the Island.

"Then Jock was called.

'What do you have to say for yourself, Mr. Ryle?'

'She's a damn liar,' Jock shouted.

'Who's a liar?'

'Mainze.'

'Did she live in your house?'

'Yes, she lived in my house.'

'What work did she do?'

'She did housework for my wife.'

'Where was her bedroom?'

'Up in the attic.'

'Did you ever go up in the attic?'

'Yes, I went up in my own attic.'

'Why did you go up in your attic?'

'To look at the flue.'

'Did you ever go up there when your wife was at Mass on weekday mornings?'

'No. I was working in the store.'

"The magistrate called Sarah Compton, Jock's store clerk. I didn't hear her come in, but she was in the back of the schoolhouse. Everybody could see that Jock hadn't expected Sarah. He blushed. He fidgeted with his glasses. Sarah was Madge Compton's eldest daughter and all the Comptons, as you know, are fearless. She was the only one asked to take an oath.

'Now, Sarah Compton. What time do you get to work in the morning?'

'I always open the store at eight o'clock in the summer.'

'Does Mr. Ryle always come in at eight o'clock?'

'For the first two years I was there he came at eight o'clock sharp and would stay until dinnertime. But last summer after Mainze came, Mr. Ryle would come in at eight, and when he saw his wife leave for Mass, about quarter after nine, he would go back to his house and stay until just before Mrs. Ryle returned. When we went on winter hours, he would come in at nine, and leave again at quarter after nine.'

'How did he look when he returned from those morning visits to his house?'

'Sometimes he would be singing when he came back and sometimes he would pass right by me and go into the office and stay there for a while.'

'Did you know there was something going on between Mr. Ryle and this child?'

'No, sir, but when you summonsed me here I put two and two together.'

'It's my job to put two and two together, Sarah Compton.'

"I saw Sarah's black eyes flash. And I thought to myself, *The Compton women have torn the face off men for less. My man it's a good thing you're on the bench.* Sarah held her tongue and the magistrate went on:

'Mr. Ryle why did you go back to your house each weekday morning after your wife left for church?'

"Jock looked like he had been struck. I thought he was going to cry. Suse was staring at her husband; her face lost its colour, and as suddenly the blood went to the roots of her hair. It was then I felt sorry for Suse, sorry for all the Ryles.

"The magistrate tore into Jock. Called him a liar. Told him he did molest the child. Asked him if he knew that he could spend twenty years in jail for rape. Called him a disgrace to the Christian family. Told him he had destroyed the life of a motherless child and begot another child that would be thrown on the world with the same prospects as its mother.

"When he finished Jock's head was on the desk.

'And now I'm going to sentence you. I'm not going to put you away for twenty years, although I could.'

"There Magistrate Wells stopped. Jock raised his head. You could see the relief on his face. Wells continued.

'I'm going to fine you four thousand dollars.'

"That was a fortune in those days. You could buy the best house on Handy Harbour for less. The blood drained from Jock's face and he actually started to cry.

'And I want you to bring the money here to me now, so this young girl will have a life for herself and your child.'

"On the word *your* he brought into the room the thunder of the Old Testament prophets. Jock stumbled to his feet. Suse got up to go with him; the magistrate ordered her to sit down. She flopped back in the desk. Jock had only to walk across the road; it took him almost a half hour to get back with the cheque. He handed it to the magistrate and this was the part I didn't expect: the magistrate asked Uncle Stephen if he would be Mainze's legal guardian. Uncle Stephen was a bachelor and must have been seventy but he took it on without a moment's hesitation."

"Grandma, wasn't it against the law to take money from a rapist to give to his victim?"

"It certainly was strange justice. Uncle Stephen and the magistrate must have been in collusion. You wouldn't get away with that now. But Wells did it, and he got away with it, and at the time I thought it wasn't a bad way to resolve the case.

"Of course, the news of the conviction went around the harbour like a wild flame. The next morning the Ryles and their eight children were aboard one of their schooners and out the harbour."

"Where did they go?"

"They went somewhere in the Boston States and set up a business. You could set up a fish business anywhere on the Atlantic coast in those times and be prosperous, and the Ryles had lots of money."

"And what happened to Mainze?"

"She went back to stay with my mother, had her baby, and gave it to one of mother's distant relatives to raise. Soon after, Uncle Stephen put Mainze in a school in New York. In those days, New York was the place many Newfoundlanders went to get a new life.

"But the strangest thing that came out of it was the Sunday after the court case our new young priest, who looked as healthy and as strapping as a boxer, announced from the pulpit he was going out to get medical attention. When he left the following Saturday he had all his belongings and he never came back.

"That winter a number of old people died and with no priest to give them the last rites of the Church, it was hard for us to bear.

"The hardest death was that of John Lamie. We were close. He was a first cousin of your grandfather and in winter he and Eugenie would drop in almost every Sunday evening, after Benediction, for a game of cards. John was a fishing captain and also Justice of the Peace. He was the same age as your grandfather but he had been ailing for a number of years. He had some problems with his innards. I couldn't help him. He went to St. John's but no doctor could give him any satisfaction.

"One evening, his young grandson Joel rushed in and shouted that his grandfather was awfully sick and would I come and bring pencil and paper. What John Lamie wanted, and it's still hard to talk about, was to tell me his sins. Because, as he said, and as I certainly knew, he didn't have long for this world. He didn't want to go before his Maker with his sins on his soul. He asked me to give the list to the first priest who came to the Island. I wrote down his sins as he told them. When he was finished I said the Act of Contrition with him.

"Then he told me another story. It had to do with Mainze. It was a shocking story and my mind is still disturbed by it after all these years. I started to write down this story he was telling me—but he stopped me. No, what he had done wasn't a sin, he said. He had taken the action in his capacity as Justice of the Peace.

"He was a dying man. I suspect he didn't see the look of astonishment on my face. He finished his story, thanked me for listening and said,

'I think I'll sleep now.'

"He turned into the wall and within five minutes he was dead. The most peaceful death I ever saw.

"After the funeral I came home, got a piece of parchment, copied out his sins in a neater hand, dated it, and sealed it. His story I committed to memory. I knew I would never forget that."

"Having that confession in your possession, did it bother you, Grandma?"

"As you can imagine, during that long winter of no priest, I often thought of that sealed envelope. The Church permits only ordained priests to forgive sin; of course, technically, I had only heard the sins. I could hardly have refused a dying man. Nevertheless, the burden harried me. As soon as the ice broke up I let it be known that I was going out to St. John's to see my mother. But, really, I wanted to rid myself of that strange freight. I decided I would bring the envelope to the Archbishop.

"Archbishop Roche was from Branch and had gone to school with my mother, and the few times he came to Handy Harbour he always made time for a visit to your grandfather and me. The day after I arrived in St. John's I went up to the Archbishop's palace. The Archbishop was very old by then but he agreed to see me, although his young priest-secretary asked me not to stay more than fifteen minutes. I was shown into his study. He was sitting with a purple cape over his shoulders. He looked frail. I kissed his ring and greeted him. I wasn't sure he remembered who I was. He nodded his head.

"I told him the story of Mainze and the young priest's role in it and the court case. He looked at me then. Held my eyes for a long half second. It was a cold look. I felt that wasn't the first time he'd heard some version of the story. He said nothing. When I realized I wasn't going to get a reply, I told him the story of John Lamie and his list of sins. I also told him the story John had told me after I had written the list.

"I took the envelope from my handbag and offered it to him. He asked me to open it. I passed him the parchment. As he read he repeated over and over, 'This is terrible, this is terrible.' He set down the parchment. Finally he said, 'I'm glad you came to me, for who else could forgive you?'

"I looked down, and for the first time in my life, I saw my hands tremble. John Lamie's sins had been forgotten. I was being regarded as the sinner because I had written down the sins of a dying man.

"The archbishop fell silent again and stared across the room for a long time, as if he had forgotten me. I was uncomfortable, wondering if something else was expected. Then I hit on it. Since he considered I had committed some abominable sin for taking down John's list of sins, I asked him if he would hear my confession. He pointed to the side of his chair. I knelt and made my confession. He gave me absolution, and as if I had been in the confessional at home, I blessed myself, rose, and walked out of his palace."

"Grandma, what was in the list of sins?"

"Well, there is still the question of breaking the seal of confession. I always feel bound by it, but I can tell you the story John told after he gave me his sins.

"It had to do with Mainze: there were more men molesting her than she had told. There was a ring; two more besides Jock Ryle and the priest. And our good friend, John Lamie, was in on the cover-up. John never told me the names of those two other men but it wasn't difficult to guess who they were. They all left on the same boat with the young priest, and like him, they never returned.

"What I never understood though was why Mainze kept silent about those other men. Nor did I understand why Jock Ryle took the blame and let the others go free. And here is the cruellest cut of all: it was John Lamie who made arrangements for those other men to leave the Island. To escape the law. I will remember that betrayal to my dying day."

"What became of Mainze?"

"I was so upset by her having kept so much of the story from me, I never wrote her, nor did she write me. And of course she was gone to New York by the time I got to St. John's. Some years later I asked Uncle Stephen what became of her. He was surprised I wasn't hearing from her, so I assumed he didn't know about the cover-up either. And I didn't tell him. He said she stopped writing him after she turned twenty-one and he had sent her the last of her money. It hurt him to be treated that way by someone he had taken such a delight in caring for.

"But I can understand how Mainze would want to forget about this place and everyone associated with her tragic life here.

"Uncle Stephen died soon after and the story closed. It's the first time I've told that story.

"All stories will out sooner or later."

Perennial Anxiety

LAURA MORRY WILLIAMS

I don't believe that I'm like Thomas
but every year I'm surprised
when the long green leaves open
on my dogberry tree

I feel the rosebuds won't open
if I don't daily watch
I'm grateful when the alyssum
presents me with its tiny blooms

I know the monkshood and peony
always grow and spread
yet I prod the ground
till they first appear

With all my doubts
of one thing I'm certain
July will surely bring
the cabbage butterfly

My Ferryland Childhood: A Memoir

LAURA MORRY WILLIAMS

THERE WERE FOURTEEN children in my family: Lillian, Willie, Douglas, Graham, Gerald, Mary, Edgar, Margaret, Robert, Ursula, Trix, me, Jack and Sheila. My parents' names were John and Elizabeth Morry. Lillian, my oldest sister, was nineteen years older than me. When I was born she was teaching school in Calvert and came home on weekends. I was born on a Sunday. That Sunday she had gone to Evening Prayers with her boyfriend, Cecil Ledwell from Calvert. The midwife, Mrs. Polly Curran, came to the house while they were gone. When they came back, Lillian sent Cecil home when she saw that I might soon be born. I was born at eleven o'clock that night. Lillian had told eleven-year-old Mary to stay out of the way, because Mom might die. Mary was frightened and hid in her bedroom, afraid to come out. Today she says she was traumatized by my birth and Lillian's warning. Father Ryan, our parish priest, baptized me. I was called Agnes after Mom's mother, Mary Agnes Bryan; she married William Sesk.

Whenever Father Ryan came by in the spring, the younger children took an enamel pan to the top of the big meadow behind the house to pick dandelion for him. When I was older and went along with my older sister, Trix, we also helped the priest by dusting books and cleaning the bookshelves. Sometimes he gave us a few books to take home which we put in the bookcase in our parlour.

Cleaning dandelion was a boring job but was made enjoyable because it meant more time spent with our mother. We cleaned the dandelion before we brought them to the priest's house. Every time Mom got any opportunity she asked us our lessons and how we were doing in school. She'd ask about our friends. I don't think we would have offered to help if we weren't asked.

In September we picked blueberries. Mom left a pan of these blueberries simmering on the wood stove until a thick crust formed on top. She told me that the jam should form a crust twice, and after stirring it twice, to leave it on the stove until it crusted for the third time. Then take it off. We let the jam cool before we ate it. It was so good with fresh cream. I cook my blueberries the way Mom said and the jam is always perfect, especially for bottling.

The children fed the new calves when they were being weaned from their mother. One evening Mom was preparing the calves' meal and I was tempted by the smell of the warm grain. When the steam filled my nostrils I tasted the feed. I thought that it must taste like porridge. It didn't!

No garbage was ever collected and there was very little in need of disposal. The wood stove took care of paper and any useless boxes, and an occasional fire down on a large flat rock in the lower meadow burnt the rest of it. Very few cans were discarded as these were used as dumpers and were great for picking berries; others were used to carry the worms on trouting trips at the farm or to Merrymeeting Pond and even to Browsy Island Pond up the shore.

Our older sisters' coats were often made over by Mrs. Kinsella in the Pool area of Ferryland. The coats were turned inside out and made to fit the younger children. When the material was taken apart, a different style emerged from the fingers of Mrs. Kinsella. Going for fittings was especially intriguing as we got to see some of the other works in progress in her sewing room. Everyone was pleased with the tailor-made coats.

Haymaking time meant that the men cut the tall grass with scythes. We children helped turn it over with sharp prongs morning and evening. When it was dry enough, we raked the hay into long rolls, then gathered it into haycocks. The haystack had to be high, and we had to be sure we didn't trample it down as that could cause it to dampen and eventually rot and spoil. Until the hay was ready to go into the stable we spread the cock of hay on the ground the first thing in the morning, tossing it loosely in a large circle. We repeated this procedure throughout the day.

Our stable had at one time been a house. When the hay was ready to go in, the children took turns at the open wooden shutter through which the hay was tossed into the loft. This opening had been a window when the stable was a house. Only half of the upstairs floor remained, and that is where we stored the hay after filling the "parlour," which had the ceiling taken off, leaving bare beams. (Daddy used the names of the rooms as they were called when he remembered it as a house.) We pulled the hay back from the prong as my father pushed it into the loft. Before we went home we were allowed to play there for a while jumping off the beams into the warm, sweet-smelling hay.

Our farm was a mile in the slide path. The area is now called Wild Rose Meadows. Plenty of pink wild roses grew on each side of the path. My father and Prince, our large black horse, brought a box cart load of cod sound-bones to the farm to use as fertilizer. We all helped spread sound-bones on the vegetables. Once, before I was big enough to help, my father sat me on a huge rock in the middle of the farm. My sister, Trix, who was two years older than me, and was helping to spread the sound-bones, took one and threw it at me, hitting me squarely in the stomach and dirtying my flowered cotton dress and making me cry. In the farm, my father grew oats for the horse. He rotated his crops. He usually set potatoes, turnips, carrots and cabbage in the rotation.

During the winter months, the men worked on their cod traps. They mended the traps in the meadows in the spring but knitted the new work in the warmth of the kitchen. The traps were then barked in a large puncheon over a fire on the beach. The smell of bark hung heavy in the air as we walked home from school.

When the men were spreading the salt fish to dry on the flake across the lane from our house near the beach, my sisters and brother and I were often under the flake with a white enamel pan pulling what Mom called chicken weed. After we brought it home, Mom cut the weed into fine pieces with a scissors and tossed a handful of flour into the pan. She then shook the pan and spread the floured weed on the ground in the backyard for the hens. This was probably to stretch along the bag of Scratch, the hens' food, that was kept in the porch.

A nice job was gathering the eggs if it wasn't from a broody hen on a nest. We usually let the setting hen alone and collected the other eggs. We washed, counted them and put them into large bowls on the pantry shelf. When someone came to buy a dozen eggs, we wrapped each egg in paper and placed them in a brown-paper bag.

We often took eggs from the henhouse, without mentioning it to our mother, to bring to Mrs. Lucy Hynes' shop. We exchanged them for apples and oranges. One day we decided, not knowing what the yellow fruit was, to get lemons. As we tried to eat it, we could hear our mother's words in our heads: "Remember all the hungry children." We weren't allowed to waste food. It wasn't easy!

Company or unexpected visitors often found me, my younger sister, Sheila, and my younger brother, Jack, running through the huge front door in our front hall or frying dried salted caplin on the newly shined kitchen range, stinking out the whole house. Neither Pledge on the piano and mantlepieces in the front room (or parlour, as we called it) nor the strong aroma of Jeyes Fluid in the upstairs chamber pots could cover the smell of the burned salt on the stove. Sheila and I, along with Jack, usually hid in the outhouse in the lower meadow until the coast was clear, or we were found, whichever came first.

In the fall of the year, when they returned in the evening on the horse and long cart, the men brought home jays' bread. We ate it with relish because it came from the birds. I don't know how long it was before we learned that it was the leftover bread from the men's lunch. Wood was often left in the woods to dry until spring and then carried out on horse and sleigh.

Our woodland lay along the right side of the farm and through it ran a river. My brothers, Edgar and Robert, and my sister, Margaret, went trouting there. Some of the times they went, they were supposed to be in school. The woodland was where Daddy and my brothers cut firewood. It was called "The Rookery." When the wood was taken out in the winter on a horse and slide or in the spring on a long cart, it was piled behind the henhouse in teepee fashion. Every day Edgar and Robert sawed and split the wood. They stacked it in the backyard. It was convenient there for us to bring in a few armfuls for Mom when she was busy. She often brought in an armful herself, "just to get out of the hot kitchen for a breath of cool air." Usually while the men were splitting the wood, we children carried armfuls, as much as was needed for the night, to the porch; we also filled the kitchen woodbox.

At a Stanley Products house party Mom won a ham slicer for getting a big amount of sales from the guests. "'Am slicer," Mrs. Representative called it. Forever after, that was how we referred to the knife, too, in fond memory of the nice saleslady. Mom kept it in a knife-holder on the wall by the kitchen stove. It was very sharp and meant to last a lifetime, which it did.

Off the porch was the pantry where all our store of winter supplies were kept—sacks of flour, sugar and boxes of margarine. On the pantry shelves pans and cake cans contained eggs, fresh butter and cakes. On another shelf was a grater, a butter print, mixing bowls, an antique bowl filled with leftover vegetables and often a platter of cold meats. There was always a gingerbread or baking powder cake on a rack covered with a clean cup towel. Mostly anything you wanted for a snack could be found in the pantry. On top of the flour barrel, under the window, was the large breadboard, and on top of that were the many loaves of freshly baked bread covered with a clean cloth. Behind the door, a shelf held many tools and cans of nails the men needed for repairs around the house or fish stage.

Mom was prepared for visitors as long as there was some good homemade bread, fresh butter and cream in the house. She could send one of us children to the shop for a tin of luncheon meat, a pound cake or a piece of cheddar cheese if needed. I don't think Mom ever considered eggs good enough to serve as a lunch to visitors. There was always a clean white tablecloth ready in the front room. For guests Mom used her bone-handled cutlery and her china cups and saucers which were kept in the cupboard we now call the china cabinet.

The porch walls were constructed, as was the whole house, with very wide, thick boards. The walls of this porch were never papered. Like the walls of the pantry, they were always painted white—as they still are today. The shelves were covered with oilcloth that had designs of flowers or fruit. The pantry door was always closed to keep out any dirt or flies. The door had a hook and eye closure and was never to be left unhooked.

The back porch had an open-beamed ceiling. A ceiling beam held a gun rack. My older brothers went gunning, catching sea birds and anything else that was edible—and sometimes things we weren't so sure were fit to eat, like seagulls. The porch had a wooden bench for furniture and nails on the wall for hanging coats. There were a few mats, or brin bags, to scuff wet boots on. These mats could be thrown outside or hung on the backyard fence when dirty, to be washed by the rain. If the mats weren't too dirty, Mom would throw them in the ringer washer and let them swish around before she emptied the water from the machine. Sometimes she would rinse them out in the rinse water of the aluminum washtub. One of us girls would be passed a broom to sweep the canvas floor.

In the kitchen, Mom always laid a canvas mat on the linoleum in front of the stove. I remember one night when I was a little older I decided to clean the oil range. I did as I had seen my mother do on numerous occasions. I took a piece of an old towel and dipped it into the paste floor wax can and proceeded to wipe the stove. The only thing I hadn't considered was that when Mom shined the stove it was relatively cool. When I cleaned the stove there was a big heat in it and the cloth caught on fire in my hand. I immediately dropped the burning cloth to the floor. It landed on the canvas mat in front of the stove. I quickly folded one end of the mat over the flaming rag and stepped on it, smothering the flames. When Mom came into the kitchen, she smelled the wax and said to me, "What are you trying to do, burn down the house?" I smiled and pointed at the black crease mark in the mat. She laughed, too. I always had wondered why there would be a cheap canvas mat over the good linoleum. I had thought it was to save the floor covering from wearing out in a heavy traffic area. I learned the mat served more than one purpose.

In the winter of 1950, we had a lot of snow. There were no snowploughs in Ferryland. My father would harness the horse and the sleigh bells would jingle as my brothers and sisters climbed on the sleigh, under a thick blanket. The blanket covered us and our school bags to protect us from the falling snow and the ice and frozen snow thrown up from the horse's hooves. Daddy would walk alongside the horse until he got in a clearing, and then he would stand on a runner. It was about a mile to the schoolhouse. The road went along at the bottom of a hill on one side and steep cliffs to the ocean on the other. There was no pavement then. The snow drifted into big banks and made the sleigh tip towards the ocean. My sisters and brother and I had to cling to the back of the sleigh and to each other to keep from falling off. At that time, when I was just ten years old, there were no seatbelts. Not everyone had a horse, either, so when my father came to pick us up at the school, he brought home the children who lived near us, too.

Our henhouse was in a small garden, called a hen's pound. It had a very high fence. The snow always piled high inside the pound, up against the fence. The children built tunnels in the snow. We built snow houses; not the igloo type with the large blocks of snow, but tunnels through which we could climb. The hens didn't come out of their house when the weather was bad. When it snowed, we used their pound as our playground.

After school we went sliding on a steep hill across the road from our house, in Mr. Paddy Crane's meadow. The Cranes had children the same ages as some of our family. We had homemade wooden slides and sometimes one of us received a bought one from Santa Claus. The homemade ones were painted red or green, but the bought ones were varnished and had steel runners. They had steering handles and they went faster than the wooden slides. At the top of the hill we lay on our stomachs on the slides; one of our sisters or friends lay on our backs and we set off down the steep hill towards the road. There was a wire fence at the bottom of the meadow. Our fear was that we would hit that fence so we would tip the slide over when we got near it.

There was very little motor traffic on the road as there were very few cars in the area at that time. Usually only the taxi drivers from up the shore and one or two cars from Ferryland would come along the road in the evening. They brought home the few people who had been in St. John's shopping. The only other cars I remember in the harbour were owned by the priest and the man who operated the co-op store, Tommy Grant. The owners of the two other smaller stores, Ede Keough and Bill Morry, each had a pickup truck. As far as I can remember, if they got stuck in the snow, they got out and shovelled the way clear. I feel there must have been ploughs on the road sometimes but I can't remember seeing them. We walked everywhere. Every step we took, we went to our waist in snow. When the snow hardened with the colder weather, we could walk on top of it. The lighter children would skid along, with the wind blowing them and they had no control at all. The heavier children ploughed through the snow and with each step it would make a scrunch sound and break under their weight making it difficult to manoeuver. We skated on the pond at the end of our lane, across the road in our Uncle Howard's meadow.

Uncle Howard was my father's brother. The ice on his meadow was mostly shiny and very slippery, as the wind blew the snow off as fast as it fell. The ice sometimes cracked and we went through and got our feet wet; the pond was really a marsh and the water seeped into a drain leading to the ocean, a few feet away. That left the space under the ice hollow. When we skated near the edge of the pond the ice cracked and our skates often went through. When we got our skates wet we crossed the lane to our meadow, went home and changed into warm socks and winter boots. We came back and continued skidding around the ice until we were called home to supper and to do our lessons. There were no computers to check our e-mail, or even television sets to watch. After our lessons were finished we went to bed. We went to bed early and got up early.

In our kitchen an oilcloth covered the large wooden table, but a linen cloth was laid over the oilcloth when Mom had a cup of tea herself or for me and anyone else who was sitting with her. A cupboard with glass doors was built into the wall under the stairs. This was where Mom kept our everyday dishes and flatware. Just inside the door on the left side was a brown hooped barrel that held the loose tea. The bottom cupboard had two wooden doors. On the top shelf were face cloths, towels, and cup towels. In the bottom of this cupboard there was anything you might be looking for, like a pair of mitts or socks and sometimes pillowcases and bedsheets. During the winter Mom kept a jug of homemade birch beer or ginger wine in the lower cupboard. When we came home from skating or playing on a cold day, she had a nice drink for us out of that jug.

Over the kitchen couch was a three-corner cupboard. In it were the salt and pepper shakers, vanilla, a package of salt, the sugar and butter dishes and a crock of molasses. There was always a bottle of Chow Chow mustard pickles. On the top shelf, a quashed package of Bugler tobacco and a half-full package of cigarette papers were wedged inside the door. These belonged to whichever brothers were still living at home. A stack of letters from my brothers, Gerald and Doug, who lived on the mainland of Canada, and letters from Mom's cousins who lived in the United States of America, and a lot of things you would never expect to find in a cupboard, like a mousetrap, were on the top shelf of that three-corner cupboard. When Daddy lay on the couch to have a nap someone was always taking something from over his head. I often wondered why he slept with the newspaper or the *Readers' Digest* covering his face.

Silver Poetry

ROBERTA BUCHANAN

My muse is too plain-spoken
to write silver poetry

On the other hand:
polishing the silver
on a Saturday morning
at Mum's house on Coper's Cope Road
when I wanted to go up to town
the silver teapot engraved
with her name
the sugar tongs
the fluted milk jug
they tarnished so quickly
our fingers stained black
with Silvo

How boring in my mother's house
semi-detached suburbia
polishing the silver teapot
"Give it a little elbow grease!"
in case the Queen dropped in for tea
(Mum's little joke, ha ha)

The brittle best china
with golden rims and handles
hand-painted flowers
imprisoned behind glass
in the mock-Chippendale cabinet
the special tongs to lift
white quartz cubes of sugar
"One lump or two?"
faking gentry with little finger
raised

The politeness of Company
precise dainty sandwiches
with crusts cut off
(potted salmon)
arranged nicely
on a doily
the iced cake, the homemade scones
with jam and cream . . .
the indigestion

How I hated the smell of Silvo
the blackened fingers
how I despised
my mother's bourgeois tastes
(no respectable home complete
without the silver teapot)

Now Mum is dead
Now I wish I could have her back
All that's left
on the highest shelf of the cupboard
is the damned
tarnished
silver teapot

Rosie

Alison Melvin

Maria's memory harbours two vivid images of Rosie Gill—their first and last meetings.

~~~

On a Saturday afternoon in November, Maria is just finishing sweeping and dusting upstairs. After four years of practice—ever since she was eight and her mother's illness had begun—she now finds this chore pleasant. It's a time to daydream and plan a fairy-tale future. She especially likes to dust the statues—St. Theresa on the hall table, and the Blessed Virgin on a corner shelf in her mother's bedroom. She kneels before the plaster St. Theresa and begins to pray to the real one: "O Saint Theresa of the child Jesus, who during your short life on earth . . ."

The creak of the downstairs door opening and her mother's, "Hello girls, come on in," interrupts Maria's pleas to her "Little Flower" saint.

"Maria," her mother calls moments later, "come down; Marcella has a surprise for you."

St. Theresa is forgotten as Maria springs up and bounds across the long hall and down the stairs to see the latest foster child to arrive at Mrs. Bennett's house down the road.

A small girl is huddled on a chair at the far end of a matching mahogany table under the window in the front kitchen. From her first
~~~

glimpse Maria is captivated. Short-cropped, chestnut hair peeks from a purple velvet bonnet, trimmed with white fur and tied by a bow of magenta ribbon under her chin. Maria has never seen anything so beautiful as the violet velvet coat with a snowy fur collar as soft as silk. Mauve snow pants and black boots complete her outfit.

Mrs. Bennett is some sweet, Maria thinks, to let the little one wear her princess-like clothes to meet the neighbours. Marcella Grace, Mrs. Bennett's blonde-haired foster daughter, sits at the front table smiling. How delighted she must be to have a sister her own age, thinks Maria.

"Rosie, this is Maria, my daughter. You'll all be walking to school together," says Mrs. Dunne, as she takes an aluminum tray from the corner cabinet and limps off to the pantry.

"Hi, Rosie, what a gorgeous coat and hat," Maria says, seating herself opposite the small stranger.

Rosie's "Hi" is a hoarse grunt as she fixes her eyes on a green diamond in the floor canvas.

"I'll bet you're going to like living in Spruce Cove. You'll make lots of new friends."

No response.

"Won't she, Marcella?" Maria adds.

Marcella nods shyly. Rosie continues to stare at the floor.

"How old are you, Rosie?"

"Six," barely audible.

"What grade are you in?"

"One," Rosie mumbles, without lifting her head.

"How are you, Marcella? You must be some happy to have Rosie living with you."

"Hi, Maria," Marcella speaks in a half-whisper.

Maria is running out of chatter, largely because her attention is glued to Rosie's face which is as still as a statue.

"Can you carry this tray for me, Maria?" her mother calls from the pantry. "We must be going to have weather; my old fingers are so stiff."

Maria hurries to help, noting to herself that her mother's hands and feet are always stiff and swollen now, even when the sun is shining. She lifts the tray and follows her mother back into the front kitchen.

"Your new mommy was so excited that you were coming today, Rosie," Maria's mother says. "Marcella, this must be your lucky day. Such a pretty new sister. You'll have lots of fun playing together. The two of you have a bite to eat with Maria now," she says, as Maria lays a plate of gingersnaps and three cups of skimmed milk on the table, and passes the tray back to her mother.

"This milk is from our cow, Bessie," Maria says.

"Mrs. Bennett has a cow too; her name is Belle," Maria's mother adds as she sits near the oil range. Rosie lifts her eyes and her cup.

With her left elbow anchored to the table, Maria rests her head on her upturned palm and crunches a gingersnap, all the while sneaking glances at the silent Rosie.

The tiny girl's eyes are darker than Hershey bars. But Maria is instantly distracted from the reminder of her favourite chocolate bar as the darkness in those eyes sends shivers along her spine. It feels just like that secret dread that filled her last St. Stephen's night when rowdy mummers had stormed into their house and dragged a scared Mr. Bob, her father's friend, out into the frosty blackness. The same pricking of shock, the same hint of something evil plagues Maria now. I'm just being silly, she thinks, as she begins to munch another gingersnap. But her taste buds have frozen under that dark stare.

She sips a mouthful of milk and swallows hard. Just a homesick child, sad and upset, she tells herself. As her mother rattles on, bringing simple replies from Marcella, silence or grunts from Rosie, Maria shrinks from the hostile set of the tiny girl's chin. Rosie removes her hat and unbuttons her coat, but her shoulders remain as rigid as the chair that holds her. Maria wishes the stony face would soften. She wants to pity the poor little scrap, torn from her home, abandoned to strangers by strangers. Spruce Cove must seem like a gravel pit compared to St. John's. But wasn't she in a pit there too?

Rumours were flying yesterday. The high-school girls had gossiped and giggled at recess about some woman in town—an "old bag" they had called her—who was stupid enough to get tangled up with sailors down on the docks. Maria had picked up most of their comments.

"No wonder," one said, "she has to be carted off to the Mental every few months. Some way to bring up a youngster."

"Just imagine Mrs. Bennett taking the daughter of someone like that. They'll probably all get diseases from the little brat," another added.

Angela Burke, the grade eleven loudmouth had taken over then. "My mother said the welfare worker found the girl alone in a dingy hole of an apartment. She'd been missing from school for days. A bit of stale bread was the only food around, and her few rags of clothes were maggoty. She was taken right away and put in the Church of England Orphanage until they could find a home for her. She'll never fit in around here."

Maria returned to her schoolwork with a heavy spirit. The girls sounded so hard-hearted. Probably they were only showing off. Just one day later, cringing from the glare of those brown eyes across the kitchen table, Maria wonders what dismal secrets they protect.

~~~

Maria's other retrievable memory of Rosie is set again in autumn, seven years later. Maria had walked home from the schoolhouse of her childhood, now expanded to two rooms. After just one year of university training she had been appointed senior teacher and principal. Back then, careers in education were as attainable as they were demanding.

~~~

On a raw November day, Maria finishes her dinner of rabbit stew and is savouring a cup of steaming coffee before trekking back to school. Her ailing father is already snoring on the couch when Tom, Mary and Blanche, Maria's younger brother and sisters, dash through the door to join their classmates in the daily race back to the school grounds. Maria's mother hobbles arthritically from stove to table, acquainting her daughter with the latest news.

Rosie has had another one of her temper fits. She must have reverted to hiding her pills, tranquillizers prescribed in ever-increasing dosages to enable Mr. and Mrs. Bennett to cope with Rosie's erratic, often violent, outbursts. A drug induced semi-stupor is the medical solution to Rosie's problems, compounded by years of avoidance of any help for her early childhood trauma.

This time the cause of Rosie's outburst is school, or more specifically, Maria.

"She's blaming you now for being put out of school two years ago," Maria's mother warns.

"But I wasn't even there," Maria counters, "I was at university."

"Tim White told me that she's vowing to go back to school," her mother adds. "She shouted at him through the raised upstairs window this morning, 'No fuckin' teacher's gonna keep me outa school.' Poor Tim said he just ducked his head and hurried on to the post office."

Maria tries to smother her growing unease, and comforts herself by rationalizing that Rosie knows deep down that she, Maria, is blameless. Whenever Rosie has a tantrum, Maria tries to be extra kind to her. She has always sympathized with her as she recalls that inflexible tot in purple velvet.

"Miss Dunne, Miss Dunne," Rosie yells as Maria latches the front yard gate on her way back to school. "Wait, I wants ya, Miss Dunne." Rosie looks much older than her thirteen years as she lumbers towards Maria. The loose black skirt and faded green cardigan offer little protection from the sharp wind. The whole cove is aware that Rosie wages constant battles about her right to dress as she pleases. Mrs. Bennett objects less and less.

Maria knew that the "Miss Dunne" is contrived; Rosie always calls her Maria.

"Yes, Rosie, what is it?"

"I'm goin' to school today." She sounds unusually affable as the brown eyes flash and her face breaks into a grin.

"Does your mother know?"

"She don't care; she's up in the garden diggin' her parsnips." A knot forms in Maria's chest.

"But, Rosie, you know you can't come to school until the school board says it's okay. I'm not allowed to let you in." Maria forces a smile.

"I don't care about them; I'll be good."

"Look, Rosie, you'll have to wait, at least until tomorrow, so that I can contact the school board and get permission." Maria scrambles for time. There are no telephones in Spruce Cove. The Bennetts will have to deal with this latest crisis overnight.

"I don't give a damn about no fuckin' school board or no fuckin' teacher. I'm goin' to school right now. No one is stoppin' me. You're not stoppin' me, Maria Dunne, you fuckin' bastard. You hates me like all them other fuckers, but I'll get ya; I'll get you all." The dark eyes glare in contempt and cold disregard. The bony arms flay the air through the nylon sweater. The clenched fists direct at Maria a current colder than the November air and far more threatening.

What can be done? Maria's mind races. Spruce Cove's men, including Mr. Bennett, are miles in the woods cutting firewood and checking rabbit snares. Mrs. Bennett's presence now would only ignite Rosie's rebellion further.

"Rosie, I have to go now. Come over to the house after school and we'll have a talk. I'll bet your mother could do with a bit of help in the garden. Tell her I'd like to buy twenty pounds of parsnips. You can bring them over this evening. I'll have a nice tip for you. See you later." Maria turns and heads off to school, pretending oblivion to the barrage of vile language that follows her.

"Ya, you all thinks ye'er so great; I can go to school whenever I likes. I'm goin now. Ain't no slut-faced, son of a bitch of a teacher goin' to stop me. Just you try to stop me, missus big shot, ya damn shagger."

Maria squares her shoulders and increases her pace.

Arriving at school fifteen minutes early, she locks the door behind her. The pupils will not think this strange as she sometimes uses the few quiet moments before class to prepare or correct work. She hurries to the adjoining classroom door. The junior teacher, Janet Cole, is already at her desk.

"We may have some excitement this afternoon." Maria tries to sound competent as she fills Janet in. A loud knock on Maria's door interrupts them. Maria is sure her worst premonition is now a reality. With knees and hands trembling, heart thumping, she rushes to unlock the door and open it a few inches.

But it's only Jeannie Chafe, one of the senior girls. Her voice quavers as she whispers, "Rosie Gill is out back, Miss. She's laughing and cursing, and she says she's coming in. The boys are egging her on. We're afraid, Miss; Marcella is crying. We wanted to let you know."

"Thank you, Jeannie. Don't worry; everything will be fine. I'll just lock the door until bell time." Maria slides the lock back in place and leans against the door to steady her shaking frame.

Janet speaks behind her, "What are you going to do? She's crazy."

"I'll open the door a few inches at 1:15. I'll stand in it, ring the bell and let the pupils in one by one. When she sees me on guard she'll know I mean business. She won't try to push past me. I can't let her in; I'll call a couple of the boys to help. I'll ask Tom and Peter to stand close to me as the others file in. I think I can trust them to do the right thing, and their parents won't make a fuss if anything goes wrong. You call the juniors in first."

As Janet hurries to summon the little ones, Maria wonders how her voice can sound almost confident when her insides are fluttering. She stumbles back to her desk and sinks to the chair, repeating over and over, "Lord, help me; Mother Mary and St. Theresa pray for me . . ."

Then, flanked by Tom and Peter, she stands shielding the doorway, bell in hand. She pretends to ignore the gaze of the wide-eyed, quivering girls who lead the entry line. Marcella, with red eyes and pale cheeks, cowers between two senior girls, who half-lift her inside. The boys come last, expectant and gleeful.

Nothing happens. The last one is in and everything's quiet. Not a sound within or without. No sign of Rosie.

Keep to the normal routine, Maria's inner voice warns. "Let's stand for prayer now, boys and girls."

As the Lord's Prayer proceeds, Maria notes that everyones's attention is torn between her and the multi-paned windows that form the south side of the building.

"Good afternoon, everyone." Maria's teeth are beginning to chatter.

"Good afternoon, Miss." Pregnant silence swallows the strained greetings.

"Be seated please; we must get to work."

Instantly, thirty-two desks are occupied and a hint of normalcy appears, but not for long. A plink followed by a pop sounds, then another and another.

"She's throwing rocks in, Miss; she's breaking the glass," Peter says.

Icy fear seizes Maria as several rocks shatter separate panes of glass, whizz over the stunned students' heads and land at random in the aisles. Glass particles crash to the floor along the window wall, inches from the first-row desks. At any moment someone will be seriously injured by hurtling rocks or jagged glass fragments.

"Quickly," Maria finds her voice. "Move quietly to Miss Cole's room; you'll be safe there." She is far from convinced, though. The junior room has similar windows on the East wall.

With nightmare speed, the students disappear into the next room. Maria, at the rear, struggles to blot out the sound of helpless glass yielding to merciless stone. How will she ever explain this to Father Flynn and the school board? Heavier thuds on the hardwood floor announce that the weapons are getting bigger. Will broken glass energize or weaken Rosie's frenzy of destruction? Maria does not dare envision the madness behind each hurl, the fiendish glee that must now consume the victorious Rosie, or the next object on which her insane fury will be vented.

Struggling against paralyzing panic, Maria notes the absolute obedience and calm of the children—all sixty-eight of them—huddled together in a space reserved for half that number. They are all expecting the assault next door to expand to the windows behind them at any moment. There is nowhere left to run.

"Let *us* go out, Miss," a confident Tom pleads. "Me and Peter'll handle her. We'll hold her down."

"We'll kill her if we get our hands on her," Peter adds.

Maria's mind is beset by images of dead bodies, vengeful parents, irate priest, plus school board and legal officials, exacting judgment on her, only her. "My God, what can I do?" she silently pleads.

Her only hope lies in Tom and Peter's compliance. She summons them and gives strict instructions. "Boys, I want you to go outside through the junior entrance. Do not go near Rosie. You could get into serious trouble if you touch her and she hurts herself. The men are still in the woods, so you must run as fast as you can to her foster mother's house. Let Mrs. Bennett know what has happened. Tell her she must come for Rosie right away. You can get a ride back with her, but she had better get another grownup to help."

Sixty-six pairs of student eyes stare in numb silence as the boys charge through the door which Miss Cole re-locks.

Maria's mind remains hazy on the events of the following twenty minutes. The plings and pops next door slow, then stop. Rosie has apparently run out of glass targets on the south wall. Wishing that she will awaken to find this a grim dream, Maria forces herself to smile and reassure the shock-ridden victims, who sit or stand as though frozen in place. Janet, who has proven her worth as colleague and supporter, still follows Maria diligently in maintaining calm.

Finally, the sounds they long to hear: a vehicle, the crunch of tires on gravel, adult voices. Maria catches Marcella's relieved glance and nods.

Tom and Peter eventually return with details of the capture. Rosie, her venom temporarily expunged, and in an exhausted stupor, had been persuaded to get into the car and go home.

After a brief consultation with Maria, Janet dismisses the students for the afternoon, telling them to take only their coats and caps. "You deserve a holiday for being so good," Janet says. "Don't worry about Rosie; Mrs. Bennett will take her to the doctor. You know she gets sick sometimes and doesn't really know that she is doing bad things."

"We'll get the windows fixed," Maria promises, as the realization of unexpected freedom produces nervous smiles.

For the seniors, the break from school will last a week, as the physical evidence of Rosie's tirade is removed. Maria knows that the emotional effects will live with them all indefinitely.

~~~

Rosie did not threaten the school or the area again. From that day on she was confined to the Waterford Hospital. Maria heard that she was
~~~

let out in her late twenties and had married. When she thinks about Rosie now Maria worries that the cycle will go on. And she still wonders what dismal secrets those dark eyes held.

The Killing-Jar

ROBERTA BUCHANAN

IT TOOK US a week by train to get from Uitenhage, South Africa, the town where I was born, to Ndola, Northern Rhodesia. We travelled first class, of course, being white; second and third class were for coloureds. The train had a powerful steam engine. "Don't stick your neck out the window," Mummy said; "if a train comes in the opposite direction it could cut off your head." We couldn't resist sticking our heads out as the train rattled on, the giraffes and elephants and kudu racing along the horizon, and we got cinders in our eyes from the coal. Every now and then, the train had to stop to get water for the steam engine.

We had a compartment to ourselves, with seats covered in green leather, bunks which let down at night for us children, and a metal washbasin which folded up into the wall when not in use. Mummy had brought a basket of food, since food on the train was so expensive. Every evening, when the sun was setting, she and Daddy went to the bar for sundowners. The black attendant let down the bunks and made up the beds with crisp white sheets. It was nice lying there and listening to the clacking of the wheels on the metal tracks. Sometimes the train stopped at a station in the middle of the night and we peered out between the blinds. The railway workers tapped the iron wheels to test for cracks. There were porters with luggage and people getting on board and the bright lights of the station and people shouting goodbye and pickanninis selling wooden toys they had made. Then the whistle screeched and we rushed off into the darkness again.

In the daytime Donald and I could run up and down the corridor for a change. But we always had to take a rest in the middle of the day. Mummy insisted on that. We hated it. We lay head to tail on the wide leather seat and kicked each other in the crotch. It was painful! Donald and I were always fighting. It wasn't fair because he was bigger than I was, and could hit harder, but if I cried I could get him into trouble.

Daddy had been recruited by a man in the Colonial Office for a really important job in Northern Rhodesia. He was Town Engineer in Uitenhage but he got sick of the politics and the Afrikaaners. Daddy designed the sewage works for the town. The Afrikaaners on the Town Council tried to guess where they would be located so they could buy up the land to sell it back at a profit, but Daddy wouldn't tell them. That made them mad! Daddy was writing a thesis on the effects of vine leaves on sewage; Mummy thought it a big joke. Mummy sold her stinkwood chairs and all her furniture to move up to Northern Rhodesia. All our china and stuff had to be packed up in wooden crates and shipped on the train. Don and I had to leave some of our toys behind to give to the poor children in the hospital.

When we arrived in Ndola we were put in a temporary house with a kitchen at the back connected by a path with a canopy over it. It was the rainy season. The cook boy had to run from the kitchen to the dining room with the food. The rain came straight down and there was thunder and lightning and everything turned to mud. Don and I enjoyed sliding down muddy slopes, even though our clothes got all dirty, especially our pants. With the rainy season came the flying ants—two ants joined together. There were thousands and thousands of them and they flew into the soup as we were eating dinner. They flew into your hair, they dropped into your gravy.

When the rain stopped and the sun shone, the butterflies came out—big, colourful, yellows and blues. Don and I chased them and tried to catch them. Daddy made us butterfly nets and a killing-jar. A wide-mouthed short mason jar, with a white paste of plaster of paris and cyanide at the bottom. Daddy said we would die if we inhaled the cyanide. It would poison us and we would fall down dead. We caught the beautiful butterflies and put them in the killing-jar. The stupid things struggled and fluttered so much they damaged their wings before they died, which made them less valuable as specimens. When they stopped moving we took them out and stuck a pin through them and mounted them in a cigarette box. Mummy and Daddy both chain-smoked, a habit they had got in the Army when they got rations of cigarettes, so we had plenty of boxes. They were good ones too, shallow cardboard with a hinged lid, they held 100 cigarettes. My favourite butterflies were iridescent blue. We never knew their names which was a pity. We didn't have a book, you see. I don't think there were such books in those days; I never saw one. At night we could get the big furry moths too and put them in the killing-jar.

After a few weeks we moved into our permanent house. All the houses were the same, built by the Colonial Office: three bedrooms with a porch in front and back. The floors were red-stained concrete which had to be polished with special red polish. The houses came with basic furniture: wooden sofas with thong seats. You had to supply your own cushions. Nobody stayed in the Colonies: it wasn't healthy. After a three-year term you got a trip Home. Home was England.

If you had a three-bedroom house you had to have three servants: a cook, a houseboy and a garden boy. But they didn't cost much because they were paid mostly in kind: mealy-meal, rice and sugar. They weren't given much money because they would only spend it on cigarettes and such. Daddy said the natives didn't have much sense. Their pay was set by the colonial office.

When the rainy season ended, Don and I turned from butterfly hunting to climbing trees. We had twenty-four mango trees in our garden, quite low and easy to climb. Also a paw-paw tree, but it didn't have any fruit because Mummy said you needed a male and a female tree and we only had the one. We had banana trees too which had small bananas called ladies' fingers. On the banana trees you could find a chameleon. If you put it on different colours it would change colour. Mummy said if you put it on Buchanan tartan it would explode! Our garden boy was called Concrete: he was a real boy, I mean a child, not like the other boys who were grown men with wives and children. He spent the day in the sun weeding the garden. The servants' families lived in a special, two-roomed shack in the back garden. The cook was called James and the houseboy was called Luke, but those weren't their real names. They were Christian names. Their real names were African but they wouldn't tell them. Donald ordered them around just like a white bwana, even though he was only ten years old.

Mummy said you had to lock everything up or the servants would steal the scissors. There were never any leftovers! The boys saw to that. On the back porch we had a meat safe with its legs in tins of paraffin to keep the ants away. Also on the back porch hung canvas bags of drinking water. Every morning Mummy had to supervise James in boiling the water to put in the canvas bags. If you drank water out of the tap you would get sick. In the back garden was our toilet. It had a bucket which was emptied very early every morning by men who came in a special cart. After you used the toilet you had to pour disinfectant into the bucket; it turned a milky white. I didn't like going to the toilet because there were spiders there and you had to keep an eye on them. Also it stank. There were spiders in the bedrooms too, but we slept under mosquito nets so you had some protection. Mummy said they were good because they ate the flies. Every evening the rooms were sprayed with Flit by the houseboy to kill the mosquitoes. You could still hear them in the night, buzzing around trying to get into your net to bite you and suck your blood and give you malaria. I was frightened that the spiders would get into my bed too, under the net. At night I watched them moving across the ceiling and the walls, big brown brutes. Mummy said they were harmless, not like the grey tarantulas. She said once a woman went into her bedroom to brush her hair—there was a tarantula on the dressing table and it jumped at her and bit her and she was poisoned and died. That scared me! I was always looking for the grey tarantula, and one day I saw one in one of the empty packing cases on the porch. James came and killed it.

We also had a black mamba on the tree by the garage. Sheila, our fox terrier, used to bark at snakes and kill them. She was very brave.

There used to be beggars coming to the house; natives, of course. One was deaf and dumb; he could only make gestures. Mummy told James to give him a sandwich and a cup of tea. She always gave something to the beggars, some food and Dad's old trousers perhaps. But she would never buy a monkey or a parrot off them even though Don and I begged her to. She said monkeys were dirty and bit people and parrots could give you a disease. The monkeys were small ones and had chains, and the parrots were green or grey.

Wouldn't you know that we had to have a rest hour in the middle of the day. Mummy insisted on it, and she lay down too to have a siesta. We *had* to lie on our beds, even though we didn't want to go to sleep. Mummy said we could read a book if we liked. My favourite was Enid Blyton. Once a boy came in the rest hour with a message for Mummy. I went to her room. She was fast asleep and although I shouted at her and shook her she didn't wake up. That frightened me. What if she died? What if she never woke up?

On Saturday nights we lay in bed and heard the drums from the native compound. It was scary and exciting at the same time. Mummy said they did ju-ju and dancing. When Mummy and Daddy went out at night, Don and I would pretend to be ghosts and try to frighten the natives sitting out back by their fire. They didn't take any notice of us, however, just went on talking in their singsong language.

Daddy's job was building new houses in the native compound. They were built of concrete blocks with a concrete floor, not like the dirt floors of the native huts which were made of dried blood and earth. The new houses were hygienic, but not as picturesque as the round huts with thatched roofs that the natives built. In the market, the natives sold dried fish, dried frogs and dried locusts. These were thought, by them, to be a great delicacy. We thought them disgusting!

Daddy was disappointed in his job. It wasn't what he was promised. So my parents decided to move back home to England for our education. Otherwise we would have to be sent to boarding schools, like their friends' children. It would be expensive, whereas at home, we could get a good education for free. Which reminds me of my first kiss. Roger, who was eleven and wore long pants, arrived home from boarding school on the train. We met and exchanged photographs. Roger kissed me on Christmas Day behind the shed, but my brother told on me and I got into trouble from my mother. I was in disgrace and my mother said I had to sit where she could keep an eye on me. I cried; I felt really humiliated. Don shouldn't have done that. What a sneak! I suppose he was jealous. I was a bad girl. Kissing was bad. Roger didn't get into trouble. I still have his photograph. He was my first boyfriend.

There was a road at the back of our house in Ndola where the sewage cart used to come. One day I saw a black woman with a stick walking down this road and she was beating a little boy who was walking in front of her. He had no clothes on and he was crying. I said to her, "Give me that stick." She did, and I threw it over the hedge. It was the best thing I ever did. I was sorry for the little boy, but I wasn't sorry for the butterflies struggling to get out of the killing-jar, beating their wings against the glass.

But I am sorry now.

New Gower Street 1962

GERALDINE CHAFE RUBIA

Life on this street
flows like brine
emptied out by the corner grocer

Little boys taunt motorists
and pester little girls
who mimic mothers in high heels
and limpsey taffeta

A window frames the wistful pose
of Chinese sister and brother
safe inside

With taverns closed
the Pinky Boys take up a collection
coppers and all
for a bootleg bottle of Port

Prostitutes fight among themselves
on the sidewalk
their curses pierce our front walls
and punctuate the family rosary

My father
a non-praying Protestant
opens an upstairs window
and christens the brawlers
with a bucket of water

Surfaces

MAGGIE HENEGHAN

IT WILL TAKE years before Claire realizes how easily bad news can slip into a home. As easily as Claire does now, crunching the snow beneath her boots, eyeing the fallen branches of the ancient maple tossed by the night wind, looking at the random pattern and yellowed corners of Jake's paw prints, the tracks of her brothers' boots. She climbs the steps gingerly, watching for the spot where the roof drips. Always a mound there, she has to move carefully or risk falling. It's what lies beneath the surface that can hurt.

It moves swiftly, this kind of bad news, news so shocking that there seemed to be all of her family standing in the back porch that day, freezing. Mother would kill them for wasting heat like that, but she's there, too. And some boy Aidan's brought home from school; he does that on Fridays, brings one of his friends home, so they don't always get stuck eating cafeteria food. He keeps his head down; still Claire can see he'd rather be anywhere else, even sitting on the front stone fence, waiting out the hour.

The puddles beneath their boots enlarge, touching all, and her mother shivers.

They eat hot dogs this Friday, another rule broken. In Claire's house, it's always fish for Friday, no matter what. And such wieners! Split and tough, because they've been boiling forever, and rock-hard buns, left too long in the warmer. The plates are enough to scald you, but no one complains. Neil serves the hot dogs. His face is chubbier than the others and sallow; his dark eyes are so enlarged he looks like he's been in another scrap, except he carries a stricken look Claire's never seen there before. It frightens her, but she still stares until he growls, "Eat your lunch."

Her mother, having told them the news, leans against the deep-freeze and talks throughout an endless string of phone calls. She winds the cord around her long fingers only to keep releasing it, although she complains when they do the same. She blinks at the ceiling, never once checking to see if anyone is eating.

"Oh! You've heard already, have you? Yes, I guess it's bound to be on the news; still we're trying to get hold of everybody first. There's just so many of us."

There are pauses in these conversations; later, when Claire is old enough she will fill them in. Now they are punctuated by her mother's sighs, the slow release of air, like an old balloon with the slightest hole pricked in it.

"A teacher, high-school. Her students loved her, you know; she was always so vivacious. Two boys, one in kindergarten, one little more than a baby. I knew something was up when I saw Father Mackay here."

Her mother's voice continues in the background, talking about the priest having come, all dressed in black, with some formal, funny, boxed hat on his head; her mother would know the name. She probably says it, but Claire is busy, tracing her fork through a puddle of ketchup, imagining his arrival, his robe making a gentle sweep in the snow. He was waiting for her mother, standing there holding a prayer book in one hand and extending the other as she got out of the old Impala. As Claire lingers at the table, she sees everything as clearly as if she, too, were coming back from Mass, not for the first Friday, but for the repose of someone's soul.

"The Mass will be on Monday. At the Basilica. Oh, in the morning, of course."

Claire hates it when the teachers insist they sing at such masses—funerals for straggly souls with hardly any family. Then, she and her classmates are trotted across the parking lot to lend their voices. It would have been Presentation's turn today, she thinks. Mercy won't have to bother; there'll be a huge choir on Monday, her mother's family so musical and so involved in the community.

"At first I didn't know who he was talking about. Shocked! Well, that's it, isn't it? You never know what the day's going to bring."

Claire's mother thinks it's her oldest boy, gone off in spite of them to work in the Alberta tar sands, determined to pay his own way. She's been wrong about her intuition before.

"Coming in for a meeting. She hasn't been in since Dad's birthday, you know. Late November. He hated her driving in over the road like that, especially in winter. A Toyota. Totalled. They say it was instant, wouldn't have felt a thing. She was wearing her seatbelt. Would you believe the car seat's still intact?"

The hot dog long gone cold, Claire all the while imagines the news, how her mother takes it, that her youngest sister was killed early that morning by some fellow, immediately made villain. Although he was probably only wrong in trying to pass in a snowstorm, and, maybe, one could say they were both wrong to drive the Placentia road that morning. But then she had young children; she just couldn't leave any sooner.

"Up in Holyrood. Next to Mom. The time they're going to have digging the ground. No, no, Tom will say the Mass. Of course, the bishop will be there and all the priests. Yes, they were so close. Thank God Mom's not around to see this."

Claire remembers the walk through Mercer's garden. She always takes the Barnes Road route home, so she can walk with her friends and travel in a pack through the narrow run of Presentation courtyard. Never know what can happen there. It's sunny, so bright; the snow holds those diamond sparkles of really cold winter. It's a gorgeous clear day for St. John's, and as her world exists only from the Narrows to the Overpass, a blinding snowstorm elsewhere on the Avalon bears no weight. The snow floats around Claire as she kicks its smoothness. She thinks about her morning, another row with the gym teacher. Claire knows her own sauce, but she didn't stop herself. She loves the challenge of authority and how her own face stays so pale while the teacher's reddens.

She scales the fence, careful to avoid hitching her coat. She has already torn two on the barbed wire on top, and her mother nearly killed her. Almost there, she pauses and sniffs the air. All she sees is the steam from the dryer vent. She can't smell any fish; Claire hates fish.

"A turkey? Why, that would be lovely. We'll go back to Dad's place. He keeps the heat on up there all winter. Good thing. Mary's cooking a ham, and Mrs. Clarke called to say she'd do a roast. Well, you know, it's going to be huge. All those people will have to be fed. Liquor? Oh, I'm sure Ned or Bob or someone will take care of that."

This is the point when Claire slows her memories. She sometimes thinks that if she never went in the door that day, if she had stayed in for lunch or been polite to Miss Baker, things would have been different. She knows better, most of the time. Still, it remains a secret wish that she could have done something, that she could have taken something from her routine life to alter the pattern of so many others. Even now, so many years later, she sometimes notices short, dark women in the mall or walking along Water Street, moving swiftly, their heads bobbing in conversation or swaying as if singing to themselves. Then, she catches herself with an ache that surprises her, that after twenty years—a lifetime, really—she can still be twelve and her aunt barely dead.

"Would've been thirty-four in March. He was killed, too. Poor man. Older fellow, married, I think. Terrible, really. No, there's not much to be done. Just get through it. My kids? She was so close to all of them, comes with being the youngest. Fifteen years between us. Yes, my flower girl. Remember how sweet she looked. Like a little pixie. Do you think so? No, I never thought Claire looked much like her."

Later, they all go back to school, Neil, Aidan, Sheila, and the friend Aidan brought home. Claire doesn't. She disappears into her bedroom and sits on Sheila's bed. She looks out over the street. It's still sunny, bright enough that the icicles on the porch roof are dripping and pushing perfect circles into the snow. Claire puts her feet up on the radiator, pressing them into the raised edges, so that her soles become imprinted with the iron. She hasn't changed clothes yet; Friday is the day her mother presses their uniforms for the coming week, but she knows that won't happen today. Claire finds the heavy, dark material strangely comforting as she fingers it. The pleats crumple under her weight; she sees a spot of ketchup on the bodice. Good thing it didn't get on her blouse; her mother rails against stains.

She no longer hears her mother; perhaps the phone finally hangs silent. The rad is very hot, and every so often Claire lifts her feet into the cold air above before she places them back again. Her good shoes are in school. Nothing she can do about that now. She doesn't wonder if Sheila will remember them. She doesn't wonder why the rest of them went back or why her mother didn't make her. She suddenly sees herself having to wear boots all weekend or walking through the Basilica in her socks. She giggles. She can't help it; it just perked from her lips.

The heat travels along her legs. Claire moves the sheers to get a better look. Her mother hates them fiddling with the curtains, but, today, everything seems cloudy. Below her are the last students rushing back to class and women walking carefully to avoid the slush, all set for an afternoon at the bowling alley across the street. Claire wants to blow on the window, press her lips to it, make some lasting sign that she was here, but she's too old for that now. There's a yawning pit in her stomach, not hunger, although she doesn't remember tasting the hot dog she forced down. She feels very old right now, or at least, what a twelve-year-old imagines is the feeling of old.

Her mother knocks on the door, even though it isn't closed. She wears her fur coat, has just applied her bright red lipstick. She never smudges. She pats her tight curls around her head as Claire turns. She doesn't look pale or too made-up, tired or refreshed. In fact, she doesn't look any different than she does on most Friday afternoons. If Claire is looking for grief, her mother hides it well. "I'm going to get my hair done," she begins. "I already had the appointment made; I might as well go."

Claire wonders if she is explaining something to her. She stares at her mother, before quickly placing her feet on the floor. Her mother dislikes sock feet. She digs her high heels into their feet whenever she catches them unshod. But her mother busies herself with tying her scarf, brilliant gold and maroon.

"The funeral is on Monday. I hope Sheila remembers your shoes." She pulls one leather glove smoothly on and then speaks as if it just occurs, "And, oh, Claire, if the phone rings, don't say where I am."

Claire hears a funny expiration of air then. Is it her mother or is it the radiator? Strange noises escape it sometimes. She looks at her mother; their brown eyes reflect each other's unspoken hurt. She wants to call her Mommy today. She won't. She wants to say, "Don't go." She wants to admit that even if they were to say nothing to each other all afternoon, that even if the phone were to keep ringing and her mother were to give the same horrible story over and over, the presence of her body, her breath in the house, the sound of her voice in the faraway kitchen would comfort Claire on a day when the sun shines so brightly it hurts her eyes. She says nothing, just blinks hard. Her mother disappears.

The radiator hisses. The sun hides for a moment behind the clouds. More bowlers hurry to their game; the sun reappears, and Claire is alone, except for the sleeping dog below. She sinks into the emerald green bedspread and watches perfectly formed circles drop onto the fabric. Tears over nothing look just the same as these, she thinks.

Summer

Garden Party

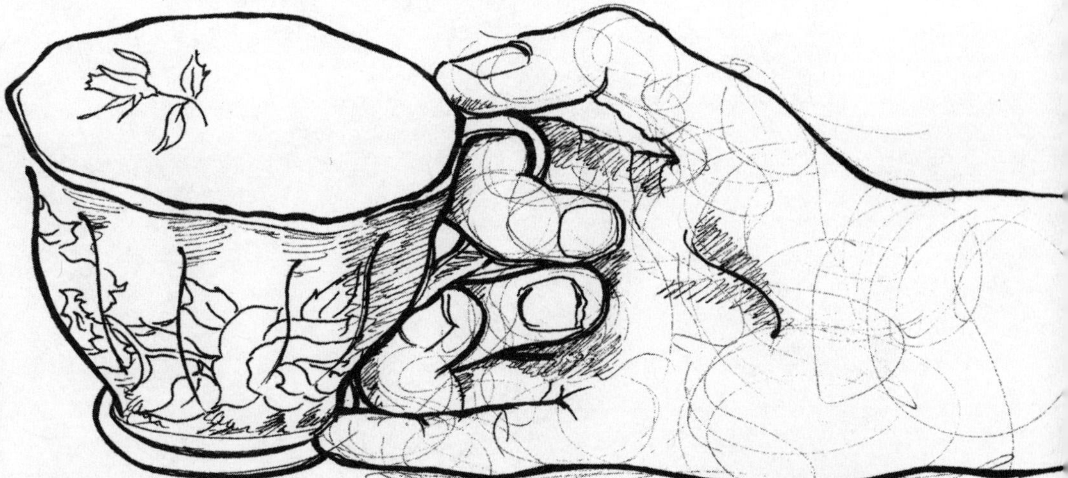

The Summer of Lannie Ramunski

M. T. DOHANEY

IN THE SOFT moments of my life I can still hear her voice. It is husky. A smoker's voice, although at the time I met her she had only been smoking for a couple of months—and even then only on the sly, out of sight of her grandmother. Mrs. Furlong had no idea that her summer visitor never left her bedroom without her pack of Lucky's hidden in the waistband of her underwear.

Lannie had a quick, easy smile. It would light up her eyes, reminding me of the forget-me-nots that grew helter-skelter in our backyard. She wore her long blond hair draped over one eye, à la Veronica Lake. Her mother, whose salad days had been spent in the forties, and who knew everything there was to know about the movie stars of that time, had told her that there was even a song about Veronica Lake's hair-do. Sometimes Lannie would sing a few bars of *A sweater, a Sarong, and a Peek-a-boo-bang* just to demonstrate that the information she was parcelling out was correct. At fifteen, I was certain that had I been given a hand in fashioning myself I would have gladly become a clone of Lannie Ramunski.

But I have other memories of her as well. Sad memories. I was with her on the day she learned her mother, while undergoing an operation for cancer, had died on the operating table. Her anguished cry when she read the telegram her father had sent from Boston is still as fresh in my memory as if no years have intervened. It is a piercing shrill sound that rises and falls like the screech of a seagull. And I can still see her crumpled form as she lay huddled at the foot of her bed, a broken creature, her hand clutching the telegram. I hadn't read the telegram and I wondered how her father had worded his condolences since he had abandoned both wife and daughter many years before.

From the instant we learned that Lannie Ramunski was going to be spending the summer in our village—a small, isolated, sea-battered clutch of houses backed up against a barren cliff—we were filled with titillating intrigue and exquisite anticipation. Just her name alone resonated with a ring of outlandishness. For some of us it even teetered on the brink of damnation.

Sister Ignatius—our tenth-grade teacher—confirmed that her research showed there never had been a Saint Lannie. A shocking revelation, indeed! Without a heavenly benefactor to intercede for her, who could she call upon to coax and wheedle favours from God on her behalf?

Sister Ignatius said that Lannie was more likely a trumped-up Hollywood name. Her lip curled when she said the word "Hollywood." She dispensed this information as she flicked her waist-length black serge veil over her shoulder with one hand, while with the other she held a book of saints and martyrs splayed open on her desk. She ran her index finger down the list of names to see if she could find one from which "Lannie" could be derived, no matter how remote the connection. But there was neither saint nor martyr whose name came even close.

She slammed the book shut and rapped her knuckles on its cover to signal her search was now completed.

"Like a favourite aunt," she explained, as if we needed an explanation as to the significance of having a saintly namesake. "The saints reside at God's right hand," she said, indicating with her own pale white hand the proximity of God and the saints. She pointed from one side of her desk to the other, measuring distance. "From their lips to His ear is only a whisper away." At this point her voice dropped so low we could barely make out her words. "How wonderful it must be to be so close to the Lord." She said this with such reverence, her lower lip trembled.

We knew of no one else who was in Lannie Ramunski's precarious situation. Certainly, no one in our village was without a saint's name. Every morning when Sister Ignatius called roll, it sounded as if she were reading straight from the Litany of the Saints. Mary, Agnes, Lucy, Cecilia, Ann, Elizabeth, Sarah, Rose, Catherine, Paul, James, Ambrose, Steven, Patrick, John. In case of duplication, other distinctions had been made, Elizabeth from the Gulch. Elizabeth from the Harbour. Patrick from upalong. Patrick from the Cove. And, of course, there were diminutives: Betsy, Betty, and Liz; Paddy, Pad, and Pat.

Our saints' namesakes had been given to us at our Baptism and usually we had two. I, however, had been given three. However, to get three, I had to separate Mary from Magdalene and include Holy Women along with the list of saints. And I had to discount the fact that I was called Theresa, not to honour the saint who dropped flowers from heaven, but to honour my grandmother—a crusty old woman who was still in this world and definitely no saint.

But it was surely understandable that with our bent of mind, it was appalling to us that our expected visitor was without a heavenly benefactor, especially in light of the fact that her surname—Ramunski—had a heathen ring to it. Our surnames could be traced back to generations of ancestors who had come to Newfoundland directly from Ireland (Saint Patrick's Ireland): O'Rourke, O'Brien, O'Sullivan, O'Rielly, Clancy, Cleary, Callaghan, Conway, Kelly, Dunphy, Daugherty, Foley, Finnigan, and Furlong. There wasn't a Smith or a Jones in the group, much less a name as outlandish as Ramunski.

I was one of the first to learn about Lannie's coming visit and I lost no time in spreading this news about. I had overheard a conversation between my mother and Lannie's grandmother who was our closest neighbour. Mrs. Furlong had been sitting in our kitchen with my mother, having a cup of tea one Saturday morning. I had left my sweater hanging over a chair in the dining room and I'd come down from my bedroom to retrieve it. The dining room and kitchen were adjacent and the door separating them wasn't fully closed. Hearing a snippet of their conversation piqued my interest so much that I stayed to listen.

"She's having a heavy operation, girl," Mrs. Furlong said, getting into the contents of a letter her daughter had written to her and which she had picked up at the post office on Friday afternoon. "On her womanly parts. She already had some work done last year. Remember?

I told you about it back then. They took out the part where the cancer had set in. Now, 'tis back agin. In another place, of course."

"The poor soul," my mother responded, dropping her voice in the way she always did whenever she talked about bad news having befallen someone. "And was that what her letter was all about?"

"Yes, partly. And she wants to know if I'm up to having her girl come live with me for the summer."

"Oh my, Missus," Mother prophesied dourly. "A lot of responsibility, ma'am. And you not well."

"Yer right in that regard, girl. Of course, I'm not up to it. Me heart hardly got enough push in it to hold me upright these days. But what can I do? Can't leave the girl alone. She's only fifteen. Same age as your Theresa. And the father not worth a pinch of henshit. As you know very well, Fred Ramunski slipped the traces a couple of years ago and traipsed off with another woman leaving Gloria and Lannie to fend for themselves." She shrugged indifferently. "I think it was with a woman who worked in the funeral parlour business with him. But what does it matter who it was. Gloria called her the Undertaker Hag. She said Fred and this hag used to get soused together on embalming fluid. But she may have made that up. Gloria was always inclined to stretch things."

"Oh I remember when he jumped the fence," my mother confirmed. "Or at least when he got caught jumping the fence. Can't say I was surprised. Right from the first I had him pegged as a gallivant. But Gloria couldn't see beyond the uniform. She was determined to get herself an American serviceman so she could go live in the States."

"Fer sure. Yer right on that, girl. I felt the same way as you did about him. Blood of a bitch, that's what he is. If I could get me hands on him, I'd rip out his privates so he'd have no reason to gallivant."

They both laughed and then moved on with their conversation about the granddaughter's visit.

As soon as Mrs. Furlong left our house that morning I asked my mother for more details on Lannie Ramunski. Just her name alone had already captured my imagination. And because we would be neighbours I was certain she would be my special friend. I would be the envy of the other girls in my class who often cliqued together and snubbed me because their houses were situated farther up the road, and they were lined up cheek by jowl, allowing them to frequently visit each other.

But apart from my girlfriends envying me, there was the excitement of spending a summer with someone who was from that magical place called Boston. I had aunts and uncles who were living there, and although I had never met any of them, their Christmas, Easter and birthday cards were always so filled with enchantment that I would stare at them for hours. I saved each one. Indeed, it was these Christmas cards that decorated our tree year after year. They had tinsel, ribbon, embossed printing and glitter that came off on your fingers and sparkled like fairy dust.

Our own cards were church-bought and were extremely basic and unadorned and always of a religious bent. At Christmas there was the Manger scene. At Easter there was The Last Supper. And on St. Patrick's Day there was Saint Patrick himself in his green bishop's robes with a few slain snakes lying prone at his feet. But there was never any glitter. Nor tinsel. Nor embossing. Nor ribbons. And certainly no extravagantly brilliant colours.

"How many times do I have to tell you to stop snooping in on other people's conversation?" Mother asked, sidestepping my urgent need for details about Lannie. "I keep telling you that people who eavesdrop never hear anything good about themselves."

"I didn't hear anything bad about myself," I peevishly countered, knowing she was embarrassed because I had overheard her laughing at Mrs. Furlong's bawdy talk. "You were talking about this Lannie person. And about her mother. And about her father. Nothing about me."

"Well one of these days, my lady," she predicted with a turndown of her lips and then immediately began a tirade on what was really on her mind.

"I'm telling you now," she said, wagging her finger in the direction of Betsy Furlong's house, "I've got enough to do this summer with your father only able to get home on weekends without having to take on the worry of you. So I don't want you hanging around with this girl this summer if she turns out to be a wild one. I don't care even if it puts Betsy's nose out of shape. Those girls from Boston can be as hard as nails. And this one never had a father to guide her."

She continued with her reasons as to why I was not to take up with Mrs. Furlong's American granddaughter. "And as far as I can tell she's not even Christian, much less Catholic. Betsy once told me that she wanted Gloria to sneak the child into a church to get her baptized or even dunk her in the sink herself. But she never made a move. Afraid of that husband of hers, I suppose. He said it was all nonsense and didn't want her baptized. Myself, I would have said to that husband 'If 'tis all nonsense like you think it is, why not let me get her baptized, just to humour me. If it's just foolishness, what's the harm?'"

Mother gave a defiant toss of her head, leaving no doubt that Gloria's husband would not easily get over her time had she been the one married to him.

"At least that makes sense to me. I say, why should he fear something that he believes is just a bunch of nonsense? Poor old Selena Cleary believed that stepping on a crack would break her mother's back so she spent a lifetime dodging potholes and frost heaves. But what harm if that's what she believed. Didn't hurt us any to see her jumping about like a grasshopper. And it helped her. Much the same with having this child baptized. If he didn't believe in it, it couldn't have done any damage just to have a drop of water sprinkled on her head. And it would have meant so much to her grandmother."

All of Mother's chatter only served to make me more inquisitive about Lannie, but none of it prepared me for that first breathtaking sight of her. Nor did it protect me from being completely enthralled with her. She was tall, but not gangly tall. She had shoulder-length yellow hair. I was to learn that her hair colour had been helped along by a bottle of peroxide. She told me this unabashedly as if bleaching one's hair wasn't the stuff of a Jezebel. Her skin was cream-coloured, and in comparison, our ruddy, sea-cured cheeks seemed common and vulgar.

And the clothes she wore were all gaily coloured—saucy clothes, mother said—but they made our paltry wardrobes, especially our black school uniforms, seem so totally dull and dowdy, so workaday. She wore her cardigan-style sweaters with the sleeves pushed up to the elbows and buttoned at the back, unashamedly displaying her breasts. Her full, waltz-length cotton skirts were the height of fashion—a fashion we had only been privy to in an Eaton's catalogue. The skirts billowed out with the help of several layers of fine, white netting, which she called "crinolines." I never tired of seeing the swish of skirt and netting as she picked her way over rocky beaches and narrow paths that were littered with sheep dung. She wore lipstick—pale pink lipstick—and nail polish to match. Compared to my unvarnished flesh, this was Mary Magdalene before her redemption.

I fell instantly in love with Lannie and my mother's severe warning to keep my distance fell on deaf ears. My powerful crush on Anthony Callaghan vanished like the fog before a gale-force wind. My future plans to be a nurse waned, and no longer did I feel the need to be in the good graces of the girls in my class. I wanted only to be metamorphosed into a dazzlingly delightful Lannie Ramunski. I wanted all of her qualities to be my qualities, and if this couldn't be possible, I was willing to settle for being caught forever in the orbit of her sweep.

I mimicked Lannie's accent until my mouth got stiff from the effort. We *pawked* the *caw* in the *pawking* lot. I also practised her walk and the way she tossed her head, her hair swinging sultrily with each toss from her left shoulder to her right. But sensual and sexy continued to elude me. Of course uniforms made of black serge and worn two inches below the knee, round-toed flat-heeled shoes and hair chopped close to the ear line don't lend themselves very easily to a provocative image.

It came as no surprise to me that Anthony Callaghan also fell in love with Lannie. From the moment he set eyes upon her, all romantic thoughts of me seemed to have vaporized. He no longer wanted to sit beside me whenever we huddled in groups on the bank of the brook that ran through our village. And if it got chilly, it was to Lannie he offered his sweater.

I blamed only Anthony for this humiliating betrayal. How could I blame Lannie if Anthony had honed in on her? Should you blame the wild rose for attracting a bee, or the light bulb for enticing the moth? Besides, Lannie had told me that she had a real boyfriend back home and Anthony was only a flirtatious fling and I could have him back as soon as she left for Boston. She showed me a photograph of this Boston boyfriend to reassure me that this was so, and I could see at a glance that Anthony was no match for the Jimmy Dean look-alike who stared sulkily into the camera.

Lannie frequently tried to persuade me to wear lipstick, and whenever she was getting dressed she would always offer me a variety of silver and gold tubes from which to choose.

"Try this one," she would say, pushing the lipstick up out of its case, a tower of exquisite and tantalizing rose pink. I could almost taste the glycerine sliding over my lips, and I could imagine pursing my lips together, the way Lannie did, to spread the colour evenly. But I always refused. I couldn't take the chance of my mother finding out and then forbidding me to associate with Lannie. To insure my continued association with her, I knew I had to be a paragon of virtue, a model of decorum. Mother did not give second chances.

One evening, however, when Mother and Mrs. Furlong had gone to a church card party, Lannie snatched the opportunity to set free the siren that crouched inside me, waiting for escape. She announced she was going to make me glamorous.

She had seen my wardrobe and knew nothing in it would be of any help. School uniforms and sweaters made from black homespun yarn do not a temptress make, so she offered her own clothes.

She pulled a white cardigan from its hanger and began buttoning it up on me—buttons in back—commenting as she worked that she had tons of sweaters because before her mother got sick, she had worked in the basement of Filene's Department Store and she had always bought clothes for the two of them when they were placed on the third markdown rack. She added a cotton skirt with two crinolines, and then styled my hair so one side fell over my eye. The glistening lipstick was the final touch.

I surveyed my startling new self in the mirror. Because I had no breasts to speak of—Anthony once quipped that I was a carpenter's dream, a flat board—the back-to-front sweater made me look as if my head was on backwards. But, despite this body flaw, my first look at my renovated self almost took my breath away. When I pushed up the sweater sleeves and pirouetted on my round-toed black brogues, I was staggered by the transformation. No caterpillar had ever surveyed his butterfly transformation with more astonishment, with more delight. Vanity aside, I knew I outshone all other girls in the village—all except Lannie.

From then on, my days were filled with exhilarating intrigue and heart-stopping scheming. The night hours were of no account because they were hours without Lannie. The wardrobe changes—the crinolines, the lipstick, the back-to-front sweaters, and eventually even the nail polish—were now everyday events and it all had to be done at Mrs. Furlong's house. Her health was deteriorating and she spent most of her days lying on the couch in her kitchen listening to the soap serials on the radio and paying little interest in our comings and goings. Each time we dodged her inspection, we felt giddy with relief, as if we had just made our escape from a prison camp. When we got outdoors and the real and present danger was safely thwarted, we would break into gales of muffled laughter.

However, not all of the times we spent together were so high-spirited. Sometimes when we were alone our conversations took a more reflective and wistful direction. One day as we were sitting on the bank beside the brook and letting our bare feet dangle in the water, Lannie said apropos of nothing that had to do with our conversation at hand that I was lucky because my father loved me. It seemed to me to be such a senseless remark, because speculating on whether or not my parents loved me was a thought so foreign, so alien to my world, that I had never even entertained it. Weren't parents supposed to love you? That was their God-given duty. It was not a thought that I had ever had need to ponder upon.

Because she, herself, had tabled the discussion on parents, I felt free to ask the question that I had not dared bring up earlier.

"Why do you always call your father 'Undertaker Fred'? Why not 'Dad' or 'Father'?"

Her answer was clear and simple and, to her, obvious.

"Because he owns a funeral parlour."

"My father is a fisherman but he's still my father. I wouldn't dream of calling him 'Fisherman Jim.'"

"Your father didn't leave your mother and you for a 'bit of stuff.'" It was as though I should have known that her father's leaving her had cancelled their relationship.

"Bit of stuff? You mean a girlfriend?"

"Yeah, Fred's Folly."

"That's what you call her?"

"That's what Mother calls her. Behind her back, of course. She also calls her Fred's Piece of Stuff. I call her Mag the Hag. Her first name is Maggie."

"Is she nice?"

"Do nice women break up families?"

I shrugged. I hadn't ever known such a woman. Or even known of such a woman. She accepted the shrug and continued.

"I've never met her. And don't plan on meeting her either. And I've hardly ever seen him. If Grandmother hadn't taken me this summer, he would've been forced to take me. I told Mom I'd do away with myself first." She made a motion as if she were slitting her throat.

"Don't even joke about that!" I admonished, half in jealous anger that she could so easily leave me behind in death, and half in morbid fear that she would go to hell and I would never be reunited with her. "Don't you know that it's a mortal sin to take your own life?"

"A mortal sin? Never heard of such a thing! I always thought a sin was a sin."

"No. There's venial sins and mortal sins."

She flashed a mischievous grin. "You mean they grade sins. Like apples. Grade A. Grade B."

She then swished her hair over her shoulder, and made a terrifying pronouncement. "If I'd rather be dead than live with Mag the Hag that's my business. Not anyone else's. Not even God's."

I instantly went to great lengths to explain what I had been taught about suicide—that it is slapping God's gift of life in His face and because there is no chance of asking forgiveness, hell is a certainty.

"Get on" she said. "You don't really believe that stuff, do you?"

The look on my face said I did, and not wishing to explore the subject any further, she immediately switched the topic to one of Fred's undertaker jokes.

"What did one casket say to the other in the dead of night in the funeral parlour?"

"I've no idea," I said short-toned, miffed at my profound conversation being dismissed so cavalierly.

She giggled and then supplied the answer. "Is that you coffin?"

When I knelt by the side of my bed that night, I released Mary Magdalene from her duty as my intercessor and turned her over to Lannie. I thought that Magdalene would be better able to understand Lannie than would Theresa. She would be less likely to be shocked by her irreverence. After all, she, herself, had had a sullied past and even had seven devils cast out of her. And despite her less than pure life, she had been present at the Crucifixion and at the Empty Tomb. I concluded from this that she must have been looked upon as a favourite and, therefore, better positioned than others to save Lannie from the fires of hell.

~~~

The telegram from her father arrived the next day. Her mother had died on the operating table. Within hours of its arrival Lannie went back home. It was the last week in August. A Thursday. The grandfather clock in Mrs. Furlong's kitchen struck the hour as I passed through on the way up to Lannie's room. Eleven mournful strikes. "She's beside herself," Mrs. Furlong said, stopping her own crying long enough to look up at the ceiling, to indicate Lannie's bedroom. "'Tis terrible that's what 'tis. A sorrow too great to bear. And I'm not well enough to travel to the funeral, even if I had the money."

~~~

My life instantly emptied upon Lannie's leaving. My days became hollow. The impending school year held no interest for me. Anthony tried to forge his way back into my affections, but I cast him away without a backward look, cast him out just as the devils had been cast out of Mary Magdalene. Over the summer my hair had grown to shoulder length and I had defied my mother by not having it cut. I now could swish it back and forth, chin lifted, head turned in haughty profile. Almost without my noticing, my breasts began showing signs that I wouldn't be a carpenter's dream forever. But all of this no longer brought me any joy.

~~~

Quickly on the heels of Lannie's departure, more news arrived from Boston. It started with a whisper that went up and down the rows of desks in Sister Ignatius' class. Sarah had gone to the convent to get coloured chalk for Sister. Mother Superior told her that a priest in Boston had called our parish priest with the news that Lannie Ramunski was dead and he was to inform Mrs. Furlong. As the story went, Lannie had a headache and she swallowed pain pills that she had brought from her mother's house when she went to live with her father. Unaware of their potency, she had accidentally taken too many.

I was stunned. So stunned that Sister Ignatius had to tell me three times to get down on my knees to pray the *De Profundis* on behalf of Lannie's soul.

As I knelt on the hardwood floor and mumbled along with the others, *Out of the depths, I have cried to You, O Lord, Lord hear my voice,* I thought what a useless exercise this is. Lannie is beyond the reach of prayer.

I staggered to my feet and stumbled to the washroom. I sat on the toilet and beseeched every saint I could call to mind to intercede with God on Lannie's behalf. I called in a special way upon Mary Magdalene. And then, because I was always one to hedge my bets, I went directly to the Deity. "Please, God," I begged. "Just this one time make an exception about Your suicide rule. You know as well as I do how much she hated living with Undertaker Fred and Mag the Hag."
~~~

Summer Love

LILLIAN BURSEY

Summer love, an immense bouquet,
blooms and fades;
each minute cherished.
We use the avenue of love to teach,
to tell, to learn . . .
too late.

Clematis

JANET McNAUGHTON

The year I thought to
pull my clematis vine down
it burst into bloom.

First Night

Georgina Olivere Queller

With hot shower-pink cheeks
and revved from aerobics
she prances
foot to foot
waiting for a Friday beer
at the Ship Inn

they talk at the end of the bar
he's too young
too drunk—too often

but saucy and blue eyes

and he likes her
she's known and resisted

but beer and chatter
chatter and beer
until his buddy comes

no longer the centre
she leaves in a weave
he follows in cold night air

you're too drunk to drive
says the town drunk
(not skid-row drunk
just daily middle-class-drunk)

At her home she offers
I suppose you'll want to tuck me in

he muses
on the unfinished beer on the bar
the friend left to guard it
half-hour at most
won't even be flat

at the end of her bed
they sway
no dancing foot to foot
just kisses like teenagers
but she's thirty-nine
and he's thirty-two

in the time before AIDS
she slurs
do you have herpes?

he thinks
if I had leprosy
I wouldn't tell her now
no says he
fumbling to find the soft passage
for a hard friend

she ignores the warning in her head
and thus begins
what he lovingly calls

her first medical miracle
at least there'll be time for me
to come she hopes
but she doesn't

she dismisses him
you can go now

he sees again
the lost beer on the bar
the lost time with a friend
but pressing his thick fingers
against her plump clitoris
he stays
for the next thirteen years

Ten Thousand Years

TRUDY J. MORGAN-COLE

LIZ: A WRETCH LIKE ME

Amazing grace, how sweet the sound
That saved a wretch like me

EVERYONE IS STANDING now, hymn books open. Kathy and Shannon both have tears pouring down their cheeks. Liz, who doesn't cry easily, wishes she could. It's more appropriate at a funeral than the wild desire to giggle that has seized her half a dozen times throughout this service. A wretch like me. Would Jeff have chosen this hymn? Probably not; must have been his mother. Wretched, lost, blind . . . that's me, Liz thinks, at least in the eyes of most of the people in this room. Kathy, no doubt, would think Liz was a wretch. Shannon might too, but she'd never say it. Was Jeff a wretch? Possibly. He once was. He and Liz were wretched, lost and blind together, and it was terrific.

She remembers the words of the Spirit to the church at Laodicea: ". . . and knowest not that thou art poor, and wretched, and blind, and naked." Yes, naked; they'd been that too. Her memory is like that, studded with random King James verses, learned from picture rolls in the Primary Room downstairs. It's a useful bank of memories for a writer to have, great for literary allusions, but uncomfortable at moments like this when she recalls how those words were once charged with meaning.

Liz rarely comes back to St. John's, the Holy City—it's only a coincidence she's here for Jeff's funeral. She knows it's really a very unholy city; there are artists and atheists here, people who inhabit the same world she does in Vancouver—but when she comes back here, the tiny church she grew up in swells to dominate the skyline like the Basilica.

The Basilica—now that would be a church worth being haunted by. Liz wishes she had grown up Catholic. She still would have lost her faith but it would have been so much more trendy. She has friends who call themselves Recovering Catholics. There's no cachet to being an ex-fundamentalist, unless you can boast a harsh, vindictive father who burned your fingertips on the stove because you wore nail polish, or a saintly youth leader who sexually abused you. Liz had neither. And her church, this building with blond-wood pews and plastic plants, has left her with nothing beautiful or memorable. Not for the first time she wonders if "Protestant" and "prose" have the same root, if she can turn some clever play on the two words into a poem. Liz longs for a more liturgical past. Today's whole ceremony would be less demeaning if a robed priest were intoning words from a prayer book: "In the midst of life we are in death." Instead she has to sit through this haphazard collection of hymns, a poem, a solo, and reminiscences of Jeff that are nothing like the Jeff she remembers.

Of course, she hasn't seen him in five years, hasn't really talked to him in more than ten. The pictures propped on the coffin last night showed a man starting to put on weight, whose hairline was receding a little. Liz sneaks a glance along the row at Shannon and Kathy. They are all the same age—thirty-two—and Liz knows she looks the youngest by a good five years—thinner, better dressed. She's the only one wearing what her grandmother would have considered appropriate funeral wear—a black dress—though cut along lines her grandmother would not have approved of. Shannon is wearing a navy blue dress and Kathy a beige suit. Kathy is starting to gain weight and Shannon's blond highlights look a little obvious. Liz knows she's being catty but doesn't care. If a whole churchful of people can label her wretched, blind and lost, she has the right to label them plump, dowdy, and middle-aged.

The hymn grinds interminably on, Mrs. Tilley at the organ missing notes. Liz, though never a good girl, was a believing one until she was sixteen. That year, in fact, she went through a phase of being intensely religious, mystical even. Her church did not encourage mysticism but she gave it her best shot. She remembers sitting here, two pews back, with her eyes closed while Mrs. Tilley played "Let All Mortal Flesh Keep Silence" at the beginning of the service, loving the minor chords and the words "mortal flesh." She wished even then that there were candles in church. She had been saved at youth camp the summer before, singing "We Are One In the Spirit" in front of the flickering campfire, holding hands with her best friend Shannon on one side and cute Jeff Fox on the other, part of the circle, bathed in the Spirit. Once lost, now found. Sometimes on Friday nights at home she used to light a candle in her room and pray out loud in front of it, trying to feel God in the room, filling her up.

That was the year Jeff broke up with Kathy and he and Liz started dating. Then, in the summer between sixteen and seventeen, they discovered sex. A warm Saturday night after a youth social at Shannon's place, hemmed in by parents and bright lights, Jeff brought her a dish of ice cream and sank down next to her on the floor in the corner. He put a hand on her knee and asked if they could leave early. He had the car.

Up on Signal Hill, in the back seat, they were sweaty and cramped and uncomfortable. Air Supply was playing on the tape deck. Liz knew the rules—Jeff pushed as far as he could and she set the boundaries—but she had decided, quite consciously, to screw the rules and see where exploration would take them. That first time, she felt guilty. The second time they were listening to Queen and it was a lot better. The third time, she came. She has no recollection of what was on the radio. Guilt, mysticism, praying in front of candles—it all dropped away. She learned that summer that the moment of ecstasy she had been groping toward, the moment of firelit spiritual transformation she tried endlessly to recapture, was there and possible inside her own body. From then on, whenever Shannon talked about God or religion, Liz wanted to laugh. *You're looking for it*, she wanted to say, *looking for it outside yourself, but I've found it. It's here. Inside yourself. Right between your legs.*

Sex that summer was simply uncluttered ecstasy, just like getting drunk had been when she'd tried that a few summers before. Too bad drinking and having sex and writing poetry all had to get messy and complicated. Still, she thinks an orgasm is a more reliable source of ecstasy than praying in front of a candle.

Soon the hymn will be over and the coffin will move outside. Do they have to go to the graveyard? Yes, Kathy and Shannon will think they should. When the three of them came in together, old Mrs. Holloway said, "Oh look, it's the three musketeers! It's so nice to see you girls together again." How little people understand. Liz and Shannon had been friends, Shannon and Kathy were friends, and all three of them had hung around with all the other kids their age. Liz and Shannon are still friends, in spite of differences. Shannon still goes to church but Liz can respect her faith because she's unsure of it. Shannon asks questions. They can argue. You can't argue with Kathy's bland bovine simplicity. Pastor's wife, homeschooling her two kids—she and Liz had never had much in common but there was nothing at all there now. And after the cemetery Shannon would want to invite them both back to her place and they'd have to make an evening out of it.

Liz wishes she felt something more for the man in the coffin. She is sorry the Jeff who made love to her in the back seat of his dad's '81 Civic is gone, but he's been gone for years now. Yet Shannon and Kathy, snotting and bawling there, never knew him like she did. He saved a wretch like me, Liz thinks, and raises her voice to sing.

SHANNON: SAFE THUS FAR

Through many dangers, toils and snares, I have already come
'Tis grace hath brought me safe thus far, and grace will lead me home.

SAFE THUS FAR. Shannon's life is more like a crazy quilt than a stained glass window, a collage of colours forming no discernible pattern, but she is safe thus far. Never, at least as an adult, has she been able to feel more than that; she isn't even sure certainty is something she wants.

Jeff understood that. She is crying for him, can only sing half a line at a time before her throat knots again and a new spill of tears wells up. Yet she almost envies him. He is safe . . . finally. No more "thus far." The next stop for Jeff is ten thousand years, bright shining as the sun.

If it's all true.

What would Jeff have said?

That's the tragedy . . . no time. A car accident leaves no time for goodbyes, for questioning and deciding once and for all between faith and doubt. Wherever Jeff was in his life's journey—at the moment his wheels hit black ice—there he is, suspended forever in that moment. Is he?

They used to debate that very thing in Youth class. In the Youth Room with its green cinderblock walls, sitting in a ring on the hard wooden chairs with Pastor Dave at the top of the circle, his Bible and Quarterly on his lap. Jeff said, "Yeah but like, what if you're a good person, you're a Christian, and you die in a car accident, right, and right before the transport truck slams into you, the last thing you think is a curse word?"

"Like you haven't got time to go, Oh God, I'm sorry, forgive me," Liz said.

"Well, your last thought *should* be something like that, like, Jesus forgive all my sins," Shannon remembers saying.

"Yeah, but it probably won't be," said Jeff. "So, are you lost for all eternity then, because your last thought was a sin and you never had time to repent?"

She had a crush on Jeff from about grade five on—maybe earlier. She can't recall a time when she wasn't writing "Shannon loves Jeff" on the inside cover of her schoolbooks. He was the best looking guy in class. And the summer before grade seven, when he started to notice girls, he noticed Kathy first, which, Shannon recognized, was only just. Kathy was the prettiest girl, and the nicest. She had blond hair that waved naturally, golden skin and blue eyes. She looked like a fairy-tale princess in lacy little-girl dress-up dresses; she looked like a Hollywood teenager in jeans and a T-shirt. She even got boobs first—but small neat ones, Shannon remembers, not big sloppy embarrassing ones.

At youth camp the summer she was twelve, Shannon stole Jeff's Toronto Blue Jays cap and slept with it under her pillow for two nights. When word got back to Jeff he was mad. Not flattered, not enjoying the attention—just plain mad. He told the guys if anyone was going to wear his cap it'd be Kathy Simms, not that scrawny flat-chested scarecrow Shannon Burry. Shannon gave the cap to Liz to give to Dave to give to Jeff. Later in the week Kathy was wearing the cap and Jeff was feeding her toasted marshmallows straight off the stick.

In spite of this, Shannon and Kathy were always best friends in elementary school. Later, in junior high, Shannon started to hang around with Liz and throughout high school she swung back and forth between them, sometimes getting into fights over who was her best friend. It was a relief to discover that she was an adult and didn't have to pick a best friend anymore, though her wedding had been tricky, and in the end she was glad she had a sister to be maid of honour so Liz and Kathy could just be bridesmaids. Apart from that one difficult bit, adulthood was easier; friendship, like so many other areas of life, could remain vague and undefined.

It's a kind of grace after all, Shannon believes—the grace that relieved her fears—that allows her not to know all the answers. Even while she admires Liz and Kathy for being in their different ways so certain and so consistent about their chosen lives, she is relieved to live in her tangle of questions. Jeff understood that. For a moment she believes that no one, not even Barry who loves and accepts her, no one will ever see the world precisely as she does. Jeff did. Now she is, she will always be, the only one who sees it that way.

She thinks sometimes she is two separate Shannons. One swears and goes to movies, attends poetry readings where the word "fuck" is used with impunity, drinks the occasional glass of wine when she visits Liz. The other Shannon keeps a spiritual journal and writes notes to Kathy on paper inscribed with Bible verses, telling about her prayer list and asking to be remembered in Kathy's prayers. Neither feels false, but she would not reveal either to the opposite friend. Barry, who does not judge, accepts both; Jeff understood both.

Her fingers trace the word "Hymnal" in gold leaf on the cover of the book she holds. She loves the hymnal and its old words of assurance, as she loves all the certainties of this blocky unlovely building where she still worships almost weekly. She does not always believe, anymore, that when all her labours and trials are o'er she will be safe on that beautiful shore, and she cannot always honestly sing that on Christ the Solid Rock she stands, all other ground is sinking sand. She knows the feel of sand under her feet and doesn't entirely dislike it.

But Jeff is dead now, and she needs certainty. She hopes he was certain, no matter what words came out of his mouth at the end. Why can she not be as certain as her teenaged self, who knew Liz and Jeff were heading for trouble because they drank and smoked? She and Kathy used to agonize over how to save them, though Shannon knew that in Kathy's mind saving Jeff involved getting him back from Liz, and that Liz's soul was, in Kathy's estimation, expendable. Shannon believed her own motives were purer. She was long over her crush on Jeff. But wrangling with him over his eternal destiny cemented their friendship: repeated episodes of picking him up drunk from parties when he called her for a ride, driving up to Signal Hill till long past her curfew, begging to know how he could do this to himself. She remembers him banging his fist on the dashboard and shouting, "Show me one shred of evidence that God exists—show me a piece of Noah's Ark—and I'll believe it! Yeah, show me a piece of Noah's Ark and I'll quit drinking!"

"Why wasn't I out driving around, having these conversations, with *you*?" she asked Liz once when reliving those years. "You were my friend, you were doing the same stuff Jeff was."

"Lure of the bad boy," Liz said. "Admit it. You still wanted him. You wanted to be the one to save him."

Perhaps true. But they grew into real friendship, a friendship strengthened by the fact that both had stayed in St. John's when others moved away, that both stayed more or less in the church, that they'd each married people the other liked. Jeff played hockey with Barry, who was a pallbearer today; Shannon took quilting classes with Jeff's wife Debbie. But Shannon and Jeff were the pivot of the friendship: their shared memories, their need to talk and make each other laugh and solve insoluble problems.

She was glad, last night, to walk into the funeral home and find a closed casket (though what else to expect, after a car accident?) Seeing the still, white face is always the worst. The pictures on the coffin were easy by comparison—Jeff with Debbie and the baby, Jeff alone with the dog. Hugging Debbie and crying with her was harder, but the hard part today will be watching the coffin lowered into the ground. Jeff in a box under earth and stone, unseeing, unlaughing, unspeaking. Ten thousand years. Let it be true, please.

KATHY: MY SHIELD AND PORTION

The Lord has promised good to me, His word my hope secures
He will my shield and portion be as long as life endures.

THE SERVICE HAS to end, must end soon, Kathy thinks. They are on the last hymn, "Amazing Grace," and as they start the seldom-sung fourth verse the pallbearers swing the coffin around and begin to carry it down the aisle.

She likes that verse. She likes old hymns, though she's sure Liz, and probably Shannon, would disapprove of her taste. Liz disapproves of her anyway. Liz makes fun of the fact that Kathy home-schools her kids; she says Kathy can't keep them wrapped up in cotton wool forever and they'll have to face the real world sooner or later. Easy for Liz to say, who has neither kids nor faith. She has nothing to lose. Kathy has everything to lose, and may soon lose it.

Jeff. If only Jeff could come back to life, help her through this, finish what he started. Now that he's dead, no one living knows what she's been through. She could let it sink back into secrecy and no one would hold her accountable. She must, she will tell Shannon this weekend. Shannon is strong; she will help. But she's not a man. It would be better if she were a man. Or worse.

Kathy is a messy cryer. She rummages in her pocket for Kleenex, finds one used and one unused, and passes the clean one to Shannon. She envies Shannon's friendship with Jeff; she envies her own younger self. She knows it's stupid to feel this way about a guy you dated in seventh grade but she often thinks things would have been better if she and Jeff had stayed together.

They were together almost four years, grade seven to grade ten, until even grown-ups started to think they might end up married. Breaking up after all that time was messy. Of course, there aren't any easy breakups, especially in grade ten. He just stopped hanging around, stopped calling, told her nothing was wrong when she asked. She cornered him after school one day outside Henry's Lunch and kept him talking till the guys he was with had gone on to the bus stop. He told her he'd miss his bus. She said she didn't care. Finally, after she tortured him for a good half-hour, he said, "I think we should break up. I just—I mean, I just think it would be better."

Maybe, she thinks, it wasn't that bad a breakup. No excuses or lies. He thought it would be better. Better for him, of course.

What was awful, what embarrasses her even now to remember, is how she went back into the school, wishing Shannon was still there so she could cry on her shoulder. Instead there was Liz, who always stayed late because her mother was a teacher. Liz bending down to take a drink at the fountain, Liz who wasn't even a close friend, just one of the girls in her class, one of the girls from church. Kathy went up to her, tears and snot streaming down her face, and said, "I need a hug! Jeff just dumped me!" And Liz had hugged her awkwardly, patting her back, and said, "Oh, that's too bad, I'm really sorry." And within a week Liz and Jeff were going out. Shannon told her later that Jeff had told Liz a month before that he'd go out with her as soon as he could break up with Kathy. She's sure Liz remembers that moment every time they see each other, even after sixteen years.

She thinks of Jeff's baby son, fatherless now, and that leads her back to thinking of her own kids. They're staying with her sister for the day. Darryn didn't understand why she'd bring the kids into St. John's for a funeral. She told him she needed to take them shopping.

She soaks one Kleenex and reaches for another in her purse. She is crying for more than Jeff's death but this is all right; it's a funeral and tears are expected. After they go to the graveyard she'll get Shannon away from Liz and tell her everything. She hates the thought of Liz finding out, partly because it'll give Liz the satisfaction of seeing one more cliché about Christians spring to life. *Liz would probably be surprised I even know the word cliché*, Kathy thinks.

Yes, of course she feels inferior to Liz and even to Shannon, who is her friend. She feels fat and dumpy beside them, and the beige suit screams "Pastor's Wife" to anyone who will listen. At least she's the only one who's kept her natural hair colour—Shannon has those awful brassy highlights, and Liz's glossy black hair always has a rinse in it with a trace of some exotic scarlet or purple shining under the black. Not having to colour her hair yet—it's not much to hang onto, but Kathy grabs consolation where she can.

"Kathy, you've done everything so right. You were the one who played by all the rules," Jeff said that day last summer when they met by accident in the mall and she wound up telling him the whole story. "It's so unfair for this to happen to you. Aren't you ever mad at God?"

"No," Kathy said. "And besides, I wasn't the one who did everything right. I was the stupid one, the weak one. I used to wonder why any woman would stay in a marriage when she was being abused. Smart women, strong women—someone like Liz or Shannon—they never would. But I did. I am."

Blame God? No, that she couldn't do. Yes, the Lord had promised good to her. But what kind of good? If He was going to be her shield and portion, there must be blows coming. Why else a shield? And why blame God for choices she had made herself? She had chosen Darryn; no one had forced her to marry him. God was the only good thing: God and her kids.

Jeff's wife Debbie was in the front, getting up now to follow the casket out, clutching her baby, looking lost. Kathy had spoken to her maybe three times, counting last night at the funeral home. What did Debbie believe? Was she angry at God? "Comfort her, Lord," she prayed, as automatically as breathing. "Wrap Your arms around her."

When we've been there ten thousand years, bright shining as the sun . . . . We'll see Jeff again, she told Debbie in her mind, *but it's here and now we need him—you to live your life and help you raise that baby, and me so I can have the courage to leave my husband. I need a friend like Jeff to stand beside me*. "Think of your kids, Kathy," he'd said, and of course she had thought of nothing else, but hearing him say it put things into perspective.

When that long afternoon at the mall was over and she had to face the drive back alone, Jeff had taken her in his arms and she remembered with a swift ache the first time he'd kissed her, in the back of the darkened church auditorium while they watched "Herbie the Love Bug." The room had smelled of popcorn and teenage sweat, and his braces had pressed against her upper lip. First kiss, first hand-holding, first hand on her breast—but that was as far as it went. The first man she slept with had been Darryn on her wedding night—the first man to hurt her, to hit her, to bruise her. And now Jeff was the first to say that it was OK to leave Darryn, that she had to do it. She had clung to his embrace, half wishing he'd try to seduce her, though she knew she'd say no.

Talking to Jeff had changed nothing. She still feared the shame, the gossip and censure, and still thought her wedding vows were sacred—but somehow that goodbye hug made her fear of Darryn, when she saw him again that night, more real and more repulsive. A man could be good and kind: Jeff was. Even when he was bad, going out with Liz, drinking and running wild, he was still good at heart.

And his sudden death had given her the excuse she needed to pack the kids in the car and drive to St. John's. She isn't going back. And she isn't alone. God stands beside her, taller and stronger than Jeff, so real she almost feels she can slip her hand into His. Whatever else she lacks that Shannon and Liz have, she has this—this shining faith, this Presence. He sent Jeff, that day in the mall. He will give her the strength to stay in St. John's, to keep her children away from Darryn. "Keep me here, Lord," she prays. "Don't let me go back. I won't go back."

The hymn ends. The last of the family has followed the casket out, and now the organ plays as everyone else follows, pew by pew. Kathy looks at red-eyed Shannon beside her. Beyond Shannon, Liz is a blur of black. "Shan, I have to talk to you later, alone," she whispers, pushing open a door, throwing away the key. Outside is a future where she can imagine herself phoning Darryn, saying, "I'm not coming back. I just think it would be better."

Shannon wipes her eyes and folds Kathy into a hug. They stand with their arms around each other.

As long as life endures.

Lost Love

LAURA MORRY WILLIAMS

But in vision
I recall a beach
in luscious summer rain.

I still journey
on smooth, wet pebbles
holding your firm, warm hand.

A Proposal

(A found poem)

LAURA MORRY WILLIAMS

"I think that you and I should stick together
like those two pigeons on the balcony
we'll take a slice of bread
wherever we can get one
and when another fellow comes along
I'll pick at him until he goes away!"

Night Train

Eileen Dicks

The 11:55 pm out of Euston Station
Fills with Service people going north
Among them a WAAF
In the crowded corridor
The young soldier outside
Eyes fixed on each other
To imprint the memory

Guard's whistle blows
Train lurches
Unsmiling, still gazing at the girl
He walks with the moving train
Until it picks up speed
Drags his hand away
Thinks of his overseas posting
How long before they meet again

Garden Party

Eileen Dicks

She is late
Approaching slowly
Mid gardens lush and green
Trying not to cause a stir
And yet she does
Dressed in white and cornflower blue
Her wide brimmed hat
Casually carried
In the warm glow of new love
All eyes turn to watch her sit
Put on her hat
Shading her lovely face
The greeting done
The talk resumes
Yet no one speaks her name.

Pilgrim of Eternity

(Excerpt from a novel-in-progress)

PAUL O'NEILL

I AWOKE TO LONDON in the morning sun.

The letter still lay unopened in the middle of the floor where I had flung it in a burst of petulance. It was the first thing I saw as I started to get up from that filthy bed. It had lain there one day? Two? Who cares? Time is merely an illusion when there is no beginning . . . and I knew the words it contained.

The room was cold, full of the bitter dampness of an English rooming house. A gas fire sat in what had been the grate of the room but it was greedy for shillings and gave back little heat. I could hear the wind whistle as it forced its way through the loose sashes of the windows. My road seemed to have come to an end in the garret of Bessie Mugford's four-floor rooming house in a rundown area of Pimlico.

Dragging myself from the tossing numbness of a drunken sleep, in which I had lain hidden from the reality of the world for a few hours, I forced myself to face the day. It acknowledged me with the seamless sounds of its own restive mood . . . the echo of children's voices calling in the street, an iron hoop that bounced against concrete steps and fell with a clatter to the pavement, the angry horn of a motorbike spitting defiance at a honking car, the voice of a barrow boy on the corner hawking fruit and vegetables.

In her room down the hall from mine, Nora Duffy, a worn-and-weary young woman from Dublin, moaned aloud as she awaited death from a painful and incurable cancer. In her early twenties, with haunting green eyes and lush auburn hair, her dreams of a better life in England had ended in prostitution. I heard her piteously beg in agony: "Sacred Heart of Jesus, have mercy on the dying."

With her look of innocence and tender ways, she seemed more suited to the Children of Mary than the oldest profession. The youngest of eight, she must have been a wildly charming and hopeful child. After Nora found out she was to die, her older sister Madge, a no-nonsense, raw-boned woman married to a dock worker, came down from Liverpool. I overheard her shout at Nora, "How could you have fallen so low?"

I might have asked myself that same question. Standing naked at the foot of the bed that morning, with nausea sweeping over me, a violent pain exploding in the middle of my forehead, I could feel my life unravelling. My throat was as dry as my mouth was raw. It tasted sour in the chaos of confused thoughts swirling in my brain. I imagined I could hear the liquor I'd consumed the previous evening slop about inside my bloated belly. Actually it wasn't mere liquor but one of the finest of champagnes—Veuve Clicquot Ponsardin.

A bedbug crawled from among the folds of my dirty sheets, clung brazenly to my thigh and gorged on my blood. I reached down to squash it ruthlessly between my thumbnails. The faded lilacs on the blue walls of the room seemed to emit the odour of decay, almost as if they were real, instead of printed on layers of mildewed wallpaper pulling away from the plaster.

I started for the stained porcelain sink (a facility that allowed Bessie Mugford to advertise my rat's nest as a bed-sitter with washing facilities) to empty my bladder without having to go down a flight of stairs to the common bathroom. My eyes only half open I stubbed a big toe on the leg of a chair.

"Jesus in heaven!" I cried in pain. "Bloody hell!"

Shakespeare was right . . . "when sorrows come . . ." Mrs. Mugford's rent was two months overdue. Just the previous day, in her earthy cockney, she reminded me of the month's notice she had given me four weeks ago. I had to be out of her place today if she didn't get her "Gawd'amn rent" by noon. The fact I was out of work nearly twelve weeks, and hardly had a shilling to my name, didn't soften *her* heart. I was two months in arrears.

~~~

That was why I met Mae Peabody. Although it went against everything I believed, I saw Mrs. Peabody as my salvation. I could not afford to be righteously moralistic when we met. A willowy matron, obviously an American tourist, "she could very well pass for fifty-three, in the dusk with the light behind her" to paraphrase W. S. Gilbert. A faded beauty, she clung to what was left of the vision of her youth by the use of pancake makeup and hair dye. But she had gone beyond the point where it was possible to restore any of what had been lost. She appeared to have an American mid-western accent.

The moment I saw the woman's eye flit disinterestedly among the merchandise displayed in one of Harvey Nicholls's department store windows in Knightsbridge, I knew she was in London for what my friend Simon laughingly described as the "English experience." He said it provided a little bit of spice in the life of some of his male students at the London School of Economics, and helped supplement meagre incomes.

I decided to make her my little bit of spice to help supplement my own meagre income. When I heard guys in pubs talk about how easy such seductions were I was disgusted . . . yet here I was, standing in the queue at the bus stop at the top of Sloane Street, waiting for a number 19 or 20 bus to take me to Soho, when she turned, smiling provocatively, and looked me full in the face. I knew she had been admiring my image reflected on the plate glass of the department store window in the early light of the summer evening. I was dressed in an open-neck shirt and slacks, with white sneakers on my feet, my short hair neatly combed.

With a certain air of affectation, she fumbled in her large handbag. I could see she was as nervous at this as I was as she searched among her things for a cigarette. She finally found a package of Camels and put one in her mouth. Again the search went on in the handbag for matches.
~~~

I happened to have a book in my pocket. They gave me the opening I needed.

I left the queue and held out the book of matches, tearing one off and striking it.

"Perhaps I can help you." I smiled temptingly.

Being good at accents I was trying my best to sound like an Englishman. It would be much easier that way. I was sure she hadn't flown all those thousands of miles to be picked up by a Canadian guy, with the sea-salt accent of my Newfoundland. The attempt might not have fooled an English woman, with a good ear, but I saw from her smile that it charmed the American tourist.

"Would you like an American cigarette?" she said.

"Thank you."

"Do women smoke on the streets in London?" she asked with a grin.

"The war changed everything." I smiled. "Women do pretty much as they want to these days," and added with a flirtatious wink, "why don't you be bad?"

"Well . . . all right."

Remembering how Paul Henreid wooed the frustrated spinster, played by Bette Davis in *Now Voyager*, I lit two cigarettes in my mouth and handed her one. I don't know if she saw the movie, but there was a note of delight as she thanked me with a titter. I thought to myself, how many affairs have begun with a cigarette since Sir Walter Raleigh introduced tobacco to Europe?

Like most people, the woman was hearing what she desperately wanted to hear. We often do that to ourselves. They say there are more lonely people in the world than hungry ones. If so, she was of the majority and I was of the minority. Not having eaten anything all day but some take-out fish and chips at lunchtime, my empty stomach was gurgling like an infant's.

After introducing myself with the precaution of a false name, I told her I was a student of history down from Cambridge for the weekend. I said because I had behaved somewhat rashly with some university friends the previous night, I was out of funds, with only my ticket back for tomorrow. Without a better offer I'd probably sleep the night away on a bench in the railway station. That elicited the invitation I had hoped it would.

"You're a very naughty young man to be looking for some place to spend the night." She admonished me with a wag of her cigarette. "Well then . . . since it's dinnertime, and we must both eat before we do anything else, let me treat you to a meal."

"I don't think it would be right for me to expect a stranger to—"

I hoped she'd interrupt my refusal of her offer.

"To hell with being polite, Greg." She stamped out the cigarette on the sidewalk and linked into me. "I'm Mae Peabody from Anderson, Indiana, a state in the mid-west of the great United States of America, and you're Greg Strickland, a student down from Cambridge for the weekend. There! See. We're not strangers anymore. Where should we eat, my Prince Charming? I don't think I'd be brave enough to visit a pub alone. Although it might be fun if I had an escort . . . a young man on my arm."

She knew I knew she was now the one who was flirting. Mae Peabody was beginning to enjoy taking part in the game.

I was still not certain I could go all the way with the charade, even as I followed her into the taxi, but I was so strapped for cash. I had the driver drop us off at the Swallow's Nest, a crowded, up-beat bistro I knew of by reputation along King's Road in Chelsea. I was sure I wouldn't meet anyone there I knew. And if I did, what matter? They would probably be on the game themselves.

After we dined on a main course of lamb chops and a dessert of strawberry pavlovas, we ambled slowly back to Sloane Square, pausing to look at the window displays when passing Peter Jones's department store. Linked arm in arm, we took the zebra crossing to the square, and sat on one of the benches in the gathering darkness, watching the play of traffic lights on the water in the fountain. Crowds were just getting out of the tiny Royal Court Theatre across the way, where several new playwrights were gaining international attention with their realistic dramas.

I could feel Mae Peabody's loneliness as she talked of her Indiana home where her husband had been an executive with some division of General Motors. In a weak effort to relax her and be funny, I asked if the candlelight still lies gleaming through the sycamores on the banks of the Wabash. She roared with laughter at that.

"I'm amazed to find an Englishman who knows our state song."

I had almost given the game away. I hastily covered my tracks.

"It was popular in the music halls over here in my parents' day."

"I'm afraid the only things that gleam through the sycamores now are neon lights."

After half an hour of small talk, during which I moved closer to her and put a playful arm around her shoulder, she finally suggested we go back to her hotel room for a drink, which she called a nightcap. She was staying at the Cadogan, just up Sloane Street. It was a short walk of ten minutes or less to the front door, where she told me her room number.

"Just in case I run into someone from home," she drawled, and added, in imitation of Blanche Dubois, "I don't want to have to explain to anyone why I am entertaining a young gentleman caller . . . so give me a ten-minute head start."

With an encouraging wink she was gone. I knew the real reason she wanted ten minutes was to use the bathroom and fix her face. After strolling up Pont Street to Beauchamp Place and back, I entered through the Lily Langtry Bar, crossed the lobby, where a tour group was booking in, and took the elevator to her floor without attracting attention.

"Why don't you get comfortable?" she urged, unbuttoning my shirt and pulling the tails out of my trousers.

At this point I was becoming a little confused as to how far I wanted to go. To give me time to think I made the excuse of needing to use the toilet. On the way I passed a framed photograph of her with three children. It was standing on a bedside table. Assuming they were grandchildren, I made no comment, went in the bathroom, and shut the door.

While I was there, agonizing over how far I would have to go to get paid for my services, there was a tap on the bedroom door. I heard her pull on a dressing gown and open the door to a waiter. She told the fellow where to put down the tray and champagne she had ordered as a nightcap. I heard the waiter pop a cork and place a bottle in an ice bucket. He thanked her for the tip and left.

When I came out, I saw he'd delivered a magnum ice bucket containing two jeroboams of chilled champagne, Veuve Clicquot Ponsardin. Mae was obviously sparing no expense in the hope of enjoying her London evening with the accommodating young Englishman, less than half her age, whom she had plucked from the street. She had removed the robe and was standing, holding two flutes of bubbly in her hand. I took one. We grinned, crossed elbows, and sipped.

As we drank, we played silly love games on the sofa, moving in and out of each other's arms. The teasing and kissing became ever more suggestive and we both became more daring as the first bottle slowly emptied. Mae confessed to feeling just a wee bit tipsy and slipped out of her shoes and began to tug at the zipper on my trousers as I cupped a breast in my hand. I wondered if she drank the champagne for the pleasure, or for the courage to become more and more bold in pursuit of her ultimate goal.

Instead of being aroused by her groping my crotch, I was amused to find myself wondering if this might have been the room in the Cadogan Hotel where Oscar Wilde was arrested so many years ago. Poor Oscar! The wages of unconventional morality are far worse than the wages of sin. What Mae and I were doing was so conventional it hardly seemed to involve morality at all.

By the time I opened the second green bottle and set it swimming in the melting ice, we were stretched out on the hotel room bed making love . . . an odd name for something so totally devoid of emotion, let alone of love. It would have been truer to say, we were making lust. At least Mae Peabody was. What I was making was money. My head was already beginning to spin and ache from the champagne. With the headache I began to resent what I was doing. Could being evicted by Bessie Mugford be any worse? I was the hired stud of a lonely widow who could have been my mom, she looked enough like her. The whole set-up, which was my own doing, disgusted me.

When it came time to leave, Mae Peabody tucked a bank note in my pocket with a lingering kiss. "Whenever I think of London . . ." she said, a touch of sadness in her voice, ". . . it is you I will always remember."

Stumbling down Sloane Street to Pimlico, in the pre-dawn melt of darkness, I felt terrible for having taken deliberate advantage of the woman. I recalled the words of Nora's sister, *How could you have fallen so low?* My besotted brain was then no more capable than Nora's of coping with such a complex question, but I did smile to myself as I remembered Kipling's line about the colonel's lady and Judy O'Grady. If not sisters, Nora and I were certainly now brother and sister under the skin. When passing Sloane Square underground station, before turning into Pimlico, I took the bank note from my pocket and examined it in the blazing light. It was twenty pounds.

~~~

The whiteness of my body glared at me from the mirror over the sink like some dead fish on a beach of stones. It was bloated from wind and too much to drink the night before, marred here and there by blemishes and bruises. But the worst bruises did not show, hidden as they were, beneath my skin. I emptied my distended bladder into the sink, turned on the tap and watched the yellow water run clear as it circled the drain.

The breadbox was empty. There was still some leftover coffee in the cold pot sitting on the gas ring. Bitter, day-old coffee was nothing new to me. There was an imperious knock on the door that could only mean Bessie Mugford had come to tell me I must clear out by afternoon. Covering my nakedness in a pair of jeans that hung over the back of the broken wooden chair beside the bed, I opened the door to stare into the quivering mole on my landlady's chin. From it there protruded a single curling hair that always enraged me. I had an overwhelming desire to grab tweezers and pluck it out, only I didn't possess tweezers. A large woman whose bones were enveloped in fat, she always sounded nasty, even when she wasn't trying to be intimidating.

"Yer outta 'ere t'day me lad," she bellowed."Two months be'ind in your rent . . . an' no 'ope o' payin'. Out you go! Do I make meself clear?"

The woman and her voice were equally repulsive. Without a word I went to my shirt pocket, pulled out the twenty pound note and thrust it in her face. Her watery, bloodshot eyes opened wide in surprise.
~~~

"Take eight pounds out for the two months," was all I said.

"What's this? Yer ship come in 'as it?"

She grabbed the note in her chubby fist, reached into the large pocket of her stained apron, pulled out a fistful of notes and handed me twelve pounds in change. Before she could question me about the money, I slammed the door in the wretched woman's face.

"Writers. Bah! I've 'ad too many o' yer kind. Poor as church mice." She grunted loudly as she heaved her massive bulk down the stairs which creaked a complaint each time one of her flat feet landed on a step.

I turned back into the room to see the letter in my father's familiar handwriting still lying on the floor, waiting to be opened. It swam into focus, flooding my memory with echoes of an earlier time in another place, where my world was a familiar house on a road that linked the upper levels of my city to its fondly remembered wharves and ships. I threw open the window, I needed the company of the workday noise. Thank God it wasn't Sunday, when London is stripped down to the holy melancholy of empty streets, empty pubs, empty bistros, empty churches and emptier sermons.

Two pigeons haggled on my windowsill like weekend bargain hunters in the Portobello Road. The light in the room changed momentarily as one of the few clouds in the sky passed between Pimlico and the noontide sun. Its warming rays made even the wretched tiers of council flats across the street look inviting. I lit the gas ring and after a few minutes poured some of the reheated coffee into a mug, or as the English say, a beaker.

Like that cloud, I felt something blocking me from coping with what my life had become. How had I ended up in such a squalid state of disorder? Was it because of an illusion that I possessed an innate gift for writing . . . a gift that now mocked me from a pile of rejection slips into which all my hopes and my ambition plunged?

I stared at my father's letter, like a person hypnotized by the snake that was about to inject its fatal venom. In my hapless predicament I saw my father stare at my shame. I yearned for some word of compassion from him, but I knew the voice I would hear coming from those pages would be pleading with me to admit my mistake and come home. He liked poetry, and in one letter called me, in Shelley's words, a

"Pilgrim of Eternity." He said there comes a time in every life when even the most devout pilgrim has to abandon the pursuit of the impossible for the reality of this world. His words, so kindly meant, overwhelmed me with the loneliness that accompanies failure. There was a poem by a minor American poet, Ella Wheeler Wilcox, one Mother cut from the *Evening Telegram*, framed and hung on our kitchen wall. It said in part "*laugh and the world laughs with you, weep and you weep alone.*" But when we cry alone it's usually a cry of self-pity, without repentance or redemption. So why even bother?

There was a gentle knock on my door, not the impatient rapping of Bessie Mugford, but a slight, almost apologetic tap. I knew it was Ellie Maywood. Nobody else knocked so gently. Ellie was a ballet student from Crewe whose father worked in the railway switching-yards there. It was her dream to dance with the Royal Ballet. Her parents' wish to see her dream come true, brought her to a back bedroom on the floor below me in our cheap rooming house. Ellie had the good fortune to have auditioned for, and been accepted by, England's finest ballet school where the famous came and talked to the students.

Ellie had the look about her of a life-size parchment doll with skin so pale you could almost see through it. Her high cheekbones and wide black eyes gave her a look of intense ambition. Her only conceit was a fondness for dropping the first names of England's ballet greats in conversation. Anton was Dolin, Moira was Shearer, Leonide was Massine, Alicia was Markova, Michael was Soames, and of course, "Dear Margot" was Fonteyn. All she ever said about them was that one of them had given a class in her school that day, or she had seen another walking on the street, or coming out of a door at Covent Garden. It was a harmless conceit that seemed to give her pleasure and helped distance herself from the workaday world of Crewe.

"I got you out of bed," she apologized, seeing me wearing only jeans and in bare feet.

"I was up. Come in, Ellie. Care for a cup of coffee? I just made some. There's no milk."

"Jake . . . your coffee is not fit for human consumption," she laughed. "I came to borrow some matches to light my gas ring to make myself a cup of tea."

"Here." I flipped her a small white satin box of gold-tipped matches I'd snatched from a table as I'd walked through the Lily Langtry Bar. "Light my gas ring and make us both a cup of tea. There's some Twinings in the cannister."

She read the name in gold lettering on the back of the matches, while delicately perking her head, rather like a bird examining something of interest. "Were you at the Cadogan Hotel?"

"Last night. I met a friend from home who took me there for a drink," I nervously improvised.

I pulled on a blue tee-shirt and a pair of loafers.

Having filled the kettle with water from the basin tap, Ellie lit the gas ring and settled cross-legged in the Morris chair, the one half-decent piece of furniture in my room. The warmth of her smile bridged the emptiness I often felt inside those cell-like walls. Although she was vulnerable, sometimes embarrassingly so, I had known for some time I was in love with Ellie Maywood from Crewe. Very much in love.

By Sliding Rock

Paul O'Neill

I still come here
each year, alone,
and watch them
gather cuttings where
green willows grow among
the feldspar
of the granite rocks.

Once we, like them,
were shadows in a sea
of spring's wild timothy.

But were we also
clouded fools
who did not see
the weeds consume
unfolding paths up which
we chased the sun?

In this eternal trysting place
of mocking mouths
and limbs that wound the
unsuspecting heart

we hid our memories
and each walked off
a different way—
alone.

Beatrice

EILEEN DICKS

I had often watched her sewing
The stitches quick and fine.
Now she sat, her dark head bent
Folding the soft blue cloth
The fingers poised and curled
She leaned towards the window
To catch the dying light.

"You'd think you were doing some fine embroidery."
She lifted her head and smiled
"There's always something to mend."

I wanted to ask about her husband
How many months in the San?
Instead I said, "I'm going away
I came to say goodbye."
The pliant hands were working fast
With her needle small and sharp
Her voice held a note of promise, not hope,
"I'm taking the boys to the sea next summer"
Was her reply.

A High Romance

BERNICE MORGAN

HUBERT DRONES ALONG in what I've come to think of as his canon voice. No one would guess from this monotonous tone that the woman lying in the mahogany coffin had been his chief confidante and advisor for fifteen years.

"Good, grey Hubert," Cynthia would have said—or would she? Sitting in the church we have so long attended together, I caution myself against my lifelong urge to reshape reality—to "remould it nearer to the heart's desire." Cynthia was sharp and funny—sometimes cutting—especially in the face of human stupidity, but I never knew her to be condescending. I must try to remember her as she was, not make her into someone else.

I am not ready to extend this charity to Hubert. I would very much like to remould his speaking voice. On more than one occasion I have suggested to him that a more dramatically presented homily might keep me awake on Sunday mornings. Must he be so controlled? For Cynthia he should be reciting poetry, pulling his hair, wearing sackcloth and ashes. Too late the thought comes to me that I should be the one giving Cynthia's eulogy—in the last terrible days it had not occurred to me—so here I sit, forced to listen as Hubert mumbles on about how Cynthia served her community, how she was a patron of the arts, a member of the vestry, the founder of a scholarship at the School of Music and so on and so on. Nothing of the living, breathing woman, just this dull, naked list that every person in the cathedral already knows. Were it not for all those eyes on my back and the sure knowledge that Cynthia would consider such a thing undignified, I would simply walk out. Equally undignified to fall asleep.

I realize then that I have been scowling at poor Hubert, perhaps even shaking my head as I sometimes do when I listen to the news. Cynthia would have enjoyed the scene; Hubert rabbiting on in the pulpit, me silent and alone making faces at him from the mourners' pew, an untidy bunch of weeds in my lap.

The first time I saw Cynthia she was kneeling in her garden surrounded by just such flowers. Remembering that long-ago day on my way here, I stopped by her place to see if I could find the mustard-coloured flowers. Overgrown as her garden is now I managed to find a few of the same flowers—although they may not be. From one September to the next I can never remember how to tell goldenrod from tansy. Whatever their name, they shed their pollen onto my black overcoat and give off a rank smell.

It was late September then too. I was walking between school and my boarding house on Hayward Avenue, where Mrs. Pickett would be dusting the hall mirror when I came through the door. It was a pleasant afternoon and I was walking slowly, dreading my landlady's cheerful curiosity and trying to dismiss the unpleasant conversation I'd just had with my headmaster. As often when I was a young man, I was lecturing myself, wondering what I could learn from the experience. Was there something in my voice that irritated people? Was it my face? Perhaps the way I stood? Had my refusal to take over a Boy Scout group or read the lesson at morning worship been that curt?

"Extracurricular activities are an integral part of what we do here at Bishop Feild—and as this is a small faculty we must all carry our weight." The headmaster had a way of phrasing statements that did not invite contradiction. Before leaving his office I had promised to oversee the Drama Society—something I knew no more about than scouting or High Anglican prayers. It wasn't so much McEwan's words that shook me, it was the grimness of his face, the flicker of dislike, even contempt I thought I'd seen in his eyes. Forget it, forget it—enjoy the blessing of a quiet street, bright fall air and leaves scrunching beneath your feet—

"season of mist and mellow fruitfulness" I thought, wishing away the tension I felt at the back of my neck.

"Hallo, Mr. Downing," a voice came from a small front garden I was passing. I turned and saw her, a woman kneeling in the grass, surrounded by a dozen or more flowers she'd cut and spread out, each flower lying on its own sheet of white paper like patients in a hospital ward. The strange flower arrangement barely registered so concerned was I with the possibility that I might have been talking aloud, scolding myself or even reciting poetry. Will she think me mad? Report me to the headmaster? She knows who I am. She could be a mother of one of the boys or even a fellow teacher . . .

The woman stood, pulled off her muddy gloves and came towards me. She must have seen my panic for she smiled and said, "I know you—but we've never met." She held her hand out across the low stone wall, "I am Cynthia Markham—and you I think are Theo Downing. I'm on the board of directors for Bishop Feild College, I recognized you from your application picture."

Her face was neither beautiful or pretty. Arresting might be a better word but not the right one. She had a high forehead, widely spaced grey eyes and good cheekbones that gave her an open, calm demeanour. Her hands were long-fingered and narrow, she wore no rings. When I didn't speak she asked if I was settling in comfortably. I stammered some reply and she began telling me the name of the flowers she had spread out on the grass; she would dry them, she said, between books.

She turned slightly away from me, pointing to the flowers, and as she talked I studied her. Cynthia Markham was a remarkable sight. She was a tall woman, slightly taller than me if you counted the puff of hair tied up haphazardly in a red kerchief. Even then, in her late thirties she had streaks of grey running through her black hair. She wore a skirt and sweater of some dark shade mostly covered with a large red, very dirty, wraparound apron with the words "Markham's Drygoods" printed in black across the bib. On her feet she wore grey wool socks inside wooden clogs—footwear I had only seen in pictures of Dutch children. We chatted a few minutes about inconsequential things—the evening, autumn flowers, stone walls, Robert Frost, and I walked away feeling immensely better. For the first time since my arrival in St. John's I had forgotten myself enough to speak to another adult with a degree of ease.

Back then my knowledge of people, especially women, was limited to my argumentative mother and sisters. Those three joking, lipsticked girls who had disappeared into marriage before I entered my Ontario high school. In the last year I'd taken a girl called Florence to the movies on Saturday afternoons and once to a wiener roast down by the lake. In university I barely spoke to a girl. Unlike my sisters, whose humour was open and obvious, the laughter of these smooth young college women, in pressed kilts and matching sweater sets, was a code I did not understand. My dateless condition was not remarkable in those post-war years when most female undergraduates were more interested in the handsome ex-servicemen who crowded onto university campuses than in callow country boys like me.

I had made no friends, male or female, during my college years. My out-of-class time was taken up with a job at The Logan, which was a men's club that had once been famous for the number of bankers among its membership. The club was run like a small exclusive hotel with a reading room, a dining room and a billiard room—the latter usually empty. No women were permitted through the club's bevelled glass doors. The old men's leather chairs were shabby, the plumbing antique, and the iron radiators gurgled and banged erratically, but the club's endowments had been so well invested that it could still maintain an excellent cook and an adequate staff. My job was to tend the furnace at night and make myself generally useful on weekends when most of the regular staff were off. In exchange I was given a small comfortable room behind the furnace and a good supper every night. It was an excellent arrangement, which allowed me to stay in university.

My diploma—that piece of vellum that had recommended me to the board at Bishop Feild—was really a farce. My degree did not represent the university experience I had imagined—a time when one attended concerts, debates and poetry readings where dons sipped sherry while arguing the merits of modern prose with angry young men. I had read far too much about the dreaming spires.

Everything I knew and was had come to me second-hand. I'd changed my name from Ted to Theo; carefully, methodically, cast off the attitudes and mannerisms of my decent, garage-owning family, then pulled on the protective colouring of the opinions and ideas of my professors. I had constructed myself like a child sticking scraps of coloured paper into the shape of a man. Even the way I spoke—with what I hoped were the undertones of English gentry—had been acquired by playing and replaying, on The Logan's phonograph, an old 45 rpm recording of Ronald Coleman reading *Lost Horizon*.

Teaching jobs were plentiful in 1950 and I only sent out three applications, each to out-of-the-way places, each accompanied by a copy of my academic record and two glowing letters of reference. I knew the letters of reference were glowing because I wrote them myself. I did not resort to total forgery, but asked both men—a lazy professor for whom I'd done marking, and one of the old bankers at The Logan (its stationery being far more impressive than its plumbing)—to sign the letters I had composed. These, combined with excellent marks, a Bachelor's degree in English, and a photograph (requested, I suspect, to ensure that I was neither black nor yellow) had recommended me to the board of Bishop Feild, a hundred-year-old Anglican boys' school in St. John's, the capital of Newfoundland, a large island that had recently become the tenth Canadian province.

Leafing through old *National Geographics* in the reading room of The Logan I discovered that St. John's was a town of about fifty thousand and that most Newfoundlanders, predominantly of Irish ancestry, still fished the Grand Banks as their forebears had. Calculating that the citizens of a small Irish town on the edge of the Atlantic Ocean would be unlikely to see through my counterfeit persona, I accepted the position of English Master at Bishop Feild, bought myself two blue serge suits at Eatons, and in late August flew to St. John's.

If my references were misleading, then even more misleading were the credentials of the place to which I had come. I knew this weeks before the day I met Cynthia Markham. St. John's was a bastion of Britishness. Bishop Feild College, second only to the Anglican Cathedral, was the institution upon which loyalty to The Mother Country (always capitalized) was founded. The student body was divided into "houses" that competed for points in debating, stamp collecting, soccer and a dozen other activities, as well as for marks in the usual academic subjects, including Latin. The boys were addressed by their last name, wore a school uniform, and morning worship ended with "God Save The King." Although the school no longer took live-in students, the atmosphere reminded me of every English schoolboy novel I'd ever read.

Beyond the school walls, streets and buildings were named after England's rulers and England's victories. Indeed, the accent of the parents was predominately English. Church Lads' Brigades marched on Sundays, there were concerts in church halls, lengths of tweed in store windows, newspapers carried announcements of the arrival of boatloads of English china, English biscuits, English chocolate, English coal and English tea. The very fog that drifted through the Narrows might have wafted straight across the Atlantic from London.

Before I had time to realize all this, to perceive how a place can be riddled with stories that both undermine and reinforce the class system, I came to grief by asking a fourth form boy if his family owned the candy store across from the school. The child's look of scorn was accompanied by a proud and highly detailed recounting of his father's family tree and the ancestry of the store owner—who, although sharing the same surname, had descended from an altogether inferior background. The genealogy lesson was followed by a curt note from the boy's father pointing out the dangers to someone who has newly come from away of jumping to conclusions.

I was unfamiliar with The Book of Common Prayer, knew nothing of Gilbert and Sullivan, had no Scout badges, and could not even discuss soccer, much less cricket. I did not own a school tie and was pretty sure that Headmaster McEwan's speech made in the staff room on the subject of Attire Befitting a Gentleman had been directed at me. The headmaster, public school and ex-British navy, not only sounded like Ronald Coleman but also looked like him.

Many nights, lying awake in my room in Mrs. Pickett's boarding house, I would listen to the foghorn and wonder if I would ever belong here or if I should have taken a job somewhere else. Yet, even while I lay there considering Yellowknife or the Orkneys, I knew it was here, in this self-satisfied little town, that I wanted to be known and respected. St. John's was an extension of my imagined England, the perfect place for the person I had created. The irony was that its being so fitting was what made it so impossible.

What kept me from total despair was an unshakeable belief in my ability to teach. I had always known that given a roomful of youngsters, a closed door and the books I loved, I could transfer the beauty of written words to the students' minds. Behind that closed door I was completely confident, and I loved it—loved the electricity in the classroom, the aliveness—and yes, the admiration on those young faces. For that I was willing to endure any number of snubs, any amount of correction from the headmaster.

Three days after our first meeting, one of my students, the son of a government member (a cabinet minister himself now, he has come down from Ottawa for the funeral, is sitting just to the left and behind me) who was a neighbour of Cynthia Markham's, passed me a cream envelope containing a note on which "Please come for tea on Saturday" was scrawled in thick brown ink with what I thought was a straight pen. I discovered later that the note, like most of Cynthia's invitations, had been written hurriedly, on impulse, with a drawing pen. Cynthia made beautiful, detailed pen and ink drawings of weeds, flowers, tree cones and seed pods. Sometimes, in the euphoria of a successfully finished drawing, she dashed off an invitation—often later regretted—for by nature she was reclusive. Cynthia never showed her work. Most of the people invited to the old Markham house knew nothing of her artistic ability; yet, most of St. John's, and certainly my landlady, would have said they knew everything there was to know about Cynthia Markham.

The day after the note was delivered to me, I screwed up my courage and asked Mrs. Pickett what an invitation to tea involved. My ignorance shocked her. My landlady nudged me into her dim front room, sat me down and set me to rights about tea—afternoon tea, she said, was not supper. I'd probably get tea with tea buns and jam. She asked where I was going to tea, and when I told her, she began tracing the Markham family tree back for generations to old Abraham Markham.

There was talk, she said, that Abraham's real surname was Mararyk, but never mind with that now, he got rich from selling jewellery, first from a handcart, then from a tiny corner store. Before

Abraham died the Markham's owned a big dry goods store that his son and grandsons expanded into a block-long department store on Water Street. They lost some of their holdings during the Depression, but even up to the war they had a fleet of ships and a fishing station up on the Labrador.

This, and much more Mrs. Pickett told me. By the time she finished she'd dusted every piece of furniture and ornament in that crowded room. I remember she came and stood looking down at me, arms folded, the duster tucked into her armpit. "Cynthia Markham is a lady, a proper lady," she said with admiration. For all that, I noticed when she spoke of Miss Markham it was in a tone of kindly condescension. Although Cynthia was rich and Mrs. Pickett was not, the other woman's failure to acquire a husband, had, I gathered, placed them on equal footing in my landlady's view.

"I can't recall her ever having a beau. Not that she's ugly—a bit plain perhaps, doesn't make the best of herself. Not like her mother, Agnes, who was a real fashion plate in her day."

According to Mrs. Pickett the Markham family had daughtered-out; "Cynthia Markham's father was the only son of an only son, and when he died the business was sold. Then Cynthia had to come home from England, where she was studying, to look after her mother."

Mrs. Pickett could not remember what it was Cynthia had been studying. "Something arty—music or poetry—anyway she never went back. Agnes Markham lingered on for fifteen years. When she finally died Cynthia was into her thirties and no one was beating her door down." My landlady looked down at me speculatively. Her face was blank. She might have been wondering if I would make an appropriate suitor for Miss Markham, or she might have been wondering if she should dust me. Then she gave a slight shake of her head; clearly I would not do. "Made a nice life for herself has Cynthia Markham—runs that big old house with whatever help she gets out of Doris Mercer, and that's not much I'd say—and she volunteers for things like the library book drive and the hospital appeal—a pure lady, born and bred."

I thanked Mrs. Pickett effusively and sincerely. Aside from clarifying the subject of afternoon tea and obtaining all that background on Cynthia Markham, I had made two important discoveries; the first was that if I'd asked my landlady's advice on other subjects I would have avoided most of the embarrassing gaffes I'd made in the last few weeks. Second: when you ask someone for advice they forget to ask you personal questions. I hoped she was right about the ceremony of afternoon tea.

She was. I also acted on Mrs. Pickett's suggestion that I open an account at the Royal Stores. "Get yourself a good English tweed jacket and ask Tom Facey to pick out your ties." Like all her advice, this also proved sound.

The tea was a success. I was clad in my new tweed jacket and a pair of flannels recommended by Mr. Facey. Cynthia Markham was dressed very conventionally in a dark skirt and silk blouse. She led me into a comfortable room where a fire had been lit and introduced me to a plump, pretty woman, who to my surprise turned out to be the headmaster's wife, and two of the younger teachers. I had met the man before. He was the mathematics teacher at Bishop Feild and seemed much more human sipping tea beside Cynthia's fireplace than he had in the teachers' room. The tall, tanned woman named Jessie was the games mistress at Bishop Spencer College, the Anglican school for girls.

The atmosphere was completely relaxed and I heard myself laughing with the others at Mrs. McEwan's stories about travelling with three Newfoundland dogs which she regularly took to shows all over North America. She was not a woman I could imagine the headmaster marrying. Delightfully frank, she spoke in what Mrs. Pickett called a bay accent—which bay I could not tell, of course. When the Spencer teacher asked if the year had gotten off to a good start at Feild, Mrs. McEwan said, "Swimmingly, I think," chewed thoughtfully on her shortbread for a minute, then added, "Of course you'd never know that from my husband—Ewan never smiles until after Christmas." She grinned at me, then at the math teacher. "New staff shouldn't take fright—my husband really is a good man—a real teddy bear despite his over-developed stiff upper lip."

I was never able to think of the headmaster again without imaging a well-dressed teddy bear keeping a stiff upper lip, sometimes while the poor creature was being pulled apart by three huge Newfoundland dogs. It helped our relationship immensely.

Within a month or two I seemed to be meeting Cynthia almost every week, either at church—for she had suggested I begin attending the Cathedral—or at the homes of other people where a committee was being formed or some celebration was being planned. I am fairly sure that Cynthia suggested I be asked to join these groups. She had the ability to put an idea into a person's mind without them ever realizing they had not thought of it themselves. Over the years I was able to observe that talent many times, for I was by no means the only person in St. John's who owed their acceptance to Cynthia Markham.

Some milestone in our relationship was passed just after Christmas when the teachers at Bishop Feild were each given two complimentary tickets to a community concert. Realizing that the concert hall was not five minutes walk from her house and that my lack of transportation would not therefore be an embarrassment, I asked Cynthia to accompany me. I remember walking through the cold, clear night, snow crunching underfoot, Christmas lights still sparkling from a few houses. I don't think either of us spoke. Back in her living room we drank tea and replayed most of the Italian Symphony. I might have been a Hottentot for all I knew of Mendelssohn, but Cynthia spoke of the music as if it were poetry, conjuring up images of sun shining on leaping dancers, on whitewalled houses and blue lakes. It was, in fact, violin that she had been studying in London when she was called home to nurse her mother. Over the years she taught me to listen to and appreciate music. It was one of many things we enjoyed together.

Shortly after the drama society's rather weak Easter pageant, the headmaster, smiling now, asked if I would be willing to extend my contract for two more years. I was happy to say yes. That first winter, seeing that I needed help, Cynthia had introduced me to two of her friends who worked for the CBC and were members of an amateur theatrical group—one of several groups in the city. I, who was faculty advisor for Bishop Feild's drama society, had never even seen a live play and was swept away when I saw Cynthia's friends in *The Browning Version*. I wanted to be part of their next production. It did not matter to me, then, if I would be cleaning the stage or passing out costumes, prompting or painting scenery. I knew that I must somehow be involved in theatre. In the winters that followed I did all of these things, eventually working my way up to direct a group that won five provincial and two national prizes at the annual drama festivals that used to be held in those days. Since retirement I've been writing reviews for *The Telegram*. It's amazing how many people read them, even people who never go to the theatre.

I stayed on at Mrs. Pickett's boarding house for three years, until I had saved enough to get a mortgage on a nice little two-storey on Barnes Road. As the years passed Cynthia and I saw more and more of each other. In fall and winter we would go for long walks in and around St. John's. I learned to use a camera in order to take close-ups of the plants Cynthia wanted to draw. We went to concerts together, and although Cynthia was not a member of my theatre group I think she saw every one of the plays I directed. When Cynthia entertained I drifted naturally into playing the part of host; in return, she sometimes helped me give small dinner parties for my colleagues at Bishops. I no longer remember when it was that I realized people were referring to us as a couple, Cynthia and Theo. Theo and Cynthia . . .

I feel the firm pressure of a hand on my shoulder and know I have spoken out loud—perhaps said our names. The hand gives my shoulder a single, firm pat, then withdraws. I wonder if the hand might belong to my old headmaster—Stew McEwan reminding me to keep a stiff upper lip. I almost smile. Stew is an old man now, we've become friends. I caught sight of him and Barbara in the vestry when I came in.

God! Hubert is still talking! But he is getting tired, his lips moving ever more slowly, like a mechanical toy winding down. I must have made some kind of noise because he's looking at me too, in that puzzled plaintive way Hubert has, apprehension that I am about to interrupt him mixed with hope that I will. Someone should call Jean—Jean, Hubert's wife, is normally a moderating influence on his verbosity; today she is sitting at the back with the junior choir which will be singing at the graveside. I hope they do a good job. I've asked them to sing something joyous, hopeful. Nothing is more moving than young voices singing in the open air. I remember Cynthia saying that once when I commented unfavourably on a cheerful but untalented group of Scouts and Girl Guides singing at the Lieutenant Governor's Garden Party.

The tone of condescension vanished from women's voices when they spoke of Cynthia. Married or not, she now had a man who clearly adored her—and I did. She had done so much for me. I like to imagine I helped her in some small ways. People said she was looking younger every year, and I know she felt more confident about her art. In the mid '60s she'd had an exhibition of her drawings in the university art gallery.

As soon as I had enough money, I began spending summers along the coast of the Mediterranean, trips that were the culmination of daydreams that began the night Cynthia and I first talked about the poetry of music. Sitting outside small cafes, a warm sun bouncing off cream walls, the warm earth smells, warm music, warm voices, cool wine, I even wrote some bad poetry. We rarely travelled together; Cynthia usually stayed home in the summer and she'd spend the fall theatre season in London. Sometimes she was already gone when I returned to begin a new school year. People would ask if we'd met while away. The town loved to speculate about us. I enjoyed their speculation and so, I think, did Cynthia. I told her once about hearing one of my students tell a new boy, "Old Downing is really one of the Royal Family—he's in disgrace that's why he's over here—and he can never marry and never, never go back to England!" We laughed together and speculated about what terrible thing would have made the House of Windsor disown me.

"I know you," she'd said that first afternoon when she reached for my hand across the stone wall. I still wonder what she knew. Had those intelligent grey eyes seen more than just a frightened boy in a cheap serge suit?

It's not completely true that I didn't speak to a girl while I was in university. During our last semester, I did date a shy, awkward girl, a girl who did not know yet how pretty she was. A girl who looked at me one night and said, "Bad luck for me, isn't it? The only guy who'll talk to me is a fag!"

Once, just after I'd come back from a summer in Greece, Cynthia leaned forward touching my hand. "Did you enjoy the summer—did you find someone?"

The question was hopeful, concerned. I smiled and nodded and she smiled back. It was as near as we ever came to discussing sex, yet we understood each other perfectly—or perhaps not. I never asked if she found someone on her trips. I regret that, I do regret that.

After I retired from Feild, having turned down the principalship (headmasters had by then vanished from the face of the earth) Cynthia and I did take one trip together. We were away for three months, saw most of the great cities of Europe and brazenly talked about it when we came back. Who could question the propriety of seventy-three-year-old Cynthia Markham and sixty-year-old Theo Downing spending the fall touring Europe together?

Hubert's voice has finally stopped. In the blessed silence I pick up the wildflowers, walk forward and place the untidy bouquet on the polished surface. I stay there, one hand on either side of the flowers, holding myself up with Cynthia's coffin, waiting for the music to begin, waiting to follow the coffin down the aisle.

After the graveside service the women will crowd around me with words of sympathy, with invitations to tea and advice about wearing a scarf on such a nippy day. Either Jean or Hubert will tell me to be sure and drop by the rectory on the way home. There will be a fire in the grate, we'll sip brandy and have Cynthia's real memorial service.

I will stay in this place for the rest of my life, putting flowers on her grave, going alone to all the events we once attended together, helping with Bishop Feild's fundraising, reading the early service twice a month, occasionally reviewing some visiting dramatic group with a venom that delights my St. John's readers: "Ah, thought they could get away with that stuff here—think we wouldn't know the difference. Old Theo'll disabuse them of that quickly enough!" people will say, thumping my column in *The Telegram*.

Eventually, I will die and be buried in the churchyard next to her. Yellow weeds will grow over our graves, and after a time no one will remember exactly who Cynthia and Theo were. "He turned up here all alone," people will say, "came from England, the bastard son of some prince, so he couldn't marry. She was beautiful, tall and stately with flowing hair, and although they could never marry, they were always together. It's said they had a son but he grew up in some foreign place."

I know just how it will be.

And when they turn her coffin I follow, moving slowly down the aisle with her. Then I can see their faces, all of those loving, sentimental people who remember ours as the romance against which all other romances must be measured. I begin to weep real tears, tears I cannot stop.

Stamp Collecting Newfoundland

Georgina Olivere Queller

I WAS ALREADY six years old when Joey Smallwood got his way and we all became Canadians.

At the time of confederation, I knew little about Newfoundland and less about Canada. Since my parents didn't own a car until 1974, much of my ignorance about Newfoundland would have continued if my father hadn't been a stamp collector. When I was young, my family depended on the kindness of friends to go anywhere we couldn't get to, by what my father always called, shank's mare. (It must have been three or four years before I realized he meant we had to walk on our own steam . . . I kept waiting for someone's horse to show up.) This limited our travel around Newfoundland to a Sunday afternoon drive around the Bay or up the Southern Shore with a close family friend who came to be the fifth wheel on our family wagon. Without first-hand experience my knowledge of pre- and early post-confederation Newfoundland was tied to my father's postage stamp collection.

He hunted partridge and rabbit, picked berries, went trout fishing, and worked hard at his job like other Newfoundland fathers. But stamps were his passion. These days it would be considered an addiction or an obsession. Every spare moment of the time he spent at home, he was at his stamps. My memory bank videotape has him sitting, with his hands over a bowl of hot water, soaking stamps. He wears a white or sometimes a blue Arrow shirt with starched collar and cuffs. The sleeves are pushed up and held by those old-fashioned stretchy, metallic arm bands. A natural gray, knitted vest is stretched over his stout middle concealing the braces that hold up his trousers. His left forearm rests on the edge of Mom's largest kitchen bowl. The ginger brown one with the cream interior that she has to steal back for raising bread. The thick square fingers of his right hand dip in and out of the bowl of soaking stamps. He has black hair on the back of his hands and down his square stubby fingers. His fingernails are large, closely clipped and shiny clean from the hot water. With his right thumb he pushes stamps from the torn corners of envelopes. They float free in the water. With his other hand he takes the emptied envelope corner and lays it on the mounting wet stack in a cereal bowl next to him.

This memory of him dates back to the end of World War II. We still lived at 77 St. Clare Avenue. He sits on a wooden kitchen chair at an old card table. The orange coils on the cone-shaped burner from the nearby Cosy Glow slowly toasts us in the small room. I sit next to the Cosy Glow. My arms are wrapped around my straw-stuffed Scotty dog pulling him tight to my chest. My chair is round bottomed, also straw-filled; periodically I loosen the grip on Scotty and pick at the grey and wine tapestry pictures that are woven into the chair's coarse upholstery. Daddy tells me stories about his stamps and the friends and traders with whom he deals. Growing up I would hear these stories over and over again. He explains to me: "You can learn a lot about Newfoundland from these stamps Puddin', about our history and geography, all kinds of things. You'd hardly credit it." He talks about the people in his stamp world. People like Fox-in-the-Breadbox Moores, the Reverend Loveys, George Wilson, George Burden and one Gilbert Higgins, who he says, "can talk the leg off a kitchen chair." Other, shady elements in the stamp world, will go nameless. But cronies of every species turned up at our door to talk and trade or buy and sell Newfoundland stamps.

From the age of about four, I joined my two older sisters in doing the mundane tasks associated with stamp collecting. As well as the usual childhood chores, soaking and drying, sorting and counting, and running and fetching stamps fell to us. Far better than Saturday morning dusting and polishing the brass ornaments on our mother's what-not table, stamp chores were more along the lines of indoor fun. Bags of contest mail from CJON and VOCM, and letters from Santa Claus, detoured on their way to the North Pole, came into our home to have their stamps removed. These stamps showed us Newfoundland's colonial history, her codfish and game, her statues and ships, her outports and towns and everything that went into her identity prior to April 1, 1949. Through them I got to know not only about Newfoundland itself, but myself as a Newfoundlander, and my father as a collector of stamps and stories.

When I was five we left the west end of St. John's for the city's first subdivision, Churchill Park. For the then fabulous price of $17,500 we became house-poor for the rest of our parents' mortgaged lives. In this modern bungalow (a new word in our vocabularies at the time) my father gave up his card table for the dining room table. The stamp hobby had by now become a business alongside my father's job as a floorwalker at the Royal Stores. Paraphernalia from his stamp world could be found throughout our new house. Magnifying glasses of assorted types and sizes, perforation gauges, elastic bands, window envelopes, paper hinges for mounting stamps, first-day covers, blunt-nose tongs, and my father wetting his index finger as he counted off stacks of 100 stamp lots, were common sights throughout the new house at 11 Sycamore. Newspaper sheets with used stamps laid out on them could always be found drying in front of the hot-air furnace registers. Drawers which in other homes held games and off-season clothing were filled with books and boxes of stamps. Mom's cupboards for the storage of homemade jam gradually gave way to more and more books of stamps and tradeable, saleable stock. *Scott's Stamp Catalogue*, with its up-to-date listing and valuation of the world's stamps, was always a successful Christmas present for our father. When we three daughters grew up and left home, the small back bedroom became his office. And the pictures on those Newfoundland stamps had become internalized and formed a big part of my conception of Newfoundland.

Aside from all the stamps that he accumulated in quantity, our father had special albums for his collections. One book each for Newfoundland, Canada, Great Britain, U.S.A. and a World Book for everything else. The Newfoundland album was the most interesting and valuable. The earliest stamps in the book, 1857 issue, looked more British than Newfoundland in origin. They were in pence. They had British monarchs and British floral emblems. If the word "Newfoundland" wasn't printed on them anyone might have thought they were British stamps. From this first series the one that I have never forgotten was a yellow green triangle-shaped stamp. It had no perforations on its sides and was a 3-pence stamp. Clustered on it were the three flowers: the rose, the thistle and the shamrock. In 1865, when decimal currency came to Newfoundland, the colony of Newfoundland, in her third issue of stamps, began to show some of her own images. A 2¢ codfish stamp, a 5¢ seal and a 13¢ sailing ship began to tell the story of Newfoundland. These exact images and variations on them turned up again and again. Their values and colours varied. The names for the colours were exact, and to me, exotic. They introduced more new vocabulary to me over the years. Scarlet vermilion, rose lake, violet brown, grey lilac, brown lilac, carmine, chestnut, slate violet, ultramarine, Venetian red, olive, and brown bistre were some of the colours. The stamps were two-colour prints: black for the typed parts, and the pictures were in soft mellow colours with those wonderful names. They were so different from the bright full-colour printing process used on Canadian stamps today. The very softness of the old Newfoundland stamp colours had an allure that drew you to them. The old Canadian stamps, though they were printed in roughly the same way as our own, often by the same printers even, didn't entice me the way the Newfoundland ones did. The pictures of all those prime ministers I had never heard about, boring buildings and their, at the time, "foreign" images held no appeal for me.

In the Newfoundland collection, I wasn't very keen on the monarchial stamps. There were a few exceptions. The pictures of the six and then twelve-year-old Princess Elizabeth available in blue, dull blue and bright blue attracted me. The profile of Queen Victoria with her famous white veil headpiece trailing down her back etched itself on my brain. As did a young Prince of Wales in uniform. He looked like the picture of our maternal grandfather in his World War I uniform. Grandfather James had died when I was one. When I think of him now I see him, both as the picture on our grandmother's, Muffer James', mantlepiece, and as a soldier on the 4¢ rose lake Newfoundland stamp.

Stamps with imprints of John Guy and one of his ships, the *Endeavour*; John Cabot and his ship the *Matthew*; Sir Humphrey Gilbert and the *Squirrel*; Sir Wilfred Grenfell and the *Strathcona II*; the statue of the Fighting Newfoundlander (which I saw on the stamp long before I got to Bowring Park); the Colonial Building; and old maps of Newfoundland and Labrador, introduced me to the history of my country of birth before I'd had any lessons on the subject at school. And those classes were for only half an hour a week in grade five. I was drawn to all of the Newfoundland dog stamps whether pictured in headshot or standing. The salmon leaping a falls on the Humber River made me fancy seeing the real thing. I first learned about other Newfoundland game and wildlife this way also. On stamps, I saw the "Willow Ptarmigan," the caribou "Monarch of the Wilds," the salmon "King of the Rivers," colonies of seals, a whitecoat seal pup and the famous "Currency of Newfoundland" stamp where the codfish filled up a whole stamp as they once did the traps. There were logging camps, paper mills, miners digging, and ships loading iron ore at Bell Island. Olive-green caribou hunting scenes, a red iceberg, blue ptarmigans, a grey sealing fleet headed to the front, and an ultramarine fishing fleet leaving for the Banks through the Narrows of St. John's Harbour caught my childhood imagination and gave a colourful testament to our environment and way of life. Newfoundland communities I didn't get to visit until I was twenty, and some I've yet to visit, were on those stamps: Cupids, Grand Falls, Shell Bird Island, Placentia, Mount Moriah, Little Rapids, and more. There was a full series of stamps commemorating the Great War in which our Grandfather James fought and was wounded. All the big battles: Beaumont Hamel, Suvla Bay, Monchy, Ubique, Steenbeck and others were there. First Flight Covers of aeroplanes travelling in and out of Newfoundland told a detailed story of our early aviation. A train, which I took to be the "Bullet," the Newfoundland Hotel, and the War Memorial were things from my own home town on those important government-issued postal stamps.

Of all the stories about my father's stamp collecting, my favourite is the story about the stamp that changed our lives—even before confederation could. It was about the two cent surcharge (printed bold, like so: **Two Cents**) on the carmine 30¢ Memorial College stamp. The stamp was issued in 1946 when I was just three years old. My father, Foxy Moores and another collector whose name I can't remember were the main dealers in St. John's at that time. They had gotten together and decided that these surcharged stamps would be in demand by Canadian and American buyers. If they stayed together and didn't underbid each other they could control the price they received. The **Two Cent** surcharge was originally done because of a shortage of 2¢ stamps at the end of World War II. The Memorial College stamp was a large one and was printed in sheets of 50, whereas most came in sheets of 100 stamps. Due to this 2¢ stamp shortage, each person was limited to buying only two sheets of them at a time. Over the next two weeks, Dad had Mom go around from post office to post office all over St. John's, picking up her quota at each one. He did the same and, after a decent interval, they made their rounds again. Thus, they were able to hoard a large number of the sheets of the locally surcharged stamps. While the price agreed upon by his fellow dealers held, he made a windfall profit of $1,500.00. In 1946 that bought us a house in the country at Second Pond, an electric wringer washing machine, and a mahogany console radio record player that could tune in FM stations (if there had been one to tune into in Newfoundland at the time). The deal they made lasted only three weeks before one of his fellow cartel members undersold the agreed price leading to its collapse. While it held, they had a wild ride, as apparently did I, according to my father, "Being wheeled in your carriage from post office to post office while your mother bought up the **Two Cent** surcharged 30¢ carmine Memorial College stamp."

From then on, we spent all our summers at Second Pond. We went there the day after school closed in June and stayed until the day before it opened again in September. Still not owning a car, my father rode to work on the Petty Harbour Bus. And I became a country child, hopping rocks, climbing hills, picking berries, living free in Newfoundland.

My father's stamps not only taught me about Newfoundland but they changed the way I grew up here. They made the Newfoundland of my childhood persist in a visual way that I would not have had otherwise. They gave me a history and geography of Newfoundland and Labrador that even Bishop Spencer College failed to provide.

Bibliography

Newfoundland Specialized Stamp Catalogue. Second Edition, by John M. Walsh & John G. Butt. Walsh's Philatelic Service, St. John's, NL, Canada, 1998.

The Hundred Black Ducks

LILLIAN BOUZANE

The hundred black ducks
driven to wait out the storm at the duck pond
dive, call to each other, rise, pattern, head due north.
Four break off, return to the duck pond:
the food, the children
the pigeons that coo under the bridge.

The Heron

(Excerpt from a novel-in-progress)

LIBBY CREELMAN

DARREN HAD COME home early from work and was in the living room reading the paper. Occasionally he glanced up to see Cooper roaming around outside, possibly looking for another stump, though Darren had already told him one was enough. It was great to see the boy walking. He was wearing a layer of T-shirts but no jacket or coat. Although it was spring, it was still cool. The wind had come around from the northeast and was cutting. Jeanette had returned home from doing errands only ten minutes earlier and disappeared into the bathroom. All was quiet. Evidently she had not opened the shower curtain.

There had been three herons initially. The crew saw them flying low above the 25-metre-high whitecaps, heading for the tanker. Darren imagined it must have been quite a sight, 500 miles northeast of the Azores and there they were: three long-winged creatures with folded necks and trailing legs, their bodies rickety as they battled 80-knot winds to reach the tanker. The five-year-old *Mattea* normally shuttled crude oil from Hibernia to the transhipment facility at Whiffen Head, but at this particular moment it was returning from France where it had been for its first refitting. From the bridge, the crew watched the birds make land on deck. They were placed in a storage room, but one died almost immediately and was cast overboard.

The tanker was another week reaching Conception Bay due to

headwinds and some nasty weather. A second heron died within a day of Newfoundland, but by then a bit of superstition had set in and none of the crew would approach the birds. Darren had taken custody of both the dead heron and the lone survivor, who was now in his bathtub, only an hour-and-a-half ago. The dead bird was in the freezer between the ice cream and fish patties. Jeanette wasn't going to like that either.

When she emerged from the bathroom, her face was shiny and scrubbed and she was already in her pre-bedtime layers.

"You're going to bed early," he said.

She sat down across from him and took some of the newspaper. He wasn't going to be surprised if she didn't speak to him. But then she looked up.

"What's in the tub?"

"A heron, but I don't think it's a Great Blue. I think it's a European species. A Grey Heron."

"Is that unusual?"

"Perhaps. It was on the ship a week and those clowns never tried to feed it. I might take it down to Byron and see what he has to say."

She snapped the newspaper. "If the doctors go on strike they're not getting any sympathy from me."

"Were there many goldfish left?"

She looked up. "Where? In the bathtub?"

Darren slowly drew back the shower curtain, and sure enough, all the goldfish were gone. He had purchased a dozen in at the mall on his way home from the tanker. Half he'd slipped into the tub; the other six were still in the bag.

Visiting the tanker had consumed his entire afternoon. He had hoped to pick up the heron and be gone, but wasn't surprised when the crew urged him to come aboard to collect the bird himself. He was ferried out via a longliner to the ship, which was enormous and freshly painted a bright, salmon pink. A crowd of crewmen followed him as he was taken to the rope locker, a spacious storage room with a number of yellow lockers where, Darren guessed, the ropes were stored, since there was not a single one in sight. A handwritten note posted on the door warned: "Live Birds Inside." Although the crew had grown fearful of the herons, someone must have been coming in to clean up because the floor was spotless. It was unusual, Darren was made to understand, that they had kept these birds; the normal practice was to toss them overboard.

The live heron was standing in a corner, beside the dead one. The crew hung back and watched as Darren seized the live heron and put it in a box, then slipped the dead one into a garbage bag. Back on deck, Darren paused to marvel at the size of the ship. Its deck was the length of a football field and the height of the ship itself was six stories. Many birds lost over the Atlantic sought refuge on such a vessel. Darren imagined the birds' attraction to such a ship: to not only its almighty size and excessive pinkness, but to its sheer presence over the unyielding seascape, as though it had been invoked not through chance, but necessity.

The heron was standing in the bathtub beside the stump he and Cooper had dug out of Darren's garden shed. Its neck and head were sunk to the level of its blue-grey wings, which were folded in such a way they resembled a cloak draped over the bird's back and shoulders, lending it an elegant Count Dracula air, despite the lavender-coloured tub. A few minutes passed, during which neither the heron nor Darren moved, and then the heron lifted its head high on its serpentine neck and with its right leg made a few leisurely attempts to scale the side of the bathtub. Darren backed away and the bird defecated. The feces was projected the length of the tub and Darren saw that among the otherwise dazzling yellow matter there were some black bits, indicative of bleeding in the guts.

He knelt beside the tub and dumped in the remaining half-dozen goldfish, but he knew he would be bringing the heron to Byron the next day.

When he returned to the living room, Jeanette's eyes were closed.

The heron survived the night, but had rejected the second course of goldfish, one of which was floating belly-up the following morning. The remaining five were moving sluggishly through the dirty water. While Darren scooped them up with a drinking glass and flushed them down the toilet, the heron stood oblivious, its black and white crest rising and falling like a toy whose batteries were running low.

For nearly two decades, Byron Prince had run the Southern Shore Animal Rescue Park. Southern Shore Concentration Camp, was more like it, Darren often told people; sure, half the animals brought to it perished. Nonetheless, he called ahead and left a message with Byron that he was bringing down an unusual heron.

Turning in at Byron's, he was concerned when he saw the parking area vacant. Byron lived alone in a one-storey bungalow that Darren had the misfortune to visit only once; the medley of odours resulting from fried meat, sour clothing and sick birds had been alarming.

The birds were kept in a long shed beside the house. But here, too, the lot was empty. The Southern Shore Animal Rescue Park, as its name suggested, served as both hospital and nature park; it was through this second capacity that Byron made his meager income. The place was looking more rundown than Darren recalled, though it had never been particularly shipshape, and then the door to the Rehabilitation Centre, as Byron called the shed, opened and Byron stepped out and waved. As usual, he was wearing shorts.

Darren had first met Byron after a summer as field assistant for a renowned seabird biologist. In truth, Darren had spent his summer sitting in a dark cabin on an offshore island blowing eggs for the biologist's illegal personal collection. He came back to university disillusioned and in bad spirits. Byron had worn his intelligence openly and, Darren thought, arrogantly. Competition between the two had been spontaneous. It took all the years of graduate school for this to wear down, though Darren remained childishly vigilant of Byron's excessive knowledge.

Byron was smiling as he crossed the lot. He was always happy to see Darren, which surprised Darren.

"Where are the school buses?" Darren asked.

Byron made a dismissive gesture with his hand and said, "Let's have a look at that heron."

Darren opened the back of his truck and watched as Byron leaned in to have a peek. He still wore his brown hair—no grey, Darren noticed—parted down the middle, an antiquated style that took some getting used to. His dark eyes were enormous, round and perpetually startled; they reminded Darren of a tree-clinging bushbaby.

"How long has it been without food?"

"I gave it some goldfish last night."

"How many?"

"Half a dozen."

"And before that?"

"At least a week."

Byron was shaking his head and frowning. "The goldfish were a disastrous idea." He lifted the box and Darren followed him inside.

The "hospital" smelled of feces, dead fish, and antiseptic. They entered the small operating room where an aluminum table folded out from the wall in a manner similar to changing tables in airport washrooms. Byron placed the box on the table and stood blinking.

"You'll have to excuse me if I seem a bit slow off the mark. I was up all night with an owl. Okay. *Normally,* first thing I do is leave the bird alone. You know that. Do nothing. Don't touch it. Put it in a dark room with the temperature a few degrees above the comfort zone. Birds come in, no meat on them—"

"I'm not sure that bird can afford to be left alone, Byron." Byron's friendly lecturing always made Darren feel defensive. He put up with it because he was the one who had landed the secure government job, while Byron was stuck here becoming yearly more eccentric and less respected.

"Second thing I do, after leaving it alone, is hydrate it. More important than food. But you know that." Here he shook his head again. He went over to a small table and picked up a large syringe and filled it with Gatorade. "If we can stabilize the electrolytes . . . Could you hold this?"

Darren took the syringe and rubber tube, then stood obediently back a few feet as Byron opened the box.

"Too late, Darren."

"What?"

"It's gone."

Darren approached Byron and the two of them stood silent for a moment, gazing in at the crumpled heron. Already, it seemed, the colours were fading.

Byron took a deep, catching breath. "When you said unusual heron,

Darren, I thought maybe you had a Cattle Egret. But now this is something. This *is* something." And he lifted the body out of the box and laid it on the metal table. "Venture a guess?"

"Grey Heron?"

Byron looked disappointed. He turned the heron over onto its back and spread the wings. The keel was clearly outlined; there was no doubt it had been consuming its own muscles for days. Here was a body crying out for forced hydration.

"Grey Heron. Yes, indeed." Byron stroked the bird's feathered thighs. "White thighs. White headlights. Very diagnostic."

Byron looked sideways at Darren.

"You see what I'm getting at? These white patches on the leading edge of the wing, just past the carpel joint. This is a Grey Heron, Darren, absolutely no question. Congratulations."

"Well—"

"At one time, this species was an improbable sighting. But in recent years several have been seen in southern Greenland, and Iceland is now averaging fifty sightings a year, evidently from Norway. What you've got here, of course, is a ship-assist. Not a true vagrant. One other thing. Greys tend to curl their toes in flight. They don't look as leggy as our Great Blues. Something to keep in mind should you see a Great Blue that doesn't look quite right, Darren, when you're out and about."

As Byron spoke, he fiddled with the heron, patting down its feathers and pulling its legs straight, then doing the same with its neck and head so the body was stretched several feet across the table. To have come all this way, Darren thought, only to die in a box in the company of two well-meaning but essentially ineffective humans. He placed the syringe on the table.

"How's business?"

Byron laid the heron back in the box and closed the lid. "They're shutting me down."

"What?"

"Operating without the proper permits. Not licensed for veterinary medicine. A few other infringements. I thought you knew."

"I had no idea. Have you been fined?"

"Good heavens, no."

This explained the lack of school buses. As well as the empty parking lot, and, come to think of it, the hand-painted sign hadn't been there at the edge of the road.

"That's tough."

Byron shrugged. "Want to have a look around? It may be your last chance."

"You bet. Who's in the recovery room?"

"Boreal Owl." Byron opened the door partway and Darren leaned in. The room was dark, but in an elevated wire cage Darren could see a creature the size of a kitten racing around, startled by their entry. It wore an orange figure-eight bandage on one wing.

"It was hit by a car and found on the side of the road," Byron said. "Broken humerus." The owl slowed and huddled in a far corner. Darren had watched Byron set bones a number of times. He said he could feel the break with his fingers. Like a piece of cloth laid over gravel, he once explained. He could "hear" it with his fingers. "There's also a gannet in the closet. It keeps getting out and scaring the owl. Maybe you could take it with you? It just needs to be released."

Darren followed Byron into the rodent nursery where, normally, families of rats and mice were housed in stacked drawers. Today, most of the drawers were empty. But the truth was, Darren was not surprised by this turn of events.

"I've had to cut back," Byron explained. "No point, with only a few weeks left."

"Have they said what they plan to do with the birds?"

"They'll be donated to the provincial museum," Byron said. He opened the freezer and spoke through a cloud of condensed air. "I didn't know what to do with all these, so I've started putting them away. They might be of use to someone."

Darren peered in at the heap of frozen rodents. The bodies were coiled around each other as though they had died huddled together for warmth, though Byron would certainly have killed them first.

"A hundred and thirteen." Byron spoke absently, as though he were speaking to himself. Darren figured he normally did a fair amount of that, anyway.

"I think I have time for a quick tour of the park, Byron."

"Excellent. I'll grab my coat. Don't let me forget the gannet when we get back."

Darren nodded, knowing he wouldn't forget, but hoping Byron would.

They exited the rehabilitation centre and took a shortcut through a boggy gully to the "nature walk" proper, which was similar to the shortcut but wider. Here and there, in response to seasonal wetness, planks had been laid down, though many had sunk below the level of water and moss and now shifted unpredictably beneath their feet. Various plants were labelled, but crudely, as with a card marked "Lambkill, *Kalmia angustifolia*" wrapped in translucent plastic and tied to a plant with string.

Darren remembered an argument that had taken place between them nearly twenty years earlier, when he had made one of his first, nosy visits to the park. Byron had incorrectly labelled black spruce as white—or was it white spruce, black?—and his sulking, uncompromising reaction had surprised Darren, who was certain his identification was correct. Darren wondered where that tree had stood and for the first time entertained the possibility that either one of them might have been mistaken.

Although the sky was clouded, when they emerged onto open field the bronzed brightness blanketing the landscape was a relief. A raised boardwalk snaked several feet above the barrens and into a compound enclosed by a wire fence. They stepped up onto the boardwalk and entered the compound through a gate that swung unevenly and whose hinges, Darren saw, were working their way out. Once they were inside, Byron fiddled for a moment with the gate, but it would not catch and he gave up.

"I always made a show of closing the gates when we had visitors," he said, "but frankly, it's not necessary."

Darren saw that the second gate, through which visitors were meant to exit the compound, was opening and closing with a soothing hush in the slight wind.

A series of whistles, descending note by note and called out so clearly they made the air seem hollow, sounded nearby. Three snowy owls were emerging from behind a stand of shrubs, half-hopping, half-walking, while a fourth, smaller than the rest, stood whistling and watching.

"The male," Byron said. "He's been here fifteen years."

One of the owls jumped and spread its wings, and the wind picked it up and carried it a few feet.

None of them could fly. One was a wing amputee; the others had broken bones that had mended, but imperfections in the healing process prevented true recovery of flight. There was also the problem of "permanent wing droop," a condition that made the birds cosmetically unviable for public viewing. Real zoological parks did not want them. Displayed inside a glass case was the most anyone could hope for them now.

The owls were densely feathered, even on their legs and toes. They were splendid, but also in some way preposterous. As the hopping alternated with clumsy walking, Darren thought they looked more like children waddling around in snowsuits than magnificent white owls. Indeed, they were like children—children placed and forgotten in a bleak, edge-of-the-world camp. Or children locked up in closets and discovered at eight years of age, unable to speak or make eye contact.

"One is missing," Byron said, looking around.

Even so, a closet, a camp—wouldn't those be better than the provincial museum?

Byron was turning slowly, scanning the perimeter of the enclosure, while the male owl continued whistling. "Now and then one gets carried over the fence if it's very gusty. Or, of course, it exits through one of the gates. But they always hang around outside and wait for me. Oh, there, look."

Several hundred metres away, outside the enclosure, an animal was coming over the hummocky ground and, like the ones inside, occasionally jumping up and attempting flight.

Byron went back out the gate and dropped onto the ground to wait for the returning owl. Seeing Byron, the owl hesitated, then continued towards the compound. It reached the fence and pressed up against it, as though there was the possibility it would give way, and Byron circled out a short distance before coming back for it. When he was just a few feet away, the owl turned over onto its back, its huge soft wings fell open and it presented Byron with its black talons. Byron tugged a heavy glove out of his back pocket and handed it to the owl, as one might hand a favourite blanket to a sleepy child, and with a motion that seemed almost gluttonous in its speed and readiness, both talons reached out to clasp the glove.

Byron leaned over and grabbed the owl's legs and carried it like a farmyard chicken back inside the compound.

During this the whistling male had grown silent. Darren was again struck by the juxtaposition of beauty and silliness. Though alive, imperious, and at this moment in no danger, the male was useless at flying, a failure at hunting. For fifteen years it had been fed rats, and not even live rats. First, Byron whacked them once or twice over the edge of a table.

The owl looked at Darren, blinked and its head swivelled so that it was facing behind itself. It did this several times while Darren stared at it. Then it leaned forward and hooted. Its body throbbed with each note.

"Don't look directly at him," Byron said. A certain tone in his voice—protectiveness, vexation—reminded Darren that huge changes were coming to Byron.

It was time to go. Darren headed back towards Byron. When he reached him he put his hand on his shoulder and was shocked when Byron flinched, as though it had been a long time since he'd been touched. Certainly not here, where instinct mandated each animal recoil from his touch.

Three Bird Haiku

Kathleen Knowles

BLACK-CAPPED CHICKADEE

Flirt, dance, tease the snow
Cheeky chatter, can't catch me
I won't marry you

NORTHERN FLICKER

Skyward, pole, strut, bow
Scarlet cap, cashmere sweater,
hammer madly, shriek.

BOREAL OWL

Dusk, a furtive swoop
Swivel, amber stare enchants
Deep green secrets kept

Historical Sites, 1992

BERNICE MORGAN

ON THE SECOND day of our drive up the Northern Peninsula, my husband and I, our daughter and son-in-law stop at the Port au Choix archeological site. It is one of those cool days we get in Newfoundland even in summertime. There is no sun, but a shimmering brightness, a luminescence that comes from pre-dawn rain, fills the little cove. On the wet bushes each leaf is distinct and the blue-grey rocks are splashed with impossibly bright, mustard-coloured lichen. Beyond the cove the ocean stretches away, polished pewter glimmering up to the coast of Labrador.

In the middle of a large square that has been cut into the bog, we hunch gazing into the cupped hand of the archeologist. It is a young hand but rough and grimy. The object she holds is small and white, so delicately carved that it might be a piece of jewellery.

"An arrowhead we uncovered this morning," she says. She touches the serrated edge; "Dorset Eskimo—2,000 to 3,000 years old—beautiful work."

We ask to hold the thin triangle, passing it from hand to hand as the young woman tells us about people who have lived on this peninsula at different times. The first inhabitants, she says, were the Maritime Archaic Indians who crossed over from Labrador at least 4,200 years ago. Three of their cemeteries have been found.

"Eskimo people occupied this particular site," she says, gesturing around us at the dig, which is carefully divided into a grid with white string. "The Eskimo came after the Indians—about 2,500 years ago. For over six hundred years some of them—a large family or group of families probably—camped right here every summer . . ."

I am the last to get the arrowhead, holding it as the archeologist talks. But I have stopped listening. I squat on my heels, the rich, warm smell of bog rising all around me, and with my scant knowledge of history try to imagine what was happening in the world on the day the object in my hand was being carved. Europe and the Americas would have been separate worlds, each undreamt of by the other. But somewhere no doubt people had been fighting, over land, over trade, over religion. The classical age of Greece was about to begin, Rome had not become a world power and Jesus would not be born for 500 years.

And here, right where I am kneeling, someone had spent the day carving an arrowhead. Man or woman, they had enjoyed the work—had taken time to incise a beautiful, unnecessary pattern into the stone. A person who could take that much time shaping something as mundane as an arrowhead must have felt safe, very secure. And why not—after setting up summer camps here for six hundred years? I, who live in a country that six days ago celebrated its 125th birthday, try to imagine what it must be like to know your family has occupied the same piece of land for 600 years.

My daughter nudges me. "We have to go if we want to see the icebergs before suppertime."

We thank the young woman (the other workers, each hunched over a square of earth, have not looked up) and walk back to the road where the car is parked. We turn back towards a pencilled sign we'd seen earlier: "Icebergs $1.00."

Until yesterday our son-in-law had never seen an iceberg. We are eager to get a closer look, to impress him with their size. He says the sign may be a joke—a dollar seems like a very small amount for a boat trip. We tell him that's just one-way, it will cost a hundred dollars to get back.

The sign is still there, brown cardboard pinned to a lightpole, pointing us down a dirt lane towards the sea. It is a short lane. On one side is the sea, grey fishing sheds and wharves—a timeless scene. The other side of the road is a small suburb, six or seven modern houses with flower beds and tidy lawns. Outside the last house two little girls sit beside an upturned box, watching as we drive up. They wear jeans and Fido Dido T-shirts. The sun has come out and the smallest girl peers at us over a huge pair of fluorescent-framed sunglasses.

My husband stops the car and nominates me to negotiate. I walk across the road. "Is this where the iceberg tours are?"

The children nod solemnly and point down to the front of the box on which "Icebergs $1.00" has been written in red marker. "What do you get for a dollar and how long does it take?" I ask.

The girls, who seem very well-organized, take turns speaking. They will lead us on a hike along the path, down past the cliffs, show us all the icebergs and a rock, "Just like your grandmother's chair." They are proud of their outport, enthusiastic about their tour—but obviously more taken with the rock than with icebergs. There is also a rock like a chimney that the sea blows right up through. The tour will take about an hour, or maybe (this after seeing my dismay) half an hour.

Knowing that I am making a decision I will always regret, I tell them that we will not have time for their tour today, that we had hoped to go out in a boat to see the icebergs up close.

"Our Daddy can do that!" the youngest one says cheerfully. She points towards a shed across the road beside which three men peer thoughtfully under the raised hood of a pickup truck.

The youngest of the three is the girls' father. He introduces himself as Jim Skanes. He is a good-looking man, brown as an Indian, with pale grey eyes and a slow smile. He doesn't seem to know how much to ask for a trip out to the icebergs. Ten dollars, he says at first, but we eventually bargained up to twenty for the four of us. He tells us that this tour stuff is the girls' idea. "It's summertime and the youngsters are a bit idle," he says.

The other, older men are amused by his embarrassment, "Go on, Jim, I knows now you don't put the young ones up to it—haulin' in money from innocent mainlanders!"

Protesting the label—explaining that only Andy is a mainlander—we follow Jim into the shed that separates the road from the wharf. Inside the shed, which Jim calls a store, nets are looped over beams, rope coiled in barrels and red floats stacked in a huge bin. When I remark on how tidy everything is he makes a non-committal sound, passes us each a life jacket and leads us out the back door onto the wharf.

Two boys, nine or ten years old, are lying on their stomachs trying to jig fish from under the wharf. One boy jumps up. "Can me and Ian go Dad? Can we go, too?" He begins to unknot the rope that ties a fibreglass boat to the wharf.

Jim leaps into the boat and we four follow slowly, climbing carefully down a ladder nailed to the side of the wharf.

"Can me and Ian come?" the boy asks again.

His father says "No"—very briskly—holding out his hand for the rope.

"Frig!" The boy tosses the rope to his father and turns away. He looks as if he is about to cry. The child's disappointment surprises me. Surely he must have ridden in the boat a hundred times.

The man catches my eye as he starts the motor. "He's used to doin' whatever I do in summertime," he says.

We pull away from the wharf, the motor roars to life, Jim makes a great, flamboyant swoop around a dozen or more fishing boats anchored midstream, then heads towards open water.

Outside the protection of the hills the bow of the boat rises on the crest of each wave, hurtles forward, pauses a second, then hits the water with a resounding thump. Coming down from one of these falls my bottom misses the seat and I topple backward.

"Rough, isn't it?" I say, wanting to be reassured.

"Not what you'd really call rough," Jim smiles as I scramble back onto the seat.

Out here on the water he is relaxed, confident. He stands in the stern, holding the tiller lightly, talking and pointing, explaining the different kinds of ice that come down the coast each season. We sit, facing away from him, looking past the bow of the boat to the icebergs, great towering things, glittering white, with gashes through which aquamarine light glows. Frightening, but beautiful and still, tall as skyscrapers even in July.

"The three over there are grounded—but that small one," he points to a low iceberg, looking for all the world like a jet plane half-submerged in black water, "that one's a floater. Deadly. We'll have to move our traps before nightfall or she'll tear them up."

This is 1992, the cod moratorium has just been announced, we are surprised there are traps in the water. We twist around shouting questions over our shoulders. Asking what people up here think of the moratorium, asking what kind of traps he's got out.

"Cod right now," he shouts back. "We hardly got any lobster this year. Now all hands got one or two cod traps out just in case—but there's no cod. I don't s'pose fifty pound of cod been caught between us this month."

"But what about the moratorium?" my husband asks.

"The moratorium stops just east of us—on the other side of the cape. It doesn't affect us—be better if it did. At least then we'd know where we stand."

"What are you going to do?" A terrible thing to ask—but how can one not ask?

"I don't know." Without taking his eyes off the horizon he shakes his head.

There is a prolonged silence until Jim remembers his duties as tour guide. "That's Cape Bauld over there, the most northerly part of Newfoundland. In my father's time used to be hundreds of fishing boats put in there every spring on their way to the Labrador." He tells us a story about some great meeting of pirates that once took place on the Cape, how they fell to fighting and, according to rumour, buried golden goblets looted from a Spanish castle. The man is a good storyteller. Andy comments that maybe he should go into the tour business full time.

"I doubt there's a living in it. Besides my mind 'ed always be on fishin'," he says and tells us the government's got a retraining program for fishermen; he doesn't think much of it. "The wife got a brother up in Ontario—a journeyman carpenter—and he can't find work. What hope's up there for the likes of me!"

Jim hopes he'll be able to get at least a part-time job on one of the boats monitoring foreign fishing inside Canadian waters. "There's lots of them out there," he says, "scoopin' up whatever's left. But then the government's cuttin' back on surveillance and research too. Last year I was lucky enough to get six months on a government research vessel. It takes me away from home but at least I'd be able to hold onto my house and boats."

As we come back into the shelter of the harbour he points to a bright blue trap skiff with a white engine house. "That's my other boat—built her myself two years ago."

The blue boat is beautiful, about thirty feet long and riding high out of the water; there is not a scratch or chip in her wooden sides. "She's a beauty," my husband says. We look from the boat to Jim with awe—to be able to say, so casually, with so little pride, "I built her"—as if it was the most ordinary thing in the world for a man to do!

"Yeah, she's a nice boat—the wife says I put too much into her—but I enjoyed the work. Hardly use her now, though—it's cheaper to run this one."

When we come alongside the wharf the boys are waiting. Jim's son catches our rope and knots it around the piling. His friend Ian helps me get up the ladder.

We are the awkward ones now. Trying to select the most palatable of the weak, hopeful phrases that come to mind. In the end we just say thank you, shake Jim's hand, pay him and scurry back to our car feeling vaguely ashamed.

The box with its sign is still there but the girls have gone. I hope they have captured someone to take on their tour.

One day travellers will find this place, tourists or archaeologists; different people in that distant unimaginable time will walk down this very lane. They will find signs of human habitation, dive for bits of Jim's boat, marvelling at the man's skill, the pride he must have felt carving out the long planks. Digging in his wife's garden they will unearth strange objects, unknown seeds, plastic toys, nails and shards of glass, broken cups and a mysterious sign that, when finally decoded, will read: "Icebergs $1.00."

Seasonal Rites

Geraldine Chafe Rubia

Walking to the car, I see I have forgotten
to remove the ice grip from the tip of my cane
though it is June and the only ice
expected—hoped for by tour operators—is bergs
along the coast to lure tourists
but I leave the winter gadget in place,
tuck my cane in the car,
drive right on The Boulevard then left and left
again, Quidi Vidi Lake on one side swishy waves,
ducks and gulls and pigeons, rowers in racing shells
practising for the Royal Regatta
and on my right Her Majesty's Pen
adjacent to the Anglican Cemetery where
I almost catch sight of my father's grave
awaiting the pot of geraniums I will anchor
there for the Flower Service in July
never knowing if they will stay in place
or be stolen for somebody else's plot
then steeply at the top of Lakeview Avenue I ease
left, pick up speed, slow to 30 when required,
slower past Historic Mallard Cottage
ANTIQUES and collectibles . . . Closed today Open tomorrow
slower again to gawk at the reds yellows pinks of real

and fake petunias marigolds bleeding hearts in beds,
pots, and planters in the yard and on top of the fence
of the house that come Christmas will be festooned
with strings of lights eclipsing the stars
making me muse if these seasonal rites will cut short
or prolong the life of the man and his house
and I give Barrows Road Brewery scarcely a glance
before I turn left to a gravel clearing, stop and gaze
out past the granite portal of Quidi Vidi Gut
to the heaving indigo triangle of Atlantic sea.

All in a Day's Work

KATHLEEN KNOWLES

"SWEET JESUS, I'M fucked." Jimmy Boyle was muttering to himself as he released a rolling billow of smoke and flicked his cigarette butt to the ground. He was crouched behind a boulder two thirds of the way up the rocky hillside that rises steeply beside Quidi Vidi Gut, a sheltered, fifteen-metre-wide pocket of the Atlantic on the eastern edge of St. John's. Squinting around the side of the rock Jimmy could see several abandoned fishing sheds down by the water's edge. Beyond them was the Flake House Restaurant, an elegant, glass-fronted structure, the type of establishment that Jimmy had never had occasion to see from the inside. He could make out at least twenty rifles balanced on the railing of the restaurant balcony. They were all manned, and all pointed in his direction. In addition, marksmen were stationed at strategic points around the shoreline, past the Quidi Vidi Brewery and down as far as the narrow passageway that leads to the open Atlantic.

"Holy shit. I figgered the entire Constabulary would be up to the Regatta all day pickin up the drunks and pickpockets. Last year I made a couple hundred bucks on Regatta Day. Sure, I said to meself. It's a perfect day for a flit—everyone up in the tower watchin the races, mad they even has to work today. Walked right through the main lobby of Her Majesty's Penitentiary and out the front door, then scooted around into the Anglican cemetery and out the other side onto the fairgrounds. Nobody even noticed. Missed the first few races, but watched a good number before headin over to the beer tent to snatch a few tickets while buddy was studyin a ripe young lady in a grand bathing suit, what there was of it."

Jimmy had been an inmate at the penitentiary several times. He was on friendly terms with the guards, who often included him in their poker games. In return he caused no trouble, and, just to show them he didn't hold a grudge, occasionally bought them a beer at the local pub when he was on the outside. His longest visit hadn't even been his fault. On a dare, he'd borrowed a car, a spiffy white Caddy, from the parking lot of The Growlers Lounge, and had been enjoying a leisurely tour around town until some fool pedestrian, drunk as a priest, had forced him to swerve and smash into a parked car. He had bounced off that car, then hit two others, the second a police cruiser, before coming to an undignified stop. He had been livid, and always claimed the police had been illegally parked.

Today, Wednesday August 4, was a large, hot day, much too fine a day to spend cooped up. Jimmy had escaped and prowled through the crowd during the morning, trying his luck at a few games of chance. He had won a fluffy pink elephant at darts and given it to a scrawny young girl who had been leaning against the side of a concession stand looking bored, hot and miserable. His reward had been her shy, delighted smile. Her mother, a spider-faced hag with a cigarette hanging from the corner of her thin, scarlet lips, was wearing shorts and a halter top that Jimmy thought would have looked more becoming on the stuffed elephant. "Dear God, please let them strings stay tied up until I'm out of sight of it," he had whispered to himself.

By midafternoon he'd pilfered a few hot dogs from a busy vendor distracted by an argument with some green-haired teenagers, and escaped to his quiet little hideaway down in the Gut. But they'd found him. "Mother o' God all I did was rob old lady Johnson o' fifty bucks for a two-four and a pack o' cigarettes. A guy has a right to a beer and a smoke. Imagine, me own landlady turning me in to the cops. She's a hard ticket, she is. It's her fault anyways. Her's and the govermint's. They cut off me EI 'pretending investigation,' whatever that's about, and she charges me an arm and a leg for me rent. What am I s'posed to do? But one night in Her Majesty's hotel is all I'm after puttin up wit this time. No, I'll not be spendin the summer months in that musty old hole. They won't take me alive. I'll just drag meself up the hill here rock by rock, slow like, till I'm over to the other side and away."

Jimmy eased himself cautiously from behind the rock, doubled over to keep as close to the ground as he could, and was starting to inch towards the next one, a couple of metres away, when an explosion tore into the silence. He hurled himself backwards to his hiding place.

"All right, me son. We're into it now. I'll be kilt for sure and me poor mother will be after findin out her only son died on the run, a criminal. For me dear Mother's sake I better give meself up."

On the balcony of the Flake House the group of twenty-four men and women that had gathered were also stunned by the booming sound. They stared at one another in disbelief. Several of the group lived in St. John's and were dressed in jeans or shorts and T-shirts. The notable exception was a lawyer who had been summoned from the courthouse for this emergency situation and was still wearing his flowing courtroom gown. The other members of the team had flown in from various parts of North America, one from as far away as southern California, and had the expensively casual dress and confident bearing that only money, buckets of money, can buy. He had arrived in St. John's on an early morning flight following a call from his local contact, the lawyer in the robes. "What the Hell was that?" he demanded. The lawyer shook his head.

"Signal Hill Tattoo," he replied. "Guns go off every afternoon."

"Well can't you stop them? The noise must be scaring him half to death."

"Stop the tattoo? It's part of our heritage, like traffic cops and church-run schools. You might just as well try to get the city councillors to agree to, well, to anything at all, in fact, as stop the tattoo."

As they spoke, Jimmy Boyle emerged from his hiding place wearing badly crumpled jeans and a Montreal Canadiens shirt he'd picked up from the grass at the Regatta. Too long in the sleeves, he had thought after he took it. I'm after losin me touch. Used to have a better eye for size than that. His peaked cap proclaimed his loyalty to Labatt's Blue. Like the rings on the trunk of a tree, the creases in Jimmy's broad face, an unshaven face that was radiating a pink glow as a result of his few hours in the sun, measured his forty-eight years. On a sunny day his freckles multiplied exponentially, so that by August of a good summer they merged to form a mask that stretched from his chin, upwards past his impenetrable eyebrows, and on to his thinning whitish-blonde hair, hair that had once been a flaming symbol of his Irish heritage. His nose, an obviously once-broken, veiny bulb, and his generous paunch described his lifestyle; and a jagged scar on his forehead, obtained when a buddy had pushed him onto the sidewalk in an unprovoked attack one night, told a large part of his history. Not visible was a tattoo, a skull and crossbones on his left forearm, the result of another dare, this time from a crew member of a Portuguese fishing trawler.

Jimmy stretched himself to his full height of five-foot-five, squared his shoulders, gave an experienced yank at the seat of his pants, and began marching down the hill and towards the guns, his arms up, his stubby, nicotine-stained fingers pointing towards the sky.

"Okay, boys. Calm down now. I'll go peaceful like."

And from the crowd at the restaurant: "Who is that? What the Hell's he doing?"

"Damned if I know."

They started waving frantically at Jimmy, but he was determined to go through with his surrender.

"I'm not givin ya any excuse t' shoot, boys. I'm not armed."

"Guy must be drunk from the Regatta. I'll try and head him off."

The speaker, a music professor at Memorial University, hurled his equipment to the floor of the balcony, descended the stairs three at a time, then virtually flew in Jimmy's direction. When he reached the shoreline he got down on all fours and bounced his way as fast as he could towards him. Jimmy was confused. Sure he was giving himself up. What more did they want? He'd pay back his landlady and everything could go back to normal. It's not like it was the first time they'd worked things out. His stomach clenched. Was she so poisoned with him that she'd told them he'd done something else? Something violent? The bitch. He'd fix her good this time. By now the professor was close enough that Jimmy could hear him.

"Get down. Get down."

There was a tension in the air that Jimmy was having difficulty interpreting.

"I said I give up. Take me back to Her Majesty's Hotel if you please. Call off your guns."

As Jimmy spoke, a very small gull flew up from the water and landed on a rock on the opposite side of the Gut. The professor gasped and then continued in a hysterical stage whisper, "What are you talking about? Who are you? You've just scared up the rarest gull in North America. You should be put in jail. Please just get out of the way so we can all get a good look in our telescopes."

"Telescopes?"

"Yes. There's birdwatchers here from all over North America trying to see it and take pictures. You're in the way."

"Birdwatchers? You're not the cops?"

"What are you talking about? Please, just stay out of the way."

"Right on, me son. You got it. I'll just be on me way then."

The professor stood up and raced back to the restaurant. By now the sights of all telescopes had been turned to the rock on which the gull had settled. It was obviously nervous, stretching its neck upwards and darting quick looks from side to side, ready to take off immediately if necessary.

Jimmy trailed after the professor, his panic forgotten, replaced by his instinctive curiosity.

"So, they'd be good eatin, then, would they?"

"What? My God no! They're just rare. We all want to look at it and add it to our lists."

"Lists? You keep lists of everythin what you eats?"

"We're not going to eat it. We just want to look at it and photograph it."

"Now why would that be, if you don't mind me askin?"

"To have the slide to look at and show to people and know that we've seen a really rare bird."

"Right on, I gets it."

Jimmy kept tagging along. "Boy, I've got me a live one here," he thought. "He's escaped same as I have, I'd say, but not from no penitentiary." By now they were back on the balcony of the restaurant. The birders were in a frenzy.

"Speaking of birds, get a load of that ripe young one over there in that grand bathing suit . . . what there is of it," he says. But his observation goes unnoticed by the birders.

"Notice that lovely subtle pink? Gorgeous bird."

"Yeah," wheezed the professor. "I thought at first it was just a Little Gull, but decided to take a closer look. When I saw the pink tinge and the remnants of a black neck ring I broke out in a cold sweat. I ran to that tiny house over there and asked to use their phone for an emergency. Within ten minutes these three guys arrived and confirmed it was Ross's Gull. The ultimate gull, and in almost full breeding plumage."

He hopped around as he spoke, illustrating his story with twitchy hand movements and knocking over a plastic garden chair. Jimmy was intrigued. He'd latched onto the professor, who, although definitely crazy, didn't seem dangerous at all.

"Excuse me, again, sir. Are you sayin that this bird belongs to some one named Ross?"

"What? No. This is a species of gull that's normally found only in the high Arctic. This is the first appearance ever recorded in St. John's."

"Oh. I gets it now. You're after tryin to capture it and put it in a cage and charge people money to see it."

"No. We're just going to watch it."

"And why would that be, then?"

Before the professor could attempt an explanation, one of the birders, a surgeon from New York, exclaimed:

"Damn. I'm out of film. Where's the nearest place I can get some?"

"Not today, me son. Pleased to meet you. James Aloysius Boyle's me name. I was out for a short stroll here this evenin, sat down there by a rock to enjoy the view, maybe jot down a few short poems if the spirit moved me, when I saw you folks up here settin up yer telescopes. Knowed right off there must be another one of them rare birds around. But about yer film. Regatta Day—ya won't get none. Oldest sportin event in North America. Every year, first Wednesday in August, weather permittin, we has a go at it just up the road at Quidi Vidi Lake. You should go up and see some o' the races. Grand bit o' fun that. And lots of food and beer."

The doctor ignored him and turned to the professor: "What about the film?"

"He's right, John. The city closes up tighter than a Pentecostal on Regatta Day."

"The whole town closes up?"

Jimmy interrupted: "Yes sir, my son. Indeed it do. Here in St. John's we have celebrated the Royal St. John's Regatta since . . .

"O my God. Look, look, it's taking off."

The extremely rare Ross's Gull flew up again, with twenty-four pairs of binoculars and Jimmy Boyle's amazed gaze following its flight line, and disappeared over the hill in the direction of the lake. Silence for a second. Then: "Well, let's go. We'll have to walk. We won't get a car back through all the traffic up there now."

With amazing speed, telescopes were dismounted and tripods folded, and the entire party took off on foot out to Quidi Vidi Village Road to cover the 0.2 kilometres to the foot of Quidi Vidi Lake. Jimmy now considered himself a member of the group and followed along, waving to the residents of Quidi Vidi Village who were enjoying their Regatta Day beer and barbecue in their front gardens.

"We're after chasin a rare bird up to the lake, boys. First time we ever got one here in St. John's. Come on, join the fun."

Most people just waved and went back to their beer, but seven or eight young kids and two dogs of indeterminate ancestry followed along, a rambunctious group, bored with their parents' partying.

And so it was a strange parade that approached Quidi Vidi Lake. The gangly professor was first, running, a large, navy blue camera bag on his left shoulder, telescope and tripod under his right arm. His binoculars were bouncing on his chest and his hat was secured to his bald head by an elastic under his chin. The rest of the birders, including the still-be-gowned lawyer, followed at varying speeds. Then came Jimmy strutting ahead of the brood of youngsters, who were darting between parked cars and dancing a jig as they sang the Regatta anthem "Up The Pond."

The lower end of Quidi Vidi Lake is usually a quiet place, home to a motley assortment of ducks that live there year-round, but today the area was overflowing with Regatta Day crowds. Picnickers lined the grassy shoreline areas, camper vans and barbecues were set up in the gravel of the parking area, and walkers and joggers of every shape known to mankind, and some never before seen, formed a steady procession along the boardwalk trail that skirts the edge of the lake. Herring gulls hovered, hoping for handouts, but the Ross's Gull was nowhere to be seen. The birders infiltrated the crowd and spread out in two groups, one on each side of the lake, and proceeded to surround it, binoculars at the ready in case of any unusual movement.

The professor led a group to the south side, and by the time they approached the boathouse and main fairground area the crowd was overwhelming. Within five seconds the professor started to twitch and hop around as he turned to the lawyer.

"There it is. On the boathouse. My God, it must be terrified."

The Ross's Gull had perched on the roof of the Quidi Vidi boathouse and was surveying the throngs of people who were moving back and forth portaging boats on their heads and hauling other rowing paraphernalia. Dozens more fair-goers sat around talking and eating, both on the balcony and on the ground level area by the chip wagon that was belting out a lively jig in competition with the Church Lads' Brigade Band that was performing at the other end of the lake.

The professor signalled to the birders close behind him, who began converging on the boathouse urging people, with little success, to be quiet and move away from the structure, and gave five dollars each to two of Jimmy's remaining band to race to the north side of the lake and tell the others that the gull had been located.

Jimmy had been following along half-heartedly, more interested in people-watching than birdwatching, and he was now observing a major domestic squabble. A large Airstream trailer with Ontario licence plates was parked in the lot by the boathouse, and a man and a woman in matching jogging suits were standing by the door having a disagreement of a calibre that only many years of marriage can achieve.

"I told you to have that camera checked out before we left Toronto. But no, you couldn't be bothered, could you?"

"I checked it myself. The test roll was just fine. Something's happened to it since then."

"O sure, now blame it on me."

"Did I say it was your fault? What do you want me to do? Kill myself?"

"You do that and leave me in this godforsaken province with the kids and I'll never forgive you. I spent all that money on film and now we have a camera that doesn't fucking work. That's great, just great. What a wonderful vacation this turned out to be."

As she yelled, the woman, her face distorted into a caricature, hurled a yellow plastic bag onto a nearby picnic table and stomped off into the van, slamming the door behind her. Her husband sighed, ran his fingers through his hair, and then followed her inside where the argument continued.

Jimmy strolled casually over to the picnic table and walked around it, eyeing the plastic bag. The tips of his fingers were tingling. Without hesitating, he deftly scooped up the bag, at the same time commenting to an elderly lady watching from a bench: "There it is. Knowed I left me lunch somewheres. I'm lucky it weren't stolen. Good day to ya, missus."

And off he strode. When he was safely behind a row of shrubs he peeked into the bag.

"Yes, me son," he exclaimed. "The luck o' the Irish is wit me today. And them from Ontario t' boot."

By now all the birders had assembled at the boathouse and were attempting to set up their tripods and cameras among the swarms of people. Amazingly, the gull was still on the ridge of the roof. Jimmy casually approached the New York surgeon who was watching the bird through his binoculars, his Nikon camera with a four-hundred-millimetre lens attached hanging like an albatross around his neck.

"Excuse me, sir. About your film problem. Just happens I have a buddy what owns a camera shop in town. We go back a long ways, went to St. Pat's together, we did. Anyways, just fer me he opened 'er up this evenin when I explained yer predicamint, so to speak. To make a long story short, I was able to get some film fer ya. Sure it might not be the right kind, mind you, but it's the best I could manage under the extenuatin circumstances." He now had the man's complete attention.

"What? Let me see. That's amazing. How much do I owe you?"

"Well, I'm not just sure now. Me buddy said I could pay him next week. He didn't want to be bothered openin up the cash and all that sort of stuff today, since he was officially closed and all. I guess whatever ya usually pays would be just fine."

"Well, let's see. I can't believe it. And a whole bag. Let's see, there's ten rolls in here. In New York these rolls sell for about twenty dollars each. So I guess I owe you two hundred dollars. Would that be okay?"

"I guess that would be about right," answered Jimmy, and watched in amazement as the man opened his wallet.

"Would you prefer Canadian money?"

"Indeed I would, me son, sir. Don't trust no foreign money."

"Right. Well, here's your two hundred plus another twenty for your trouble. I really do appreciate it. Newfoundlanders are as friendly and helpful as everyone says."

"No trouble at all, me son. Glad to help out."

Jimmy was about to take off when the crowd suddenly became very quiet. He shoved the money into his back pocket just as a tallish man holding a microphone approached the surgeon.

"Hello, sir. My name's Karl Wells and I'm doing a live television report from the Regatta. I understand there's a very rare bird on the boathouse."

"Yes. That's correct. It's a Ross's Gull, normally found only in the Arctic."

Jimmy was trying to back into the crowd, but the birder grabbed his arm. "And I want to publicly thank this gentleman here who saved the day for me. I was completely out of film and he managed to get a friend of his to open up his shop and get some for me so that I didn't miss the chance of a lifetime for a picture of a Ross's." Jimmy pretended to be removing something from his left eye and turned as far away from the camera as he could.

"Nuttin at all," he mumbled, and ducked into the crowd, this time successfully.

"I guess he's shy, folks. Well that's it at the Regatta for this year. And now back to Debbie in the studio."

The crowd thinned out a bit as the television crew moved off. Jimmy was already at the far end of the lake crouched behind a dumpster outside the stadium.

"Jesus! All I need is them guards at the Pen to be watchin the news. And me all over the screen. I better get outa here. Maybe I'll go back home. They'd never look for me there, what with the old lady so riled up at me."

Stopping only once to rest and have a few beers at a poorly lit pub on an alley off Duckworth Street, he made his way back over to Springdale Street. He coaxed open the door of Mrs. Johnson's rooming house as gently as he could, and tiptoed into the vestibule. She was ready for him, all five-feet-eight of her, and she was spitting piss and vinegar. She started in at him in her harsh, brassy bawl.

"I knowed you'd show up here Jimmy Boyle, ya sleeveen. I seed yer ugly mug all over the TV screen, ya actin like a hero. 'What's he been up to now,' I says to meself. I'm callin the cops right now. Ya won't rob me again."

"Well now Mrs. Johnson. Just a minute here. S'pose I was to give ya back yer fifty, and fifty on top of it fer bein so kind to the likes o' meself."

"And where'd ya be after gettin that kind o' money, Jimmy Boyle?"

"All in a day's work. All in a day's work, missus. Ya want it or not?"

"Give it here, then."

"Not so fast, now, duckie. Tomorrow when the cops comes lookin fer me, you'll be after droppin the charges, I guess."

"Jimmy Boyle, you're a sly bugger. All right, all right. Give me the money then."

"Deal."

Jimmy left the house and headed straight to The Growlers. The bartender greeted him with surprise.

"How's she goin, Jimmy? Thought you were back inside."

"No way, Skipper. It was just a misunderstandin. A misunderstandin, that's all. A round fer all hands now, on me."

Writer Wanted

Anne Ferncase

I want to write a poem,
one that stops the heart,
has the focus of a ruby-throated
hummingbird
feathered and sweet breathing
hovered over
honeysuckle

Here I sit, rattling paper,
not writing
that perfect poem
but thinking about it,
thinking very hard,
almost tasting
that perfect
word.

Practical Catholics, Budding Atheists

PEGGY SMITH KRACHUN

EVEN THEN, HOW much did I really believe? I know people suffer horrendous psychological damage, sometimes even physical damage, from religious beliefs and rituals imposed on them when they're young and impressionable. I may be more fortunate than many of my generation. That's not to say I don't have my share of unsavoury memories—but looking back, I'm just not sure how seriously I took it all. I do know that by the time my moment of truth arrived—when a priest refused me absolution because I was taking birth control pills—I felt no great wrench in deciding that this was it, I was finished with all that nonsense. It was as I vaguely remember, a real non-event.

Maybe my particular religious upbringing made it easier. I grew up in a small town in eastern Newfoundland that was almost 100 percent Roman Catholic at the time. There was some piety floating around, to be sure, but people were definitely not fundamentalists or Bible-thumpers. We paid lip service. We obeyed the rules, in varying degrees. In church we knelt, stood, sat, prayed and blessed ourselves on cue. At Mass the priest read a passage from one of the Gospels or Epistles, sometimes followed by a related sermon. That was the extent of my knowledge of the Bible. I'm not even sure if we had one in the house, but if we did, it wasn't dragged out to hit anyone over the head with (literally or figuratively). The fear of God was not instilled in us to keep us away from sex, for example, because sex was never discussed.

I took Latin for five years in school; it was an accomplishment to know another language (albeit a dead one) and I liked the fact that I understood some of the church liturgy. I sang in choir and loved the hymns; I still think that if you ignore the words, the melodies are amongst the most wonderful music ever written. I hung on to Midnight Mass long after I ceased any other practice of religion, but when they moved it from 12 a.m. Christmas morning to 9 p.m. Christmas Eve, my reason for going ended. Celebrated at the witching hour, it added magic to the season that I've never felt since.

Within my family, religion was not very oppressive. Some things were taken for granted, of course. We had to go to Mass every Sunday, under pain of mortal sin, and besides, where else could we show off a new hat or coat? My mother—who, I know now, struggled with unbelief, although she would never come out and admit it in those years—made some attempts to get us to do more, like go to Mass on weekdays, or (boys only, of course) serve on the altar. The fear of God may have played some small part in this. But much more compelling motives, I think, were to keep on the good side of the priests and nuns—who could make or break us—and to try to earn the same respect they gave the "better" families in town (who were, coincidentally, also the most well-off families in town).

We were, above all, practical Catholics, my mother being the most practical of all. Her genuine wish for us, her children, to don the cloth and habit cannot be accounted for in any way but by other-worldly fervour. It was, again, partly to keep up with the Joneses (in this case the Mahers and the Murphys), but mainly because she desired a better life for us. To a woman who had given birth to eleven children in the space of fifteen years, the sterile, safe and comfortable convent life was something to which any sensible girl should aspire. (In later years, when many priests were found to be pedophiles, and women—some pregnant—left the convent in droves, we were vindicated, and took great pleasure in bringing it up: "Now, Mom, aren't you glad I didn't disgrace you *that* way? I only got divorced.")

Remember the Catholic campaign with the slogan, "The family that prays together, stays together"? During that period we all had to say the Rosary every night, out loud, en famille. My father, as head of the household, took his responsibility for this fairly seriously, and more so when he was drinking. He would become solemn and pompous, demanding absolute quiet during the recitations of our respective Mysteries (one Our Father, ten Hail Marys, and one Glory Be in each Mystery—utter boredom multiplied by five). The quieter it got, the more uncontrollable became the urge to titter and giggle. My father would rise from his knees, stand ominously over the offenders, silently take us by the hand and lead us to the bedroom, where he would shut the door on us with a meaningful click, leaving us finally free to collapse into the mirth we'd been trying so hard to hold back.

So went my family upbringing, where I was fed, but not force-fed, religion. The official Church organization was another story. My hometown, like millions of others in those days, was ruled by a priest. Father P. was a true ascetic, whose eyes, my mother said, were fixed on heaven. Unfortunately, this made him extremely intolerant of human failings. Coughing in church, for instance, was an insult to God and strictly forbidden; Father P. did not hesitate to make a public example of anyone who broke this rule. He would pointedly stop in the middle of his prayer or sermon and wait for the coughing to cease. Many a poor faithful nearly choked to death trying to hold it in; if they just couldn't, Father P. publicly berated them from the pulpit and ordered them to leave. One older man in an advanced stage of tuberculosis was banished in disgrace, and had to attend church in another town for the brief time he had left.

Females were not allowed to wear slacks in public, even in the dead of winter, because the Blessed Virgin Mary had never worn slacks. (Jesus hadn't either but I never thought of that at the time.) Father P. would drive around at night, looking for lawless girls, ordering them off the street immediately. I don't remember ever getting caught, but I also was not one of the girls he commandeered to help him find those who were breaking his fashion rules. I think this is an illustration of why I escaped without too much damage: I was good but not too good, obedient to a point, but not obsequious. I walked a thin line. I followed the rules but not to the extent of becoming a "pet," which would have ostracized me from my friends who were not from the "respectable" families. In other words, I was *practical*.

We were given the usual line about sin and eternal damnation, but if we ever took it seriously, it lost most of the impact as the years wore on. Hell sounded awful, but to tell the truth, heaven was nothing to look forward to either. Eternity was a scary prospect when you really thought about it. Who wanted to live forever in a place where there was nothing to do except sit around adoring God and listening to angels playing harps? I could see *that* getting old pretty fast. Apparently, there would be no softball, movies, or even food. We were told we wouldn't need any of these things. But the idea of endless time, even in heaven, boggled the mind; I knew I'd go crazy if I kept thinking about it.

The worst punishment for the damned, they told us, far worse than hell's fires (terrible as they were), was to never see the face of God. I thought, well, that's not so bad, I think I can handle it. However, none of this really mattered much, because when you're ten or twelve, you're never going to die anyway.

By the time I was in my teens I must have been suspecting it was all a crock. Every couple of years, Mission Fathers from one order or another paid a visit to terrify us back into holiness. One who made a lasting impression on me—but not for the right reasons—was Father M., a Jesuit and a regular hellfire-and-brimstone preacher. He roared down from the pulpit the sentence that God would roar at us on Judgement Day if we died suddenly and didn't have a chance to repent: TO THE LEFT YOUNG CATHOLIC WOMAN! (The left was hell-bound, while the right was reserved for those going to heaven.) The words did strike fear in me, but only for the moment. Father M. was fortyish with a long sallow face. He was no Elvis Presley; yet there was "something about him" and he was the one we libidinous teenaged girls fell in love with that year. (We were always on the lookout for "hunks," and found them wherever we could; priests were not exempt.) When he talked about impure thoughts and deeds, well, we knew what *that* meant—sort of. This, and the passion with which he thundered his denunciations, fired our imaginations and more, and we'd joke among ourselves about how we'd like to go parking with him in the gravel pit. This is how reverent we were; this is what all the attempted brain-washing did to us.

My mother, though beset by agnosticism, never stopped going to church. She continued to hedge her bets. "Well, why not believe?" she asked me in later years. "It can't hurt. If there *is* something after all, you'll be sure of going to heaven. And if there's not, what's the difference after you're dead?" I said that it probably wouldn't hurt you, *if* you didn't let it rule your life. But, I told her, "I can't just *choose* to believe. I can't *make* myself believe if I don't." She didn't quite agree; she thought we should be able to will ourselves to do it—and no doubt felt some guilt if she couldn't.

It may have been her own ambivalence that helped point some of her children in the direction of atheism or agnosticism. She wondered where she had gone wrong. "Mom," I said, "we got it from you. You raised a family of thinkers. You shouldn't be sad, you should be proud." It's a legacy I appreciate.

I realize that my relatively liberal upbringing must have mitigated most of the adverse effects organized Catholicism had on me. I haven't yet felt the need to be "un-indoctrinated." But I'm sure some damage was done. Persistent guilt, many years later, over the ending of my marriage might be an example ("married in the eyes of God, marriage is forever"). But some have suffered much more than me, and I would never want to downplay their pain.

People living on the east coast of Canada, and particularly in Newfoundland, have always been a pretty practical lot. We've had to be, to survive; it's now in the genes. And we are no less practical about religion than about politics, economics, or anything else. I can't speak for everyone, but I suspect there are many like me. As long as religion served us, fine. And when it no longer served us, we no longer served it. Perhaps that's as good a philosophy as any.

Who I am

LAURA MORRY WILLIAMS

I have taken the words of my life
gathered them into a pile
stacked them,
sorted them, filed them.

I have read them
rearranged them
added them together.
I have taken them, explained them,
studied them, critiqued them.

I've left them
bundled together on a disk
and walked away.
Now that I am away from them,
I don't know if I am here or
home in a drawer.

Only One Regret

FRAN BAIRD INNES

ALICE AND MABEL, two of my mother's sisters, lived in America, but even from that distance, one of them was a constant presence in my life. Her name, Alice Frances, was passed on to me, and as a child I hated it almost as passionately as I loved my aunt. She was Sal to her sisters except when they were mad at her. Then it was— "For heaven's sake, Alice, stop." or "Alice, why did you?" or "You can't do that, Alice."

I first became aware of Aunt Alice one Christmas Eve, when a large parcel arrived at our house. "Oh thank God!" exclaimed Mother. She picked me up and swung me around. "It's a Christmas box all the way from Boston from your Aunt Alice. I was afraid it wouldn't get here in time." She hugged me as if I had performed this miracle. Together, we pulled the box into the parlour and left it under the bare fir tree.

I was three that year. No doubt the parcels from Boston had been arriving regularly before I was old enough to understand how important they were to our family during the Depression. I don't remember what my brother or my parents got from that box but I will never forget my present: a tall-as-me, red stocking bulging with surprises. Hanging out over the top was a blue and white polka-dot elephant with pink floppy ears. Squealing with delight, I danced around with my el-e-flimp. Beautiful and lovable, that toy was my most prized possession throughout my childhood. I still have a thing for elephants.

Aunt Alice spent most of her adult life in Boston, and the boxes, tied up with catgut, a practical adaptation from her nursing profession, kept coming at Christmas, Easter, birthdays and other times for no apparent reason at all, except for the pleasure she got from sending them.

At times, Mother was less than enthusiastic about their contents, like the year she got a half dozen bottles of capers. "What wasteful extravagance," she complained. "Why couldn't Alice send me something sensible like silk stockings?"

I wasn't always pleased with my gifts either. One year I got a one-piece, navy blue snowsuit with pea-green stripes across the top. That may have been the latest thing in Boston to keep an active girl snug and dry, but in Grand Falls it was a curiosity. The boys made my life a misery.

"Here comes the zebra. Run for your life!" they yelled every time I wore the darn thing. Then there was the straw, stovepipe hat which, as a teenager, I was forced to wear to church to my dying shame. But most of the time Aunt Sal managed to bridge the cultural gap between Boston and Grand Falls with things which were only slightly out of the ordinary.

One summer she came back for the first of her many visits. Before she hung up her clothes, she had the household in an uproar. Never one to travel light, her suitcases bulged with everything from the latest fishing gear to her "respectable" bar. Liquor was a touchy subject in our house. Dad, coming from Glasgow, had the Scots love of a wee dram, while Mother and her sisters were brought up by a strict father who was a Methodist lay reader. Mother and I watched as my aunt tossed underwear, the likes of which we had never seen before, on the bed with her sweaters and shoes.

"Oh, here you are," she said, holding up a bottle of Johnnie Walker whiskey.

Mother was shocked. "Alice, what are you doing, bringing liquor into this house?"

"Harry and I are going to have a drink. Now where are those capers I sent you? I'll fix us a few canapes."

"Alice," Mother said, "have you gone square to the devil since you went to Boston? Drinking and smoking and heaven knows what else."

"My cigarettes are menthol; they're good for my hay fever," Alice snapped.

"All I can say is," Mother continued, "that poor Father must be turning over in his grave. And look at the example you are setting the children."

"For heaven's sake, Elsie, there's no harm in a sociable drink. Don't be such a prude. You should have one yourself. It will help you relax."

I adored my Aunt Sal. Curled on her bed (normally my bed) I watched entranced as she unscrewed the cap from a small bottle and painted her nails blood red.

"Can I paint my nails too?"

She showed me how to dip the brush, squeeze it against the side of the bottle and draw it over each nail. The brush kept slipping off my nails onto my fingers.

"Here, let me help you." She gently took my hand, wiped off the mess with some clear smelly stuff and painted my nails. "Now blow on them before they get all smeared." I felt like a queen.

She drew the line at letting me paint my lips. "You know your mother will kill me," she said. So, I had to content myself with watching her open small pots of lip rouge, rubbing a little on each cheek, then choosing the right shade for her lips, to match whatever "creative outfit" she was wearing. "Outrageous outfits" according to my mother. One of Aunt Sal's favourites for an evening party was a grey satin dress with an uneven hemline (de rigueur at that time). The dress was elegant and so quite acceptable to Mother.

"Too dull," said Alice as she draped a fuchsia and red triangular scarf over one hip and added a large sequin pin where it tied at the waist. To complete the look she wound a matching turban around her head of blond, curly hair. For Mother that was the last straw.

"For pity sake, Alice, all you need is a long cigarette holder dangling from your mouth and you'll look like one of Al Capone's molls."

"Oh I have one of those right here." She rummaged in her oversized purse, pulled out a long, black and ivory cigarette holder and stuck in a king-size, menthol cigarette. With a defiant flourish, she flicked on a silver lighter, lit the cigarette, took a deep draw and blew several smoke rings into the air. Mother was speechless at first, then the feathers flew.

"You can't go traipsing around here like that, Alice. People will think you are crazy or even worse, a loose woman."

"Frankly, I don't care what they think. If it's good enough for Boston, it should be good enough for Grand Falls." And so the argument went until Aunt Sal offered a compromise. She took off the turban.

Most of Aunt Sal's fights with her sisters were over clothes. With Mother, because they were too far-out for Grand Falls, and with Mabel, because they were not elegant enough for Detroit.

By the time I was a young woman in 1947 I had gone to live in Toronto. I received a letter there from Aunt Mab urging me to come to Detroit for the wedding of her favourite son, Douglas. "It will be a formal affair," she wrote, "his bride comes from a very wealthy family. She is a lovely girl and I am so thrilled. Do come and don't forget to pack your formal gown. This is strictly black tie and tails."

How could I turn down an invitation like that? I drove to Detroit and arrived at Aunt Mab's house the day before the wedding. Alice had already arrived from Boston. Mabel, who like Mother, was ever suspicious of her sister's choice of clothes, said, "Now that Flick (her pet name for me) is here why don't you model your dresses for the wedding." Alice trotted off upstairs and returned to make her grand entrance. Her ensemble was a 1920s flapper style, emerald green, short silk dress which she wore over a dyed-to-match, long satin slip, added to meet the formal requirement.

Mabel went into hysterics. Crying, pacing, banging her fist in her hand, she screamed at Alice, "You can't wear that thing. I won't have it. You'll make fools of us all and disgrace poor Douggie."

Never as willing to tangle with Mabel as she was with my mother, Aunt Sal muttered, "OK then, I'll stay home because I haven't anything else to wear."

That was not an option for Aunt Mab. Alice, a frequent visitor to Detroit, was well-liked among Mabel's friends and a favourite with the family of the bride.

I managed to restore peace by sending Aunt Mab to bed with aspirins and hot tea after I agreed to take Aunt Sal downtown to buy a suitable, long gown. She found one at Marshall Fields and charged it to Aunt Mabel's account.

Alice had never married, although she did get engaged once. She said she decided not to marry the man because he couldn't stand it if his handkerchief wasn't straight in his breast pocket. She kept the engagement ring, explaining, "I thought I deserved it for putting up with him for as long as I did."

Devoted as she was to her nursing career, Sal pursued many other interests with equal vigour. One of these was horse racing. Come spring, she headed for Suffolk Downs. I visited her in Boston several times while I was a student at Mount Allison University in New Brunswick. On Saturday morning, rain or shine, we went to the races. The leisurely lunch at the track was second only to the serious business of studying the racing forms which she explained to me in great detail. Then we were off to the paddock to look the horses over before she placed her "surefire" bets on the first race of the afternoon. Actually, I got a lot of my education from Aunt Sal.

For many years she was a live-in, private nurse to one of Boston's wealthy families. She was sixty when her last charge died and left her a few thousand dollars for her retirement. She decided if she was to retire, she would do it in style by doubling her money at the race track. Within two years she was broke but unrepentant, having thoroughly enjoyed the gamble and the first years of freedom from responsibility since she was eighteen.

She quit the horses after that and adopted the Boston Red Sox. She became something of a mascot to the team and they named her their number one fan.

Moving out of the uptown neighbourhood where she had spent most of her adult life, she took a modest apartment near the hospital where she nursed for the next ten years. She intended to retire at seventy, but patients kept asking for her, so she stayed on as a private-duty nurse until, at age eighty, an ulcer operation forced her to retire.

The doctors didn't think Aunt Sal would survive the operation but she nursed herself through that one as she had nursed so many of her patients throughout her long career. She returned to Newfoundland where, after eighty-eight years of living, she died of old age.

Shortly before her death, Aunt Sal confided to me that she had only one regret: "I'm going to my grave with my old cherry intact, can you beat it?"

I suspect that was the only Methodist dictum Aunt Sal's rebellious soul couldn't overcome.

A Life Well Lived

ESTHER SLANEY-BROWN

HE REACHED INTO his pocket and pulled out his old pocketknife. He opened the knife, gave it a swift wipe on the leg of his pants. He then bent over and pulled a bright, red beet from his garden. He peeled the beet and passed it to me. I had never seen a beet straight from the garden before.

"Go ahead, try it." He was grinning; his blue, blue eyes twinkled as he watched me as I bit into the bitter, earthy-tasting offering. I tried not to disappoint him as I chewed the most foul-tasting thing I had ever experienced. I continued to gnaw as my hands turned dark red from its juice. I watched as he performed the same task, this time for himself. He bit into his like it was the sweetest apple he had ever eaten.

I lagged behind him as we perused his garden, taking tiny bites as he showed me his carrots, turnips, and blue potatoes growing in perfect rows. He finally noticed my discomfort.

"Just throw it over there where the birds will get it." He always took care of the birds.

"It's OK, they have to eat too." I threw what was left of the slimy mess into the grass at the edge of the garden. He pulled his handkerchief from his pocket and wiped my hands. It didn't do much good. My hands remained dark red.

"Don't worry about it. That'll be gone in a few days." He was a man who worked the soil, and a bit of dirt on his hands only meant he was doing his job. I knew I had to go back to the house where my mother was having tea. My mother—whose vocation in life was to keep her children spotless.

"Come along, I'll show you where the brook is." I had never seen a brook before. My father always brought the water from the back garden at home in Freshwater. I was never permitted to go to that garden.

We trudged along the path till we reached the wooden enclosure. He opened the top and let me look down. I remember how dark and forbidding it looked.

"Whenever you come over here," he told me, "you must stay well away from this place."

It was a good lesson taught by a wise man. He satisfied my curiosity. There was no need for me to wander too close to the brook after that. We walked forever, it seemed, over his land. He showed me where the wild strawberries grew on the side of the hill. I know we talked on that first day when I met him, though I don't remember much of the conversation. I know we talked because we always did. We had become inseparable, that day, my grandfather and me.

What I didn't know at the time was that my parents had bought an old house here in Chapel's Cove and we would be moving in with my mother's parents while my father worked on our new home. For the next three years in his house my grandfather stirred my imagination, comforted me with his presence, and instilled in me a great love for history.

My grandfather had a wooden bench built on one side of the kitchen. When his day's work ended he stretched out on his bench and lit his pipe. My grandparents conversed about the day's happenings as he puffed on his pipe and Nanny put the finishing touches on supper. It became my habit to curl up on the bench with him.

I waited patiently while my grandparents discussed marvelous things I had never heard before. How long more before they sold the calf, which hens were "laid out" and would become Sunday dinner, how the lambs were growing, and that it looked like it was going to be a good year for the potatoes. On and on they chatted while I sat there absorbing the comforting atmosphere. My father worked on "the base" in Argentia. There were potatoes growing in the forbidden back garden, there were a few hens up there somewhere, but the talk about animals and gardens was all new and fascinating to me.

When supper was finished, I would have my turn. While Nanny cleared away, my grandfather and I would escape to the front yard. He would lean over the gate puffing on his pipe. I had to pull myself up to the bottom rail so I could peep over the pickets. With the pipe secured in the side of his mouth, he told me stories.

Stories of caves and dead soldier's bones he found in those caves on the far hills when he was a boy. He told me about the old money and one soldier's medal he found in one of the caves. One day he promised me we would go to the caves and search for treasures. But he was growing old then and his legs would never get him up the hills of Blow Me Down. What he didn't know was that I already had my treasure.

For the next nine years of our lives I followed him every chance I got. We made hay together with handkerchiefs, knots tied on each end, plopped on our heads. I sat with him in the cellar while he cut his seed potatoes. I stood quietly in the stable as he combed Nelson's mane and brushed the sides of his beloved horse. I sat quietly on the bench absorbing his sadness the day he had to sell Nelson. As he grew older and frailer, I sat and listened to the greatest storyteller I will ever know.

I heard stories of his parents' trip from Ireland. He told me our very own family ghost story about his father serving Mass for a dead priest. He told me about the black thornbush in Ireland where his father cut a walking stick for his grandfather—the stick he now used to get around with. He told me of the day when he buried his third baby.

"I promised myself that day," he told me, "I would never again fly in the face of God." No more babies died in his family after that day. I try to remember that lesson when things don't go my way and I want to get angry with God.

One day I had to meet the priest at the door with a lit candle. That day he came to give my grandfather the last rites of his church. I sat with him on a hot, stuffy day in July as his life on this earth ended.

My last memory of my friend is looking at his work-stained hands encircled by his well-worn Rosary beads as they lowered the lid on his coffin. I'm sure there is a special place in heaven for those who come home with a bit of dirt under their fingernails.

Swimmer's Prayer

Laura Morry Williams

Strands of kelp,
like a woman's hair,
washed gently by the spray
as the sea wraps itself around the shore,
rest on the necks of beaches.

Let me, while swimming
rise with the tide,
allow the waves to caress my hair
as I stroke the water
or, feeling tired, fall inward
assured of being lifted again.

Let my hair flow so gracefully,
resting lightly on the surface
as I swim safely
onto distant shores.

Hard Light

(Inspired by Michael Crummey's book of the same title and begun at a WANL Open Reading when he was the featured reader.)

GEORGINA OLIVERE QUELLER

After the hard light, before the dark night
here in the uncertain hour,
spruce trees grow furry.

Rough chortles from a green pond
frogs' evensong. No-seem-'ems furious
dance, mid-air pliés.

Day-dust settles on rocks
my mother calls stones.
"Rocks are
too big to carry," she corrects.

But these are not smooth or round
like the word stones—instead
they are misshapen, pointed, trapezoid.

Some of my rocks, like gems,
fit into a child's pocket,
hard as light can be.

I Have Forgotten the Way to Beachy Cove

ROBERTA BUCHANAN

I have forgotten the way to Beachy Cove
to the hidden cleft, the stony path
that plunges downward to the sea.
I have forgotten the way to the waterfall
the sound of water rattling over pebbles
through banks of green, and the wildflowers—
purple flags, asters, butter and eggs.
I have forgotten the way to the high rock
where we lay on our bellies in sunlight
and watched connors in the clear water
below;
and the cold, cold water
where we dived for mussels to roast
on the beach; how the blue shells opened
to reveal orange flesh.
And the time I came with my pen and notebook
to write the tree on the edge of the cliff
how its tenacious roots wound gripping a huge boulder
how it must topple down in the next winter storm
and die, to the soft dirge of the icy brook.
And the time I came to write in my notebook
the *hieramos gamos* of fresh water and salt
how the yearning waves tumbling embraced

and embraced the rushing brook
throwing herself amorously
into the arms of her bold salt cousin—
O sweet merging of waters!

I have forgotten the way to Beachy Cove
its hidden cleft, the stony beach
the waterfall, the wildflowers
the tree hanging over the cliff's edge
the sound of water
swirling and gurgling, rattling
over the stones, over the beating
of my heart.

Intemperate Zone:

A Suite of Poems About Belonging

Janet McNaughton

I. HERE

The land diminishes as you approach the sea,
contains less earth,
sustains less life,
until you leap off the edge of the continent
to find yourself in a place where the blue above
is the same as the blue beneath
a tenuous band of cloud all that maintains
a sense of up and down,
of sea and sky,
of equilibrium and being.

It goes on like that
until you could believe
you are heading for the end,
where everything will fall into the void—
and then you are here.

Here is a place just newly clawed by glaciers,
ancient rock wounds still fresh and bleeding water

into a thousand mirror ponds.
Here is empty and naked,
unwalked upon, still waiting to be touched.

II. INTEMPERATE ZONE

This is the season of night.
Mid-afternoon
the sky begins its short decline to darkness,
my energies wane.
Sleep, my body tells me,
sleep, the day is past.
But I ply myself with cocoa,
extract day labour, light denied.
Moleing on under the incandescent light
my body's chemistry reads as void.

Looking at me you can see
my people have lived
in intemperate zones like this for millennia.
My skin paled to capture a sunlight
that is pure poison to me now.

But I consigned myself to this latitude of extremes
where summers are measured by light,
and winters by darkness—
accidental exile that I feel most keenly
in this season of night.

III. LEAD COVE

Why would they call this Lead Cove?
Still a stranger after all these years,
knowing I will never have

that knowing that is bred in the bone,
my imagination fails me
when confronted with this place that is that question.

Flat rocks angle gentle from the water
to an abrupt crescendo of deadly cliff.
The mossy barrens cupped between
clipped by the wind and neat like something tame,
not tame in any way.

Days when the seas are calm and flat
the sun probes into tidal crevices
fed by the pure cold salt of sea-
faceted pools paved with coralline algae
unlikely pinks and bathroom tile green,
sea urchins shelter here sometimes
and once, a starfish.

In the shelter of a ring of tuckamore
the blueberries are warm on this cool day
living on my tongue until I crush them—
sweet, dead pulp exploding in my mouth.

It is enough to be alive
in this place where no one who engendered me
has ever walked, has ever died,
or been laid cold in this cold ground
as I one day will be.

My passion for this place begins with me.

Stone

GRACE BUTT

She places a small hard object
in my hand
then with a smile
she is gone

What she has given me
is a stone
not an ordinary one
but one from a beach
where it has been smoothed
and smoothed and smoothed
by the pounding and grinding
of the ocean

It is grey black
but not the colours of
greyness and blackness
it is flat but not totally flat
it is oval but distortedly so
it has sides
but it does not have edges

Within my hand
I turn my little beach stone
from one side to another
over and back
over and back
its surfaces clean and even
either way fitting
the centre of my palm
I want to retain it

It gives me something to hold
The assurance of its formation
The comfort of its smoothness

Autumn

Starlings Everywhere Then Gone

The Series

With thanks to Steve O'Brien and Steve Porter

HELEN FOGWILL PORTER

SPRING 1997

Looking up a number in the phone book
I come across your name
there it is on Page 262
G. Whitty 1 Calver Street 579-6951

FALL 1953

In your office at the Justice Department
across the hall from mine
we listened to the World Series
on the radio you smuggled in
later I caught hell from Miss Bartlett
for not being where I was supposed to be
when she came prowling
Was that the year Duke Snider became
the Dodgers' hitting star?

You told me all about *The Dizzy Dean Story*
the only movie you'd seen in years

you watched it four times

The Brooklyn Dodgers were soon
my team too
though I'd hardly heard of them
before that summer
they fitted the ordinary guy image
that was so much a part of St. John's
and of you

You organized your bookkeeping
without missing an out
Mr. Howley turned his hearing aid off
while he worked
he didn't follow baseball

SPRING 1997

They tell me you're at the Miller Centre
that if I went to visit
you wouldn't know me
you've forgotten Roy Campanella
Pee Wee Reese
and even Jackie Robinson

but there's your name leaping out at me
I want to dial the number
instead I stare at the page
and think of Ebbets' Field

Driving to Maberly

HILDA CHAULK MURRAY

A late September road-flash of red maple, yellow birch.
The setting sun goldens the road we've passed, casts
our long shadow ahead, fills our back and side-view
mirrors with dazzling light.
Each roadside pond reflects the rainbow-tinted sky.
In the twilight at journey's end, we watch a pink-gold
moon emerge from the calm dark ocean.

Harvest Sounds

HILDA CHAULK MURRAY

I pick blueberries
Across the narrow valley Michelle's dog barks
fights for the last word with Madame Echo
A bee zooms close
Three boisterous crows berate me
All around is the constant grumble
of the sea

Guilty as Hell

(Excerpt from a novel-in-progress Finishing School *written as diary entries)*

HELEN FOGWILL PORTER

TRUTH IS STRANGER than fiction. I been hearing that all my life and whoever said it first knew what they were talking about. What's been going on the past few days you wouldn't believe if you read it in a book. Or the *National Enquirer*. First I got a call from the Health Science saying Herb was a patient there. His neighbours noticed he didn't have his garbage out. They phoned him and got no answer and then they phoned the police. I spose they didn't know how to get ahold of me. They're mostly new people up there now; Mom's old neighbours are all gone into senior citizens' cottages. Or dead. Anyway, the police found Herb in the cellar at the foot of the stairs. They're more like a ladder than stairs, really—you go down through a hatch in the pantry. Like mine. He was half-unconscious, probably fell over the stairs when he was going down to look at the furnace or something. His right hip is broken.

I feels as guilty as hell. Why didn't I phone him when he didn't come around for a while? That wouldn't have stopped him from falling but at least we might of found him quicker. Dr. Noseworthy figures he must have been there two days. I still can't understand why he haven't been here to the house for so long. The doctor thinks he might've had a weak turn or a mini-stroke, said his blood pressure was right high. He could've got weak before he fell, she said, was probably getting giddy off and on for a while and never said nothing to nobody. That must be why he haven't been out around.

Of course I went right to the hospital when they phoned, called a taxi. He's okay, in a room with three other men. They all got something broken. He filled right up when he saw me, thought about Mom, I spose. I didn't know if I should give him a kiss or what. Finally, I just caught hold of his hand and said, "What have you been up to, you bad boy?" Why do we say such foolish things to people when they're sick, especially old people? He liked the card I got him, religious, of course. While I was there a few Salvation Army people came to see him. He was right proud of himself then, showing off a bit, especially when Major and Mrs. Bradbury come in. You got to give your religion when you're getting admitted to hospital. What would I say if I had to go in? When I had my hysterectomy I said United but I haven't been to a United Church for years. Or any other church, for that matter. Except for a few funerals.

While Herb was talking to the Bradburys I glanced around the room, just for something to do. The man in the bed by the window looked familiar but I couldn't place him first. It was only when I was on my way home that I remembered who he was, and then I got the shivers. When I was a youngster, eleven or twelve, I suppose, I was walking home from school kinda late one day, probably had to stay in for talking. On my way I went into Picco's shop to buy an exercise book and when I came out this queer-looking fella was standing just outside the door. He must of been from another part of town; I never saw him before. He was probably around nineteen or twenty. When I passed along by him he sang out, "Hallo, honey, how is your cunny?" I took off, and then I could hear him running behind me. Well, I never ran so fast in my life. If I had to run like that on Sports Day in school I woulda won all the ribbons. He was close behind me, and he kept on shouting the same thing over and over. Of course there wasn't another soul on the road.

When I got in the house I ran right upstairs to the bathroom and vomited my guts up. I was shaking like a leaf. Nothing like that ever happened to me before. Or since. I could be as saucy as the next one and was always pretty good at taking care of myself. But this was different. I only got the one look at his face when I came out of the shop; he was standing right under the light. He was cross-eyed and he had a long white face. I thought he might be what we used to call simple.

I saw him a few times after that and he always looked at me funny but he never said anything to me again. The only person I ever told was my cousin Clarice. I wouldn't dare tell Mom. Clarice is three years older than me, or she was. She's dead now, poor girl, kidney trouble. She said it sounded like John Taylor, that he was harmless and wouldn't hurt a fly. I never saw him again until tonight. He looked exactly the same, although that must be nearly forty years ago. He had his leg up in traction, probably broke it chasing a youngster. He had no visitors.

Herb is finding it hard to get used to having a woman doctor. He keeps calling her Nurse, Dr. Noseworthy told me, but she just laughs. She's sweet. Herb is worried to death about his door—the policemen had to break it down to get in the house. I said Fred would fix it for him. I hope Fred won't give me a hard time over that. The police should fix it, by rights.

Only for that, Herb seems fine. The nurses told me he's eating good—they got a real pet made out of him. Of course he loves that. Perhaps when he gets better we can ease him into a home.

When I got home the phone was ringing while I was unlocking the door. I wasn't going to answer it first, thought it might be another one of those hang-ups, but I finally did pick it up. "Hallo," I said. I'm sure I didn't sound the best. I was beat out, after working all day and then going in to see Herb. Someone was definitely on the line but there wasn't a peep. "Hallo," I yelled. I was getting really mad. "I know you're there. Speak up or hang up, will ya, for the love of God. I haven't got time for this."

"Is this Mrs. Eileen Novak?" It was a woman's voice, or a girl's. Sounded high and nervous.

"Yes, this is Eileen Novak." Hardly anyone calls me Mrs. All the customers in to work calls me Eileen, and so do the girls. Mr. Snell is the only one says Mrs. Novak, and he always sounds like he's making fun of me. She didn't say anything else for a few seconds. "Hurry up, will ya?" I said. "I haven't got all night."

"This is Marie Chalker." Her voice had dropped to a whisper. "I goes out with Tom Soper. You knows him, don't you?" My stomach turned over.

"Yeah, I goes to school with Tom at Avalon Community College." Watch yourself now, Eileen, I said to myself. Don't spill your guts. I was just about to put the receiver down when she spoke again. "I heard you does more than go to school with him." She sounded so young, like she was gonna start crying any minute. "I heard you were down to that new restaurant with him. What's that they calls it—Rapunzel's?"

"Rumpelstiltskin's." I knew it. I knew that news'd be all over town.

"Okay, Rumpelstiltskin's. He never took me to no Rumpelstiltskin's. He thinks Leo's or Ches's is good enough for me." She sounded like she was getting mad. That's better than bawling, anyway, I thought.

I didn't know what to do or say. I should've just hung up. But I couldn't help pitying the poor girl.

"What's wrong with going to supper with a friend?" She didn't have to know everything. All the same, I wouldn't be surprised if half St. John's knows what time Tom left here that morning. "He told me you and him were broke up."

"Oh, he did, did he? Wait till I gets ahold of him." She was really mad by then. "Let's cool it, Marie," he said to me two weeks ago. "Give each other some space, see other people. All that garbage, after going out for five years and supposed to be getting engaged Valentine's Day. That's my birthday, too."

I didn't know if I was supposed to start singing Happy Birthday or what. I knew something like this would happen. Kelly in to work is always telling us to trust our own instincts. She got a year university, studied psychology.

Marie wasn't finished yet. "It was after he met you that he started all that nonsense. What've you got a spell put on him or something? I heard you were old enough to be his mother."

Then it was my turn to get mad. "What's age got to do with it?" I asked her. I musta sounded like Tina Turner. "Anyhow, I think this is something between you and Tom. You can't hold him if he really wants to go. It's nothing to do with me." Did I read that in Dear Abby? Then

I took pity on her again. "Listen, Marie girl, he's not the only fish in the sea. There's lots more where he came from."

"Yeah? Well why didn't you find one of em then?"

It was time to put a stop to this. "Marie, I'm hanging up now. And don't you go phoning me any more and not saying anything. I'm too busy to put up with that kind of stuff."

"You're Lorraine Follett's mother, aren't you? Is she still in Kirby House?"

Gentle Jesus meek and mild, I said to myself. Look upon a little child. Does everyone in the world know my business? Lorraine's and Heather's too, I spose. I wish I never laid eyes on Tom Soper.

Stranger than fiction, there's no doubt about it. Day before yesterday all that happened. I don't know what I was like yesterday. We were busy into work but I had it arranged to get off early to meet Lorraine and them for supper at the Big R. Heather came too. She loves the chips over there, even though she's always running down junk food. She even had a bit of fish tonight, batter and all. I had a lovely big piece. Lorraine looked pretty good, had herself done up nice. She was wearing a lovely dark green coat with a little black fur collar. Probably had it given her. It really suits her.

The youngsters were okay. Jason seemed a bit quiet. Lorraine told me in the bathroom she can't say a word against Mike in front of him. Ashley was a darling, as usual. She thinks the world of Heather. Heather is having the two of them down to her place soon, to watch a video. Mike don't know how lucky he is to have such beautiful children. Smart too.

While I was watching them tonight I remembered how much I used to worry about Ashley when she was a baby. I was afraid of my life she had Down's Syndrome. I was at the hospital when she was born; Lorraine wanted me to go with her. She's a real sook about pain. Mike was gone off somewhere as usual, though I must say he came to the hospital as soon as he got home. She *was* a few days early. I wouldn't stay in the case room once the bad part started, but Lorraine made me promise to wait in the little room outside till the baby was born. Lorraine wanted a girl so much. I don't know who looked after Jason that day, I spose it musta been Mike's mother. Or Judy.

I saw Ashley when she was a few minutes old. Her eyes were really slanty and her head looked all squished in. All babies probably looks like that first when they're born. I can't even remember what my own looked like. I figured she'd look different in a few days.

Ashley never did get rid of that look around her eyes. She's right pretty though, always was. A little bit oriental looking, like that movie actress Leslie Caron. I still kept wondering, but I never said a word to no one. She seemed bright and alert. I was always watching her, not letting on to anyone. I was afraid to put it in words, and I didn't want to worry Lorraine.

When Ashley was about five months old Lorraine took her to Sears to have her picture taken, got a special deal on it. She gave me a big framed picture for my wall. Ashley looked gorgeous but I could still see the slanty eyes. One night when Mollie was here with a neighbour of hers the other woman looked at the picture and asked me if Ashley had Down's Syndrome. Just like that.

I got right flustered. It seemed really ignorant for her to come out with it like that. Mollie told me after she's a student assistant like Jean. They takes stuff like Down's for granted. I still never said a word to Lorraine or anyone else. I was always reading stuff about Down's Syndrome in the magazines in to work. One night I even went into the Reference Library in the Arts and Culture Centre. Heather told me you can find out anything you want to know in there. The girl at the desk got me some articles about it but I didn't find what I really wanted to know.

There's a nurse, Mrs. Edgecombe, comes to me to get her hair done. I asked her one day if you could tell if a baby had Down's Syndrome as soon as it was born. I just kind of worked it into the conversation, told her a friend of mine wanted to know. She said the doctors knew right away and they always told the parents. That relieved me a bit but I never stopped worrying, especially when Ashley wasn't as quick learning her colours and letters as Jason was. And Mom did have a baby with something wrong with him, the one she lost.

I don't know exactly when I stopped worrying. Ashley is as smart as can be now, gets a great report card. She's in grade one and she loves school. On the concert they had last spring she had a part to say all by herself. Heather had a puzzle book for her last night, and a chapter book for Jason. Heather said she had a job keeping up with Ashley on the puzzles, she was so fast. I can finally breathe a sign of relief.

What about if there *was* something wrong with her, though? I'd still love her just as much, maybe more. But the way I looks at it there's enough hardship in life without having something like that. When my girls were small Mom had a neighbour whose only child had Down's Syndrome. Never let her play on the street, even when she was a big girl. They always kept her in the garden. She was about three years older than Lorraine. When Lorraine was three or four she loved to play with her, but as she got older she didn't want to go over there any more. Shirley went over one year, and then Heather, but they all gave it up after a while. And Belinda wanted them to come so much. She'd bring out all her toys; it was a real sin. Haven't seen her or her mother for years. I think they moved.

Jean'd eat the head right off me if she knew I was going on like this. Heather wouldn't like it either. But I can't help what's in my mind. I wouldn't dare mention it to anyone.

I'm some tired tonight, stressed out, I spose. I feels like crawling into bed and never getting up. Poor Nell, I can almost envy her, over there in the hospital with nobody to worry about only herself. That's a sin for me; I don't know what the poor girl is going through. Jean said she heard she'd soon be out.

Bev had the car tonight and gave me a run home. Her husband didn't need it, for once. "You're awful quiet tonight, Eileen," she said when we got to my door. "Anything wrong?"

"No, girl, only the usual." Her and Jean knows all about Herb and Lorraine and Mike and everything else. Everything else except Tom.

I didn't intend to write anything in here tonight, thought I'd have to go straight to bed. But I knew I'd be too wound up to sleep. I'm calmed down a bit now. After I lets the cat in I'm going to bed. Hope I don't have any stupid dreams.

Last night I dreamt me and Tom were going at it in his car. I looked up and saw a face staring in the window. It was that John Taylor. I was trying to tell Tom he was there but I couldn't get a sound out. That often happens to me in dreams—feels like my mouth is full of sawdust or something. I pulled away from Tom and started to bawl. When I looked at the window again John Taylor's face was gone and Tom's was there, looking right sly. There was tears in my eyes when I woke up. What in the name of God can I do to give myself a good dream for a change?

Untitled

Joan Scott

They celebrate the scarlet leaves
But for my sanity I need
To see beneath November boots
The green inside the maple seed

My Mother's Poem

Bernice Morgan

I thought the Cape would stay
always as I left it,
sea-locked in time.
The black stove, the lamplit kitchen,
a narrow house,
a graveyard,
a neck of sand.

I sat by the window
until dawn,
sewing a sailor suit
for my youngest brother.
Watching the headland,
waiting for the steamer
that would take me to St. John's.

I thought they would always be there,
a family to return to.
But they followed me,
passed me—went out in all directions.
The house crumbled,
the kettle rusted on the beach,
headstones sank in the sand.

They followed.
My mother to lie in a city graveyard
among strange names.
The sailor to drown in another sea.
Others to send Christmas cards
with stamps my children save.

I Curse this Body

Georgina Olivere Queller

I curs
e this bo
dy that no
man loves.
The
stret
ched tautness of its
eighth-month belly on a post
menopausal woman. I damn this
body that seeks to put itself out of the
way of abuse by abusing itself. I rage
against those hormones that still
call out to those rejecting men
and—forgive me—I cannot help but condemn
the little death that always ends in tears. But
afterwards, I love this body that all men curse
and I caress the roundness of its development
post men pausing there. I admire this body that has
survived and flourished
and I court the hormones
that linger still and reach out for
release. Then I cannot help but
love the tears that come . . . life,
after the little death.

Three Poems about My Relationship with My Body

Marilyn Porter

Start the day with muesli, yogurt, fruit and nuts,
a light snack, two small crackers and
a carrot stick.
lunch a bit of fish (not fried)
another snack, maybe a morsel of cheese.
supper then a tiny meal (two veggies) and a herbal tea.

~~~

glistening
and glowing with grease,
fried potatoes, garlic buttered carrots
special chocolate, stored in the fridge which is ever
open. Nibbles of fresh-baked bread and buns
with cream and jam.

~~~

A CHARM AGAINST THE PAIN

After so many years of ricocheting
from bulge to dip and back again
here I am in middle age, without
much shape at all. So free at last
from tyranny, let's warmly welcome
stretchy waistbands and comfy shoes.

when I finally saw an elephant

GEORGINA OLIVERE QUELLER

elephantless in Newfoundland
i dream of taut grey hides
glossy-picture-book-smooth beasts
their rumps as smooth as my own
back then

unnatural here
they weren't brought in
like moose and Brunette Island buffalo
they didn't steal over the gulf ice
like the rabid red fox
or the chattering grey squirrel

elephants are so big that
when i was small
circuses wouldn't bring them here

bridges are too narrow
mothers don't fit
fathers are too heavy and
babies can't come alone—
or so they said

A CHARM AGAINST THE PAIN

at thirty-four i meet an old grey elephant
a sawdust-bound mammoth
stranded behind an Antigonish fair tent

transfixed i concentrate
not on the height of her soaring over me
not on the fatness of her stubby feet
or the silliness of her tiny tail
swatting everyday Antigonish flies

i am not even taken
by the sight of this gargantuan
being washed down
by a small grey-uniformed man
with a bucket and brush

amazed i see instead
there is no taut grey hide
no glossy-picture-book-smooth skin
but wrinkles—
her whole skin
a bag of big and little wrinkles

did she get this way
from constant lounging
in mud baths
or is it the pattern of her life

the same one
i see on my own hands
criss-crossed leatherlike
harbinger of the wizened woman
i will become

as the woman I met
on the geriatric ward

at 999 Queen Street—
Toronto's asylum

shed of 100 pounds
she stands
her back to me
her nightgown swaddles her feet
wrinkled-empty-buttock flesh
hangs in loose folds
large-boned shoulders outline
the pattern of her former self

transfixed i stare at
those pendulous folds
while she is washed down
by a small grey-uniformed woman
with a basin and brush

Work Poem

For Jim Hardenbrook

MICHAEL BRUCE-LOCKHART

I don't know how to make a poem of this.
It's not poetic,
except inside of me.
It still sings inside of me, sometimes,
in the night, like now.

Ol' Jim.
I can see him now,
in his engineering uniform:
white shirt and tie, sleeves rolled up to
just below the elbow,
grey hair, and glasses on the end of his nose,
the inevitable cold cup of coffee clutched in his hand.

I handed him his board, my new circuit installed,
a little crab tucked away in a crevice between two chips.
"Give it a try, Jim," I said,
and walked away,
feeling my stomach tighten.
"It probably won't work the first time."

I wonder why I did that?
Not disclaim, I mean
(circuits seldom work the first time);
walk away. That was not usual.
Maybe it was because we'd had that problem
for so damn long.
It had stumped us both for months
and the cheese was on our backs.
(that's an old game—
what they want yesterday, we promise tomorrow
and hope we can show them enough next week to keep
them happy—but there's no doubt
it was getting warm in the kitchen)

Then I'd seen it.
I guess, in fact, it had been there a while,
but suddenly that needed piece
came cruising in from out the mind mist
and popped into place.
That's some feeling!
When you've got an answer
and all that remains is to get it down.
Sharpen the pencil.
Reach for the pad.
Lines slashing down,
shift and rule and rotate,
lead flowing like ink.
No call for the eraser,
it's all there.

This time, next time, tenth time,
it didn't matter.
Sooner or later, it would work.
I could feel the exultation rising.
I'd walked, not to let it show.

I've no idea
how long he took to hook it up and turn it on.
I only remember Jim
whooping it up,
turning the power on and off, on and off,
his eyes locked to the screen,
and each time his yell across the lab,
"Look at that!
Why that little mother just locked on,
Slicker . . . than . . . seal shit!"

Dear Jim.
An engineer's engineer.
Twenty-five years of nights
and weekends
solving other people's problems
for 30 gs a year.
Not even upset that some young upstart
had solved his problem
but just enjoying the solution.

A Woman's Work . . .

Masonic Park Nursing Home, Mount Pearl c. 1985

HELEN FOGWILL PORTER

Mary is scrubbing again, her practised hands
half clenched, move back and forth
across the smooth surface.
She looks up and says: "Don't you track mud
over my clean floor," but then
her green eyes light up with that leprechaun grin
she asks for a cigarette.
"Busy today?" I ask, as she takes
short happy puffs.
"Don't be talkin'; I never stopped a minute
had to mix the bread and wash the quilts
and you shoulda seen the ironing; I had a job to keep the fire goin'."
She finishes the cigarette and begins
to scrub once more.
A nurse comes by, straightens the strap
around Mary's waist and says
"Time for bed now, my love."
As she pushes the wheelchair
down the hall, Mary turns and winks at me
as if she and I are the only ones
who really know what's going on.

on retiring

ANNE FERNCASE

one day I woke up
realized
I had nothing
if not time

what was I going to do with it

I fetched the morning
Telegram
perused the Community
Calendar
stuffed with its dinners
dances
bingos
meetings

There were the self-help groups—
        AA for the Drinkers
        Support for Families of Schizophrenics
        Alzheimers' Anonymous
        Parades for Veterans
        Books for Babies
        Fats Incorporated

        Gays for Life
        Swimmers in Search of New Shapes
        French for Francophiles

it was exhilarating
even intimidating

was I crazy enough for
the mental health social
on Friday afternoons
literate enough
to bring books to newborns
too blessed old to be a Big Sister
could I dance at the Columbus Club
if I wasn't a couple

oh merde

there had to be
some black hole
for this square peg

I'd had my dreams
        money I once thought I'd make
        dudes I'd wanted to date
        a family line I had hoped to create

yet time
faces me every morning
leans on me
throughout each day
fights with me for sleep

tomorrow
begin
with the
Obituaries

Blood-Red Poppies

FRAN BAIRD INNES

Blood-red poppies bounce up and down
as people remember, gather round the War Memorial.
Across the harbour from Signal Hill, a cannon blast.
Hundreds of foam-white gulls forsake rocky roosts,
take to the air, wheel higher and higher,
over the top and out to sea and safety.

Music to Lie in Bed By

Geraldine Chafe Rubia

Lying still
upon my bed
I hear concertos
in my head

Tinnitus programmed
in my ears
continuous
for years and years
soughful as
a summer breeze
louder when
I've had a sneeze

Heart a-thrumming
under that
now dub-a-dub
now pititta-pat

Waters piped
along the walls
rush and plink
like Rattle Falls

confused with gurgling
of my guts
borborygmi
from eating nuts

Insistent on
the windowpane
tip-tapping beads
of autumn rain
accompanied
by wind in trees
inciting tinnitus
like a sneeze

And then a gift
a wanted word
beneath the clamour
clearly heard

Who needs TV
or radio
with this performance
on the go

Lying still
upon my bed
I hear concertos
in my head

Starlings Everywhere Then Gone

JOAN SCOTT

Finishing my supper this August evening,
starlings rush at my house, fly
low, then rise to clear the roof.

As one flight narrows to nothing,
another appears over opposite chimneys.
From lofty aerobatics, a large group descends and hurries after.

It's time to head outdoors,
to the wide skies of this eastern town.
Where are they all?

Back, and up high, I see the birds.
The round amoeba moves into its own pseudopod,
then surges towards me.

I hear their beating wings,
they curve away and around, everyone scurries to catch up.
Then it is up, up, and far away, out of sight.

I am bereft.
Waiting.
I don't know where to look.

The sun sets over a dark hill,
The sky is gold, white and blue.

Suddenly, they are back,
pouring down behind buildings and trees,
giving themselves to gravity,
with no restraint.

I turn a corner.
Only trees without birds rustle in the wind.
I miss that racket of an audience of children before a show.

I turn another corner to sweet bird gossip.

Noisy. Restless. Latecomers dart in.
Here are two, then one, then fifteen.
They overflow the trees
on an island in a pond.
Together now with friends and family.

Again a sudden silence.

Skeins of birds,
wind out and up,
leave the island,
tuck down for the night
in pond-side trees.

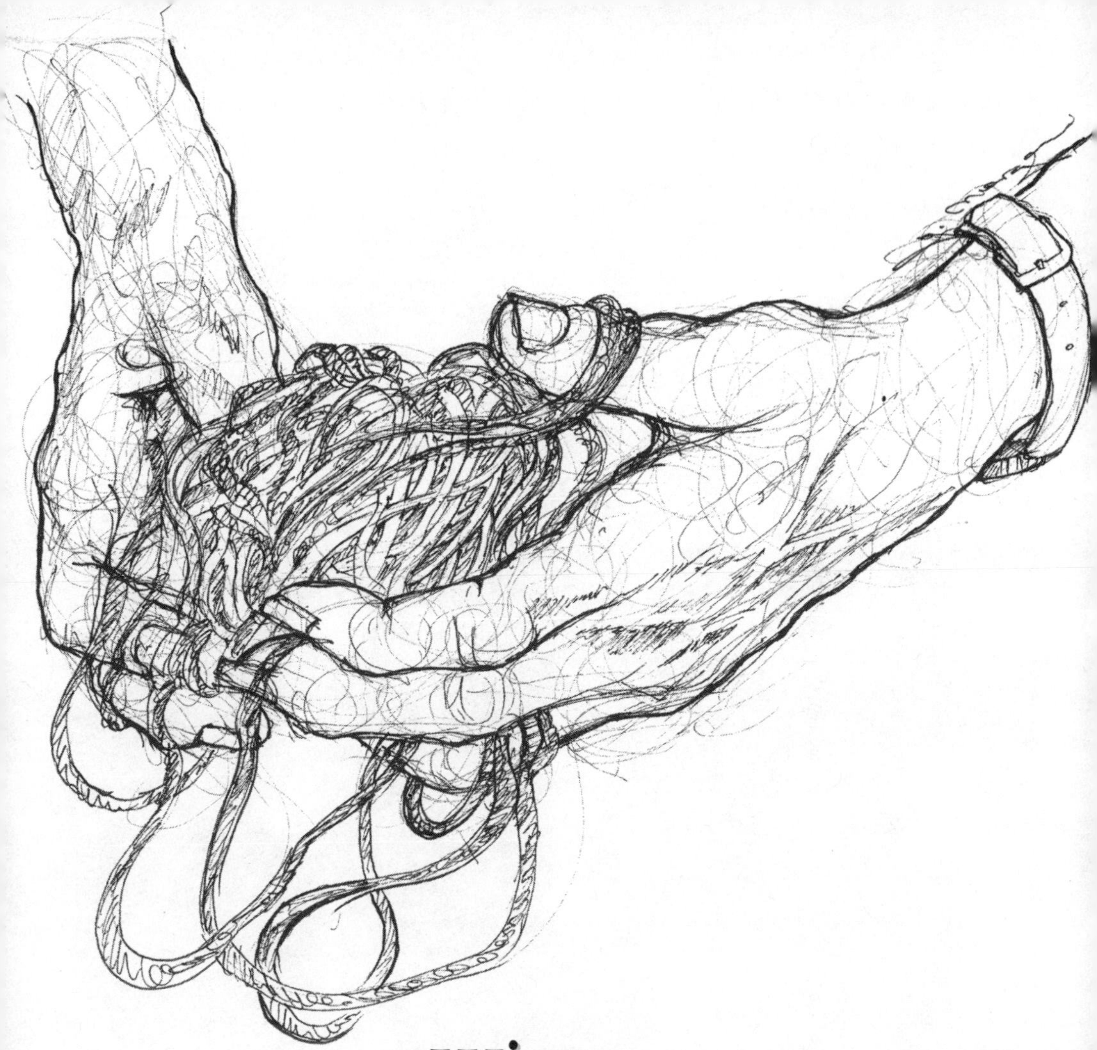

Winter

Shivering Thoughts

Two Haiku

GERALDINE FLANNIGAN

shivering thoughts
sweep my mind the long night through
snowy december

~~~

scented pine cones
scatting around the yard
my christmas wreaths
~~~

Speaking as Settlers

PAUL O'NEILL

We were brought west
by tattered sails of tired ships
and rescued on this curve of seaweed
from the shipwrecked dreams
of those who braved
the barbarous waves
to redefine their hopes
in unfamiliar suns
and brittle stars shrouded in
shadows of the dark.

They came unto a land
possessed by snow and ice
and thirsted for
the songs of harbingers
with morning breathing spring
upon the barren pastures of the dead.

Who knows
what things were learned by
those nameless few
who lie with friends and enemies
in broken ground

where time has pulled the weeds and
wild grass over them.
They listened in abating storms
to alien winds on wasted shores
that shaped their joys and sorrows
with tears grown old.

Now there is music in the solitude
of these forbidding
and foreboding crags where
webbed feet nest among the mists
and burning eyes foretell
what now is seen and heard . . .
a fragile tribute
to their lost complexities . . .
a homeland born . . .
a unity of man and wilderness
taking our loves and hates
and welding them into a common fate.

The Ghost of Cim

North Welsh Ghosts

MARILYN PORTER

Always a nice lady, she was,
In her pale lilac gown.
Soft footsteps up the kitchen stairs
Or down the alley between houses.

Discreet, restrained, unobtrusive—
Except for that time just after she died,
When she was angry,
Behaved quite badly
Occasionally even throwing things.
Until a visiting preacher sat up all one night,
With his hand on the Bible.
She came—some trouble with the will,
Which he had sorted out.
After that she was content
Just to stroll, in her lilac gown.
She played the piano sometimes.
Brahms, usually. Quite well too.

Then we modernized the house.
Took away the kitchen stairs and

Blocked up the alley.
So she went away.
Quietly in her silent slippers
Making no fuss.

Trapped

KATHLEEN KNOWLES

THE SEAVIEW HOME for Seniors sprawls over an acre of land on the top of ancient, brooding cliffs, ten kilometres north of St. John's, Newfoundland. Here, high above the North Atlantic, herring gulls scream as they glide overhead on the constant winds, and occasionally a bald eagle soars by, almost at eye level. The two-storey nucleus of Seaview is a whitish, square structure that was built by the provincial government twenty-seven years ago during an election campaign. Subsequent governments have funded additions to it, and now four extensions, linear, single-storey buildings of blue, yellow, green, and turquoise, stretch to the south, giving the home the appearance of a multicoloured squid. The salt air has gnawed sores on most of the tentacles, wounds in the paint that often penetrate right down to the wood, and the shade of red on the roof varies from a flamboyant crimson on the newest limb to a tired rust, almost brown, on the body. The roof, as roofs are destined to do in Newfoundland, leaks steadily when the winds of April lash out from the northeast.

Monday morning is marching into action at Seaview, but for Rose Parfrey, slumped in her wheelchair, it is just one more in a tedious procession of mornings. Gently, as though stroking a favourite cat, her left hand moves back and forth on a paper on the table in front of her, making lines with a blue felt marker. The exertion forces the only sound she can produce, an occasional muted grunt, to erupt from her throat. Day after day, Rose is abandoned to draw lines at this table in a corner of the common room. The stroking motion soothes her, and she's discovered that as long as she keeps making marks on the paper they leave her alone and don't relocate her for singalongs, or crafts, or wheelchair exercises. Her son-in-law, Mike, calls her wheelchair her hot rod. She hates its sinister black vinyl, its handles that stick out like horns on a bull. She offers it no friendship as it carries her through her new life.

Rose has been at Seaview for four months. Her daughter Patsy found her, on a distant Monday morning, unconscious on the floor of her kitchen. Fragments of a crystal juice decanter had littered the floor, and tomato juice, red and thick, had been splattered over the lower cupboards and the floor, a thin red snake of it inching its way towards the dining room. Her sixteen-year-old black cat, Miffy, had been lurking on top of the fridge. Rose doesn't remember falling, or the ride in the wailing ambulance. She can only recall the six long weeks at St. Clare's, and now the confinement of this nebulous place. Patsy tells her she has had a stroke. Stroke of luck keeps running through her mind, but she knows that's not what Patsy means.

Rose is a delicate woman, wiry it was called when she was young, a perfect build for track and field. Now they call it frail. Age and gravity have compressed her frame to only five feet, and already nine-year-old Stevie, the youngest of her three great-grandchildren, reaches up to her shoulder. She has a rounded hump between her shoulders, and her head drops forward, making it necessary for her to focus her eyes upwards in order to see the world around her. The strain of this gives her a headache, and so usually she doesn't bother. She knows what's there.

For thirty-three years, every month, Rose had coloured her hair a warm, chestnut brown; but now, in this place, they don't bother, so that the two inches of hair closest to her scalp are an unpleasant yellow, the yellow of a smoker's front teeth. Her complexion, though, is clear. Patsy makes sure the attendants use special cream, and she has instructed them never to use soap on her face. She says you could strip paint with the stuff they use here. Rose's husband, John, always said her skin was like that of a porcelain doll. The memory of his gentle touch as he stroked her cheek is so much a part of her that when she closes her eyes she can still feel the softness of his skin.

The area in front of Rose is littered with an assortment of chairs, mostly discards from local homes, all drab and faded, one, like Rose, with an arm hanging lifeless at its side, a silent victim, perhaps, of some domestic skirmish. In the corner behind her, a bookcase sags under the weight of dust-covered copies of *The Newfoundland Herald* and *The Downhomer*. A partially finished jigsaw puzzle clutters a nearby table. Several escaped pieces are hiding underneath, camouflaged by the mottled linoleum. A few metres to Rose's left, a young girl sits pumping a dilapidated rocker at the tempo of a fast jig while staring blankly at a muted television screen. Rose has seen her often, and assumes she is the granddaughter of one of the residents, waiting to escape the obligatory visit. The girl is about twelve, and has lovely auburn hair, straight and shiny. She is wearing a pair of bright green shorts and a yellow T-shirt with some sort of picture on it, and sneakers, but no socks. Rose has taken a liking to the girl and has named her Violet, because it is a name she has always loved. Even in silence, she finds Violet's companionship more comforting than that of the other residents.

The routine smells of disinfectant and bodies are being infiltrated by a third, more aggressive aroma advancing from the direction of the kitchen. Soon the smells will converge in a taste, and Rose will be wheeled out of the common room, through the foyer, past the statue of the Virgin Mary, and into the cafeteria for lunch.

Rose's coloured markers are kept in a clear plastic case. Stevie gave them to her on her last birthday, her eighty-seventh. His mother had been embarrassed. "You know kids," she had laughed. Stevie had helped her open the gift, and as the markers had touched her weathered hands she had felt a spark of excitement. At night she hides them in the third drawer of her dresser, under the half-dozen nighties sent by family members. People have already been stealing money from her purse, even though she hides it in her closet. The last time money was missing, Patsy had counted everything for her and assured her that it was all still there, but she knows differently.

At first Rose had tried to draw familiar objects—houses, trees, flowers—but her hand just wouldn't obey orders. They usually place her right hand, the one she has always used, in her lap where it rests, oblivious to its responsibilities. And so she settles for lines—thick, thin, wavy, however they appear. She has developed an intimate sense of the character of each of her colours and feels a surge of power as their energy flows into her fingers, through her hand and wrist, up her arm, and then diffuses throughout the rest of her body. There is one colour she never touches. The black marker terrifies her. The one time she did pick it up her whole body had started to shake and she had dropped it as though it were burning. The blackness is always lurking close by, waiting impatiently for its chance to grab her again and drag her deeper into its depths.

Patsy humours her by bringing her proper artist's paper, large, heavily-textured sheets. Rose loves the new packages. They come in canary yellow wrappers. Yellow birds, yellow flowers. Was there once a yellow dress? Patsy brings her everything she needs, but never mentions Rose going home. Her son Kyle and her other daughter, Erin, have moved away to the mainland and she rarely hears from them, although Patsy insists that they call every week. She'd certainly remember if her own children called her. Wouldn't she? Sometimes a gremlin gets inside her head and fools up the wires to torment her. Rose's days trudge through the labyrinth of her mind like the shapes and colours in a kaleidoscope turning slowly in the light. Images sparkle, then change shape and disappear before she can claim them.

On warm afternoons, they often move the residents outdoors to a spacious patio that is covered by a billowy awning of red, white, and blue striped canvas and faces the sea. A wooden railing, painted white, encloses the area. When the capelin used to roll in, residents could watch the frantic scene of people collecting the slithering fish with nets and buckets while their dogs rolled in the stinky mess on the beach. They could also watch the fishing boats come and go. Those residents are gone now. So are the boats. And the fish. The only diversion these days is the tourists who clamber along the rocks in July and August in hopes of finding a broken lobster pot to take home to use as a planter. A pair of binoculars still hangs, lopsided, next to the front door.

One afternoon, as Rose sits on the porch absently making lines, she senses that she is being watched. She turns a bit to her left and recognizes Violet, her silent ally, standing at the edge of the porch watching her out of the corner of her eye. When Rose looks up the girl immediately drops her gaze to the floor. As Rose watches, she wanders over to the binoculars and lifts them carefully from the hook. They are large for her small hands, and she has difficulty holding them steady. She watches for a few seconds only, replaces them so that they are now hanging evenly, then moves to sit in the chair opposite Rose. She stares at the floor and chews on a finger. Rose can see that her nails are bitten to the quick, and raw. The blue sky soon becomes moody and a cold, grey mass of fog swirls in around them. They have placed her white sweater on the chair beside her, beyond her reach. Violet walks timidly around the table, and, without looking directly at Rose, picks up the sweater and drapes it around her shoulders. She then settles back into her chair.

As they sit, a weary looking woman, maybe thirty, in a once-white uniform, approaches from across the porch, the heels of her scuffed loafers clomping at each step. She sighs and leans against the railing. "How ya doin, Kimmy, girl? Tomorrow best bring a book or somethin wit ya. And be sure ya don't leave the porch, now. I don't want no trouble." She greets a woman approaching from the other side of the porch. "Hi, Theresa. Bout time for a break, I'd say."

"How's it goin, Mary? Sacred Heart it's some hot in that kitchen. This your girl here?"

"Yeah, this is my Kimmy. Mrs. O'Brien says she can stay here if she don't get in the way."

The two women furtively take cigarettes and tiny lighters from their pockets and light up, facing away from the windows. Rose keeps her eyes on her paper. Mary continues, "Remember in the old days we used to hang out over to the wharf all summer? The boys'd wander on down after dinner and we'd sit around smokin and laughin all afternoon."

"Yeah. I remembers them days."

"Nuttin ta do now. Sure, Kimmy'll be bored to death sittin around here with the old ones, but I don't know what else I'm sposed to do. If I didn't need this friggin job I'd be able ta spend more time wit er, right? And I hates havin to ride out here every mornin with that lech Jake. Reminds me too much of my old man."

"Where's her father to these days, Mary?"

"Aw, Gerry's not real regular, like. He's crazy over Kimmy, though, and when he comes to take her to his place he can't wait to get goin. He takes her every weekend 'cept when he's off checkin his snares. He's got a job now out to that big new furniture place by the overpass, but he never keeps a job for long. Not his fault. Cutbacks, right? He's some lucky, though. Always has just enough weeks for his E.I.

Theresa looks over at Kim. "She don't seem too happy today, do she?"

"Right gloomy, she is. Not like my boy, Jason. He's away at camp and lovin it altogether. Always the life of the party, he is. Sure, he drives his teachers cracked. They're after phonin me about every other day. Friggin nuisance, they are."

"I knows what you mean. I'm after gettin a few calls myself about my Tracey. Sure, they got nuttin better to do but be botherin us."

"Anyways, Gerry says boys and girls is different so you have to treat them different. He has the knack of it. Startin next week he's gonna be able to come early for her on Wednesdays, and take her for the night. That'll give us a bit of a break from each other, right?" She sighs a large balloon of smoke. "Maybe I shoulda stayed with Gerry. I guess men have to have their drink now and again, right?" And looking over at her daughter: "Maybe you should start colouring with Rosie, here. She do go on wit it don't she, Theresa?"

"Indeed she do. That Dr. Sage says it's good for the mazes in her head or some such foolishness. Any idiot with half a brain could figger that out. Give me the money he's after makin and I'd sort out a few o'their problems."

Dr. Sage, the psychiatrist who visits Seaview every two weeks, is a Resident at the Health Sciences Centre in St. John's. Rose has heard them say he's from Vancouver. He explains her condition to her, tells her she must continue with her physio and speech therapies, and talks about making adjustments in life. He has told the staff that studies have shown that Rose's artwork—he always raises two fingers of each hand, bent at the tips as he says this, sometimes so close to his head that it looks like he's trying for bunny ears—could work as therapy. He thinks it possible that her choice of colours is a reflection of her feelings and moods and assures them that it will prevent her from feeling depressed and isolated.

The next day Violet appears on the porch soon after lunch and sits with a thin paperback book in her hand. The cover picture is of a woman with flowing, blonde hair, wearing a frothy, low-cut gown, like something from the deep South. Eyes closed, she is lying back in the arms of a dark, intense-looking man in a blousey white shirt open to the waist. Violet reads for a while, turning the pages very slowly. Most of the time she just watches Rose or stares at the floor. Rose and Violet settle into a routine of sharing the afternoons comfortably, weaving the days of the summer into a predictable pattern.

One August afternoon, Rose looks up, sees that Violet is watching her draw, and attempts to push a piece of her paper across the table. Violet stares at it for a few seconds, then begins to examine the markers intensely, as though the choice of colours were extensive, and Rose is surprised when she reaches for the purple. Rose has trouble controlling purple. She uses it only rarely, and it always leaves her feeling shaky.

Violet makes a few short tentative lines, as though testing to see if the table is solid, then immediately her stroke becomes aggressive. She draws a small, solid purple circle and surrounds it with a larger circle. Pressing harder, she makes thick, jagged spikes stick out of it all around the outside. Inside she draws three triangles at the top, with circles inside them, as for eyes, a distorted, amoeba-shaped nose, and a mouth that sneers from the bottom centre of the page up to the triangle eye on the right side. When she is finished she falls back in her chair, breathing heavily. They stare at the drawing. Rose is shivering.

From the direction of the parking lot, a medium-height, heavy-set man, about thirty-five, approaches and steps up onto the porch. He is casually dressed in black cotton pants and a faded red shirt, the top four buttons undone. His hair is clean, but has been blown into a frenzy by the wind in the parking lot. As he comes closer, Rose catches a whiff of cigarettes and stale beer and notices his veiny nose, a nose with a crooked bridge that hints at lost bar room debates.

"Hey, Kimmy. How's my special girl today?" He flashes a cock-eyed grin, looking sideways at both of them. With the tips of his fingers he strokes Violet's arm, slowly and very lightly, from her wrist to her elbow, pauses a second, and then continues up to her neck. His hand lingers on her shoulder. Rose has dropped her marker. Her left hand is gripping the arm of her wheelchair. Mary appears from the front door, hair fluffed up, lips scarlet. “Hi, Gerry. Kimmy here’s made friends with this old lady. They sit together every day. Seems right boring to me, but she don’t seem to mind. I was after thinkin maybe we could all go to a movie together tonight. Whadya think?”

Violet has grabbed the black marker and is slashing her drawing with strong strokes. She attacks it until the paper tears.

“Na, girl, no good. Me ’n Kimmy got a lot on the go, right, Kimmy? Leave that stuff be. Let’s go.”

Meticulously, Violet replaces the marker in the row of colours, and for the first time she stares directly into Rose’s eyes. The abyss that Rose has been dreading is in those eyes, two bottomless pools of blackness, darker, more profound than the horror of her worst fears. Slowly, hand in hand, Gerry and Violet walk toward the parking lot.

A Privilege of Birth

JENNIFER MORGAN

HE HAS BEEN declining again. Passive. No sparks of interest, very little initiative. Whispering. Forgetting. Sleeping. I couldn't get him to work on the shelves with me in the garage. Not that I need him to help me put them together, any more than at one time he would have needed me to help with his projects. What bothers me is his excuse. He is convinced there's a connection between standing on the hard concrete and "dysentery," his word for diarrhoea. But it is his medicine which brings diarrhoea. The last time I got him down there he had to run to the basement bathroom. We were alone, so, trying to protect the father-daughter privacy, I handed what he needed around the door. New Attends, I put them together for him, but through the crack in the door I could see him having problems, taking them apart . . . no, wait, that was earlier, that was in Coley's Point.

The time he had trouble putting the Attends together was a week ago this past Thursday when I took him to Coley's Point. We dropped Mommy off at a meeting. He'd been up and fully alert at a reasonable hour. When I suggested that we go out for breakfast and then to Coley's Point he was happy, he'd gotten dressed with enthusiasm. He put everything on over his pajamas of course, but "It's a cold day," Mommy and I said to each other, "the extra layer won't hurt."

We arrived at MacDonalds and I left Daddy to range free for a table. As I gave our order I kept glancing over my shoulder, monitoring his shuffle around the tables, that vague childlike look in his eyes. He looked like Trudy's boy, Christopher, surrounded by people he doesn't know very well.

The next time I looked I saw Uncle Don. Sure enough Daddy was sitting with Don and Sue.

"You think you have an original idea and then half the world turns up!" I complained when I reached the table with our food.

"Other people go to MacDonalds, you know!" Uncle Don retorted. "That's how they stay in business."

The conversation was lively. We analyzed last week's funeral of the Queen Mum, which, it turned out, they had also gotten up early to watch—Anglophile fanatics—just like us. My republican mother slept in.

"Well, I tell you, I figure they must have had that crown bolted on to that coffin with something!" said Don.

We speculated on how the crown stayed on through the lifting from the horse-drawn wagon and then into the hearse. It was Sue who caught Daddy's whispered comment.

"They said, ''ere Mum 'old on to that!'" He imitated the old woman in the coffin, grimly clutching her crown.

"Her last duty for the family," I added.

"Or maybe it was with her teeth?" he said, biting the air, that gleam of humour in his eyes.

Glimpses of my Daddy. They make me wonder what we did right, what we are doing wrong when he recedes . . . our intermittent reward. Sometimes it works, sometimes it doesn't. But if you think it's related to what you do, if you think your actions are powerful enough to keep him alive, you are torturing yourself.

We drove in silence to Coley's Point. His eyes were so watery I kept looking at him, wondering if he was okay. As we approached Tim Horton's, I asked if he wanted to use the bathroom there, but he said no. Walking up the path to the house, I reflected on "the old man's pride." I could almost hear the phrase in my dad's voice, like it was him who was describing this stranger on my right. Gently, excusing the foibles of the elderly.

"He was proud, you see," my father would say if he was me

describing him, "he was proud of the job he'd done, installing the plumbing in Coley's Point. He wanted to use his own bathroom!"

Unfortunately, both of us forgot that he'd turned the water off back in January, the day before his terrible spell. The toilet was full of pink antifreeze, so my father went ahead and used it. But when he pulled the handle it wouldn't flush. He was in a panic. He couldn't remember where the valve was to turn the water on. He turned the taps under the toilet, he went to the kitchen to turn on the source, then back to the bathroom. That was when I remembered.

The fire in the kitchen stove had warmed things up quite nicely. I settled Daddy there to change. Mommy keeps a bag in the trunk packed with clean clothes. I sorted through what he needed, laid clean underwear on the daybed. That was when I put the Attends together—although through the crack in the door I saw him take them apart and reassemble them. I saw his black cords circling his feet, his skinny pink legs. I wanted to look away but he was doing it wrong. He is used to my mom being with him, helping him put them on so he doesn't have to take his cords off.

"Daddy, you have to step out of your pants. Step into the Attends like they're a pair of shorts. Daddy, take your underwear off before you put the Attends on. That's right . . ."

From behind the door I pretend that I can't see. On his side, his back to the door, he pretends I'm not looking. Always I am wondering, how long can we keep this fragile false privacy?

As long as possible.

After our excitement, my father elected to lie on the daybed and enjoy a nap in the warm kitchen. I addressed our non-flush toilet. The plastic garbage bucket seemed an excellent solution. But it liberally leaked all the way up the path from the beach. My gallon of water was only a quart when I got to the toilet. The next time I used the plastic wastebasket from the bathroom. A perfect one-flush wastebasket. It was a pleasant day to be making trips down to the beach for water. I saw myself from another era, the Morgan maid, fetching water. However, this toilet was making bedpans look efficient; one trip and my great aunt Lizzie would have been done, whereas my job took three. At the beach the water was dotted with chatty seagulls enjoying the community's warm sewage piped into the bay from the concrete under my feet. A fine way to pass the time, the sun on my back, my hands only a little cold from the salt water, the cheerful calls of the birds.

That job done, I wandered around the house with my dad's camera: sunlight on rusted bedsprings in the children's room, the angled view from the upstairs window of the path between the two houses, the beach beyond, and the dark, always disappointingly empty attic, a few oil cans and glinting bottles in front of the one small window.

I picked up one bottle. Small enough to lie on my palm. It might make a gift for David in California. Despite stains and rips, the label still spelled its contents: "Lemon Crystals." Downstairs I photographed it on the windowsill, lit by sunlight wavy through the melted-glass window.

That was when I went outside and sat in the sun, between the two houses, and enjoyed the shelter from the wind, the rough rock foundation biting into my back. I moved here and there until I and the foundation met with a compromise. The light on my face and the smell of salt water, the rock-gravelling waves, coupled with the cry of gulls! If I moved my head to the right I could see the beach—or I could just sit straight and look at Harry Dawe's house, the shed on the hill with the green crescent painted on the door. When did those little pine trees grow up? It will soon be as forested as when Abraham Morgan arrived from Port de Graves, bringing Rachel Andrews as his wife. I must have sat there an hour enjoying Abraham's wall, before pangs of hunger led me back to the house. My dad was lying on the daybed, his eyes open.

"What would you like to do for lunch? A trip to a restaurant, or home delivery?"

"Option two," he said, his speech slurred, but his mild humour still shimmering behind the tumor.

As a young adult I thought my family were crazy people. Coming over to Coley's Point to work like dogs—shingling, painting, doing yard work. Or like today, coming all this way to use the toilet and lie on the couch. But even at my most cynical, I have always been under the influence of this place.

We all are.

I'd seen it that morning in my Uncle Don's eyes.

"Oh, are you going to Coley's Point?" The light, the pleasure, the brief considered look (shall I go along?), the remembered duties (my car's in the garage, we promised Trudy we'd meet her), the expedition postponed.

When we get here we don't do much. Light the fire. Sit and talk. Eat a lunch. Some, like my mother, or the younger ones, who itch to be doing something, will go for a walk across the beach or up the hill. In the fall I picked blueberries like a madwoman, obsessively trying to beat invisible rakers who use plastic rakes that destroy the bushes. Listening to the gulls cry, feeling the wide bay stretched out behind my back, facing the hill, smelling the soil.

But my dad and his generation are always happy to just sit in the house. In the kitchen. Talking. It is only these last months that I named what this house means to us. The Coley's Point house is our totem. We were not artisans like the Haida. But my people built this old house. By hand.

My dad used to point out the beveled edges of the wooden beams inches above his head. Hand-planed. Someone, some man, decided it needed to look fancy, or at least fancier than a shed or a boat. Maybe it was his concession to a woman he loved, or his own internal idea of fancy, but he took the time to hand-bevel the beams. That man was my great-great-grandfather, Abraham Morgan, who built this home in 1867, the year Canada, the country next door, was founded.

When David came to visit he understood this.

As we ate the deli food I'd bought at Dominion, Daddy asked me, "What was it that David said about this place?"

"David said he couldn't believe he was in a house that had been built by my ancestors, people related to me. He said he had no continuity like that. To think that one family had owned this land for five generations."

My dad smiled with pleasure. He liked that story.

Earlier that afternoon, leaning against the old house, I had been aware of the fragility of this structure my people once built. The sway of the foundation stones, the dip as the well settles into its underground hole. The crooked clapboard. Its eggshell white paint flecking off the silver-grey wood beneath. It looks transparent. Suddenly I was reminded of other totems. The piles of rocks on barrens, wind whining through the holes. Nepalese prayer flags on Mount Everest. Ragged, bleached, flapping human artifacts holding on to this beautiful earth by one thin, unravelling thread.

Then I feel the burden of this house. Its urging imperative. I want to bring fresh paint and new clapboard, to mend and fight this growing transparency, this fading I see before my eyes.

Not just for Abraham and Rachel, but for George Henry, who drove Morgan's company car all the way from St. John's. And Mac who bought the 1950s-style lawn chairs, whose armchair sits in the living room. For Great-aunt Violet who planted the trees that now block the view to the beach. For George, my dad, and Greg, my brother, who built the deck. Like the bear and the frog and the raven, I feel their eyes on me when I sit in the sun, with my back to this house, enjoying the privileges of my birth.

After lunch, my father and I pack up. We padlock the door and walk to the front lawn. My dad has a plan. He holds the car he bought at Toys R Us— "to photograph." It is a model of a 1940s car which he has painted green to look like the company car he remembers riding in when he was a child, during the war. Except now he is confused. He brought it to photograph in front of the house on Kenmount Road. But we are at Coley's Point.

"Daddy, let's photograph it here." It will be a trick photograph.

Daddy puts out his hand, the toy car resting on his palm. My job is to photograph the car and the house, not showing his hand.

"Like the hundreds of photos all over North America of soldiers in Europe holding up the leaning tower of Pisa," says my dad.

But at the last minute I see him. Holding the green car in his hand. Smiling down at it in delight. The old house behind him, soberly watching. I back up a step, and take a photo of my dad, enjoying his joke.

It's only after we've left that I remember the bottle on the windowsill. Remember that I was going to give it to David.

"The Lemon Crystals." Looking at the photos later that week my mother will say, "Every Newfoundland household had some. If you were offered a drink you could always ask for a glass of Lemon Crystal. I hated it even as a child. Remember the Lemon Crystals George?"

Haiku

MARILYN PORTER

monochrome landscape
all brightness expunged till spring
one lost scarlet glove

Viewing Not Advised

M. T. DOHANEY

THEY HAD TO take out the parlour window and pry off a couple of clapboards to get Paddy's casket inside his house. And they had to hack off most of the branches of the lilac tree. Everyone said cutting back the tree was a real shame because only days earlier it had come into full purple bloom. But there was no other choice; the branches were so ungainly they were completely blocking the passage to the window.

Mrs. Josie, Paddy's mother, wanted her son brought in through the front door as would befit any slain soldier. However, she had failed to take into account the professionally-made casket that had been freighted out from the military hospital in St. John's. It was so much larger than anything that would have been cobbled together in Bloated Gut; it was impossible to squeeze it in through the narrow door, no matter how it was twisted and turned.

Within an hour of his arrival, Paddy had been set up in the parlour. Two candles—special ones blessed by the priest on Candlemas day—had been lit and placed on a small table at the head of the casket. A pickle bottle, overflowing with the lilac blooms that had been salvaged from the hacked-off branches, was on another small table at the foot of the casket. Mrs. Josie, herself, had draped the Union Jack over the casket and she had tenderly tugged at it to make certain it fell in even folds to the floor. When it was smoothed out to her liking, she placed her husband's pocket watch on the top, rubbing her hand over it as she laid it down as if in a caress.

Paddy had only been a little boy when his father died, and he had claimed that watch for his own. He never left it out of his sight. He even took it to the war with him, and someone who had visited him in the military hospital in St. John's said he had it laid on his nightstand, within a hand's reach.

When the makeshift viewing room was in readiness—the candles lit, the casket draped, Mrs. Josie's rosary beads laid on top of it, on the spot where Paddy's hands were surmised to be folded—Father Reardon, the parish priest, led the gathering in saying the rosary for the repose of Paddy's soul. He then left immediately afterwards, saying he had to get back to the rectory in time for Friday evening devotions.

As soon as he left, Mrs. Josie went up to her bedroom, exhausted from the day, and once the wake keepers had the kitchen all to themselves, they set about livening up the place. Mary Frances, a neighbour, and Bridget Cleary, Paddy's girlfriend, began preparing vegetables for the pot of salt beef that was already in full boil on the stove. Earlier in the day, Phonse, the oldest of the wake keepers, had smuggled in a keg of homebrew and had hidden it under the kitchen table. He brought the keg out into the centre of the kitchen and invited Austin Lannon, Mrs. Josie's brother-in-law, and Paddy's best friend, Neddie Nolan, to fill up their glasses.

"Come on, b'ys," Phonse said, releasing the bung from the keg. "Let's get a few drinks into ourselves so things'll look brighter."

He singled out Neddie. "Me son, yer not here jest fer yer good looks. Pick up that accordion and give us a tune."

"Yes, b'y," Austin seconded. "We needs things livened up a bit. In honour of Paddy, play the Regiment's tune."

Neddie began playing "The Banks of Newfoundland." Phonse, holding aloft his full glass of beer, got up and step-danced around the beer keg. The beer from his glass sloshed over the floor. At the end of the tune, he dropped back into his chair, exhausted. Neddie put the accordion aside.

"Don't put that thing away, Neddie!" Mary Frances ordered. "Bridget is going to give us a song."

Bridget shook her head. "I don't feel much like singing."

"Sure you do, girl," Austin coaxed. "Sing Paddy's song. Sing 'Come Back Paddy 'Reilly'."

"Come on, me love," Phonse cajoled. "We all loves that song."

Mary Frances put down the turnip and clapped encouragement. "Come on me darlin, sing 'Come Back Paddy 'Reilly'." She coached off-tune and just above a whisper. "*The garden of Eden has vanished they say . . .*"

Neddie played a few bars of the tune. Reluctantly, Bridget began to sing, her voice unsteady. Austin and Phonse swayed their beer glasses, keeping time to the music.

The garden of Eden has vanished they say
But I know the lie of it still
Just turn to the left at the Bridge of Finea
And stop when halfway to Cootehill.
Tis there I will find it I know sure enough
When fortune has come to my call
O the grass it is green around Ballyjamesduff
And the blue sky is over it all.
And tones that are tender and tones that are gruff
Come whispering over the sea

Bridget's voice quavered and Phonse hurriedly waved everyone to join in.

"Come on fellows. Join in. Help her out."

They all obliged and chimed in on the chorus.

Come back Paddy 'Reilly to Ballyjamesduff
Come home Paddy 'Reilly to me.

Bridget began to sob uncontrollably and Mary Frances went to comfort her. She put an arm around her shoulder.

"There, there, me darlin'. Let it all come out. You've a right to that. Not being able to see him even in death. That's the hard part."

Neddie got up out of his chair and went to refill his beer glass. "That's a bunch of bloody foolishness," he said, addressing the room at large. His voice took on a mocking tone. "'*Viewing not advised.*' Who in the hell do they think they are—telling us we can't see our own Paddy?"

Phonse quickly backed him up. "I'm with you there, b'y. We should be able to see him. He went away August 1914 and here it is June 1919. Never clapped eyes on him in between."

Mary Frances went to the stove and lifted the cover on the salt beef pot. She jabbed at the salt beef. "That's done," she said. "Time to get the turnips in."

She looked over at Bridget. "Too bad, girl, you and Mrs. Josie couldn't have gotten in to see him this spring after he was sent back from that hospital in England. But I knows well enough about the expense. Ye'd have to stay a week in St. John's on account of the train. Everything costs money."

Bridget wiped her eyes with the back of her hand. "They kept telling us Paddy was doing as well as could be expected. If we'd known he was at death's door we'd have found the money somewhere to go see him."

"Sure you would," Austin consoled. "They kept the truth from you." He mimicked the information the nurses in the military hospital had written to Mrs. Josie. "'Y'er son is doing as well as can be expected.' Sure that tells you nothing. As well as can be expected for what? For a corpse?"

He waved his empty glass at Neddie.

"While y'er up, b'y, fill mine up, too. And I say let's open up Paddy as soon as we gets a few more beers into us. Hell's flames with 'viewing not advised.'"

Mary Frances had been bent over a counter chopping up a head of cabbage. She quickly straightened up and jabbed her cutting knife in Austin's direction.

"Not while I have a breath in me body will ye open him up!"

She looked toward the ceiling, beyond which was Mrs. Josie's bedroom.

"Ye 'ent going to hurt that poor soul any more than she's already been hurt. Her only child dead and she blames herself. She says if she hadn't signed Paddy's enlistment papers he couldn't have gone to the war, him being underage. But he pestered her so much she finally gave in."

"Get some sense into you, woman, how can it hurt her to see her own son?" Austin asked testily.

"You're the one who needs to get sense," Mary Frances retorted. "Maybe he's all smashed up. Ever think of that?"

Again she pointed to the ceiling.

"No need to place more guilt on that poor soul's heart."

Phonse quickly interjected. "I tried to get her to stop blaming herself. I said if she wants to blame anyone, blame the Newfoundland Government—sending our young boys overseas to spill their blood on foreign soil."

He added scornfully. "And for *England*! I bet no one in England could find Bloated Gut on a map if you gave them a magnifying glass. And I bet they don't know Paddy 'Reilly is lying dead in that parlour in the prime of his life. All on their account."

"And hundreds more than Paddy got slaughtered," Neddie confirmed. "Bill Ryan's father told me that at the battle of Somme—and that's where Paddy met his comeuppance—the bullets were as thick as hailstones—Bill told him he turned up his collar and marched forward as if the turned-up collar could protect him."

Neddie reached for Phonse's glass.

"Might as well fill up yers while I'm up here."

He sniffed the air appreciatively and looked in the direction of the pot of salt beef and vegetables.

"Beginning to smell some good, Mary Frances." He held up Phonse's full glass of beer for inspection. "And this beer tastes some good, too."

"Yes, good beer all right," Austin allowed, "but don't swell his head with too much praise. Meself, I feels so good right now, I thinks we should open up Paddy and let him get a sniff of beer and a whiff of that salt beef and cabbage."

He turned to Bridget. "You'd like to see him, wouldn't you, girl?"

"Sure I would, but the Government said the casket was sealed and we shouldn't tamper with it. And the telegram said 'viewing not advised'."

"The *Government*," Neddie mocked. "We should give a pinch of hen shit about the government? Did it care about Mrs. Josie when they took Paddy away to be slaughtered?"

He slapped his legs. "And I'd be slaughtered too, I s'pose, if it weren't for these crooked legs of mine. I knows very well I'd have gone with Paddy. Me and him were good buddies. That's why I'd like so much to see him."

"Here's to Neddie's crooked legs," Phonse toasted, raising his glass. "And I say let's open up Paddy and let him have one last look around."

Mary Frances faced down the three men. "Now listen here, ye fellows. Jest because yer bellies are filled with hop beer, is no reason fer ye to do something foolish. Yer not opening that casket and that's it. Ye saw the sign on it. 'Sealed' it said. And ye read the telegram. 'Viewing not advised.'"

"Who pays attention to that stuff, girl," Austin Lannon sneered. "I bet they says that to everyone. Jim Barnes' boy had the same thing on his box. Meself, I thinks the Government probably made up a whole bunch of stickers saying 'viewing not advised' and some others saying 'sealed' and now they have to use them somewhere. Ye knows how it goes with the Government. Got to hide yer waste."

At that moment, a flash of lightning shot in through the kitchen window, followed by a loud clap of thunder. Mary Frances made a rapid sign of the cross over herself.

"Blessed Lord. There 'tis. The storm they threatened. And all the windows in the house are wide open. Every last one."

She started for the hall door that led to the upstairs bedrooms. She stopped and beckoned to Bridget.

"Give me a hand, girl. If the casings get wet they'll swell twice their size and we'll never get the bloody things closed."

Bridget quickly got up and followed Mary Frances up the stairs.

As soon as the door closed behind the two women, Phonse jumped to his feet.

"Now's our time, b'ys. I knows where Mrs. Josie keeps her crowbars and stuff. Just out here in the back porch."

He raced out through the kitchen door, followed by Austin. Within a couple of seconds they returned—each one carrying a crowbar. Austin also had a hammer and a chisel. These he handed over to Neddie.

"This'll do it, b'ys," Austin said, brandishing the crowbar and heading for the parlour. "Hurry! We haven't got much time."

Within a few minutes, the casket was pried open. The three men looked inside.

"Sweet Redeemer! Oh Mother of God!" Phonse said and staggered to a chair and dropped into it. Neddie and Austin stayed looking in at the body as if they were riveted to the spot.

Mary Frances came downstairs. She noticed the open parlour door. She looked in. She saw the raised lid on the casket. She saw the men staring at the corpse as if transfixed.

"Oh Merciful Mother! Oh Hand of God! Ye drunken fools. Ye went and opened it."

Scowling, she strode into the parlour, toward the casket, past Phonse who was sitting as if stupefied in his chair.

"'Ent him" Phonse mumbled as she passed by. He spoke without looking at her.

"Don't talk so foolish, b'y," Mary Frances dismissed and kept on going. She stopped beside the casket and looked in. She saw the body of a young man dressed in the uniform of the Newfoundland Regiment.

"Oh Holy Saint Joseph," she whispered, and made a rapid sign of the cross over herself as she staggered back against the wall. "'Ent him. Fer sure, it 'ent him."

Bridget entered the parlour doorway. Phonse came out of his stupor and tried to stop her from going any farther.

"Go back, girl! Don't look at him. Fer the love of God, don't look at him. 'Ent Paddy at'all. Nothing like him."

Bridget paid no attention. She hurried to the casket.

"Ohohoh," she gasped. Her hand rushed to her mouth. "Ohohoh!"

Austin grabbed her and helped her into a chair.

Neddie was the first to get himself under control. "Close him up, b'ys." He grasped the casket lid to pull it closed. "Let's not say a word. Close him up and pretend he's Paddy. Stove polish the cracks in the box."

"No!" Bridget wailed, struggling to get out of her chair. "We have to find Paddy. We have to let them know they didn't send us Paddy."

"She's right, b'ys," Mary Frances said heavily, moving towards the casket and once more looking down at the stranger. "He 'ent Paddy and we can't say he is. Besides we can't let Mrs. Josie bury a complete stranger, thinking he's her son."

"But if we tells her, it might kill her," Phonse objected. He, too, staggered to his feet and joined the others around the casket.

"Should've thought of that before ye sprung it open." Mary Frances' tone held no sympathy for their predicament.

"And what if that fellow is a Protestant?" Bridget put in quickly. "We can't bury a Protestant in a Catholic cemetery. We could be excommunicated for that. Ye got to own up to what ye did and then send Buddy back."

"Send Buddy back!" Phonse repeated and looked at Bridget as if she had lost her mind. "Where's y'er head, girl? How can we send him back? The train don't come for six more days. If we keeps him in the parlour that long, there won't be enough disinfectant in Murphy's store to cut the stench."

"He's right, girl," Neddie said. "He's already startin' to go. See! He's leakin' at the mouth."

Austin stared down at the body, scrutinizing it and then latched on to a solution. "Are we all sure he 'ent Paddy? Perhaps 'tis Paddy and we don't recognize him. War changes people. And he's several years older."

"Of course that fellow 'ent Paddy," Mary Frances snapped. "That poor divil in there has a nose on him as long as the Burin Peninsula."

She pointed to Paddy's photograph hanging on the wall above the casket.

"Besides, Paddy was as freckly as a tom cod and had red hair, like his father, Lord have mercy on his soul."

She turned her gaze back to the casket, and asked cantankerously, "Do any of ye see freckles or any sign of red hair on this fellow?"

One by one they slumped into the parlour chairs.

"In the name of all that's good and holy, what are we goin' to do?" Austin asked. It was more of a statement than a question. "We're in some mess now. Some bloody mess."

"Some bloody mess fer sure," Phonse agreed. "And there's something else we should think about. If we tells the priest that Buddy 'ent Paddy, he won't be allowed to be buried in Paddy's grave. He'll have to be put outside the cemetery fence. No soldier deserves that. And when the Government finds out what we done we'll be in fer it. We might even end up in jail."

"I'd rather be in jail than in the fix we're in now," Neddie lamented. "We can't keep him in the parlour for a week even if we owns up to what we done. And we can't get him exchanged for Paddy until a week from today. By then he'll be rancid."

"We could send a telegram to the hospital," Bridget said hopefully, certain she had found a way out. "Fer sure ye'll have to own up to what ye did. But ye did no worse than the government did when they sent out the wrong body."

"Telegraph offices are closed on Saturdays," Austin snapped. "You knows that as well as I do." He could feel the situation getting more hopeless with every suggested solution. "Besides, what can the hospital do? They can't make the train come any faster."

"And what do we tell poor Mrs. Josie?" Mary Frances bemoaned. "Ye liquored up fools, ye got us into some bloody mess. If ye had left the box closed the fellow in there would be Paddy. But, no, that wasn't good enough fer ye. Ye had to open it up. Now that poor fellow 'ent Paddy and he is goin' to have to get buried outside the fence like an old bloated horse and we'll have to go lookin' all over the place fer Paddy. And for all we knows, and that's takin' into account there was a straight swap made, this fellow might be from up the coast and Paddy might be on the mail boat right now, halfway to St. Anthony's."

Neddie groaned. "Lord dyin', I jest thought of something else. If Buddy is from St. John's he's buried by now. We can't very well go around to every boneyard in town and say, "Up she comes, b'ys. That might be our Paddy down there."

He swiped his hand across his forehead and down his perspiration-coated cheeks. Then he jumped up as if he had just been given the answer. He snatched up the hammer from where they had laid down the crowbars and other tools.

"I'm goin' to hammer him shut. As far as everyone is concerned, we never opened him up. 'Tis the only way out."

Bridget let out a loud wail. "Ye can't do that. We got to send him back so we can find Paddy." She raced out of the parlour and up the stairs to Mrs. Josie's room. Mary Frances ran after her, hoping to waylay her, but she couldn't catch her. Bridget already had a couple of seconds of a head start and she was pushing open Mrs. Josie's bedroom door by the time Mary Frances got to the top of the stairs.

~~~

Immediately upon hearing Bridget's version of what was going on, Mrs. Josie got up out of her bed and headed for the parlour. Mary Frances tried to keep her from going into the room by blocking the doorway. "Don't go in there, Mrs.," she pleaded. "Don't torture yerself. He 'ent Paddy. That poor divil in there has a nose on him as long as the month of March. And he's got hair blacker than the stove."

Mrs. Josie shoved past her. "I wants to see fer meself."

She pushed up the coffin lid and stared in at the inert body. She stared for several seconds, taking in every detail of the uniform and of the pale face and the clasped hands of the coffined soldier. All eyes were on her, but no one spoke. No one suggested she should look away because she wasn't looking at Paddy. She was simply looking at a dead soldier. No one offered an apology for breaching the nailed-down coffin lid.

"I wants his uniform opened," she ordered. "I wants to see if he has a wound in his lung."

"Mrs!" Neddie protested.

"Do it!" she said, pointing to the long row of brass buttons on the uniform coat. "Or I'll do it meself." She immediately began undoing the buttons. Mary Frances and Phonse came over to help. There was no shirt under the coat, just swatches of bandages.

"Get me a scissors!" Mrs. Josie barked, beginning to pick at the end of a bandage to loosen it.

"Oh fer the love of God, Mrs. Don't take off his bandages. That may be the only thing holding him together. They're right down his waist and up to his neck. See! He's swaddled in them."

Fearing the truth of Mary Frances' words, Mrs. Josie stopped picking at the bandages and began buttoning up the uniform coat. The others rushed in to help, and without saying another word Mrs. Josie left the parlour and went back to her bedroom.

~~~

In the morning when she came down to breakfast, Mary Frances made room for her at the table where all of the wake keepers, along with Bridget, were eating.

"I've been doin' a lot of thinkin'," she offered, after she had taken several sips of tea. Her voice was far away and forlorn. "A lot of thinkin'."

"I'm certain ye have, Mrs.," Mary Frances said softly, placing a plate of buttered toast beside Mrs. Josie's cup of tea. "There's a lot to think about. We've been thinkin' too. All night in fact. But we're no closer to a solution than we were when we started."

"I thinks I've got the solution. I thinks there's only one thing to do. And that's the right thing. My Paddy wouldn't want to cause pain to anyone, and if we goes searching for him, graves are going to have to be dug up. Mothers who've gotten the funeral over with, will have to do it all over again. And I knows Paddy is dead. I've no doubt about that. The telegram said so. They wouldn't be likely to make two mistakes with the same soldier. And that watch would never have gotten away from Paddy if he was alive. And the government says 'tis Paddy in there. And 'tis been years since we saw him. And maybe he doesn't look like himself because war changes people. That soldier in there could be my Paddy. And if 'tis I certainly don't want to send him back to the Government. Don't want to turn him out of his own house and rout him about more than he's already been routed about. Don't want to deny him the comfort of being buried beside his poor father. So I sez we should keep our mouths shut and bury that poor soldier in Paddy's grave. Nail the lid shut. Not a word to anyone. Even if he 'ent Paddy, he's some poor mother's son."

A Mostly One-Sided Dialogue

GERALDINE CHAFE RUBIA

a poet in a how town said
love is most mad and moonly
in a wow town let me add
love is tao typhoonly

boffo and bassoonly
cosmic and cartoonly
brio and balloonly

once in a vow town banners read
love is jess and junely
after all is lost and had
love is most wry and runely

I am strange?

seeing you blue-jeaned
with the kitten in your arms
soft-contoured as in summer haze
I am unloosened
to July imaginings
your voice delicious dewberries

almost at my lips—
what did you say?

I should not be indulging in fantasy

well I know
why I get no kiss in greeting
the way your countless friends and kinfolk do
well I know
we have small chance of meeting
in any but a crowded rendezvous

well I know
why you will not nestle near me
and why it is we're never far apart
the chiefest reason that you have to fear me . . .

any day now you'll say

you have no intention of changing the status quo

squandering or not squandering
I give you bits and pieces of myself
pondering or not pondering
you store them in odd receptacles

I wonder will they settle
and meld at last in your heart
or crumple bit by bit
in your litter bin

you suppose you love me a little

the sonnets that I memorize
are the I'll-be-damned depths of your eyes

your Harlequin hair
and offhanded air
unzipping my epic disguise

see you in the movies

I tell you now
if ever you diminish in my sight
if there comes a day
when a bird in flight
does not remind me of you

if my wings stop beating
at evening on your windowpane
if there comes a dawn
when my old refrain
falls silent in the air

I tell you now
if ever your brightness dims to me
it will only mean
your light is everywhere

take it easy

I unlikeliest jenny of all
picturing still past fifty-three
some swift spring or endless fall
verging on senility
you'll turn to me
and then we'll see

Fir Trees Dark Against the Sky

EILEEN DICKS

Fir trees dark against the sky
Deep snow crunches underfoot
As man and boy walk through the woods
This one Dad? he stops and looks
No it's too young and slight
The fir tree waved them out of sight

Goodbye Percy Janes

(March 12, 1922–February 19, 1999)

DANETTE DOOLEY

THE MAN WALKED in, glanced around the room and slowly approached the closed mahogany-coloured casket. After reading the inscription on the brass nameplate, he turned and asked hesitantly:

"I wonder, is this Mr. Janes a writer?"

"Yes, he is," I replied, looking toward the only other person in the room.

Helen Fogwill Porter was busy thumbing through the United/Anglican Hymnal for an appropriate hymn to be sung during the service that evening.

The man nodded, crossed his arms, cleared his throat and spoke again.

"My name is Don Gough. I think this man is my uncle. My father Clayton Janes had a brother named Percy. I never knew my father." He hesitated before continuing. "Myself and my brother were given up for adoption shortly after we were born. We're children from my father's second marriage. Do you know if this man ever mentioned a brother named Clayton?"

"Yes, he did," I said, thinking back to that sunny afternoon in July, 1997, when I sat drinking Tetley tea and eating Purity Jam Jams with Percy Janes in his small cottage on St. Thomas' Line.

"Everybody in my family is dead now, except me," Percy had said, staring straight ahead. "I never thought it would come to this. I'm the last leaf on the tree. I miss them, my family. I miss Clayton, he's the next one to me—Crawfie in the book." (Janes's *House of Hate*).

As if a faucet had been turned, Don Gough's story now spilled from his mouth.

"I never knew my birth parents," he said, still standing near the casket. "Besides putting myself and my brother up for adoption, my father had already given up the five children he had by his first wife. But that's not for me to question. I'm not here for that."

He said this firmly, as if trying to reassure us he wasn't out to cause a racket.

"By the time I found my birth mother and my brother a couple of years ago, my father had passed away. I just happened to see this death announcement in *The Telegram* this morning. When I read about him being involved in the writing community . . . well I'd heard my father's brother was a writer. What can you tell me about this man?" he asked, taking a seat beside me.

By this time a handful of other writers had gathered in the funeral parlour. Unsure whether it was my place to speak, I did so anyway.

"I know he spent his summers in his cottage on St. Thomas' Line and his winters in St. John's. Percy had been suffering from Alzheimer's for a while before he died. Sometimes he rented an apartment in the Churchill Square area. He . . ."

"My God, I live on Smithville Crescent, we've probably passed each other on the street and didn't know it. I could have spent time with him, taken him for drives. I could have been a friend to him, had I only known."

Percy's nephew wasn't the only person who'd never met the man, yet showed up to pay their last respects. Later that evening, about halfway through the tribute organized by the Writers' Alliance, a middle-aged woman sitting alone at the back of Barrett's chapel dabbed at her eyes with a Kleenex. When asked if she was a friend of Percy's the lady replied, "No, I've never met the man, but I used to work at the University Library. I've read most of his books."

Only the most gifted writers among us possess the power to stir such emotion within a stranger. Percy Janes was one of the best.

Just as Percy had so often brought our dialect to life through the written word, Boyd Chubbs accomplished a similar feat during Percy's tribute by strumming his guitar to a medley of Newfoundland tunes. "For you Percy," Boyd smiled, looking toward the casket.

Percy would have been particularly pleased with the words spoken by his long-time friend and fellow author, Paul O'Neill.

"I remember one time going on a bus with Margaret Laurence," Paul began.

"Margaret, to my mind, was probably the greatest Canadian writer of this century. We got to talking about Percy and how he went to live with her in England. She took him into her house, cared for him and gave him room and board. Margaret said to me, 'What do you think of his novel?' (Janes's *House of Hate*). I told her that I thought it was the greatest Newfoundland novel that's ever been written. She said, 'I didn't realize when I took Percy in that I was giving room and board to a genius.'"

When I visited Percy in 1997, he told me about his travels throughout England and his time at Margaret's "Elm Cottage." Laurence wrote the foreword to the New Canadian Library Edition of *House of Hate* published in 1976—something that pleased Percy immensely.

"As far as *House of Hate* is concerned, the best review, by far, is Margaret Laurence's introduction, which is all opinion, no gossip," Percy said as we chatted at his kitchen table.

"I never had any knowledge that she was going to write about the book. It just came as a very pleasant surprise. It was an excellent review and as good as I could expect to get from a person far more experienced in writing than I was. I believe Margaret's comments still give the book a boost today," he said proudly.

Although *House of Hate* caused much dissension in his family when it was first published in 1970, nearly three decades later Percy had no regrets about publishing the novel.

"My father and my eldest brother disowned me, another brother threatened my life. So it was traumatic when the book was first published. But that only lasted a short time," he said.

"And the worst was I was condemned by a Canon—Canon Loder. He wrote a letter to the *Atlantic Advocate* very heavily condemning the book, saying it was a disgrace and should be de-published. He appears in the book indirectly through his daughter. There was nothing bad said about her. It's just that she was a little in love with Racer. But that's not wrong; that's normal."

While writing *House of Hate*, Percy focused at times upon amusing incidents to address the subject of a working-class family coping with an oppressive father.

"I intentionally included a good bit of humour. Otherwise, it would be too grim for words," he said.

"I didn't have a technique to do that at first. Sometimes when I'd get stuck I'd say to myself—now how would Crawfie react to that? Or I'd say—would my mother consider this unseemly? She was very old-fashioned, you know."

As another hymn ended, *TickleAce* editor Bruce Porter stepped back from the organ to take his turn at the microphone.

"Like many of you, I got to know Percy after his return to Newfoundland in the mid-seventies," Bruce said. "I came to know him first as a writer, then later as a friend; first as a novelist, later as a very stimulating dinner guest; first as a fellow gardener, later as the witty and insightful poet. Cogency and an impeccable ability to coax the magic out of words, were only two of Percy's wonderful traits. We will all remember him in our own distinctive way. I will remember him as a writer who captured supremely the dialect of our outport tongue. And I will recall him, as long as I retain a memory, for his profound, relentless honesty . . ."

Listening to Bruce's tribute, I thought how proud Percy would have been to hear such praise from one of the people he truly admired.

While we strolled about his garden that afternoon, Percy pointed out the different trees and shrubs he'd planted many years before. He also mentioned Bruce Porter several times.

"Technical ability isn't something that's stressed much these days, Danette. Character is stressed and even structure, but technique is a little different. Bruce Porter had a few good words to say about me on that subject. Bruce has worked hard to get *TickleAce* where it is today, you know. That's the only literary magazine we have now. *The Newfoundland Quarterly* is okay but not too exciting. It's been around for a long, long time. What I find now is that, unlike years ago when nobody would know what *TickleAce* was, these days it has really grown in popularity. And that's good. It stemmed from practically nothing. We need very much a literary magazine and I've been happy to contribute to it. I also served for two terms as one of their editors, you know. I sat at a desk in an office and . . ." Percy's eyes sparkled as he broke into song, his right arm waving through the air, as though conducting music.

> "I cleaned the windows and I swept the floor
> And I polished up the handle on the big front door
> I polished up that handle so carefullee
> That now I am the Ruler of the Queen's Navee!"

"Gilbert and Sullivan, do you like them, Danette?"

"Oh yes," I said, laughing along with him. Though I was familiar with the duo, I didn't have a clue what song I'd just heard. But if Percy Janes sang their praises, well, I liked them, too.

"Yes, my days with *TickleAce* were good ones, that's for sure," he said, settling down to more serious conversation about his work.

"People may not realize this but *House of Hate* was rejected by several publishers in England and the States before Jack McClelland said, okay," Percy told me.

"I almost had an offer from the States. Doubleday. Almost. But what happened was that somebody who read it said it was a good book but it was too original. Said there were no sales for it in the States and that was the market he was thinking of publishing it in," Percy explained.

"I've written a number of plays too but you don't know about them because they were never produced. They never got on stage. That was a real disappointment. I used to think about taking my girlfriend at the time to my first night but it didn't work out that way. She was working at the University's Department of Nursing at the time but she went to Tanzania. She—"

"My gosh, she went far enough away, didn't she," I interrupted.

"That's for sure. I used to say to her, you're going far enough away, have I got leprosy or something?" he laughed.

Percy Janes was all talk that afternoon. I was all ears.

"I feel that I did a good thing by getting this land, Danette," he said, stretching his right arm out toward the green, carpet-like grass.

"I had it for two or three years and I couldn't afford to build the cottage. But through the influence of Harold Horwood—this is not dropping names, this is a true account—I received a $6,000 grant to continue work-in-progress, so that was very good. I sent in a synopsis as I recall. I'm talking now about the Canada Council. They've been pretty good to me, you know. So I feel that kind of got me over the highest difficulties that I faced and I'm grateful for that. Because without that money I wouldn't have been able to build this little cottage."

As I sat in the chapel listening to writer after writer talk about how the man resting before us had influenced their career, I knew I would remember Percy Janes first and foremost as a man with a terrific sense of humour. A man who made me feel at home on his turf. Seldom one to mix with a group, Percy seemed more lonely than reclusive as we chatted in his cottage about his daily routine.

"I don't have a wide acquaintance among writers, you know, Danette, but Peter and Carolyn Harley are very good to me. They pick me up and take me to Churchill Square a lot. My neighbour, Mrs. Lawlor, is good to me too. She brings up my meals quite often. Now, if I was here (St. Thomas' Line) during the winter it might get a bit claustrophobic because you can't get out and sometimes the wind is so bad that it would cut you right down. But in the summer I write in the morning, I garden in the afternoon, and I get the news on television in the evening. So I don't feel that I'm skimping."

"No, you're not doing without," I said, looking around the unfinished room that served as his office, living room and kitchen.

"Oh, yes I am," he grinned.

"You are? Then what are you doing without?"

"The three-letter word," Percy laughed, slapping his right hand on his knee.

Feeling my face flush, I quickly moved on to my next question. I asked Percy about his health. Spending a good part of his day gardening left him tanned, trim and handsome.

"I might as well give you the truth of it, Danette," he said, getting up from the table and gazing out the window toward the distant sky.

"I've had operations, two or three altogether. Trouble with diets, miscellaneous complaints. Nothing that's going to kill me but enough to slow me down."

It was at this point that Percy remembered the tape recorder on the table.

"Oh, you've got the tape on, I'd forgotten about it," he said.

"Yes, the tape has been on but that's okay. Don't worry, I'm not going to tell anyone that you're doing without the three-letter word."

"I'm not worried about that, Danette," he laughed. "What I'm giving you here is carte blanche. It's yours to do with as you wish. And if you say that I said that, I'll just say yes, I'm guilty," he joked, raising his right arm in the air, as if swearing on the Bible.

Becoming serious again, Percy spoke about working on a long essay. He wasn't prepared to elaborate further.

"All I can tell you is that it's about a subject dear to my heart. I have other things in mind that I'd like to write, too," he said. "But God knows and God will dispose."

Back in the chapel, the celebration continued. Ron Rompkey stood to bring condolences on behalf of Memorial University.

"This is the second opportunity I've had to say something nice about Percy Janes," he began. "The first time was several years ago when I was a member of the Senate at the University. Somebody decided that Percy should receive an honourary degree. I remember being asked to make a public statement at that time, so I went through all the details, which you've heard tonight, and I spent quite a bit of time preparing something about the contribution that Percy Janes had made to this province. The Senate voted, without any doubt whatsoever, to give him that degree, and I had been looking forward to the next spring when Percy would arrive to receive his degree. But he never arrived. He did not give us the opportunity to honour him at that time and that's something which I, personally, have regretted ever since . . ."

Percy Janes didn't not just show up, I wanted to stand and shout.

He battled with his decision not to accept the degree—a decision he took the time to explain to me as we chatted in his garden.

"It's just as well to be honest about it, Danette. I thought it was premature," he said when I asked why he'd declined the honourary degree.

"When I got the letter, it was a little bit disturbing. I knew I didn't want to do it, yet I didn't want to offend the University. It was a little hard. I had to walk a thin line but I finally had to say no. I wrote Mr. Collins and he said, That's okay, Mr. Janes. The argument against not accepting it is that I'm seventy-five now and I might not have time to have another shot at it. Nevertheless, formal honours I don't crave but good criticism I really appreciate."

And Percy Janes received his share of positive criticism over the years.

"Several people in St. John's came down very well on my work, you know," he told me.

"People like Pat O'Flaherty. O'Flaherty liked my work, not just in connection with *House of Hate,* but with all my work, especially my poetry. He's consistently written good opinions and meant them because we're not close friends or anything like that. It's good to get the opinion of a person you respect. There aren't too many of them around. Tom Dawe wrote a review, too. It was not a bad review but it was a little timid. He didn't want to hurt my feelings and he didn't want to say that he knew it was a good novel. He was a little shy about taking the plunge. I find that Newfoundlanders are very reluctant to praise Newfoundland writers. I tell you, as a Newfoundland writer, you don't get spoiled," Percy smiled.

Agnes Walsh hesitated just a moment before approaching the front of the chapel. Poetry book in hand, she began reading from her latest collection, *In the Old Country of My Heart*.[1] Her poem "Percy Janes Boarding the Bus" sums up well my novice writer's awe at being in close proximity to the likes of Percy Janes.

> I was going to the Mall for a kettle
> Waiting on the number five,
> When the number something-or-other
> pulled up.
>
> I was looking past it for mine,
> when I saw him, an arm raised,
> running softly.
>
> I jumped to life, beat on the bus door,
> said to the driver: "Mr. Janes.
> Mr. Percy Janes wants to get on."
>
> He raised a "So what?" eyebrow.
>
> Mr. Janes straightened his astrakhan hat,
> mumbled thank you and stepped up.
> As the bus rumbled on
> I continued under my breath:
> "Ladies and gentlemen, Mr. Percy Janes,
> Newfoundland writer, poet,
> just boarded the number something-or-other."
>
> If this was Portugal,
> a plaque would be placed
> over the seat where he sat.
>
> As it is, you have me
> mumbling in the street
> like a tourist in my own country.

I know exactly what you mean, Agnes, I thought, as my mind wandered again to that afternoon in Percy's garden.

"I just love it out here, Danette," Percy said, breathing in the hot afternoon air, his eyes squinting in the brightness of the sun.

Walking toward a huge tree, he sat down beneath his beloved maple. I took a place beside him on the grass. As he talked about his roots, both family and garden, I sat overwhelmed that this author I'd long admired would take so much time to talk to me.

"What advice would you give a new writer like me, Percy Janes," I asked, holding my breath for his answer.

"That's a dangerous question to ask me, my dear," he said.

"Oh, you mean it's a bad question, do you?"

"Not from my point of view it's not, but from yours it might be. Okay, I'll try to make this as simple as I can for you to understand. When I was younger, quite young, in my twenties, I thought you got famous with your first work, like Ernest Hemingway or F. Scott Fitzgerald. But I wasn't as fortunate as them. They had a literary culture all ready to dip into when they became writers. Canada is a generation or two behind. That's why we have never caught up with the Americans," he said.

Percy stopped talking long enough to run his hand over the grass as if smoothing the wrinkles from a blanket on a freshly made bed. After a few minutes he continued.

"People thought I was crazy when I told them that I wanted to make a living as a writer, Danette. So my point to you now is, just like this tall tree we're sitting under, it takes a long time to build up soil that the new writing can develop in. So don't expect too much too soon. Don't get disheartened if it takes a while for your work to be recognized and, whatever you do, don't give up," he said, pointing his right index finger close to my face.

"I'll give you a little test here, Danette. Did you ever hear of George Gissing?"

"Ah, no, I haven't," I answered, reluctantly admitting my ignorance. "I guess I failed your test, Percy Janes."

He smiled, plucked a few blades of long grass that had escaped the lawn mower's teeth and stroked them between his finger and thumb.

"I think it's rare to be totally discouraged but not unheard of. George Gissing is an example of that, though. He just gave up. He was quite talented but he was lacking in blood and guts. Don't let that happen to you, my dear."

"You're not like that at all," I said.

"No, I don't worry about that now. I'll do what I can and that's it."

"I can't believe I'm sitting here talking to Percy Janes," I whispered, before realizing my thoughts had been spoken out loud.

"Why do you call me Percy Janes and not just Percy?" he asked, getting up from under the shade of the tree.

"Whenever I've heard your name mentioned, you were always called Percy Janes. Never just Percy. Never Mr. Janes. I guess I've come to think of it as just one name, you know, like Mary-Ann," I said, standing on cue.

"Goodness, don't call me Mary-Ann whatever you do," he laughed, nudging my arm. "If that's the case you can stick to Percy Janes. No worry, no sweat, no sweat in that at all," he said, walking toward the house.

Inside his cottage, Percy boiled the kettle for yet another cup of tea. Having spent an hour or so in the afternoon sun, I was tempted to ask for a cold drink instead but didn't want to, just in case he didn't have any soft drinks in the house. Besides, watching him prepare more tea told me that the afternoon had not yet come to an end. I was grateful for that.

"How long is it going to be before we get to see more of your work?" I asked, as he puttered about the kitchen.

"That's very hard to say, Danette. I might finish that long essay in a rush—you know, the one I told you about earlier. That's something that has happened to me, when I'm at work. Then again, I might lose faith in it and have to put it aside—not as work-in-progress but as unfinished work," he explained.

"I must have three novels that somebody might read sometime but they're only apprentice works. I'm glad now, and I say this sincerely, I'm glad now that they weren't published because they would have taken the glitter off some of the others. Does that sound egotistical, Danette?" he asked, pouring boiling water into my mug.

"No, I think you know yourself what's your best work," I answered.

"Oh yes. Although they say very frequently that an author, or any artist, is not the best judge, and I'm half inclined to think that's true—that you can be too close to your own work. But I've never been seriously held up by this. And, when I finally got to admitting that these three novels weren't going to go—I said, 'Okay, buddy, let's decide what we're going to do next.' Because I always wanted to write. I didn't want to be idle."

Hating for our time together to end, yet knowing I had to drive back to town soon, I finished the rest of my tea before standing to leave. Like the perfect host he'd been all afternoon, he followed me down the path to my car.

"I just hope you have enough information to use," he said, hurrying to catch up with me. "You know—where was he at this time—what was he doing and so on. It would be a good guide for anyone who was doing something like a biography, but I don't want to hear about that. And I don't intend to write an autobiography. I just don't want to do it. There's lots of material around if people want to use it. Not now but after I'm gone."

The funeral parlour was almost empty except for those planning the evening service. Don Gough stared down into the face of an uncle he'd never known.

"Thanks for letting me look at him," he said to Percy's executor and friend, John Ryan. "I wish I knew more about my father's family. This man looks a lot like my brother, Pat."

Reluctantly he moved away from the casket.

"He looks just like himself," someone whispered, the usual comment made at such times.

But Percy didn't look like himself one bit. At least not in my book. He'd looked much better a couple of days ago when Lillian Bouzane, Helen and I visited him in hospital.

"He's close to death now," the nurse warned before we entered the room.

Percy looked as if he was merely sleeping. Perhaps resting after a hard day's work in his garden. The only sign of his illness was the paleness of his skin. There were no tubes, no monitors, no nurses popping in to take his blood pressure. Just as he'd lived, Percy was being left alone to die a peaceful death.

Although Percy wasn't a churchgoer he always enjoyed listening to the old-fashioned hymns.

"Let's sing *Shall We Gather at the River*[2] for him," Lillian suggested.

I stood next to the bed and held Percy's cool left hand as Helen and Lillian sang softly.

> Yes, we'll gather at the river,
> the beautiful, the beautiful river;
> gather with the saints at the river
> that flows by the throne of God.

Now, three days later, too much pink powder has been plastered on tissue-paper skin pulled over protruding cheekbones; too much orange lipstick has been painted on too tight lips. I overcome the urge to reach into the casket to loosen the navy tie choking Percy's bird-like neck. Closing my eyes, I inhale deeply, trying to recapture the aroma of dark soil mixed with freshly cut grass—an earthy smell that will always remind me of Percy Janes.

I remember Percy traipsing about in his garden, his clean, though wrinkled, white cotton shirt unbuttoned at the neck, haphazardly tucked into his full-of-hitches black polyester pants.

"So you'd like to see something done with your work later, would you?" I asked that afternoon as he opened my car door for me to head home.

"That's right. No worry, no sweat, no sweat in that at all," he smiled.

Moving back a few feet, Percy stood with his hands on his hips watching as I backed out of the driveway and headed the car toward Paradise.

"Goodbye, Percy Janes," I yelled, waving through the open car window before pressing on the gas.

But he'd already turned his back to me and was heading up the garden path.

Notes

1. *In the Old Country of My Heart*, Agnes Walsh, Killick Press, 1996.
2. Words and Music by Robert Lowery, 1864; www.cyberhymnal.org/htm/s/w/swgatriv.htm

And a Wife Shall Cleave to her Husband

ANNE FERNCASE

I go to bed,
hours after my snoring husband,
so cold
my frigid toes with vampire nails
crawl around
beneath the covers
cry out
for leg meat.

Slaughter on Franklyn Avenue

A Beast Poem

HELEN FOGWILL PORTER

Why do I hate you, tiny beast,
What have you done to me?
You do not bite or scratch or pounce
Why can't I let you be?

I fill my cat with gourmet food
She's soft and fat and round
Yet you I drag beneath my feet
And crush you to the ground

Your brother comes to take your place
And I slay him as well
Your mother father sister too
I send them all to Hell

While Kitty purrs upon my bed
And dreams the time away
I toss the corpses in the trash

And kneel at night to pray

That morning will bring no more beasts
To slither on my floor
In search of warmth and sustenance
Why can't I like you more?

Beast-ridden

(Double Haiku)

HELEN FOGWILL PORTER

Feline at my feet
a live hot water bottle
snug and cozy, warm

My ankle itches
as a blood-red blotch appears
cat's crafty cargo

Erotic Lines in the Junior Common Room

BERNICE MORGAN

The poet, icicle thin, dressed all in black, walks to the podium, thanks her audience for coming out on such a cold night, sips her wine, begins . . .

"There are bloodlines,
and heartlines,
and lines of soft flesh stretched
over hip, and thigh, and groin,
and all lines lead to you . . ."

The Carpenter's Daughter arrives late (steaming from battle lines at Chester Dawe's) longs for chilled wine, scuffs to a chair and sits, brooding on . . .

"Fault lines and credit lines,
chalk lines skilled builders flick onto clean lumber,
and those long lines of cribbing, that thirty years ago
fixed wood to concrete,
house to rock . . . ."

The Poet, in tones of modulated detachment, describes her lover's penis . . .

"Rich mushroom rising out of dark earth,

out of damp and distant caves,
tasting of soil, and salt, and shadow,
of past and future . . ."

Drugged by the smell of wet wood, the Carpenter's Daughter watches slush melt off her boots, trickle across a beige carpet, recalls . . .

Sewer lines that snake below sub-zero ground,
lines that heave, bulge, split
back up into bathrooms and kitchens.
"These things happen," her lover said,
sighing,
praying for escape lines . . .

The Poet, fingering her fringed shawl, shivers,
speaks of warmer, kinder places,
of forsaken lovers, discarded wedding rings . . .

"And lifelines and passion lines,
burning taut lines of phone wire,
steel singing over ice, over sea,
crossing prairies, continents—
Unwinding like Theseus' thread,
calling from warm islands
where, in sea-green caverns,
Cretan gods wait . . ."

The Carpenter's Daughter, stubborn disbeliever,
rejects divine intervention.
Insists that rotting boards be pried up, pulled out, replaced.
Has dragged her lover through icy streets,
through lines of thick traffic,
hounded him into Dawe's, where, in a check-out line
he spoke of trust . . .

"There are things mere mortals must accept,
they have stopped making 2 by 4s!"
he said, and scowling left.
Abandoning her to 1 ½ by 3 ½ inch boards,
to walls and ceilings and floors
that will forevermore remain unaligned.

The Two Dresses

ALISON MELVIN

IN MY MOTHER'S meagre wardrobe the cinnamon, tub-silk dress hung in quiet dignity. Flanked by her two Sunday best—also tub-silk, but floral—this one quickened my childhood imagination. Its texture, soft and smooth, enticed my six-year-old fingers. Its vivid colour awakened images of princesses and castles from my storybook world; of cinnamon buns with raisins and molasses, from my real one.

I knew why this gown was only worn by a wire hanger. My questions always met with the same response from Mother, as she bent over her grey washtub in our narrow downstairs hall, "Oh, that's my wedding dress, remember?" Her blue-green eyes would become reflective, her face transformed in a glow of treasured memories. Embarrassed by this hint of emotional weakness, she'd add, "I felt it was a bit loose on me then; it's a size twelve, you know."

Her attention appeared to return to the brown woollen sock lathered with lye soap. Her vigorous scrubbing on the ribbed-glass washboard creaked its wooden frame against her sawed-off pork-barrel washtub. These faded socks were a reminder of passing time. Still, I wanted to believe that she was seeing, as I was, a raven-haired young woman, stately and sure in flowing cinnamon, rapt in the emotion of her wedding day.

~~~
~~~

Forty-five years later another dress of mother's absorbs my attention. One hundred percent rayon and deep aquamarine to match her eyes, this one I have the pleasure of choosing led by my mother's counsel. "Don't forget a high collar to cover my neck." I steal one more glance at the protruding bones, the indigo blotches of her ruptured blood vessels.

"Make sure the sleeves come to the wrist."

Good thinking, Mother, my silent response. Cloak those mutilated arms, those shadows of muscled limbs that had excelled in the relentless toil of fish stage, flake, garden and home. How can I shroud those arms that I can still feel warmly embracing your baby girl? I hold back my tears and force myself to take a robotic stance. No garment could hide those hands, though, her fingers like hens' claws from her thirty-year battle with her demon—rheumatoid arthritis.

Size presents another dilemma. "I suppose I need about a twelve," she says. How can I suggest that even a size eight will enfold her fifty-seven pound frame twice?

So guided by Mother, I trudge downtown to her favourite store, Wilansky's, determined to complete my mission.

The next day Mother questions me and smiles contentedly from her nursing-home bed as I describe my purchase in the minute detail that the sightless require. Specifics of colour especially intrigue her. Just what she wanted!

Yet, nothing can induce me to bring in the dress for her inspection. Like its cinnamon predecessor, my mother will wear this frock only once. I see her adult life framed in these two dresses—the cinnamon tub-silk and the aquamarine rayon—chosen with care for her two major public appearances.

The Visitor

GRACE BUTT

THE VISITOR. MOST people don't talk about the visitor—you know, the guy who visits everyone in the community, one after the other. You never know when to expect him, you can't tell when he'll arrive. There are indications he is in my area. But I haven't seen him.

I have had other callers. One left a card announcing a new ailment. Another presented me with a package of multicoloured worries, though I couldn't remember having ordered them. And another walked into my room and began questioning me like a census taker about my age, my living conditions, my financial circumstances, my next of kin. I had a problem getting rid of him, and he said he would be back.

The day before yesterday I thought I heard the visitor just outside lifting the latch of my door. The expectation was so great that my chest wound up and my breath panted in excitement. But I was mistaken. The sound I heard must have been a neighbour unlocking her door to let her dog out.

Hanging around and waiting for an arrival is so boring. To occupy my mind, perhaps I'll look through my collection of photographs. Here is little me blowing out my three birthday candles. Here I am with the other singers in the school concert. There's me with the gang at the beach. Here I am with my bridegroom in the midst of the guests, both of us looking very formal. Here we are with the children, a family group to be inserted into Christmas cards. This is me leaning on my cane after sustaining a menopausal imbalance and fall. And here I am old, surrounded by my grandchildren and great-grandchildren, looking somewhat dazed. But as I say, I've seen it all before.

Maybe I'll fill up the kettle and lay out some baked things so I'll be relaxed in his company, drinking tea and eating tiny pieces of white cake. Some people have told me that this guy is arrogant, taking charge of the whole conversation. Others say he is gentle and soft-spoken. I'll see when the time comes.

CONTRIBUTOR BIOGRAPHIES

LILLIAN BOUZANE: Poet and novelist, her novel about John Cabot, *In the Hands of the Living God*, was selected by the *Globe and Mail* as one of the one hundred best books of 2001, and as editor's choice 20/01/01; it was also long-listed for the International IMPAC Award, and the British edition nominated for the Booker Prize. Two books of poetry, *Point Blank*, with Grace Butt, and *Back to Back*, with Harold Paddock, were followed by a suite of poems, "In the Time of Wolves," which won an International Gabriel Award in 1992, and a bronze medal from the International New York Festivals, 1993.

MICHAEL BRUCE-LOCKHART is a professor of Computer Engineering at Memorial University, where he holds the President's Award for Distinguished Teaching. A graduate of M.I.T., he was admitted there more for his skills in English than in Maths. Alas, nowadays he spends more time writing software than poetry.

ROBERTA BUCHANAN was born in South Africa and educated in England before immigrating to Canada in 1964. She taught English and Women's Studies at Memorial University and is now Professor Emerita. Poet and memoirist, she has published a book of poetry, *I Moved All My Women Upstairs*. A non-fiction work, *The Woman Who Mapped Labrador: The Life and Expedition Diary of Mina Hubbard*, co-authored with Anne Hart and Bryan Greene, was shortlisted for the Winterset Award for excellence in Newfoundland writing. She is a co-editor of *A Charm Against the Pain*.

LILLIAN BURSEY was born in British Harbour, Trinity Bay. While raising six children with her husband, John, and to maintain her sanity, she pursued university studies. She eventually graduated from Acadia

University with a Master's degree in counselling, and hung out her shingle in Dartmouth, NS. Lily is the current president of the Newfoundland Writers' Guild.

GRACE HUE BUTT was born in Brigus in 1909, but grew up and lived in St. John's. She wrote the first local newspaper column on the arts; founded the St. John's Players; and wrote and directed the first full-length Newfoundland play. Her prize-winning play, *Part of the Main,* was performed at the Abbey Lane Theatre in Dublin. She was awarded an honourary doctorate from Memorial University and received a NL Arts Council Award for her writing. Grace died in 2005 shortly before her ninety-sixth birthday. Her published works include: *The Road through Melton*; *Point Blank* (with Lillian Bouzane); *To Toslow We'll Go*; *An Ear and a Fear: Plays*; and *Persons*.

LIBBY CREELMAN: Libby has published a collection of short stories, *Walking in Paradise.* Her stories have been published in literary magazines across the country and have been included in *99: Best Canadian Stories* and *The Journey Prize Anthology,* numbers 10 and 11. She has been Executive Director of the Writers' Alliance of Newfoundland and Labrador since 2003.

EILEEN DICKS was born in London, England, and came to Newfoundland in 1946. She has been a copywriter/production assistant in radio and television, wrote drama for both media and co-produced a TV documentary on the History of the Sisters of Mercy in St. John's. Eileen continues to write poetry and short pieces on her wartime experiences in England. Eileen is one of the Guild's Honourary Life Members. She is co-editor of *We Came From Over the Sea* and has published a young adult book *Only for the Weekend.*

M. T. DOHANEY: Born in Point Verde, NL, Jean has lived in Fredricton, NB, since 1954. Mother of two, and a teacher of technical writing in the Faculty of Forestry at UNB, she received a Doctorate of Education in English at Boston University in 1978. She writes novels, short stories, and plays, including *The Corrigan Women*; *To Scatter*

Stones; *A Marriage of Masks*; and *A Fit Month for Dying*. Her journal of her first year as a widow, *When Things Get Back to Normal*, has recently been reprinted with an introduction by Helen Porter. A new novel, set in Newfoundland during confederation, is coming out in spring 2007 with Flanker Press.

DANETTE DOOLEY: Danette got her start in writing over a decade ago when she took her first creative writing course. The instructor, Helen Porter, has since become her mentor and friend. As a freelance writer, Danette's work has been published provincially, nationally, and internationally. She is a past board member of the Newfoundland Writers' Guild and the Writers' Alliance of Newfoundland and Labrador.

ANNE FERNCASE, winner of the Hilroy Fellowship Award in 1989, is a poet, playwright, environmentalist, and wordsmith. Her children's play *Running With Dragons* has been produced both in Vancouver, BC, and Newfoundland and Labrador. Born in California, sojourned in France, then immigrated to Canada, she has lived in the province since 1984.

GERALDINE FLANNIGAN was born and grew up in Chapel's Cove. She has been writing poetry and prose for many years and won several poetry contests. She is published in *Take a Deep Breath* and in the Canadian National Migraine Newsletter. She has been a member of the Writers Guild for about twelve years.

MAGGIE HENEGHAN grew up in St. John's where she lives with her husband and two daughters. She teaches English at Holy Heart High School.

FRAN BAIRD INNES was born in Grand Falls in 1924, graduated from Mount Allison University in 1946, had two children, and worked as a journalist in print, radio, and television, including CBC's *Here and Now*. Fran was a founding member of the St John's Status of Women Council. She is the author of a children's book, *Mae's Night Flight*.

KATHLEEN KNOWLES: Since she began writing in 1984 Kathleen Knowles has participated in workshops within the St. John's writing community and has attended courses at Memorial University and at the University of New Brunswick. She has served on the Board of the Newfoundland Writers' Guild and the Writers' Alliance of Newfoundland and Labrador. She is the compiler of *To Honour the Holiday* and is the author of *A Rock and a Hard Place*.

PEGGY SMITH KRACHUN: Born in Argentia, she lived for many years in St. John's and Ottawa. Besides her literary work, Peggy contributed a great deal through her work on pay equity in the federal civil service. Her literary work appeared in two anthologies and many magazines and journals. Before she died prematurely in 2001, she had published *Doors Held Ajar* with Isobel Brown and Nellie Strowbridge, and *Beside Myself*, a collection of humourous essays.

JANET McNAUGHTON is the author of six novels for young people, one picture book, and one junior novel: *Catch Me Once, Catch Me Twice*; *To Dance at the Palais Royale*; *Make or Break Spring*; *The Secret Under My Skin*; *The Saltbox Sweater*; *An Earthy Knight*; *Brave Jack and the Unicorn*; and *The Raintree Rebellion*. She writes historical fiction, science fiction, and fantasy. She is currently working on a fantasy about a dragon from Orkney who lives in St. John's. Her work has won eleven national, regional, and provincial awards.

ALISON MELVIN has lived in Burnt Cove, NL, all her life. She is a retired highschool English teacher. In addition to her writing, she enjoys family, church, and RV'ing activities.

BERNICE MORGAN was born in pre-confederation St. John's. She is a founding and Honourary Life Member of the Newfoundland Writers' Guild. Bernice has been writing since she was in her twenties, had her first book published in her fifties, and hopes to get a fourth book out in her seventies. Her short story in this anthology was written thirty years ago proving she should have published a book long before her fifties!

She is co-editor of *From This Place*. Her two novels, *Random Passage* and *Waiting for Time*, made into a popular movie, were followed by a book of short stories, *The Topography of Love*.

JENNIFER MORGAN is a freelance writer and printmaker. (The graphic art on the section title-pages of this anthology are by Jennifer.) The essay included in this anthology won the Newfoundland and Labrador Arts and Letters Competition for non-fiction, spurring Jennifer to write a full book which remains in her closet. With no date on its possible release from that closet, fans are encouraged to watch for it.

TRUDY MORGAN-COLE is a prolific St. John's writer who also teaches English and creative writing to adult learners at The Murphy Centre. (Not to mention raising two young children with her supportive husband Jason.) Trudy has written two spiritual books for young adults, *Connections*, and *Esther: A Story of Courage*, distributed in North America by Review and Herald Publishing. *The Violent Friendship of Esther Johnson*, a novel about Samuel Johnson's friend and confidante, was published by Penguin.

HILDA CHAULK MURRAY grew up in Maberly, Trinity Bay, but has resided in Mount Pearl since 1963. She taught English and mathematics in high school for fifteen years and English at the College of Trades and Technology (now College of the North Atlantic) for seventeen. Since retiring in 1989 she has devoted her time to volunteer work, research, and writing. Her published works are *More Than 50%* and *Cows Don't Know It's Sunday*.

PAUL O'NEILL: Born in St John's in 1928, he grew up there and in Bay de Verde, his ancestral home. Graduating from the National Academy of Theatre Arts in New York in 1949, he spent five years as a professional actor in the US and England. The offer of a job as a CBC executive producer brought him home. Having written his first four novels in grade nine, his first book of poetry in 1974, *Spindrift and Morning Light*, led to fourteen more books and over three dozen contributions to magazines and books. His books include: *A Gift of Heritage*, with Shane O'Dea; *Everyman's Complete Guide to St John's*; *The Legends of a Lost Tribe: Beothuk Folk Tales*; *Ten Historic Towns*, with Shane O'Dea, with illustrations by Jean Ball; *Breakers: Stories from Newfoundland and Labrador History*; *The Seat Imperial: Bay Bulls Past and Present*; *Upon This Rock: The History of the Roman Catholic Church in Newfoundland and Labrador*; *A Sound of Seagulls,* poetry; and an edition of his father's diary, *No Need to Wear Rubbers: The Travel Diary of James O'Neil.* His two-volume history of St John's—T*he Oldest City* and *A Seaport Legacy*—has recently been reprinted in one volume as *The Oldest City: The Story of St. John's, Newfoundland.*

HELEN FOGWILL PORTER was born and grew up in St. John's where she still lives. She was educated at Holloway School and Prince of Wales College. She has been writing steadily since the 1960s and has published prose and poetry across Canada and overseas. Helen has been a member of the Newfoundland Writers' Guild since its inception in 1968 and is now an Honourary Life Member. She is co-editor of *From This Place*; and has written a memoir of growing up on the Southside, *Below the Bridge*; a novel, *January, February, June or July*; and a book of short stories, *A Long and Lonely Ride*.

MARILYN PORTER: Born in North Wales, educated in England and Ireland, Marilyn arrived to the province in 1980. She has taught and researched sociology and women's studies at Memorial University. She has a son (living in Halifax), a daughter (living in the UK), and two grand-daughters. She is the co-editor of both *Their Lives and Times*, with Carmelita McGrath and Barbara Neis, and *Weather's Edge*, with Linda Cullum and Carmelita McGrath.

GEORGINA OLIVERE QUELLER: Childless and now dogless she has run out of excuses for not doing things. A member of the Guild since the beginning of the last decade of the last century, she likes to read, write, play games online, and spend time with her friends; all of which she does in an obsessive manner. She is a co-editor of *A Charm Against the Pain.*

GERALDINE CHAFE RUBIA writes poetry, plays, and prose. She has won awards in each category and is published in periodicals and anthologies. Her plays have been performed on stage and on CBC radio. With the Longside Club she has initiated performing arts opportunities for persons with disabilities. She is co-editor of *From This Place*, and has published two books of poetry, *A Poem in My Soup* and *Skating Among the Graves*. She is a co-editor of *A Charm Against the Pain*.

JOAN SCOTT: Come-from-away (so long ago nobody knows when) and a Newfoundlander by choice, Joan is a mother and former teacher, who takes great pleasure from quiet places, and from interactions with family and friends and other species. Now retired, she taught biology and Women's Studies at Memorial University.

ESTHER SLANEY-BROWN: "I grew up 'around the bay' so from an early age I was exposed to many great storytellers, the greatest being my grandparents, especially my grandfather. I think I would rather be known as a good storyteller than a great writer."

LAURA MORRY WILLIAMS, a member of the Guild since 1996, was born in Ferryland and developed an interest in writing when a student of the Sacred Heart Convent School. Laura enjoys reading, writing, gardening, and caring for her three cats. She has self-published two books, a collection of poetry, *My Many Moons*, and a novel, *Becoming Sarah*.

CONTRIBUTOR INDEX

Bouzane, Lillian 34, 67, 181
Bruce-Lockhart, Michael 259
Buchanan, Roberta 87, 99, 230
Bursey, Lillian 127
Butt, Grace 235, 331
Creelman, Libby 182
Dicks, Eileen 145, 146, 160, 308
Dohaney, M. T. 115, 294
Dooley, Danette 47, 66, 309
Ferncase, Anne 38, 62, 212, 263, 323
Flannigan, Geraldine 35, 61, 273
Heneghan, Maggie 107
Innes, Fran Baird 3, 219, 265
Knowles, Kathleen 192, 201, 278
Krachun, Peggy Smith 213
McNaughton, Janet 128, 232
Melvin, Alison 89, 329
Morgan, Bernice 161, 193, 251, 326
Morgan, Jennifer 286
Morgan-Cole, Trudy 15, 132
Murray, Hilda Chaulk 39, 241
O'Neill, Paul 147, 158, 274
Porter, Helen Fogwill 65, 239, 242, 262, 324, 325
Porter, Marilyn 29, 254, 276, 293
Queller, Georgina Olivere 129, 175, 229, 253, 256
Rubia, Geraldine Chafe xxii, 105, 199, 266, 305
Scott, Joan 250, 268
Slaney-Brown, Esther 30, 225
Williams, Laura Morry 77, 78, 144, 218, 228